Singled Out
Copyright © 2015 Julie Lawford
First Published: February 2015

Publisher: Woodhill Goodings
ISBN-13: 978-1505207514
ISBN-10: 1505207517

The right of Julie Lawford to be identified as author of this work has been asserted by her in accordance with sections 77 and 78 of the Copyright, Designs and Patents Act 1988.

All characters in this publication are fictitious and any resemblance to real persons, living or dead, is purely coincidental.

All rights reserved. No part of this publication may be used, reproduced, stored in a retrieval system, copied in any form or by any means, electronic, mechanical, photocopying, recording or otherwise transmitted without written permission from the publisher, except in the case of brief quotations embedded in critical articles or reviews.

Find out more about the author and upcoming books online at
www.julielawford.com

Singled Out

Julie Lawford

DEDICATION

For my mother, Irene
And my friend, Suzanne

Without whom I would not have attempted,
much less achieved this dream

ACKNOWLEDGEMENTS

SINGLED OUT is my first novel. But for the support and encouragement of so many people, it may never have happened.

I'm in awe of my mother, Irene Lawford, who, at a time of life when most people have their feet up in front of the fire, wrote and published two books of her own. It was her depth of commitment and passion that inspired me to try this *writing-a-book* thing for myself.

On Arvon Foundation courses, tutors Catherine Smith and John Siddique showed me how to *just do it*, and Jill Dawson and Kathryn Heyman opened my eyes to the intricacies of structure, character and dialogue. As my Gold Dust mentor, Kathryn's critique of my early draft was invaluable. At Circle of Missé Wayne Milstead showed me what was missing from my story, in the most sublime of settings.

My test readers, Suzanne Bellenger, Amanda Lewis, Dylan Hearn, Anne Buchanan, Chris Smith and Tracy Rolfe, gave me their time, their insightful critique – and their typo-spotting eyes.

Talented and passionate, my cover designer Alessio Varvarà brought a visual and artistic creativity to the project that exceeded all my expectations for Singled Out.

I'm grateful too, to friends who have been infinitely supportive of this crazy project and to readers of my blog www.awritersnotepad.wordpress.com who have joined the conversation.

I reserve my deepest gratitude for Suzanne; my *writing buddy* who became my dear friend and who has over the last five years, selflessly imparted bucket-loads of inspiration, motivation, encouragement and rigorous critique.

Finally to my readers; for giving Singled Out a chance, I thank you most sincerely.

SATURDAY

1

HE STANDS OVER her, fastening his jeans. Then he scans 360-degrees, checking for any disturbance – evidence of his presence. Like so many hotel rooms these days, it's a paean to minimalist urban chic; all feature walls and faux walnut veneer. You could be anywhere from New York to Bangkok.

He notices an indentation on the bed between her parted thighs – where his knees have depressed the waffle throw. He tugs first one side then the other, smoothing and flattening.

It was a bonus, finding a lone female in the hotel bar a few hours earlier; an American, an advertising executive en route home to Boston. She was pencil-thin, pale flesh sucking her bones like a famine victim. But she was classy – expensive tailoring, silk shirt – quality underneath too. It was always gratifying to uncover La Perla or Agent Provocateur, Rigby & Peller on the older ones. Like an extra reward for having chosen well.

Nobody saw them beneath the amber glowing downlights, tucked into a corner booth, backs to the room as he summoned round after round before settling the tab in cash. Nobody noticed when he slid her key card into his pocket and guided her to the lifts, moments before she couldn't stand up any more; so finely judged these days, assured and precise.

Good job he'd pocketed a little of what he needed before he left home, just in case. He tells himself if it hadn't been put to use he'd have flushed it before the flight. Truth is, once it was there burning a hole in his groin, he'd have found someone – anyone.

The first time on the spur-of-the-moment, he'd taken a photograph; a souvenir. It set a pattern, one he won't break – can't break. He points his camera at the woman and clicks off a couple of shots before drawing her legs together. A tight smile laces his features as he rearranges her clothes, rolling her on to her side; the recovery position, they call it. But she looks like she's sleeping and she won't remember a thing when she wakes. She'll probably miss her flight but by then he'll be long gone.

The bedside clock glows 02:00. He pulls the door shut behind him and slips down the back stairs and out of a side exit, collar high, head down against the CCTV. Moments later, jacket slung over one shoulder, he strides through the front entrance; a nod to the night porter, a few words about how hard it is to sleep in hotels and in minutes he's back in his own room with time to rest before his wake-up call.

2

THE NIGHT HAD been a cacophony of slamming doors, muffled conversations and ripples of raucous laughter in the hallway. Restless as ever, exhaustion had finally delivered Brenda Bouverie from the waves of *what-ifs*, *why-didn'ts* and *if-onlys* which pummelled her mind into the small hours. At 05:00 the tsunami made landfall; unstoppable.

She sat on the bed gripping the dog-eared envelope, staring as if willing the words within to rewrite themselves. Sliding her fingers inside, she withdrew a missive scrawled across three sheets of paper. She read every word before returning the letter to its envelope and sliding it into her bag. *No tears, not now.* She bit hard on the inside of her cheek.

A phone rang in the neighbouring room; another early start. Pausing only to flick the switch on the kettle, Brenda manoeuvred herself into the capsule bathroom to shower. Emerging in a towel which struggled to meet in the middle, she made instant coffee then lowered herself on to the dressing stool and set to work. Bronzing powder to the décolleté, illuminating foundation, concealer to hide broken veins, blusher, three shades of eye shadow, eye liner, mascara, lipstick and a satin gloss; finally a dusting of translucent powder. Next the hairdryer, on a low setting to preserve the integrity of her tumble of toasted copper curls; then heated tongs to tweak the look here and there; head down, a generous burst of *is-she-or-isn't-she* fixing spray. Finally she spritzed a mist of *Cashmere Cloud* into the air and let it settle around her, enveloping her in the subtlest suggestion of sandalwood, musk and jasmine which would linger about her all day long.

Mask applied she was armed, ready for anything. It had taken a full 60 minutes and three coffees to attain that elusive *all natural* look. Women might grudgingly admire her devotion to the task. But men would look twice at Brenda now; sometimes they'd stare, captivated without realising why.

From her case she pulled an overshirt the colour of candyfloss, bedecked around its neckline with a thousand iridescent seed pearls. She drew on a pair of palazzos, slipped the shirt over her head and slid her feet, ankles already puffy from the shower's heat, into diamante embellished sandals.

Brenda wedged her bulging sponge bags into the suitcase and leant on it to bring the two sides of the zip into line. The contents protested as she slid a security strap round the case, pulling the clasp together and giving the dials on the combination lock a stir.

She shouldered a matching travel bag, heaved the suitcase to the floor and lumbered out of the hotel room in the same instant that her neighbour, the other early riser, emerged from his own. Baggage and bodies tangled. Grappling with a suitcase and camera bag, the man let go of his book. It clattered on to the remains of the breakfast tray by his feet. He'd made time for breakfast, but the eye-watering odour which clung to him suggested he hadn't troubled the bathroom.

'Oops,' Brenda said. It was all she could utter without breathing in. She trundled off down the corridor as the man stooped to retrieve his book.

Brenda waited outside for the airport bus alongside a fractious family, a sleep-deprived business traveller, a woman clutching a patchwork bag out of which poked a pair of knitting needles, and a man in ripped denim and a cheesecloth shirt which barely restrained his forest of chest-hair. The malodorous man joined the kerbside gathering just as a police car drew up, jerking to a halt at an angle to the kerb. Trendy cheesecloth guy immediately swivelled on his heels to face the wall. As two female uniformed officers got out of the car, he pulled a handkerchief from his pocket and sneezed into it before dabbing it repeatedly around his face. He didn't pocket the handkerchief again until the officers were inside the hotel.

Was he hiding his face from the police?

Singled Out

As the thought arrived uninvited, Brenda annihilated it. When would she learn to ignore the everyday quirks of human behaviour, like normal people did?

More travellers emerged as the shuttle bus drew up. Several of the cases now lining the kerb bore blue and orange tags – an identical one was stowed in Brenda's handbag. But as the passengers boarded she chose to ignore her tour operator's branding and its invitation to interact and postpone the moment when introductions would take place and first impressions would be drawn.

She couldn't face company yet.

3

HENRY LAY ON top of the sheets wearing yesterday's underpants. The reek of stale crotch and sour armpit smothered what little air there was in the room. His wake-up call and breakfast tray weren't due for a few minutes but he'd been awake for an hour.

'Never skip breakfast' his mother had urged. It was a rule he'd followed all his life thanks first to her maternal devotion then the compliance of his wife. Until her failing health sapped her energy and then her will to live, Sadie had served him a pleasingly imaginative selection of breakfast platters over the years: toast of all kinds with spreads, sweet and savoury; crunchy home-made granola; porridge in the winter; a nice fruit compote when she'd been to the deli; croissants once a month when the French market was in town; waffles and maple syrup for several days after Obama got elected; prunes soaked overnight whenever he was having trouble with his bowels and always, always a fry-up on Sundays. It was the one, the only good thing she'd done for him, without fail and without complaint, for the whole of their dreary 25-year marriage. Even in those last few months when the cancer all but overran her skeletal frame she still managed it most days. A quarter of a century, but his sentence was over.

Theirs hadn't been a bad marriage, just dull and devoid of intimacy. They couldn't have children and he'd realised she didn't care for sex for its own sake. Thus Henry claimed his conjugal rights – tense, frenetic fumblings – only rarely. He could recall few occasions other than birthdays, his alone, never hers. But he'd adapted, found ways to attend to a man's natural urges which didn't involve her; the odd appointment at the massage parlour and blow jobs from the tarts who hung about round the back of the station. Habits established years ago, unaltered by her demise.

Henry rose and pulled on the slacks and shirt he'd slung over the chair the night before. In the bathroom he scraped damp fingers through his thinning hair and slooshed his mouth with water from the basin tap.

There was a knock on the door; outside he found a tray on the floor. He brought it in and examined the contents, a cluster of packets and sachets; cereal, a carton of UHT milk, crispbreads, margarine and a scrape of jam in a pot with a peel-off lid. He chewed his way through it all then sucked on his greasy fingers before shoving the tray back into the corridor.

He returned for his belongings. He'd not disturbed his suitcase since dragging it into the room last night and this, along with a camera bag, was ready for his departure. He hitched the camera bag on to his shoulder, grabbed his holiday reading and reversed out of the room, tugging the case. He didn't notice the woman from the next room bundling into the corridor and they collided. Her mountainous bosom cushioned the impact and overwhelmed Henry's field of vision; he rebounded, dropping his paperback. The heat of blood flooded his neck as he recovered the book from the breakfast tray. The woman's smile and its implied apology radiated a heady intensity – warm and earthy – and he realised he could hardly breathe.

Minutes later Henry found himself sharing the airport bus with the same woman. Intoxicated by their encounter and the aromas of sandalwood and musk in her perfume, he strained to win her attention, but she would not look up. Instead she busied herself rifling through a handbag the size of a house. At the airport she took off at speed and vanished like vapour into the crowd.

As Henry dragged his case towards the entrance, his camera bag swinging like a wrecking ball from one shoulder, a black Porsche swept up the ramp forcing him to leap on to the kerb. It clipped the corner of his case and ground to a stop beside the valet parking desk. The windows rolled up; the roof unfolded from the boot and clunked into place. A young man with rakish hair the colour of straw and a skim of stubble sprang out. He hoisted a case from behind the seats, tossed his keys to the valet and strode through the revolving doors.

Poncy twerp, thought Henry.

4

AT THE CHECK-IN desk an overpainted attendant reviewed Brenda's travel documents. Her badge read *Cindi*; strangely apposite for such a doll-like creature, Brenda thought. Cindi nodded towards the conveyor scales and Brenda reached for her suitcase, bracing for the strain.

'Allow me,' said a voice at her ear, making her jump. The man was so close she felt his breath on her neck. In my space, Brenda noted, but he was trying to be helpful. He heaved her case on to the scales with ease. 'That's some load,' he said. His voice was like butternut squash soup, silken and spicy. He was easy on the eye too, with his granite frame and lion-paw hands; a splash too much cologne, but only a splash.

'Every woman needs options in her holiday wardrobe,' she responded with a guarded smile before turning her attention to Cindi.

'You're overweight,' said Cindi. Brenda stared at the girl, saying nothing. 'I'm sorry, I mean your case is overweight, Miss, er... Bouverie.' Cindi's cheeks coloured under layers of orange foundation. 'Your allowance is 20 kilos and you have 24.8. There's an excess charge.'

Not since her twenties, riding pillion to Cornwall for a naughty weekend, had Brenda travelled anywhere with under 20 kilos of luggage. Familiar with the rules and loath to compromise, she handed Cindi a credit card. Only then did she liberate the blue and orange tour operator's tag from her handbag. Cindi affixed it to the suitcase and set the conveyor in motion, swallowing Brenda's holiday wardrobe and 24.8 kilograms of essentials into the bowels of the airport. Passport and boarding pass in hand, Brenda turned to find herself nose-to-chest with the man-mountain.

'I look forward to checking them out,' he said, his gaze locked on her cleavage. 'Your wardrobe options,' he added, with a smile that tweaked upwards at the sides. 'I believe we're keeping company.' He waved his own blue and orange tag at her and his face broke into a broad grin. 'I'm Turner.'

Play nicely, she told herself. He looks like one of the fun ones.

'Is that Turner something, or something Turner?' She looked him full in the face, urging his eyes away from her breasts.

'Just Turner,' he said. His face seemed familiar, but good looking men did tend to bring to mind the faces of actors and celebrities.

'Brenda,' replied Brenda and left it at that. There'd be time soon enough to size up her holiday companions.

5

HENRY FOUND A seat in the lounge within sight of the departure screens. His close encounter with the bosomy woman had unsettled him. You don't see a rack that size every day. In a porno movie maybe, but even then it'd be a boob job. Hers were real, all flesh and blood. You could die happy down a cleavage like that.

A toddler waddled towards him and tumbled over his outstretched legs. The boy's mother rose from her seat to rescue her charge. She stooped in front of Henry gathering the boy into her arms, her t-shirt gaping at the neck. Lips pursed, her irritation needed no words. Henry pulled his feet in. You wouldn't want to end your life between those desiccated little titties.

Henry stared at the screens flickering overhead. His flight wasn't even on the end one yet. His eyes trawled the hall; the place was a shoppers' paradise. These days you could buy anything you needed at the airport. Things had changed since he'd last been abroad. That was 15 years ago, the only time he'd persuaded Sadie to venture further than Norfolk. They'd gone to Benidorm, to a tower of bedrooms graced with a triangle of Astroturf and a pool the size of a bathtub. Sadie had made his life a misery for the 14 days and nights he had apparently *trapped* her there. As per usual she didn't say much, but every word she uttered was a moan; she didn't like flying, she couldn't bear the heat, the food was full of garlic, the balcony had no view – she'd gone on like a drumming bunny. So he'd learnt his lesson and the next year it was back to *that nice little B&B* in Cromer. At least he saw some peace there, even if it did rain every day.

He glanced at the logo on the tag tied to his camera case. At first all you saw were two orange semi-circles, a blue line and a few squiggles. But if you stared long enough, what emerged was an impression of the sun setting over the ocean behind a cocktail glass. Arty, he thought, though he was hardly an expert. But it was eye-catching, which was the point. A letter accompanying his booking confirmation had urged him to look out for fellow travellers at the airport bearing the same brand.

Ensuring the tag was in view Henry tiptoed between the lines of chairs, the hoards of people, the hand-luggage, carrier bags and babies, searching for matching tags. After a few minutes his eyes found a flash of blue and orange attached to a flight-bag at the coffee bar. Its owner was a muscular figure, easily a decade younger than Henry. Olive-skinned, his hair was tarry. He wore shorts covered in pockets and a polo shirt that outlined bulked-up biceps. Rooted, both feet to the floor astride a bar stool, he was necking a trio of espressos. Between each shot he scanned the departure area, alert like a tiger downwind of prey, finely tuned and flawless; a virile, overpowering Alpha to Henry's shambolic, ageing Beta. Henry stepped forward then hesitated, nerves deserting him. No.

He spotted the twerp with the Porsche who'd almost run him over sitting alone, guarding a cappuccino and fiddling with his phone. He was good-looking in a pretty-boy kind of a way – like a fashion model. He considered sidling round to see if he had a tag on his bag. On second thoughts, he looked a bit poofy with his mint green pullover slung around his neck. Henry didn't want to end up being chased around by a nancy-boy all week just because he'd been sociable at the airport.

He'd noticed a tag on a suitcase on the bus but he wasn't sure who it belonged to. Now he realised two of the bus passengers were sharing a table in the coffee bar; a stocky looking bloke in ripped jeans and a woman, knitting as if her life depended on it. She tugged at a ball of wool in a bag by her feet as her companion leant into her. He was obviously trying to chat her up but anyone could see she was more interested in her wool. Three's a crowd, Henry mused. But when the woman appeared to excuse herself and exited the coffee bar clutching her knitting, Henry thought the better of joining the man, whose features had mutated to a brittle scowl.

He continued to meander around the hall and eventually spotted another tag, attached to a striped beach bag lodged between the feet of a slip of a girl. She wore a flowery skirt which covered her knees and surrendered to a demure hem near her ankles. Mousy hair without an identifiable style framed her face. Plain-featured, she wore no make-up; a dab of lipstick would have helped.

This was more like it. She had her head in a glossy magazine but there was an empty seat beside her. Henry approached, attempting a smile but achieving a leer. He pulled the camera case off his shoulder and flapped his luggage tag under the girl's nose. She looked up.

'We're on the same holiday,' he said. 'Mind if I join you?'

'Of course,' said the girl without smiling, as if it were her duty to consent. Charmingly submissive, thought Henry, as he pressed himself into the seat beside her.

6

THE COVEN OF shag-hags was cackling in the office kitchen. Normally he'd have ignored them, but as he nuked his lunch that day, he was disturbed to find himself absorbed by their chatter. One of them – he could never remember which was which – had just come back from a singles holiday. A holiday for people with no friends, he'd thought at first. The silly cow had gone to Greece with 30 strangers. She'd been keeping it quiet but the coven dragged it out of her. They were caught between admiring her boldness and mocking her desperation.

But he had to admit, the format had possibilities; a holiday somewhere far away, with a dozen or more unwary women, their defences diluted by the sun and the sea. So a few weeks later he'd road-tested the concept, embarking on his first *holiday for the independent traveller* to a sprawling complex in the Dominican Republic. It had paid off handsomely and other trips followed; Zante, Crete, Cancun.

He returns to the counter for a top up and continues to siphon up caffeine as if it's the last thing he'll ever drink. With nothing else to occupy him, his eyes scan the hall; everywhere he looks, slappers slathered with shiny make-up, their pink and red lips glistening and engorged. Blatant displays like this disturb him; so much tawdry flesh screaming out for sex.

It's no good, this kind of thinking. It's making him restless. It'll be hours before he can self-medicate with anything more potent than a coffee or an airline miniature. In the meantime, he can't afford to draw attention.

So he counts. It's a good distraction. Something easy to start with: how many shops? He gets to 18 that he can see round the departure lounge perimeter, plus another six if he counts the booths in the middle – sunglasses and pens. How about something a bit harder: how many people in the coffee bar? It's tricky to get an accurate number as people keep coming and going. That's why it's good – he has to count the people whilst keeping an eye on two different access points. He gets to 48... 49... 47... 46... 45... 48..., keeping his mind focussed. His breathing slows. Inside his head he visualises a steamroller smoothing yard after yard of sticky black tarmac. He keeps counting, one in, two out, two in, three out, until it becomes like a sub-process, running in the back of his mind, keeping it flattened out.

A girl wanders in from Passport Control. Is that the singles' luggage tag? She's on her own with a beach bag, so it's a fair bet. She's wearing a modest skirt and a t-shirt that isn't too tight like so many in the hall. An ingénue, the sort he likes best. She finds a seat but isn't alone for long. A man, scruffy son-of-a-bitch, approaches her waving the tag on his bag. That's a sure sign they're headed in the same direction, his direction.

The man settles beside her, sleazy sod.

7

BRENDA SQUEEZED ON to a banquette in the mezzanine restaurant overlooking the melee. She glanced at the menu before ordering then braced herself as, one by one, the memories detonated.

The *all-day-breakfast* had been their holiday tradition – a sinful spread ahead of the flight. With breakfasts of yoghurt, bread and honey ahead, they'd delight in every morsel of their cholesterol-laden platters. They'd savour every taste like children let loose in a chocolate factory and eventually hoover up the lot, mopping the dregs with spongy white bread. Not that there was anything wrong with yoghurt, bread and honey; every mouthful would be relished when the time came, served al-fresco as it would be, under the shade of climbers and vines.

The server brought her order. Brenda stared, paralysed by the gargantuan platter of shiny fried eggs, bacon, fried bread, black pudding, tomatoes and congealed baked beans – and the raw burn of bewilderment.

'Why couldn't you stay out of it? You ruined... everything.'

'What happened to us, Jack?' she whispered, addressing the empty seat across the table.

But even laced with sour notes of pain and regret, a fatty feast could hold Brenda's attention. She laid into the coagulated carbs and willed herself into a holiday frame of mind. As devastating as the past months had been, Brenda's expectations for the coming week were elevated – some might say too far. She'd finally given herself permission, to try at least, to regain some perspective.

The last mouthful savoured, Brenda turned to observe the ants-nest of travellers below. They were mostly holidaymakers, betrayed by a plethora of gaudy beach bags and sandals laced around spray-tanned ankles.

Turner straddled a stool at the coffee bar. Deep-set eyes beneath abundant eyebrows suggested Eastern European origins, though his accent was pure middle-England. Solid and toned, he radiated the confidence of a man who knew he had it all going on. Brenda gazed at him, certain her pupils were dilated. She ran her tongue absently over her lips.

Jack would have slapped her wrist for that.

But it was no secret; men like Turner had little interest in cuddlesome women. Their attentions went to lithe and slender girls. Those hands would tease at micro-bikinis, not cover-all kaftans.

She noticed the odious man from the hotel, gripping his luggage tag as he wandered the seating area scanning for the telltale marker. He moved in on a young woman and she must have invited him to sit for in a moment, he had shoehorned into the seat beside her.

Too close too soon, Brenda thought. With strangers, you tread with care. Were holidays like this a magnet for the socially maladroit?

It was more bearable on the mezzanine than in the swarming hall below, so Brenda held her ground for an hour. The price was tolerable; a second cafetière and a cinnamon bun for which she had little appetite. On top of breakfast the dough lay like a slab of concrete in her gut. It did nothing to alleviate the far deeper ache inside her.

8

HE STANDS BY the motionless carousel keying the number he's been given into his phone. They – whoever they are – can wait for him, not the other way around. He lets it connect then hangs up. The arrangements are in place, nothing more is needed.

As the travellers process through to baggage claim he keeps an eye out for the ingénue, but she's nowhere to be seen. A buzzer sounds and the carousel begins to rumble round. Bags appear one by one, lurching up the ramp, tumbling on to the conveyor. People jostle for position wanting to be first away. He'd stand back and wait for the crowd to subside if he didn't have business to conduct; as it is, he presses his way to the front and when his case looms into view, he makes a grab for it.

'Oi!' whines a man beside him, elbows flailing. It's the dirty old boy he'd seen moving in on the girl – he's already thinking of her as *his* girl – at the airport. Sweat oozes from the old man's pores like sewage from a broken drain. He grinds his case against the old man's ankle.

'Who the hell do you think—?' The man turns and immediately realises his mistake.

'Go on,' he says, challenging the little prick eyeball to eyeball. It isn't a contest, just pathetic.

'Sorry... sorry, I didn't mean—.'

'Sure,' he says. Let it go. There's scant satisfaction in crushing a nobody.

His baggage retrieved, he ambles through the exit, eyes scanning left and right. He's looking out for a man dressed like a porter but wearing a green baseball cap. He spots him straight away leaning against a wall, smoking a cigarette. They make contact, the most imperceptible of nods.

He follows the man to the coach park keeping a few yards between them. They wind their way to a spot between two larger unattended vehicles. At a brief glance it would look like an innocent transaction, a porter getting paid for doing his job. However the man hasn't carried his bag and it isn't a few coins that passes between them but a wad of notes exchanged for a small package, swiftly secreted. They shake hands and the green baseball cap slips away.

Job done; he's been in the country less than 30 minutes and he's sorted, and for half what he pays at home. It's because he plans ahead, making sure before he leaves the UK that he can obtain what he needs. You arrive clean and leave clean wherever you travel, but especially Turkey, if you believe the movies – you don't want that *Midnight Express* experience. It's never a problem since he's connected. His dealer always knows someone who knows someone, gets him a number, sometimes a name to ask for – it's the same whenever he travels and he travels a lot. Works like clockwork every time.

He boards his coach, fully loaded with a week's worth of recreationals.

9

A WALL OF heat hit Brenda as she exited the air conditioned hygiene of Dalaman's international terminal and even as it commanded a vigorous flush to her chest and neck, it lifted her spirits. The late afternoon temperature hovered in the low 30s, the humidity only slowly draining from the day. She threw back her head and breathed in. The warm air hugged the back of her throat and flooded her lungs. She loved this place.

If only Jack were here.

Arriving unbidden, a rush of memory slammed into her, momentarily depriving her of breath. Brenda stood rooted to the spot, suddenly unsure of what to do next.

It might have been seconds or minutes before she spotted the travel rep decked out in navy blue and day-glo orange and her brain stirred. She confirmed her name and was directed to a bus amongst a clutch of identikit vehicles.

As Brenda hauled herself aboard, rivulets of perspiration were already carving channels across her immaculate foundation. Ignoring a weak smile from a man in the front row, she manoeuvred to the rear of the bus. From here she would get a good look at the other passengers – her companions for the coming week – as they boarded. She dropped on to a pair of seats alongside a slender woman barely wearing micro skirt and cropped t-shirt. Brenda pulled a fan from her bag and wafted it vigorously.

'This heat!' she exclaimed to her neighbour.

'We'll acclimatise,' the woman replied. 'I'm Adele.' She smiled.

Brenda sipped water from a bottle whilst Adele kept up a wry commentary as each passenger clambered on board. Wide-eyed, she singled out Turner – it was hardly surprising; she sneered at another less wholesome specimen, pale as a spectre, absorbed by something on his mobile. More women arrived, all ignored by Adele. She smiled too desperately at the next to board – the man in ripped denim from the airport shuttle bus. He returned the smile but found a seat several rows forward. A blonde man wearing a mint green sweater knotted across his shoulders was next; expensively attired, casually assured. By now Brenda expected an expression of lustful desire from Adele, but instead got subdued silence. Adele pretended she had something in her eye and hid her face until the man settled further forward in the bus.

By the time the door swung shut, the coach was full with more women than men and an abundance of thinning scalp. 'Two out of 25,' Adele sighed.

As the coach moved off, a pungent odour bloomed in the cabin. Several people reached to twist open overhead ventilators. Others sniffed, coughed and cleared their throats. The man from the hotel, Brenda surmised, though she couldn't see where he was seated. Someone begged the driver to activate the air conditioning.

The coach bounced across road humps and jolted through an automated checkpoint overseen by a guard in a military-style uniform. As it picked up speed, a pixie-like woman in blue and orange got to her feet. Her hair was lynched into a high ponytail; her make-up looked caked and chalky, applied for day-long durability. She had the crisp manner of a teacher in charge of a school bus. In perilous heels, she tottered up the aisle and back brandishing a basket of moist wipes. The air stung with synthetic citrus as foreheads and necks were blotted. Perched by the driver, the pixie-woman tapped on a microphone.

'My name is Hakima and I welcome you to my beautiful country of Turkey for your holiday with Solasoni Singles. I hope you have a fun time. Today you are all strangers, but soon you will become friends so don't be shy. Introduce yourself to your neighbour. Maybe they are the next love of your life, eh?'

A few passengers complied with hushed introductions. Brenda rarely welcomed being told what to do and appreciated being patronised even less. At least she and Adele were already chatting like old friends.

'For people who are coming on Solasoni Singles holiday for the first time, I have a few words,' Hakima continued. 'This is not a group herding-about holiday. You can do anything you like. Spend time with your new friends or go by yourself, all is fine. In the evenings we prepare a delicious feast for you, in local style, to share and be sociable with your fellow guests. I will come to your hotel three times in the week and you can ask me any questions or book with me to go on excursions. We have trips to special places like the ancient city of Ephesus and the hot springs at Pamukkale. And this week we have a special two-day gulet trip to tempt you. I love you to enjoy my country but it is your choice what you do. I take your booking for trips, or you spend seven days on the beach. Only one thing is important, enjoy your holiday. Now we drive to your hotel.'

The bus sped along humming ribbons of tarmac and Brenda gazed out at the panorama-in-motion. Tinder-dry landscape stretched out on either side; hills layered with pine, valleys patchworked with fields of citrus, figs and pomegranates.

For her first holiday alone Brenda had spurned the popular resorts, their streets scarred with all-night clubs and bars, gutters swimming with adolescent vomit. As she and Jack had always done, she'd sought out one of the unspoiled resorts frequented by Turkish city dwellers and serviced by independent tour operators. Her heart fluttered in anticipation of her first sight of the coastline which was so familiar. But there was trepidation too; how would she *be* in this place, without Jack?

'There were holidays. We had fun. But that wasn't enough for you.'

A flurry of activity commanded her attention; it was Turner, stumbling towards the front of the bus. One hand covered his mouth whilst the other waived back and forth, pointing to the roadside.

'Sit down,' ordered Hakima. 'You have to be seated, is the law.'

'Sorry but you have to stop. Stop now please. Right now!'

Turner's body convulsed and the driver got the message. The coach jerked to a halt in a spray of roadside gravel. With a hiss the door opened and Turner lurched out, still clutching his mouth. Bent over the crash barrier, he heaved several times into the undergrowth. He hung over the dripping vegetation until his stomach stopped retching. Wiping trails of bile from his mouth he turned to see the coach load of passengers staring out at him and his sallow eyes met Brenda's. Poor man, she thought. How embarrassing.

Turner climbed back into the coach. 'Travel sickness,' he mumbled unnecessarily. 'I forgot my pills. Sorry, everyone.'

The coach rumbled on. Away from the main arteries the vista changed; mini-marts piled high outside with an eclectic assemblage of foodstuffs, holiday accessories and hardware; dusty cars and battered pick-ups; a horse and cart laden with misshapen vegetables; a bar with a half-dozen whiskery old men swigging raki.

Rising up every few miles like a mirage in the desert was the ubiquitous mosque, its minaret, a narrow finger of faith, pointing heavenward. Brenda loved the exotic mystery of the call to prayer. It evoked centuries past, ancient times and age old traditions. She loved how the hypnotic chanting tumbled around the hills and suffused her senses, even as it signposted an opportune moment for food or cocktails.

The coach turned off the highway, doubling back as it climbed upward, hugging the cliffs. Passengers with a sheer drop beside them became restless; one or two reached for previously ignored seatbelts.

When it came, that longed-for first view of the Aegean took Brenda's breath away. Far below them, inky water stretched towards the horizon, unbroken but for the wake of an occasional gulet. These majestic twin-masted schooners were designed to sail, but at this time of day expedience overrode aesthetics and it was diesel, rather than wind which powered them.

The road dipped and twisted and as one boat after another sped towards the inlets and coves which fringed the ancient coastline, a deceptive serenity reached out to claim her.

10

THE COACH WOUND its way downward to its destination, a village nested on the coast, sheltered by hills lined with pine. Tarmac gave way to crusted clay and the coach slipped once or twice, its wheels skidding on the unmade path. It halted by a white stuccoed arch, festooned with boughs of bougainvillea. Beneath the foliage, a pair of iron gates stood open, leading to a courtyard and a two-storey building beyond.

Awaiting their arrival stood a local man and woman. She might have been middle-aged or younger, it was impossible to tell. She stood, arms crossed, an unconvincing smile on otherwise immobile features. He was tall, at least six feet. Ramrod straight, his body only curved at the neck where his head dipped forward. A mop of dark curls was swept back from his face by an almost invisible black comb headband.

Hakima stepped off the coach with her clipboard.

'Welcome to Hotel Erdem,' she chirruped as the travellers disembarked. 'I hope you are happy with your journey.' A few withering smiles didn't put her off. Pointing to the local couple she continued, 'Say hello to Mehmet and Defne – they run Hotel Erdem for us. They are always here and can help, whatever you need.' More withering smiles. 'Identify your luggage and Mehmet will show you to your rooms. You have time to rest before we have a cocktail drink by the pool.'

The bedrooms were in the two-storey L-shaped building which overlooked the patio. Its roof was cluttered with solar panels and water tanks. Stems of creeping ivy layered the walls, clutching angles and grasping across cracked plasterwork. The scent of bougainvillea and jasmine draped the air.

Mehmet escorted Brenda to a room on the upper floor via an external concrete staircase at one end of the block. It was air conditioned but basic. It smelled of insect repellent – someone had left an anti-mosquito gadget plugged in by the bed. A small fridge scarred with rust buzzed disconcertingly; inside she found a bottle of water and a tray of ice cubes.

Brenda pulled the muslin curtain aside and stepped on to the balcony. A black-shelled beetle skittered into the gulley and disappeared. Down below the patio was dotted with wooden tubs planted to overflowing with begonias and marigolds. In between were clusters of sun loungers, furled parasols and low tables. A swimming pool formed a focal point and to the far side of the pool stood an open-air bar shaded by a bamboo roof. Tables were dressed with tealights in colourful glass holders. Alongside the bar area a pair of refectory tables beneath a pergola were lined with wooden chairs. Strangling the pergola were the twisted boughs and peeling branches of a mature grapevine, weighed low with ripening fruit. A mass of raggedy vine leaves rippled in the breeze.

It was all serviceable, not unattractive and much as she'd expected. But as Brenda contemplated the next seven days and the gaping hole where Jack should have been, she couldn't feel – anything.

'Fancy a slug to get things started?' The voice came from the neighbouring room.

'Don't mind if I do,' said Brenda.

'Pass me your glass then. Southern Comfort ok?'

Brenda smiled – Adele might be just the kind of holiday companion she needed. She found a tumbler in her bathroom and handed it over the waist-high balcony wall. From inside the room came the clink of ice cubes. Adele appeared clutching two glasses and the bottle of golden liquor. She passed them across, swung her legs over the wall and landed with a thud in Brenda's domain. The women settled at the balcony table. Adele snapped open the bottle top and poured generously into each tumbler. Glasses connected in a salute to their nascent friendship, but before Brenda had taken a sip, Adele had emptied hers in two unladylike gulps.

'You won't let me embarrass myself, will you?' she sniggered. 'I've eaten sod-all since yesterday. I didn't even get my airline peanuts.'

When it came to food, Brenda could always make a contribution. She slipped into her room and returned bearing a tub of pistachios and a giant bag of potato chips.

'These'll have to do until I can get into town for some proper cocktail snacks,' she said.

Although Brenda's was not yet empty, Adele replenished both glasses and again slugged back the contents of her own before the ice had melted. She stared at the empty tumbler.

'You might have to look out for me this week,' she said.

11

THE SCRAWNY TURKISH guy shows him up to his room; it's close to the stairs, which is handy. He mutters on for a few moments about the fridge or the shower or something and eventually lets him be. Travel days always leave him wasted and as gratifying as the previous evening's diversion had been, the lack of sleep hasn't helped.

But he's made it; light-headed, pulse racing, he's made it. Like an escaped prisoner-of-war stumbling over the Swiss border he flops, exhausted, on to the bed. He'll have to get his shit together before dinner.

He unzips his case and extracts a shaving mirror from his spongebag. He pulls the package from his carry-on bag and tugs at the tape and brown paper until it gives way. He separates the contents, spreading them out on the bed. There are three smaller packets wrapped in polythene. He selects one, a pillow of white powder. He balances it on his right hand and bounces it up and down. It's lighter than he was expecting. They've screwed him, the peasants; there isn't much he can do about it. He pierces the corner, pouring a mound on to the mirror. He pushes the powder into two lines then rolls a new 50TL note into a straw and sharply snorts first one, then the next. He sits motionless on the bed, eyes-glazed and blinking, breathing hard through his nose, his jaw slackened.

It's a motley collection on this trip as far as he can see, more women than men. But he can hold his own. He knows how to get onside with the women. Not much competition either, one or two, tops; then just geeks and geriatrics trying to pretend they're not past-it, fooling no one. It won't be too tricky to pick off the ones he wants. Stand by for a good time and a bit more besides.

He rises from the bed, arranges the remaining contents of his spongebag on the shelf in the shower room and unpacks his clothes. He downs half a bottle of water from the fridge then extracts another line on to his mirror before carefully re-wrapping his stash and placing it in a carrier bag in the room safe at the foot of the wardrobe. He selects a combination and locks it away.

Then he strips to his boxers and executes 30 press-ups, 30 sit-ups and 30 crunches before taking a shower, dressing for dinner and doing the line he'd set by.

12

DUSK SMOTHERED THE last blush of sunset. Behind the bar a tail of wood-smoke curled out of the kitchen, teasing with its earthy tang and diffusing into a star-spattered sky.

One of the first to convene as instructed and dressed in the same clothes that had seen him through the last 48 hours, Henry positioned himself at one end of the pool bar under its fringe of fairy lights. He ordered a glass of the chilled fizz that passes for beer in foreign parts and leaned, one elbow resting on the counter, in what he hoped was a casual, approachable pose. This had the unintentional effect of flaunting a spreading underarm tidemark.

One by one other guests emerged from the bedroom block, hopping over low walls from the downstairs rooms and navigating the graphite shadow which cloaked the concrete steps from the upper floor. No lights on the steps, Henry noted. *Elf 'n' safety* would have a field day, he chuckled to himself. But then this wasn't England.

He maintained a fixed smile but no one joined him.

The two long tables beneath the pergola were set for dinner and Defne wandered between them, laying out platters of dips in dishes and grumbling to herself, seemingly oblivious to the bonhomie blossoming around her. Every so often she turned towards her husband and shook her head.

A middle-aged woman emerged from the bedroom block. Wearing a short-sleeved blouse and a grey skirt, she looked dowdy and old, like a dummy in a dusty frock in a charity shop window. She reminded Henry of Sadie. A smear of rouge on each cheek was her only attempt at make-up.

As she approached the groups of guests, Mehmet came towards her bearing a tray of glasses filled with a layered concoction of orange and red, loaded with ice and slices of orange.

'Welcome, Madame,' he said in a thick accent. 'Will you like Tequila Sunrise?'

'Yes. No. I mean, does it have alcohol in it?' the dowdy woman asked. 'I don't drink, you see.' Her voice was clipped home counties, well-spoken but nervy.

'Yes indeed,' replied Mehmet, 'but if you wish, I can make you same drink, no Tequila. Will you like?' The woman said she would, thank you, and Mehmet returned a few moments later with another glass, identical to those on the tray.

'That's not half so much fun,' said a mellifluous voice. The dowdy woman looked up. Henry jumped, heat flaming his cheeks. It was the woman he'd bumped into that morning. No longer in candy pink, she shone like the sun in antique golden silk – a fluid shirt and pants which tapered to strappy sandals. Around her neck hung strands of hammered beads, the light firing off them like sparks of static electricity. Her hair was a mass of curls. She radiated all the abundance and fecundity of a goddess – Aphrodite, the Goddess of Love.

How had she evaded him? He hadn't seen her at the airport, nor on the plane. How could he possibly have missed her on the bus? And she was on *his* holiday. Henry's hand instinctively reached towards his groin.

Things were looking up. He'd be able to gaze on that bosom for seven whole days and nights. Maybe she'd go topless by the pool – women did that on holiday, didn't they? He'd be able to watch her, flesh moist from the pool, smoothing creams on to those curves. At night he'd imagine her lying naked and sweaty – naughty thoughts to wank over. If he was clever he might catch a shot or two; a glimpse of secret flesh, something to take home and play with later.

'Yes. No. I know. I mean, it might not be much fun, but it's a lot safer,' sputtered the dowdy woman, gatecrashing his fantasy. Was she relieved to be rescued from the awkwardness of standing alone and ignored, or terrified of the attention? He was alone too. Why couldn't the goddess have rescued him instead?

The dowdy woman gulped shallow breaths and sputtered a few more words. 'I've never been. On a holiday like this before you see. It's all a bit daunting. At the moment.'

'Nor have I,' said the goddess with genuine warmth. 'So we're in it together, aren't we? Booze can oil the wheels though. Do you really not drink?'

'It's not that I don't drink. But my husband. Sorry. My ex-husband. He told me I behave like an idiot when I do. It made him so angry. He used to... to—' the woman's voice tapered off. She didn't want to explain. 'Anyway, I've rather stayed away from it,' she finally blurted. Henry understood the sub-text — her ex-husband bullied her, maybe even knocked her about. Thanks to his reporter's nose, he didn't miss much.

'But he's your *ex*-husband. He doesn't count any more, surely?' The sight of that valiant bosom rising and falling with every breath made Henry giddy.

'I... I guess not,' responded the woman and before she could sputter another word, Aphrodite relieved her of the non-Tequila Sunrise, helped herself to another glass of the boozy version from Mehmet's tray and thrust it into her hand.

'What's your name?'

'Veronica.'

'Well hello, Veronica. I'm Brenda. Shall we get the party started?'

And Henry's heartbeat went into overdrive.

13

THERE WAS JOSTLING as the call to be seated went up – three bangs of bottle against counter, courtesy of Mehmet. Adele commandeered chairs for herself and Brenda and Brenda in turn encouraged Veronica to join them. Despite Adele's urging that Turner take the seat next to her, he claimed a place opposite Brenda then pulled out the chair beside his own for a girl with a gentle Suffolk burr and a shy smile.

As she sat, a man materialised behind the girl. He slid a solid forearm across her shoulders as he took hold of the chair beside her.

'Is this one going spare?' he queried, leaning close to the girl's ear. Only Brenda noticed the flicker of discomfort that flashed across her face. The girl was the same one she'd seen being imposed upon at the airport; too youthful to be overlooked and too polite to rebuff inappropriate approaches.

With a baritone that would have been at home in a concert hall, the man introduced himself to the table as 'you guys can call me Matt'. He'd swapped cheesecloth for a t-shirt and sleeveless hoodie. With his froth of chest-hair under wraps, Matt exuded an altogether more wholesome impression. He grabbed a bottle of red and filled his glass, drank it down and refilled it. He and Adele would make quite a pair, Brenda imagined.

The wooden chair with its coarse straw seat was too small for Brenda's ample rear and the tops of the chair legs had already begun to press into her flesh. It was one of those things she was accustomed to tolerating on holiday, like the wadding mattresses, humid nights and ever-present insects. You couldn't have the Aegean's voluptuous caress without bugs and sweat. She and Jack would always laugh about those little trade-offs.

You should be here Jack. You should be here, with me.

'Is this your first time?'

'My first time?' said Brenda, blood seeping into her cheeks.

'On a singles holiday,' said Turner.

'Yes,' said Brenda. 'I've not come away by myself before. You?'

'Once or twice,' said Turner. 'There's something delicious about not being known, don't you think?' Brenda concurred. Anonymity and the absence of well-meaning friends was a bonus.

Turner's evening look was a studied casual, overworked by an abundance of designer brands – a Gucci watch, a Ralph Lauren shirt, a pair of Ray-Bans hooked at the neckline though the sun wouldn't be seen again for ten hours. Rough-hewn features and espresso eyes lent him an intensity that was as unsettling as it was stimulating. And he was fit too; Turner had the body of an athlete and the aura of a renegade.

A late arrival joined the table, the man Adele had hidden from on the coach. She identified him as 'James double-barrelled something or other'. He flopped on to the remaining vacant chair, beside Adele, throwing his iPhone and camera on to the table. He was in his thirties with unblemished caramel skin and cobalt eyes. His shirt was monogrammed; four initials, *JPW-B*.

'Hello all,' he said to the table at large, his accent a laconic *upstairs*. He let a half-smile tease his lips before stretching across Adele to grasp a bottle of wine.

'Hello, James,' said Adele.

'You know me? Do I...? Have we met?'

James's response was evidently not what Adele had anticipated. She stared at him incredulously for a moment then turned away, her neck a carpet of burgundy blotches.

'Christ, you shit,' she hissed.

'Steady on,' said James, eyebrows elevated. 'What did I do?'

Notwithstanding the odd awkward moment, conversation hummed, lubricated by bottles of house plonk. Introductions followed the 'what's your name and where do you come from' format, with the inevitable follow-on, 'what do you do'. This prompted Matt to confess to having just purchased 'an upmarket new-build in deepest Surrey' as one of many rewards of a career spent 'selling really big computers'. Brenda took a breath but before she could speak, Matt put his hand up.

'Don't ask, you won't understand it,' he announced, 'and anyway, I'll bore myself stupid – and you too – if you get me going on resilient infrastructure.' That seemed to be the end of the matter, so the conversation moved along. Chloe, cheery and petite, announced she was 'working her way down the career ladder' to a non-specific job in retail, prompting much good-natured laughter. Another woman, a narrow-lipped bottle-blonde with an empty furrow in her ring finger announced she was living off a healthy divorce settlement and 'making the bastard pay for being a duplicitous shit'. Turner lived in Central London and wouldn't say more than he was 'something in the City' and Brenda successfully dodged the question of career by asking everyone else about theirs. It was an oft-deployed tactic and Brenda was an accomplished defender of her privacy.

Turner addressed the girl beside him.

'And you are?' he asked, presenting a mannered smile.

'Well,' she began, 'my name's Lilly and I'm from Beccles.' By now Brenda fully expected Cilla Black to leap out. The girl continued, 'But I live in London now, in Notting Hill. Do you know where that is?' Turner responded politely that yes, he did know. 'Nothin' happens in Beccles and you can't stay in a place where nothin' happens forever, can you? So I came down to London to do my nanny training. And then I got myself a job.' The girl spoke as if the act of finding employment were a triumphant achievement. But Brenda warmed to her, ingenuous as she seemed. Turner and Matt too appeared charmed, as Adele's face creased.

'Now I'm at this house in Notting Hill,' Lilly continued. 'Mr and Mrs Barrington and their little ones. It's a big place – it has eight bedrooms and five bathrooms. He's an *entrepreneur* and she's, well, she does charity stuff and has lunch mostly.'

'Do you enjoy it?' asked Turner.

'It's hard work. I do the nannying of course. The children are two and four, so they're not at school. They need me to do babysitting too, because they can't find the right sort of girl where they live. I get their evening meal, since they're out such a lot and don't have the time. They say they would never eat properly if it weren't for me doing the tea. I do the food shop too because Mrs B is always so busy with her ladies. And I keep the place tidy. Oh, and I do the ironing.'

'That's an awful lot of work for such a pretty girl,' Matt said.

'I couldn't agree more,' murmured Turner. His lion paw connected momentarily with her fingertips. 'Hard labour for young hands.'

'Oh, you're a pair!' laughed Lilly. 'But don't be wasting your time on me, either of you. I'm an old fashioned girl with old fashioned values.'

'I guess we'll have to control ourselves,' said Matt, a vulpine smile lingering a moment too long. 'What do you reckon, Turner?'

'God knows, Matt, there's only so much temptation a man can stand.' Turner replied. He licked his lips theatrically.

'And I'm spoken for too,' Lilly interjected. 'Well, nearly anyway. Almost.'

'Fair enough,' smiled Turner, leaning back in his chair. 'I give in. You're a lovely girl, but I wouldn't want to piss up another man's tree.'

Oblivious to the look of shock on Lilly and Veronica's faces, Turner leaned across the table to Brenda. 'Far more fun to have one all to yourself.' He laughed.

Mehmet and Defne emerged from the kitchen bearing platters of tomato and feta salad drenched in olive oil and baskets of steaming pides. The bread was seized upon, ripped and shared.

'So, Lilly,' said Adele, too loudly, 'you're spoken for, you say?'

'Nearly,' said Lilly.

'What's nearly?' asked Veronica, her voice little more than a squeak. It was the first thing she'd said since sitting down.

'His name's Danny and he works for Mr B, at his office. He drops in for papers and files a couple of times a week and stops for a brew. We've been walking out together, the two of us.'

'Walking out?' said James. 'That sounds frightfully proper.'

'What if it does?' replied Lilly.

'So how come you're on holiday by yourself?' said James.

'Because we're not... because we don't... Because he told me I should. I was having a horrid time a few weeks back. The children were playing up and Mrs B had left me a note saying she wanted me to work my night off again. And I was tired, right tired. I was sobbing my eyes out when Danny came by for his folders; just at the right moment – or the wrong moment, depending on your view. Danny said I needed a holiday, time to think about what was going on in this house.'

'Sounds like your Danny had a point,' said Matt.

'True,' said Lilly, 'but it's my first job and it's too easy to get taken advantage of, when you don't know what's what.'

'Indeed,' said James, pensively. 'Still, now you're on a break, making new friends, enjoying new experiences.' He dropped his head to one side and let another uneven grin drift across his features.

'It'll be fun,' said Lilly. 'I've never been abroad before. But it's safe with a group, isn't it?'

'So they say,' said Adele.

'Let's hope we can find some new experiences for you.' Turner's eyes narrowed.

'Lucky girl,' chuckled James.

It was like watching hyenas toying with a stray fawn. Even so, it made Brenda wish she were 21 again and a narrow-waisted slip of a girl, unaware of the lure of her own unadorned beauty.

'I'm up for new experiences too,' said Adele, her head tilted coquettishly towards Turner and Matt. Then, finding herself ignored, 'I'm a free-spirit.'

'Is that so?' said Turner, his voice flat.

Defne served the main course, lamb casserole with tomatoes, aubergine and garlic. Brenda consumed like a ravenous castaway.

Throughout the meal, James's iPhone on the table buzzed on silent several times. Each time he downed his glass and refilled it from the nearest bottle before checking the caller's identity and rejecting the call. He seemed to be playing his own private drinking game. Brenda wondered why he'd brought the device to the table if he didn't intend to answer it.

'I wish they'd leave me alone,' he moaned after the third call. It was the first flicker of anything approaching emotion from the languid James.

'Who?' Brenda asked.

'My father, his PA. I've come on holiday, for god's sake, not gone to the moon. I'll be back in a week, I told them. Okay, I didn't tell them, but it's none of their business.' He let go the bottle of wine he was holding and it dropped to the table. It toppled, its contents spilling, spreading like a blood pool and splashing on to Turner's food. Turner's lips tightened but he said nothing. He righted the bottle then deployed his napkin to absorb the puddle of wine seeping across his plate.

'Won't they want to know where you are?' asked Lilly.

'It doesn't matter where I am. I'm not there and I'm not on company business – that's what's bothering them.'

The phone buzzed again. This time, James grabbed it.

'Yes... yes... It's great, thank you, just what I needed – perfect. I'm sure I'll have a fine time. Top marks again, guys. Oh, one thing – you couldn't give my Pa a buzz could you? Tell him I'll be back in a week and not to bother ringing me again. But for god's sake don't say where I am. No. I don't want him chasing me down. Okay... okay, thanks. Bye.' He ended the call and leaned back in his chair. 'My concierge service,' he announced.

'Concierge?' queried Lilly. 'What's that?'

'It's like having your own personal manservant,' said James. 'I tell them what I want and they sort it out, holidays and everything, wherever I want to go. I said, book me some fun with a few new people, not my usual type. They know what I like.'

'You've been on holidays like this before,' said Adele. A statement, not a question.

'Yes, if I didn't squeeze in a couple of getaways a year, I'd go nuts.'

'Ever met anyone nice – anyone worth staying in touch with?' she asked, pointedly. James reflected for a moment.

'Nope,' he said. 'No one comes to mind. Have your fun if you must, they tell me, but don't bring it home. So I don't.'

'*It?*' spat Adele.

'So you're here for some fun,' said Lilly.

'That's the plan,' said James.

'He's a shit,' muttered Adele to Brenda.

'So tell me,' said Lilly, addressing the table. 'How does this kind of holiday work? What am I supposed to do?'

'You do what you like,' Adele pouted. 'You can go off by yourself, but if you like company, there are people to go to the beach or the bar with. People to... Just figure out who you like being with and make friends.' She stared at Turner, but his eyes were black holes, sucking in the fire in her own and smothering it.

Conversation ebbed and flowed, one moment faltering on first-night nerves, the next, made fluid by the surfeit of wine. The main course over, Mehmet paraded platters of baklava to the tables; a sticky climax to the first-night feast.

After dinner a few guests chose to venture to the beachfront bars; others retreated to their rooms. Most of the guests, their herding instinct intact, stayed around the dinner tables. Gradually they circled, as if caught in a vortex, around the Alphas. Animated and evidently in a competitive frame of mind, Turner and Matt entertained with one tale after another; stories of wild holidays, extreme challenges, adrenalin sports and other testosterone-powered activities. Brenda stayed, content for a while to enjoy the verbal jousting.

Drink flowed and laughter billowed. The two men's mostly genial competitiveness was infectious. When one had a story, the other had a better one. When one came up with a witty punch-line the other produced a coruscating put-down – all in the name of the game, of course, as they were quick and respectful enough to acknowledge. Keeping such banter bubbling and winning the hearts and minds of strangers was no easy task. Yet like leaders of a cult, Matt and Turner subdued and then manipulated their followers. Never mind the competitive sparring, this was a masterclass in subtle dominance – their performance was captivating.

But having given the men a generous 45 minutes, Brenda was ready to pull herself away from the vortex. As she circled the pool en route to her room James appeared, sniffing loudly, stumbling down the last few concrete steps.

'Going so soon?' he said. 'The night is young. Come on, old girl, don't be a party pooper.'

'Less of the *old girl* thank you,' she said. 'But I've had enough cheap booze for one evening and it's been a long day.'

'Nightcap?' said James, unwilling to yield. 'I've got a lovely bottle of, um, *nightcap* in my room.'

'Your room?' queried Brenda. 'I don't think so.'

'Oh, no!' smiled James. 'I mean, I'll bring it down. We can have a glass here, under the stars and all that, or get something from the bar. Don't make me go back there.' He tossed his head in the direction of the table party.

Brenda was determined to embrace the entire holiday experience though it made even her bones ache. So she obliged and they selected a poolside table.

Mehmet approached, clapping his hands together.

'You like drink?' he said warmly.

'Two brandies, please,' said James. 'Proper ones – top shelf. Have you got Courvoisier, or Martell?'

'Very sorry,' said Mehmet with a frown. 'Only local brandy today. If you like, I get best brandy for you tomorrow.'

'The local stuff, is it any good?' asked James. Brenda feared it would be caustic.

'Not so good,' Mehmet said, pulling a face. His honesty was refreshing.

'I have best brandy in my room,' said James. 'Would you mind if we drink it here, just for tonight? We'll buy your best brandy after tonight, I promise.' Mehmet hesitated. Brenda dropped her head to one side in a plea. There'd be plenty more nights.

'I bring glasses. But you no tell the others, okay? We keep secret.'

'Deal,' said James. He made for his room again, returning with a bottle of Martell XO Cognac concealed inside his shirt. Mehmet brought two brandy balloons and James poured. Brenda took a sip from her glass, rolling her eyes appreciatively. Rich and mellow, the spirit elevated her mood as it banished the wine's rasping aftertaste.

'I'm afraid I don't do *local brandy*,' said James, as if an explanation were needed.

'Not your usual type?'

'What?' said James, quizzically.

'Like your new holiday friends. Not your usual type.'

'Oh, that,' said James. 'I wondered if I'd rubbed anyone up the wrong way. It's not what I meant.'

'What did you mean?'

'I'm part of what you'd call a set. I go to the same places with the same crowd, year in, year out,' he said. 'So for me, for my private and personal amusement, I like to change it up, get away somewhere I'm not known, not part of the set.'

'So you're slumming it for a week?'

'It's not like that,' said James. 'I just want to put my needs first every now and again – what's the harm in that?'

'None, far as I can see,' said Brenda. She looked over to where Turner and Matt continued their charm offensive. 'Why didn't you want to go back to the table?'

'I'm not sure about that one, the tall guy, what's his name?' said James.

'Turner, is that the one you mean? Why?'

'I can't put my finger on it,' continued James. 'He's looked at me in a weird way once or twice, like I'm getting up his nose even though I haven't done anything.'

'Don't you think he might have been annoyed at you?'

'Annoyed? Why?'

'Oh, you know, when you slopped wine in his dinner.'
'Did I?'
'Yes, honey, you did.'
'That would account for it,' sighed James. 'I didn't realise. I guess I am a bit sloshed.'
'Don't worry,' said Brenda. 'I'm sure everything will be fine in the morning.'

SUNDAY

1

HE LIES ON his bed, naked, a corner of the crumpled sheet twisted, wrapped about his abdomen like a loincloth. The air conditioning rattles; a chilling blast assaults him, dripping on to the dresser beneath. Despite the air, he's drenched in sweat; an irregular watermark stains the pillow beneath his neck. The sun pierces the flimsy curtains in a thousand places as breakfast time chatter rebounds around the courtyard below.

The first evening had gone well – it had actually been surprisingly good fun. He'd been engaging, good company, flirtatious; up to the line but not over it; all in all, a solid foundation. He'd drunk too much – but so had everyone else. The wine was rough but the food wasn't bad. The other guys seemed alright too, mostly. They'd had a laugh winding the girl up. Skinny tart was a weird one though; putting it out there one moment, spitting bile the next. Hormones, probably.

What about the fat one? What was her name? Bertha? No, Brenda. Women her age – and her size – are always so grateful for any attention. What's she all about? Matron? Earth Mother? No, Mother Ship. She looks like a do-gooder. Great tits though – a rack to be proud of. Bet she's one of those long-term singletons – independent and in control. Uncontrollable. She doesn't look bad on it, to be fair; nice face, steely eyes – quite a picture. But her clothes, Jesus. All those sequins and crystals, like a gigantic puff-ball ready to explode. Like the birth of a new galaxy, when there's a massive flashpoint and everything accelerates outwards in every direction. You wouldn't call it attractive, but then in some kind of a way, you would; bold, without being slutty – not even a little bit slutty – and boldness is always a draw. Bet she knows what's what in the bedroom too.

He'd found a woman like her on a dating web site once. Her hair was the same colour, golden brown with a few red-blonde streaks; dyed, but not tasteless. It was the first time he'd gone after someone online.

He pulls his camera from the drawer and locates a photo. She was older than the women he usually went for but well preserved. Nice skin. Silk and lace.

He pulls the top sheet away and feels for his flaccid cock. A morning ritual since it first sprang to life a few weeks after his twelfth birthday, he hardly registers what he's doing any more. He twitches and jerks compulsively at it until it begins to respond – at least it still does that for him. Taking a firm grasp with his right hand, he pulls rhythmically at it for a minute or so at first slowly, then faster and more vigorously. When the anti-climax comes he utters a guttural grunt. Only now does he look down. A dribble of jism oozes from the tip. Not for him the egg cup, nor even the thimble full. It used to shoot up his ribcage, warm and sticky. It made him feel connected and vital. Years in thrall to narcotics and his body is choked with toxins, depleting his output. These days he chases confirmation of his virility in other ways. He stares at the cloudy droplet for a moment before swabbing it with the sheet.

He showers, shaves and spends several minutes massaging cocoa butter into his body, top to toe. He selects shorts and a vest. Then he unlocks the safe, unwraps his stash and rolls two joints which he stows in a leather pouch. He drops the pouch into his satchel, stuffing his beach towel on top. A glance over the balcony tells him things are getting going below. He grabs the satchel and lets the door slam behind him.

2

SWATHED IN A multi-coloured sarong, Brenda was amongst the early risers drifting down to breakfast. A feast awaited; strawberries, figs and slices of banana drizzled in honey, yoghurt, platters of cheese and cold meats, two colours of bread and slices of cucumber and tomato. A warmer contained scrambled eggs and baby sausages, cut and curly. Alongside, an urn dispensed hot water for tea and coffee. However much she consumed, Brenda knew it would not fill the void inside her, but consume she did.

The sun climbed, flittering the pool's surface, as conversation and caffeine mellowed Brenda's private pain. As guests ate, Mehmet pushed a broom listlessly around the courtyard then fired up a tinny stereo and opened the bar. The citrus juicer hummed like a swarm of bees as he began processing a sack full of oranges for the day's cocktails. Heat radiated from the uneven flagstones, scorching lines of ants which trailed back and forth bearing a payload of breakfast crumbs.

Fed and watered, Brenda set about organising herself by the pool. She dragged a sun lounger, table and parasol to the spot she desired. She spread a towel across the bed and rolled another into a cylinder, placing it at the head-end. One by one, a book, a bottle of water, a sunglasses case, a notepad and pen appeared on the table, all neatly aligned. A firm stroke across the bed to eliminate creases and Brenda's corner of the world was in order for the day – at least, the things she could control.

She unwound the sarong and re-tied it about her waist, revealing a well-engineered swimsuit. It cupped her breasts securely, whilst still managing to reward any bystander with a payload of cleavage.

'Mind if I join you?' said a voice behind her.

'Sit yourself down,' said Brenda, smiling. James – or perhaps it was his bottle of cognac – had mitigated her melancholy the previous evening. Quiet time and the book could wait.

He pulled a lounger over as Brenda began the task of skin protection.

'I'll do your back,' said James, holding out his hand for her bottle of lotion.

'I can manage,' Brenda responded, unprepared for physical contact.

'Nobody can do their own back,' said James. 'Anyway I thought we were friends.'

'If you're sure,' said Brenda. He might be; she wasn't. But there was no point making a scene.

'Of course,' said James, as he prized the bottle from Brenda's fingers. 'Now I'm armed and dangerous.' Mischief crinkled his eyes. 'You wouldn't let a willing pair of hands to go to waste, would you?'

Brenda's heart heaved. What had happened to her in the past months? Since Jack went, her emotional landscape had become parched, her sense of self uprooted, like tumbleweed in the desert. She barely knew what to think or feel any more. But what was done could not be undone. She had to pick herself up and move on and until she felt it, she would have to fake it.

You pretend you care, but the only thing you care about is you. You're a fake.

'Alright, James, but I expect you to be thorough.' Smothering self-pity she set her voice to mellifluous. 'I want your platinum concierge service, nothing less.'

'Steady on, old girl!' said James.

'And less of the *old girl* please,' replied Brenda. 'I warned you about that yesterday.'

'You did,' laughed James, 'and I consider myself wrapped most deservedly across my knuckles. Now, do as you're told. Turn around and let me get my hands on you.'

James attended to every inch of Brenda's back with the lotion. Then he drew the straps from her costume down her arms – slowly, as if anticipating an objection, which never came.

Singled Out

He massaged the lotion across her shoulders, letting his fingers drift a little too close around her breasts, finding fleshy creases. Far from objecting, his touch ignited an unexpected wave of pleasure in Brenda. She yielded to her instinctive response as James squeezed more lotion and worked it into her skin. When he could prolong the exercise no longer, he snapped the lid back on the bottle with a cheery, 'there you go'.

She reciprocated the kindness, understanding it to be part of the unspoken deal, and rose to the mood of the moment. James lay on his front as she executed sweeping strokes across his back, around his shoulders and down his spine, striking the perfect note which went beyond perfunctory but stopped short of sensual. Brenda felt him uncoil under her touch and was gratified when he did not sit up for several minutes.

Over the next hour several guests broke cover to make camp in the pool area. The bolder ones, first out of the traps on the first morning, paraded like peacocks, displaying questionable physical credentials in ways calculated to look confident, but which bordered on the desperate. The later arrivals, the tentative ones, hugged the walls and hid beneath wraps and sunhats, their very presence an apology.

Henry emerged wearing a crumpled short-sleeved shirt. Hairless milk-white legs poked out beneath its hem and drew the eye reluctantly down to feet clad in scuffed sandals and, in the long tradition of the English by the sea, a pair of beige socks. Flabby buttocks had been poured into a pair of Speedos and a frizz of grey hair peeked from beneath a sunhat. He hovered by the pool shifting from one foot to the other as he scrutinised the sky. Eventually he settled on the far side, away from James, Brenda and most of the others. He clattered a lounger across the concrete to his desired spot before throwing a frayed bath towel across the bed. He pulled a bottle from his beach bag and slathered the contents on to his arms and legs. Finally he smeared a greasy sheen on to his face. He spent too long adjusting himself inside his Speedos, then squatted awkwardly on the edge of the lounger and rummaged in his bag, bringing out a dog-eared paperback.

Adele appeared in stiletto sandals, executing a perfect catwalk strut across the courtyard. She settled on a lounger by Brenda. Her lithe frame was barely adorned with a stringy red bikini; her hair was scrunchied into a loose ponytail, stray feathery strands framing her face. She still had her looks – mostly – Brenda observed, but there was little subtlety to Adele, no mystery.

'Morning Brenda,' she said. James got a grimace.

Next to show was Turner who, as the sunlight hit the back of his eyes, applied a pair of impenetrable Ray Bans. He stood over the empty lounger by Adele.

'Anyone snapped this one up yet?' he said to the group.

'Yours for the taking,' smouldered Adele, her thighs drifting apart as she spoke. Turner settled on the lounger without acknowledging her.

Lilly, barefoot and fresh as morning dew, padded to the pool's edge. She stretched a toe into the water, sending ripples across its surface. Brenda couldn't help but notice how tiny and child-like her feet were.

'Morning all,' she chirruped.

'Hey sweetie, come and join us,' said Turner, signalling to the bed beside his own.

'Later,' she said. 'I need to be kind to my skin for a day or so.'

'Suit yourself,' said Turner. Brenda noticed his lips tighten as Lilly settled in the shade beneath the pergola.

Matt wandered across the courtyard. He greeted the others, chucked his bag on a lounger and made straight for the bar.

'I see it's not too early for a beer anymore,' Turner chuckled. 'Anyone else want anything?' No one did. Turner joined Matt and in due course the two men returned, stony-faced, clutching bottles of Efes Pilsner.

'Peasant,' grizzled Matt.

'What's up?' asked Brenda.

'He chased us for our bar tabs,' said Turner. 'It's only been one evening.'

'It's not as if we're going to do a runner, is it?' Matt boomed. Several heads turned his way. Behind the counter, Mehmet put his hands up, a pained expression creasing his face.

'I only ask. I no offend, ok? No problem, no problem.'

'I guess he doesn't want to lose track,' said Brenda. 'We did all drink rather a lot last night.'

'You're right,' said Turner. 'But he's a prick all the same.'

'Peasant needs to rein his neck in,' huffed Matt. Brenda thought it best to pretend she hadn't heard.

'Anyone fancy a swim?' said James; a valiant attempt to disperse the cloud which had descended on the group.

'Not now,' replied Brenda, who never swam in company. 'You go on.'

'You?' said James, addressing Adele.

'Piss off,' said Adele.

James got to his feet. Throwing his book aside he kicked his bag beneath his lounger. He dropped his shorts, stomped as heavily as bare feet would allow to the pool's edge and executed a faultless dive, piercing the water with the faintest splash. He swam several lengths in a perfect front crawl before raising himself out of the pool on strong arms. He grabbed his towel and without a glance in Adele's direction, wandered over to join Lilly in the shade.

Over the next two hours the courtyard fell silent but for the whirring juicer, the clattering ice machine and the see-saw screeches of a million cicadas. Brenda lay on her lounger as if it were a rack in a morgue. Only the rise and fall of her chest betrayed her state – technically animate, though she felt dead inside. If she concentrated, she could order herself to embrace the sun's warmth and even appreciate the way it made her own flesh smell simultaneously sweeter and muskier. She could engineer positive thoughts about new friendships and the possibilities afforded by a few days away from work and life. But as soon as she let her mind drift to what had happened – and how it had led to her being here alone – as soon as these thoughts invaded, any pretence of tranquillity evaporated.

Brenda reached instinctively into her bag, to the pocket which held the letter. She let her hand rest on the envelope for a moment, connecting with its contents.

'You destroyed my life. This is down to you.'

3

'I'M STROLLING INTO town for a bite of lunch. Anyone fancy joining me?' Brenda's emptiness had mutated from psychological to physical. This at least, she could do something about.

'I'll come,' replied Adele. She'd spent the last 15 minutes fidgeting with her bikini straps in an effort to attract Turner's attention. Brenda was glad of the company and they set off towards the town.

The sun scorched the earth and the scrubland hissed with cicadas. Brenda and Adele meandered along the dusty path towards the beach and the shimmering sea, listening to the baglama's intoxicating strings and the eerie wail of the zurna entwining with the thrum of drums and tambourines. The music floated up from the waterfront, growing louder as it drew them in. The sound was sensual and exotic – centuries-old instruments marking the heady rhythm of contemporary Turkey – and Brenda inadvertently fell into step with the beat.

They followed their noses towards the aromas of shish kebab and grilled sardines, and soon found themselves at the start of a boardwalk which ran alongside the beach. By the steps which transitioned the walk from gravel to sandblasted decking, a couple of hoary old men sat on a bench. Their faces leathery, eyes squinting against the sun, they smoked pungent cigarettes. One muttered something through a forest of tarry whiskers and the other responded with a wheezy laugh as they gazed on the women sashaying past.

The boardwalk tracked the sweep of the bay and was home to a strip of bars and restaurants, their tangles of bougainvillea, bunting and multi-coloured awnings flapping in the breeze. Shaded patios were packed with tables overlooking the sand, with its regiments of parasols, loungers and semi-naked bodies. Culinary odours fought with sea-salty air, iron-rich seaweeds and sun-baked flesh. Music rattled from speakers along the strip, children on the beach laughed and cried and waves chased on to the sand. To Brenda, this chaos of sight, sound and smell was as familiar as a favourite novel or a much-loved old film. Only this time her companion was a stranger, the voice unfamiliar, the mannerisms jarring.

At the far end of the boardwalk a harbour with berths for a dozen gulets lay empty. By now all would be anchored in inlets within a couple of hours' motoring or sailing distance, serving up freshly-caught fish and salads to parties of day-trippers.

Behind the bars and restaurants lay what passed for a main street in this tiny town. Several alleyways ran towards it from the boardwalk and wall mounted signs and A-boards pointed the way to jewellery, leather goods and faux designer souvenirs as well as mini-marts where holidaymakers could replenish supplies of snacks and sun cream.

Brenda and Adele walked the line of restaurants. As they passed each one, waiters leapt in front of them holding out menus, sample dishes and bread and dips to taste. Mostly they tried their best to engage the two new faces in conversation.

'Hello, pretty ladies.'

'You just start your holiday?'

'Please, my restaurant is the best – no need to walk any further.'

'Where you stay?'

They strolled as she had often done with Jack, slowing to check each menu and chat with the waiters and owners. It hurt to be doing this with someone else, but they worked it thoroughly, covering the entire boardwalk before turning back and stopping at a pretty restaurant halfway along.

Its sunshine yellow awning was cheery – a giant, flapping smile of a welcome. Under its shade the tables were dressed with cloths and sprigs of wildflowers in vases – a distinctive touch in a line of identikit restaurants. Having watched the women turn around at the harbour, the patron seemed determined to capture them on their return pass. He emerged to greet them.

'Ladies, lovely ladies,' he said, his arms outstretched. In his hands were two sprigs of wildflowers, the same ones which adorned the tables. He bowed theatrically. 'Beautiful flowers for beautiful women,' he said. 'You may walk on if you must, but I think you will enjoy to come inside. I have good food, lovely table for you. Perfect to start your holiday.'

'What makes you think it's the start of our holiday?' asked Adele.

'Ah, is because I have special gift,' he said. 'I know many secret things about women.'

'Or maybe because it's the first day after changeover?' said Brenda.

'Indeed, maybe this too,' said the patron, undiscouraged. 'But you come in, yes? Emilio make nice for you.'

A bold smile and a wink sealed the deal. Emilio guided Brenda by the arm and she allowed herself to be escorted inside. Adele followed and Emilio sat the women at a table overlooking the beach. He brought hot bread and garlic butter with their menus and reeled off his list of specials. Emilio's voice was like gravel swaddled in velvet. His descriptions had a rhythmic quality, a mesmerising counterpoint to the music playing around them. It made Brenda want to feast on everything and she eyed the multi-layered meze for two, willing her companion's complicity.

But Adele disappointed, choosing a salad. So Brenda selected a mixed grill platter accompanied by rice, chips and salad, stuffed vine leaves and a selection of creamy dips.

Emilio deposited frosted glasses and bottles of Efes on the table. Having brushed the menu aside without enthusiasm, Adele slid her beer into her glass, expertly avoiding a build-up of froth.

'What's going on with you and James?' said Brenda, never shy of getting straight to the point.

'You noticed.'

'It was hard to miss. You know him?'

'Yes. We were on the same holiday two years ago in Crete, although it's abundantly clear he doesn't remember. Which wouldn't be so bad if we hadn't—' Adele's voice trailed off.

'Hadn't what?' said Brenda, her interest piqued.

'Played around a bit,' said Adele with a sigh. 'I think we managed two, it might have been three nights.' She said this as if it were some kind of achievement. 'He took my number too, for when we got home. He never called. And now he doesn't seem to remember... me... at all. He's a prick.' She shrugged.

Adele was in her forties and slender to the point of skeletal; shoulder-blades protruding, hands like the claws on a bird of prey. Years of summer sun were extracting a price from her skin, which was papery, surrendering to patchy discoloration. The rigidity around her mouth and the barren sheen of her forehead screamed Botox. No wonder Adele was wounded at not having been remembered by the younger man.

'He was drunk last night – we all were. Perhaps the booze fogged his memory,' said Brenda, but Adele wasn't convinced.

'It was bound to happen one day; running into someone I've met before. I've been coming on these holidays for years and I like to have fun. It's easy enough to find someone to play with, even when the numbers are out of balance. You have to work it, but it's there for the asking.'

Working it had been the leitmotif of Brenda's twenties. Grit and hard graft had taken over as she matured and now she had a professional persona to guard. Fold the dead-weight of personal crisis into the mix and Brenda's sense of her own sexuality was but a memory; like a wisp of smoke from a Gauloises.

But wasn't this holiday supposed to be a turning point?

The food arrived, Adele's plate as sterile as Brenda's was mouth-watering. Brenda attacked her feast methodically at first, tasting each element separately; succulent pieces of chicken, blackened in lines and crisped around their edges with char-grill; cubes of aromatic lamb, skewered with onion and red pepper; grainy kofte sausages which crumbled beneath her fork; and a slender cutlet edged with softly rendered fat which melted against her tongue. She sampled crispy, salted chips and forks of fluffy rice – you shouldn't have both, but both were delicious – and she drenched her salad with unctuous yoghurt and garlic dressing. Once she'd tasted each flavour individually she mixed and blended, combining tastes and textures, relishing every mouthful in a way that drew Emilio's attention as he worked the tables around them. Adele meanwhile picked at a sliver of lettuce here, a slice of tomato there, restricting herself to a teaspoon of the yoghurt dressing. Every time Brenda glanced in Emilio's direction, he was watching her.

'We had quite a time,' Adele continued, regret tingeing her voice. 'One night out on the beach he took me, flat-out on the rocks over the road from the hotel, 20 yards from the bar. All those dreary stiffs – they were such a boring bunch that year – sitting around cuddling their drinks with their noses in the air, couldn't bear to see a girl having fun. And he's giving it to me just feet away in the dark, you know what I mean?' Brenda nearly choked on a forkful of chicken, but Adele's mood had picked up and her mouth was running like a sewer in a thunderstorm.

'He's alright when he's not drunk. You'd think he'd be a bit lazy, wouldn't you? But he gave it everything he had. No finesse, edgy as hell, but top marks for effort. He roughed me up a bit, ripped the buttons off my shirt. Oh god, I hope I'm not putting you off your food.' Adele stopped, suddenly embarrassed.

'It takes more than that,' smiled Brenda. The lurid account had begun to sabotage Brenda's enjoyment of her meal, but it was a shame to put Adele off her stroke. 'What's wrong with a bit of fun?' she said.

'That's what I'd have said too,' said Adele, 'until now. Now it all looks like a big mistake. I hate that he doesn't remember me, but what if he realises – remembers what we did? Then it'll come out the wrong way or at the wrong time – and if he's drunk, who knows what he'll say?'

'I see,' said Brenda, wondering what the fuss was about.

'So I know he's hot and all that, but as far as I'm concerned he's a liability. And to be frank,' Adele concluded, 'it's a bit shit, to be forgotten so easily; to be... unmemorable.'

Brenda's plate was clean, every morsel devoured, whilst Adele had barely touched her salad. Emilio cleared the table.

'Good to see shiny white of plate,' he said, pride flooding his features. 'You like my food?'

'I do, Emilio.'

'I have special dessert, I make for favourite people. You want I bring you?' Never one to refuse special desserts, Brenda accepted whilst Adele ordered coffee with skimmed milk. Delivered to the table was a milk and syrup pudding on a sweet oatmeal crust topped with honey glazed walnuts and slices of sticky cinnamon flavoured apple. Brenda took a spoonful and slid the concoction slowly through parted lips. It was a delight. Emilio watched from a respectful distance as she devoured every mouthful of his special pudding.

He brought Brenda a glass of apple tea. The women continued to chat and when the conversation finally ran dry, Brenda suggested they return to the hotel via a mini mart to pick up provisions for the next few evenings' balcony cocktails. As they left the restaurant Emilio took their hands; first Adele's, a courteous gesture and then Brenda's, a lingering caress.

'I make you promise to come again,' he instructed. 'You visit to Emilio again, I give you special service,' he assured as he waved the women off.

'I'll bet that special service of his goes further than a quick flip-flop on the grill,' chuckled Adele. 'That's you sorted, if you want it.'

'I don't think so,' said Brenda. 'I doubt he has anything more on his mind than a week's worth of lunches.'

4

HENRY LAY BY the pool alone. He'd tried to chat with Veronica, the only person who'd settled in his vicinity, but she returned to her room on some pretext and didn't reappear. Most of the guests seemed happy to lie about all day doing nothing, but he was bored. Seven days of tedium loomed.

At least he had his cameras. He could pass a few hours taking shots around the town, assuming it wasn't too risky venturing out alone – you never know in foreign parts. He felt a bit silly asking, but Mehmet promised it was 'ok, ok, very safe' and pointed out the path for him so he fetched his kit and took the plunge.

The sun blazed down on the exposed path, but Henry managed to grab a few wide-angled aspects of the shoreline before his neck began to burn. Then he made for the boardwalk in the hope of finding a subject or two. He spotted a couple of craggy old men on a bench and fired off a few shots. He trained his lens on a bird's nest up on the roofline of one of the restaurants, but after ten minutes during which nothing happened, he moved on. He was on his way towards the harbour when something caught his attention; Brenda and that skinny streak of a girl having lunch.

Henry's mouth went dry. His spine fizzled.

He scanned the area, afraid he'd be seen. But he was neither too close, nor too far away. He could easily set up for a few telephoto shots without being noticed. It was too good an opportunity to miss. Henry clambered down on to the beach by a flint wall, then crouched low on the sand. He said a quiet prayer of thanks it was Brenda and not the other one who faced in his direction.

Singled Out

He watched the women sipping their beer, ordering from the menu, laughing and chatting; Brenda, so outgoing and bold. She showered delight wherever she went. And she was hot. Even the bar owner could see it; he was all over her. Henry reeled with the sting of self-knowledge. Where she was glowing and abundant, he was faded and crumpled. Where she was overflowing, he was empty – a solitary stone rattling around a jar. Where she was generous and giving, he was tight and dry.

He claimed some comfort in the photos. The sun was in the right position and Henry affixed a telephoto lens to his digital SLR camera. Whilst the women enjoyed their lunch, oblivious, he fired off a series of shots, mostly of Brenda. He avoided pointing his camera anywhere near children – that was guaranteed to cause trouble he didn't need. He clicked away, stopping every few minutes to review his haul of images. As he saw the women depart towards the shops, he packed up his camera.

He shuffled back along the path to the hotel and settled on his lounger in the shade. To complete the image of casual repose Henry dug out his holiday reading; a pot-boiler he'd picked up at a charity shop. Its pages were curled and creases scarred the spine; it reeked of stale cigarette smoke. The front cover was sticky with the remains of yesterday's breakfast jam. He licked it and wiped it on his shorts; that seemed to do the trick. He pressed it open.

The furtiveness of this unexpected photographic challenge had excited him. It was years since he'd been involved in any clandestine reporting and he recalled the thrill of sneaking about under cover of darkness and poking around in bins for evidence of dodgy deals and naughty liaisons. He'd been good at finding people who knew more than they were supposed to and wheedling it out of them, and taking photographs with lenses as long as his arm. He remembered how he'd revelled in the pressure of a deadline and loved putting the clues together and digging up stuff no one else could make sense of.

That had been his time; all those years ago.

5

THE SUN DROOPED towards the hills behind the hotel and a breeze teased the air. In the distance, loudspeakers at the mosque crackled into action and the muezzin's moans drifted across the bay, stirring the sun-worshippers. Mehmet launched into a competition with the faithful, piping contemporary Turkish hits through the speakers at the bar. He did a walk-around for orders and occupied himself cracking bottle tops, mixing cocktails, clinking and clanking about; the soundtrack of day transitioning into evening. Hakima arrived, stilettos click-clacking across the flagstones.

Brenda, Adele, Matt and Turner had passed the last few hours on a line of loungers, sweat glossing their flesh, barely moving except to increase or reduce the degree of shade around them. Restless, Brenda was the first to stir. She wandered over to where James and Barry, a sickly type with a moonscape of acne across his back, were seated at a bar table playing backgammon. A line of shot glasses and a fistful of 10TL notes on the table bore witness to their state of competitive inebriation. Cloistered under the pergola, nursing her magazine, Lilly looked up.

'Come and join in,' urged Brenda and the girl obliged. Both settled at the table with the backgammon players, as James claimed a victory. He punched the air and pushed his sunglasses up on to his forehead.

'I'm going on the Ephesus trip tomorrow,' he announced to the table. 'Anyone join me?'

'Ephesus,' said Lilly. 'That's in the Bible, isn't it? I'll come.'

'Capital,' said James. 'Anyone else? Brenda?'

'I don't know, James.'

'Come on, it'll be fun. A spoonful of history, a soupçon of archaeology, a bite of lunch and back home in time to drink away the evening; what's not to like?'

Brenda had walked the cobbled streets of Ephesus before; she'd run her fingers along its crumbling walls, clambered around the amphitheatre. Jack hadn't wanted to go, but Brenda argued it was such an important historical site, they shouldn't miss it. It was pretentious of her, but Jack had given in. They'd gone by taxi, not coach, followed someone else's tour guide around the site and finished off with a gourmet picnic. They'd had an amazing day.

'Bren?' said James, puncturing the bitter-sweet memory.

'Alright,' she said. 'Let's book it before I change my mind.'

James, Lilly and Brenda wandered over to Hakima, perched like a sparrow at the bar.

'You like Ephesus,' said Hakima, 'I think you will like also our wonderful two-day gulet cruise. It's very much fun – two days at sea with our most experienced Kaptan Barbar and his crew, with lovely places to visit and nice food. A good trip for the end of your holiday, I think. I sign you today with a special discount?' Hakima's manner blended amiable with officious and this seemed more like an instruction than an invitation. But the idea of a couple of days at sea and barbecues on the beach was appealing, so all three signed up for the cruise.

Brenda spotted Veronica on the far side of the pool. She hadn't seen her during the day and wondered if she'd hidden herself away. Veronica was wrapped in a floor-length garment that resembled a cotton dressing-gown. It was doing a poor job of covering her modesty and the faded swimsuit beneath and it billowed about her as she fussed with her beach bag. Every so often she tugged at the fabric, attempting to trap it between her knees with little effect. Nearby Henry toyed with the buttons on his camera as Veronica fretted and fiddled. Then he held the camera up, pointed it at Veronica and as the breeze parted the flimsy gown he clicked two shots then dropped the device into his bag.

Henry's invasion of her privacy had gone unnoticed by Veronica. Once, like Boudica in defence of her lands, Brenda would have ridden forth, chariot wheels ablaze, sword aloft, without a second thought to consequences, forced by her sense of justice to defend the vulnerable and expose the wrongdoer. That had been Brenda's landscape – once.

But not here, not now.

Brenda was on holiday for herself. She would be nobody's bodyguard, confessor or social worker. And what she couldn't help noticing, she intended to ignore. The petty activities of near-strangers in a faraway place were of no consequence.

What had mattered was long gone.

6

HE OBSERVES THE seedy little tableau from behind his shades. The flappy gown, the sleazeball snatching his grubby photos – that was a clumsy move. First rule of a game like that? Don't get caught in the act. The man's an amateur.

He sees Brenda watching too, staring at the little guy like he's dog shit. For a moment she looks as if she'll make a scene about it. Then she looks away.

That's a result.

The flappy gown woman is interesting. Her jumpy self-effacement fascinates him. He notices the ones that lack worldliness and she's the epitome of timid naiveté. The way she frets and fusses and avoids making eye contact engages him. She's middle-aged and pallid, but she looks like she might have been pretty once. Whatever she had, life has squeezed it out of her.

The sleazeball has thrown him an opportunity.

He orders two glasses of juice then makes his way to where the woman sits on her lounger, fiddling with her bag.

'Have one on me,' he says, keeping his voice soft. 'Orange juice,' he qualifies, holding out a chilled glass glistening with condensation, ice cubes fighting to stay alive in the heat. He sees a spasm flash through the woman's shoulders, as if she's received an electric shock. When she lifts her head the look in her eyes is one notch from terror.

'Oh. No. It's alright. There's no need,' she sputters, cutting in and out like a radio with poor reception. The sun's in her eyes, her left eyelid twitches.

'May I sit down?' he says. The courtesy will reassure her. He holds out the glass of juice and the woman finally takes hold of it.

'Yes. No. Sure. Of course. Please – do sit down,' she says eventually. There isn't enough room on the lounger next to her and that would probably be too much for her anyway, so he pulls up a chair. 'I'm sorry. I'm such a feeble thing sometimes,' she offers.

'Nonsense. Are you alright though?' he says.

'No. Yes, Yes, I am.' Nervy. Intriguing.

'So,' he says. He's forgotten her name. 'What brings you on a singles holiday?'

'I'd never have come on a... holiday... by myself, but my daughter... made me do it.' She stares into her lap as she speaks, her hands strangled by the shredded remnants of a tissue which she pulls and twists.

'Made you do it?'

'Yes, after the divorce. I don't have much... anyway... She paid for it so I had to come. She said it would do me good to get away, but I'm not so sure.'

'You're here now,' he says. 'Let's see if we can't give you a good time.'

'You don't need to worry about me. A cup of tea and a book and I'll keep to myself until it's time to go home.'

Can't have that, he thinks.

'Have you noticed your Peeping Tom?' He tips his head towards the sleazeball.

'Who? What? Peeping Tom?' Words struggle to escape her mouth on tight breaths.

'You need to know,' he says in a conspiratorial whisper. 'He's a sly one.'

'What? Henry?' she blurts. So that's his name.

'He was taking photographs of you a few minutes ago, whilst you were having a fight with your... beach robe. A bit... intimate... if you ask me.'

'Was he?' she says, eyes wide like a deer in headlights. 'Oh my word! That's not nice.'

Oh my word, he thinks. How quaint.

'No, it's not nice. He might be harmless – might be – but you should know what he's up to. He shouldn't be taking shots like that, not without your permission. We should keep an eye on him.' He's milking it, he knows. But it won't do him any harm to be on-side with this one and the more she worries about the sleazeball, the more she'll trust him.

'He. He. He tried to talk to me. Before.' Her strangled breathiness is becoming wearing. He lets his hand rest on her knee. As she looks up at him, he smiles. That one always works.

'Calm down,' he says with quiet assertiveness, and the woman surrenders to his command. 'Trust me, you've... probably... got nothing to worry about. If he bothers you again, tell me. I'll sort him out.' He removes his hand. She takes a breath and whispers so quietly he can hardly hear.

'Earlier. There weren't many people around. I was happy by myself, but he dragged his lounger over and kept trying to talk. He asked me why I'd come away on my own. I thought, it's none of your business. Then he asked me to rub cream on his back. I'm sure he hasn't had a wash in days. I couldn't refuse – it would have been rude. But I didn't like having to touch him. When I finished, I couldn't bear to sit with him, so I went to my room. I've only just come out and now he's taking photographs. What should I do?'

'Don't worry. I'll keep an eye on him,' he says. That'll make her feel indebted. But he's had enough now. 'Why don't we go and join the others,' he adds, and he's already gathering her things into her bag, so she joins in. As they get up, he fires a look at the sleazeball that would freeze the surface of the sun.

He's had a good day. His energy levels are up and the sun on his bones is therapeutic. But he needs another drink. So he escorts the woman to the others, finds her a chair then wanders back to the bar for a short.

As he approaches the group round the table, he fingers the camera in his pocket.

7

HENRY WATCHED VERONICA, plain and sallow, fiddling and fretting, her flimsy wrap doing a sorry job of protecting her modesty. He was so close he could smell her and he breathed in deeply. She smelled like Sadie, all coal tar soap and cold cream; frigid, workaday odours meant to camouflage the vivid scent of a warm body and not the slightest waft of perfume or indulgence. He was so close he even caught the track-lines of silver-pink stretch-marks at the top of her thighs with his camera. They weren't pretty, but it excited him to capture her frailties. He wanted another shot – he was sure he could get those little brown pubes peeking out from her worn out old swimsuit; in the end, he thought the better of it.

As the man approached him, the blood siphoned out of his cheeks. What did he want? Pustules of sweat amassed on his forehead.

But it wasn't Henry he was after. For some unfathomable reason, he made for Veronica. Henry was stunned. Why would anyone seek out a fluttery little bird like her? Yet she accepted a drink from him and they talked.

The cold stare on the guy's face as he stood said it all. He'd seen him take the pictures.

The man put a guiding hand on Veronica's back and she didn't shake it off. Before he went to the bar he found her a chair with the others. Henry watched as they chattered, glancing occasionally in his direction. Then a mocking rattle of laughter rose from the table, echoing around the courtyard.

Why were they treating him like this? He hadn't done anything wrong. If they didn't want to be photographed, they shouldn't be parading around in their underclothes. How was he, a red-blooded man, expected to deal with all that bare flesh? He hadn't committed a crime – he'd only taken a photograph or two. He gathered up his belongings. He wouldn't let them get away with it; he would join them, force them to be friendly. He sidled over to the table.

'Only me,' he said, finding an unwanted tremor invading his vocal chords at the critical moment. 'Mind if I join you?'

'No offence,' said the spotty guy, 'but you need to take a shower first. Know what I mean?'

'Barry!' hissed Lilly, clapping a hand to her mouth. Brenda remained impassive, in tacit support of the speaker. Had she seen him too?

'Hot day,' he spluttered, his voice tight in his throat as he backed away from the table. Stung, he fled to his room as the sound of other people's laughter rattled around the courtyard.

8

THE GUESTS BEGAN to drift away from the pool, stoked with anticipation for the evening ahead. The ranks of solar panels marshalled across the roof had laboured all day to heat vast water tanks. Now they released their payload in two dozen steaming showers. Guests would spend the next hour in preparation for the evening. The women, thirsting for love and aching for someone, somewhere, to be *the one* – but prepared to quench their desperation with a holiday fling – would apply layers of creams and powders; bronzing shoulders, airbrushing cheeks and glossing lips. The men would wash and shave as perfunctorily as they did at home and wonder if tonight would be the night they got laid – the first in weeks, months or for a hapless one or two, years.

The subtlest of faces painstakingly applied, Brenda layered her neckline with strands of seed pearls. Their iridescent cappuccino and magnolia tones came alive in the warm blush of her flesh, like meadow flowers in morning sunlight. As she gazed at her reflection, tears welled in Brenda's eyes.

Jack would have been hopping from one foot to the other by now, always so impatient for the evening to begin.

She filled bowls with nibbles as the depleted bottle of Southern Comfort made an appearance on the balcony wall, accompanied by a soft *coo-ee*.

'What do you think of it so far?' said Adele as the women drank.

'Not bad,' replied Brenda. 'Not as uncomfortable as I feared.' This was an untruth but as Brenda's pain had little to do with the experience of the holiday itself, it wasn't for sharing.

'What do you think of the men?'

'I haven't paid much attention,' Brenda lied again. Like every woman on the holiday, she'd instinctively appraised the gathering of mostly older, rheumy-eyed men on the first night.

'Really?'

'I know it's a singles holiday, but I'm not here to get laid.' Another untruth; getting laid was integral to Brenda's self-imposed vacation therapy. 'Besides, why would anyone be interested in me?'

'So why are you here?'

'I needed a break and... and there wasn't anyone to go on holiday with.'

'But you wouldn't turn it down, would you?' Probing again.

'A kiss and a cuddle wouldn't go amiss,' responded Brenda. This time, an understatement; just to be held would be a comfort to her desolate soul.

'There's the one with the Burt Reynolds chest wig – know who I mean? He's not bad.'

'Matt?' queried Brenda. 'I suppose he's alright. But he's not my type.'

'Or what about the one with the squint, says he's left his kids with their grandparents? Or perhaps he's a bit young for you.'

'Thanks,' said Brenda. Thanks a bunch, she thought.

'What about Barry – the spotty guy?'

'Are you serious?' This was beginning to depress her.

'There's the guy at the bar – where we had lunch.' So that was where she'd been heading. 'Don't pretend you didn't notice. He couldn't take his eyes off you.'

'I told you, it's customers he has his eye on, not me,' said Brenda, dismissing the notion with a wave of her hand.

'Every man needs a woman,' said Adele. 'He's up for it, I'll bet my shirt.'

Brenda counted herself a realist. The owner of a beachside bar would be expert in deploying his charm to swell his coffers. He'd flirt with the older women and they'd encourage their husbands to drink at his bar. He'd overlook any liaisons pursued by the younger men in his employ, for these too would bring business to the door. Getting a woman into bed might be an occasional fringe benefit, especially with the presence of a hotel dedicated to single travellers.

It was wrong – anathema to dignity and self-respect – to pursue a fling with a local man, especially one in the tourist trade. But it was an engaging thought and it hung around in Brenda's head as Adele chattered on, summing up the merits and shortcomings of more male guests and the few locals they'd encountered. Appealing too was the realisation that breaking her own rules and escaping from the strictures that came with always doing the right thing, might be just the therapy she needed.

The right thing wasn't always right, so maybe the wrong thing wasn't always wrong.

But why would anyone – even a hard-working bar owner – be interested in her, when the beach was an abundance of younger, slimmer more desirable bodies. To imagine a moment when she might be held and be allowed to forget even for an hour or two was to court disillusionment.

Dusk shrouded the courtyard below. Mehmet flicked the switch on a cascade of fairy lights then wandered around straightening loungers and tidying tables.

'There's James too,' continued Adele, as if presenting further evidence at a trial. 'You've made friends with James.' An observation or an accusation?

'Not the way you mean,' Brenda smiled. The thought that James might entertain her on the beach in the manner in which he'd apparently seen to Adele, was as unlikely as it was disturbing. 'But he's good company and he has a bottle of the most exquisite cognac tucked away in his room,' she added. She wanted to say he had firm fingers too, but thought better of it.

'I'm having Turner,' announced Adele, as if it were a *fait accompli*. 'He's fit and he must be loaded. I'm front of the queue for Turner. Him or Matt. If you don't want Matt, he'll be my *first reserve*.'

The women sipped their drinks and watched the early arrivals gathering by the bar. Mehmet was on form, opening bottles, pouring spirits and crushing ice, a genial smile welded to his face.

When guests laughed he laughed along, as if he got the joke. He was affable and easy-going; no doubt it was good for business. But it was when he mixed a cocktail that Mehmet flourished. A Long Island Iced Tea? Hawaiian Punch? Margarita? Sex on the Beach? Whatever you wanted, it was in Mehmet's repertoire. A measure of this, a squeeze of that; and when he rattled the cocktail shaker over his head he wore the look of a man ecstatic in prayer. Then he would drizzle a soupçon of the mix into a bottle top to taste, to make certain it was perfect, before he poured and then dressed any one of a dozen shapes and sizes of glass or even on occasion, a scooped-out melon or pineapple. Then the creation, an explosion of fruit balanced on its rim, a straw twisted into a heart, a coil or a flower, would be delivered like gift of gold, frankincense or myrrh, presented by a king, to a guest who couldn't possibly appreciate it enough to justify the care and precision with which it had been engineered.

'What do you do when you're not sunning yourself?' Brenda asked.

'I'm a PA in a Mayfair property company,' said Adele. 'It's run by someone my father knows.' Brenda wondered why this fact would be relevant.

'Sounds interesting,' Brenda said. Small-talk, one more-or-less harmless untruth layered atop another.

'It isn't,' said Adele. 'It sounded alright 15 years ago and it got me out of a hole. But I don't know what I'm still doing there. The money's crap; the people are okay, I suppose. And I get time off for good behaviour; summer holidays, skiing and stuff. I expect they let me get away with it because of Dad.'

'What? They don't want to upset your father?'

'Yes. They did him a favour, taking me on, after... well, anyway. But I don't think they expected I'd still be there 15 years later.'

'After what?'

Fixated on the cocktail theatricals below, Adele bit her lip.

'I'm sorry,' said Brenda, 'I didn't mean to intrude.' She placed a hand gently on Adele's arm. It was ostensibly a kind gesture but it had the intended effect.

'It's nothing – it's nothing now,' she said.

'But then?'

'It was the wedding that never was. I got stood up at the altar.'

'What, literally?'

'Literally, absolutely and in every mortifyingly humiliating way, yes,' said Adele. She drained her glass. 'But I'm over it.'

'What happened?'

'Apart from the obvious, you mean?'

'If you don't want to talk about it,' said Brenda, hoping to hear more.

'It was all pretty perfect,' Adele continued. 'Giles owned a telecoms company, drove an Aston Martin. We were introduced at a party. I was heading for 30 and everybody – me included – thought I should be married. Everyone was trying to pair me off, my little sister especially. Jess is two years younger; husband with an inheritance, big house in Oxfordshire, tennis club membership and a social calendar to kill for. We all thought with Giles, it would be the same for me. But he had a different idea.'

'What was it? Cold feet?' queried Brenda.

'Arctic. Pity he didn't have the guts to mention it to me. We might have worked something out. In the end, he just didn't show up. I was there, he wasn't. Dad and I did two dozen circuits of the village green in that ridiculous horse-drawn carriage, by which time the guests were all outside the church, staring at the freak show – me dry-retching into Dad's lap, him in *rigor mortis* beside me, not a clue what to do.'

'How awful,' said Brenda quietly.

'Giles resurfaced two weeks later having been on *our* honeymoon in the Seychelles by himself. Wanted his grandma's ring back – my engagement ring. He communicated through a friend. Never even said sorry.'

'And you?'

'I lost the plot. I drank too much, screwed any bloke within reach; I blew my savings. If it hadn't been for Dad, I don't know what would have happened. He sorted me a flat-share and a job; then he found reasons to come up to London every week to see how I was doing. He paid my rent a dozen times when I couldn't and I'm sure he paid my flatmates too, to keep an eye on me. He only stopped when I convinced him I was getting myself straight.'

'And were you?' asked Brenda.

'Sort of,' Adele said, refilling her glass for the fourth time.

'Wow,' said Brenda. 'That's a story.'

'It is. Okay, now it's your turn.'

'What do you mean?'

'Come on,' said Adele. 'You're in your 40's and you're on holiday on your own. You must have had some crap rain down on your parade too.'

'You could say,' said Brenda. 'But everyone's downstairs now. Let's join them. Come on, stories another day.'

9

BRENDA WAS MINDED to make a night of it.

After dinner, like a figurehead on the prow of an ocean-going vessel, she led the convoy into town. A contingent of Hotel Erdem guests followed in her wake, happy or relieved to attach to a vivacious personality. And that evening, Brenda's personality was little short of explosive.

Pre-prandial cocktails followed by rivers of wine at dinner had also set Adele on the road to an uninhibited evening. Positioned between Turner and Matt, she interlocked arms with both. She dragged them onward, dispensing flirtatious chit-chat between them, deterred by neither man's apparent indifference. Veronica and Lilly chattered, tripping along to keep pace. Others had tagged on; backgammon combatants James and Barry, and a man with a squint who seemed to have his good eye on downwardly mobile retailer, Chloe. Henry, washed and shaved, but back in the shirt Brenda recognised from the day before, brought up the rear.

The convoy stumbled along the darkened path from the hotel aided by wavering beams of light from a couple of torches. They pulled up on the boardwalk beneath the yellow awning.

'Wonderful, wonderful!' Emilio exclaimed as he counted the assembled group, eyes wide. Brenda had delivered him a pearl of great price – a host of new customers. Emilio moved to embrace her but she stepped back, so he took her hand, bringing it to his lips. As he looked up, he winked at her.

'Have you got room for us all?' Brenda asked.

'Of course,' Emilio smiled. 'I make special tables for you. Wait please.' He gesticulated to his waiters. They pulled tables together and dressed them with tea-lights. They set out bowls of pistachio nuts and Turkish Delight. Emilio beckoned the group in. 'I make VIP area for you, special friends!' he said, radiating delight – or perhaps it was triumph.

Having seated everyone, Emilio distributed cocktail menus.

'I make anything you desire; I can do everything,' said Emilio to the table, his voice laced with innuendo. 'I make excellent *Sex on the Beach*,' he added, a smile tweaking at his mouth as he commanded Brenda's attention. 'Or I can make giant bowl of mystery – very potent with spirits – and many straws, and everyone can get drunk and have fun. You like maybe?'

Emilio spoke slowly, his words curling around the group like wood smoke on a windless night. But this was a party of near strangers, mostly not young, where the dominant emotions were still wariness and restraint. The mystery bowl was declined in favour of more predictable refreshments.

As diners around them finished their meals the staff cleared tables and turned up the music. A few people got up to dance. Adele writhed and wriggled but to little avail. After several minutes of being ignored she returned to the table, where the only accessible seat was on a banquette beside James. She squeezed along the bench, scowling.

'Budge up,' she said, elbowing him in the ribs.

As James turned he was dealt an unexpected eyeful; Adele's breasts, bobbing unfettered beneath her camisole, inches from his face. Watching from across the table, Brenda wasn't certain if it was a lurch of delight or a shudder that flashed across his face. He recovered swiftly.

'Last night,' he said. 'I'm sorry if I offended you.'

'No problem,' said Adele without looking at him.

'Friends?' asked James.

'I don't think so.'

'Fuck me, Adele,' James huffed.

'What?'

'Whatever I've done – and I haven't a clue what it is – I apologise. I humbly and sincerely apologise. Come on, bygones. I'll buy you a drink.'

'Whatever,' returned Adele. 'Or better still, why don't you just leave me alone.'

As the drinks flowed, voices grew loud and laughter rippled; hands touched, eyes met; here and there arms found shoulders or waists and were welcomed or shaken away. Emilio approached Brenda, crouching beside her chair. He'd applied cologne since their arrival – citrus and cedar overlaid the odour of his warm flesh and the scent of garlic and thyme.

'You like?' he said, casting his eyes towards the Turkish Delight. Brenda nodded. Emilio picked up a cube of the sticky sweet between his finger and thumb and held it to Brenda's lips. She opened her mouth, accepting his offering and curled her tongue around the soft cube as he let it go. Emilio's eyes, dark bitter-chocolate pools, mature and real, connected with hers.

'You are beautiful,' he whispered close to her ear. 'I want.'

10

THE MOTHER SHIP reels everyone in before he can suggest going into town, making him a participant. He feels his mood crash and his bile rise, even before they depart. As they walk the path towards the beachfront bars, he finds himself locked into the middle of the gaggle of lumbering imbeciles. He has a pain in his temples and his jaw hurts; he realises his teeth are clenched. Everyone chatters and shrieks around him. He must stay calm, can't afford to lose it. It'll ruin things if he loses it.

They reach the bar, the one Brenda insists upon despite passing a dozen others that would do just as well. It's rammed with tarts in tottering high heels, spray-tanned and overpainted. They strut and wiggle; they perch on bar stools in their tight skirts, legs splayed, willing the men to cop an eyeful. They're all bare midriff and tits flopping about, overloaded with market-stall gold chains and plastic watches. No style, no substance; they're sex on a stick. They look like they've been had by a hundred men. Fucking one of them would be like eating a piece of meat someone else had chewed and spat back on the plate. Who'd want to do that?

Not him. But he wants to do something – someone. He wants a scalp – first blood of the week. That means he needs to stay composed, operate with subtlety.

Let the games commence.

He's already chosen his mark – a quiet one; no slap, fresh and clean; the girl from Beccles. It makes his cock ache to think about getting at her; especially after what she said the night before. As the evening progresses and everyone loads up with beer and cocktails and stops watching each other so carefully, he dances with her, engages her in conversation. He begins to work out his moves. But before he can make it happen, he's screwed.

It's the slapper; she gets right up his nose.

Whichever way he turns, she's there smothering him in a cloying miasma of oriental musk. She's in his face, so close he can see the creases around her pulpy lips leeching trails of pink gloss. Her breasts jiggle under a shred of chiffon, nipples protruding like puss-filled boils. She's mutton. She's *whatever happened to Baby Jane?* Everything about her disgusts him.

But still he tries to stay calm, camouflage his loathing. After all, the game is the game.

Now she's squashed against him, pouting and bleating, buzzing in his head like a mosquito; interrupting his flow; knocking him off course. She needs to be taught a lesson and there's only one way to do that. She's not what he wants; she's old, chewed meat. But the urge to cut her down is overwhelming. It pounds at his chest, hisses in his ears. That's the way it is when something – or someone – gets to him.

She's forced his hand. It means putting the other girl on ice, and he'll do it. What happens now is all her fault.

He excuses himself and slips past the bar into the Gents toilet cubicle. It smells of stale cooking oil, disinfectant and shit. A gel-filled ornament is failing to camouflage the rancid odours. The floor is wet; is it water, or piss? He can't kneel on it, so he squats on the toilet seat facing the cistern, his knees wedged against the wall. He pulls a wrap from his left sock and unfolds it. He pours the contents on to the ceramic in a neat line, using his nail to tidy the edges. He rolls a note from his wallet and siphons the line in a sharp snort, nostrils flared. With a wet finger he mops up the remaining powder and rubs it into his gums. He squats for a few moments, staring at the toilet wall, before pocketing the note and dropping the wrap down the toilet. He pisses a long, hard stream on to the paper and flushes it away. He pulls another wrap, this time from his right sock, and returns to the bar.

He's primed.

11

AT THE YELLOW bar, Henry hung back. Whilst everyone else crowded the table anxious to be in the centre of things, he occupied a stool at the end of the bar and ordered himself a beer. Still smarting from his earlier humiliation, he had no taste for the rowdiness and no intention of paying for everyone else's drinks. Like so often, he would observe from a distance.

Jollity bubbled around the table. Nobody glanced over to him at least. Perhaps they'd stopped ridiculing him – moved on to someone else. He pulled a soiled handkerchief from his trouser pocket and snorted into it, wiped a trail of escaping mucus from his fingers, then crumpled it back into his pocket.

The bar was crowded and noisy. All around him were young women in skimpy skirts and shorts, their bare arms, thighs and titties pressing in on him from every side.

Screeching laughter soared from the gaggle of singletons. They were older, mostly, than the bitches and bucks on the other tables. A few cliques had formed and that artless Adele woman was working her scrawny body like a pro. With her titties bouncing around and her little frill of a skirt, she wasn't leaving anything to chance.

His half empty glass of beer had reached the same temperature as the claggy evening air. As he took hold, it stuck to the counter top for a moment before surrendering. He was making it last. Brenda rose from the table and floated past. She didn't acknowledge him; he might as well have been invisible. A few minutes later she brushed past him on her way back to her friends. A thousand prickling charges exploded down his arm.

'She too much for you,' said the owner, nodding in Brenda's direction as he prepared another tray of drinks for the table. The man had a point.

He watched the guy – the one who made him so uneasy – go to the toilets and return a few minutes later, eyes wide like a fox in headlights. He watched him order a G&T and a beer. Then he covered the G&T with his hand for a moment before picking up both glasses and returning to the table. Did he drop something in it? It certainly looked like he had. Why would he have done that?

Henry continued to prop up the bar, sipping from his beer, undisturbed by the other guests. He saw the guy put the G&T in front of Adele and watched as she gulped it back over the next few minutes. Unnoticed, he watched as the guy slipped a hand provocatively between her legs. Her eyes rolled and his arm found her waist as she began to topple to one side. When he lifted her away from her chair he wrapped her own arm around his shoulder, taking her weight. They left the bar, she stumbling a little whilst he gripped her. Nobody else seemed to notice.

They manoeuvred along the boardwalk. Something about the scene didn't feel right. Adele's feet were dragging and Henry felt sure she would crumple to the ground, were it not for the hold the man had on her.

Henry weighed up the situation. Part of him – the reporter part – wanted to follow and see what was going on. But another part – the spineless Beta – didn't want any trouble. After the incident with Veronica that afternoon, he fancied there was only one possible outcome from getting on the wrong side of that one.

He watched until they evaporated into the blackness. Then he summoned the barman and ordered another beer.

12

HE HOLDS HER up as they progress along the boardwalk towards the dimly lit path. She can just about put one foot in front of the other. The path leads only to the hotel and he knows nobody else will pass by for a while. Half way along, unseen from either end, he pulls her off the gravel and into the scrub. Thirty yards from the path and they're smothered in darkness; only a sliver of light escapes from the crescent moon.

He lets her drop to the ground. He can hear her mewing as he grapples with his trousers. He kneels beside her and reaches out in the blackness until he can feel her hair. He lifts her head and what light there is silhouettes her pinched features. Her breath is heavy with the vapours of cheap wine and gin – disgusting.

He rolls her over and her face presses into the grass. Heaving her up on to her knees, buttocks high in the air, he pushes her skirt back over her waist. He lines up behind her as he rips into a condom wrapper with his teeth. She's a slut and he doesn't need a dose. At first he can't feel any panties. Then he realises she's wearing a thong; the soggy string carves into her butt cheeks. He yanks it aside. His thumbs press deep and hold the crease of her flesh wide. Her odours reach his nostrils and like an animal on heat he draws on their earthy scent. With one hard thrust, he bores into her. Her involuntary grunt of pain or shock is stifled by the dry grass and as he jerks into her again and again, her body collapses further towards the ground with every stroke.

He feels his cum rising. *Shit*.

His orgasm is fast and weak and unsatisfying; a feeble flutter and no overwhelm of release. Bitch. She wrecked it for him by her behaviour at the bar.

He feels for his trouser pocket and locates his camera. There's little elation in his usual trophy shot – she's hardly a trophy. But he'd begun taking photographs with the first one and he doesn't want to miss one out; the lack of order would aggravate him. Bony buttocks and her ravaged slit – that will do. He puts his hand around the camera to camouflage the flash. Then he hauls her to her feet, straightens her skirt and drags her back to the path and the hotel. He drops her on to her bed and draws the curtains.

He strides back along the path to the bar with the yellow awnings to rejoin the others. As he walks he smokes a joint. The others will smell it on him and assume he's been sitting on the beach.

By the time he gets back, less than 30 minutes have passed. When he realises he hasn't been missed, he doesn't know whether to be pleased or angry.

MONDAY

1

BRENDA WAS PRESENT – but only just – when a coach drew up outside Hotel Erdem at 7:00am. Hakima teetered off the coach steps, crisp in her corporate livery and looking fresher than the early hour could justify. Finding the gravel beneath her fragile heels, she wriggled and swivelled in her pencil skirt, smoothing out invisible creases and earning a cock-eyed grin from James.

The previous night Brenda had partied as if it were the end of the world. At Emilio's bar, as round after round lubricated her mood, she'd danced with vigour and flirted without inhibition. Later at the hotel she'd engaged in drinking games; a spin-the-bottle truth-or-dare (she never went for truth) and a few rounds of poker. Hers, as the others discovered to their rising dismay, was an impenetrable poker-face. She had without any real challenge recovered the evening's expenditure in the bar from her fellow guests before retiring, unbeaten, at 3:15am.

On emerging from her room after 3 hours sleep, she coaxed Mehmet to boil a kettle and fill a thermos mug with strong coffee. Now she slouched against the wall, clasping her prize in both hands like a communion cup. Immaculate in linen, a beach bag rested against her legs, out of which poked a sunhat, a packet of caramelised almonds and a bottle of water. Behind sunglasses destined not to be removed for several hours, Brenda's eyes were bloodshot pits, bereft of their usual subtle cosmetic; her head throbbed and her fingers twitched.

Adele was to have been on the Ephesus trip too, but she wasn't in the gathering of passengers. Brenda had knocked for her but got no answer. Nobody even knew whether she was in her room and crude speculation on her whereabouts diverted the assembled party for several minutes.

Without Adele, there were eight Hotel Erdem guests boarding the coach, joining others from nearby hotels. Brenda squeezed along the aisle past Veronica and Lilly, who were deep in conversation.

'Glad you made it,' James whispered as she pressed into the seat beside him.

'Only just,' she croaked. 'Mind over matter.'

Executing a jerky 3-point turn the coach manoeuvred up the driveway. Hakima blew into a microphone. Brenda winced.

'Good morning all,' she said. 'Welcome to our tour to the magnificent ancient city of Ephesus. You make early start, so well done for being on time. We drive today for three hours to reach Ephesus. We go fast, but in one hour we take a break for breakfast. I will tell you more about our wonderful city of Ephesus when we get close. Right now you sit back, enjoy our journey.'

The coach rattled out of the village and on to the highway, where it picked up speed. As Brenda's tender eyeballs acclimatised to the daylight, she took gulps of coffee from her thermos mug whilst James sat silently alongside. Eventually, she was ready to be human again.

'How was your night?' she asked.

'Oh, you know,' he replied. The hint of a smile creased the corners of his mouth. 'A bit of fun – nothing serious.'

'A holiday romance?'

'I wouldn't call it that.'

'A one night stand?'

'Heck, Bren. That always sounds so... dismissive.'

'Indeed.'

'Watch you don't throw the first stone, Bren. I'm not the only one who noticed your man Emilio at the bar last night. You might score a one night stand of your own before long.'

'I don't think so,' dismissed Brenda. 'I brought him a dozen customers. I expect that was worth a chat-up.'

'Don't put yourself down, Bren. Under all... You're still a babe, anyone can see it.'

'Thanks – I think,' sighed Brenda. 'But I don't feel like one this morning.'

'You don't look like one this morning, but you know what I mean. Give him a chance. Heaven knows, you might enjoy yourself.'

'What about your... whoever it was? Are you going to do it again?' asked Brenda.

'I don't think so,' he said. 'Not with her anyway.'

2

THE COACH RUMBLED northward, snaking through grey-green hills of pine and fields of olive and citrus. They passed roadside stalls selling bags of oranges, lemons and watermelons and gazed open-mouthed at the sight of a woman hunched beside a stall selling straw donkeys in a dozen different sizes. When they stopped for breakfast, it was at a shaded *locanta* where a table was laid for them in the garden. There they feasted on cold meats and cheeses, tomato and cucumber, bread and olives and drank their fill of Turkish tea and Nescafe, whilst a trio of unamused police officers and a clutch of workmen ate nearby.

When the coach pulled into the parking area at the main entrance to Ephesus, archaeological treasure-trove and tourist money-spinner, Matt was the first to disembark after Hakima. Full of smiles and genial charm, he assisted each woman in turn out of the coach.

Access to the site required visitors to traverse an avenue of stalls and endure the assault of a phalanx of sellers and their insistent patter. Not like when she'd come here with Jack. How many years ago? Back then, the arrival of a coach was greeted by nothing more than a gaggle of scruffy urchins waving trinkets, woven bracelets and bottles of water. Keen to intercept any visitor willing to slow their pace, they had smiled and squealed, chattered – and charmed.

As the memories swarmed, the air seemed to be sucked from Brenda's lungs. For a moment she couldn't breathe.

'This is the end. It's over.'

From left and right, a clamour of voices pulled her back into the day. 'Hello lovely ladies', 'you want sunhat?', 'bottle water?', 'nice necklace for you', 'best quality bags, you want?', 'nice leather belts here', 'Turkish t-shirts for you' and more, on and on they gabbled, vying for attention, pushing Jack out and forcing Brenda to put one foot in front of the other. As she took in the circus of modern-day merchandising, she found herself wondering if the owners of 'Genuine Fake Watches' or any of the other cluster of cramped stalls, were the children of her memories.

The sun flittered through the canopy of trees and canvas above their heads as Hakima drove the group forward towards the ticket booth. Only Veronica let herself become distracted, moving from one side to the other responding to each and every 'yes please, you come look'.

'I don't want anything,' she implored, as she delayed the group with yet another stop.

'Ignore them,' murmured Matt.

'But that seems rude, when they work so hard, and in this heat,' said Veronica.

'You've got a big heart,' said Matt. His hand rested on Veronica's arm for a moment, urging her forward. A vivid flush swept across her cheeks.

'Or maybe you're a sweet little sucker they can see coming a mile off,' James whispered in Brenda's ear.

At the entrance, Hakima marshalled her group.

'After entrance is avenue of trees,' she said. 'This is your last shade until you come out again. Inside you will meet your Ephesus guide; her name is Fatima, she is nice lady. Then you will see all there is in this wonderful site, and Fatima explains the history. Then you have time to explore by yourself and then at one thirty exactly you come back to our coach for the next part of our day. All clear?'

The party filed through the turnstiles and was handed off to Fatima. Petite and pretty, the guide wore jeans and stout walking boots. Around her neck dangled her tour guide pass and a woven sling cradling a bottle of water. She knew what Ephesus in the noonday sun was about, thought Brenda.

The group stood under the pine trees' shade whilst Fatima recounted the history of Ephesus, a great seaport of the ancient world. Then she herded them out into Harbour Street and the blazing sun, giving them their first glimpse of the Great Theatre. Brenda's ample frame was already on fire. Breathing heavily, she loitered at the rear of the party, sipping constantly from her water bottle. Her heart fluttered in response to the combined assaults of alcohol and caffeine; she already yearned for the forthcoming lunch stop.

'I can't believe we're actually here,' said Lilly, her voice breathy and high-pitched. 'It's like we're actually in the Bible. We're walking the streets that were actually trodden by Saint Paul and look at the places he actually visited.' Each time Lilly uttered the word *actually* it was louder than the last. The final *actually* clattered around in the fragile space between Brenda's ears and she winced. It was unusual for her to be so fractious, even after a heavy night. Make an effort, she instructed herself.

'What about you, Veronica?' she said. 'Are you into this archaeology business?'

'I love archaeology,' said Veronica, eyes alight, her face overrun with the creases of a permanent smile. 'My husband – ex-husband – never understood. He said he didn't know why I wasted time reading about ancient history. This is the first time I've seen any of it for myself. Until now, it's been library books and TV. I want to soak it all up.'

James too seemed to have come alive. Like a sand crab emerging into the sunlight, he skittered back and forth, orientating himself and scanning his guidebook. Brenda watched, fascinated by the transformation in James's customary laissez-faire demeanour. Eventually he noticed the look of bewilderment on her face.

'What's up, Bren?'

'I was wondering where you've hidden the James I thought I was on holiday with,' Brenda laughed.

'What?'

'You. This.' She swept her arm out across the dusty panorama. 'Are you into this stuff?'

'Yes, actually,' James replied. 'I always wanted to study architectural history. But... well, you have to do what people expect of you, don't you? So I joined my Pa's empire like the good son he always wished I was. It kept everyone happy.'

'Everyone except you?' said Brenda.

'That's right. But I'm here now and this stuff is amazing.'

The group clambered up the steps of the Great Theatre and sat for the next part of Fatima's presentation. James fixated on Fatima, hanging on every word she uttered and gazing open-mouthed wherever she pointed. Accompanied by an equally animated Veronica, he criss-crossed the sweeping arc, snapping photo after photo.

The group moved up Marble Road, treading with care and jostling with the ever tighter crowds. Around them tour guides spoke in English, French, German, Swedish and Japanese to visitors unbalanced by loaded backpacks, while others brandished sticks to aid their movement or umbrellas to shield them from the sun. They stopped randomly and without warning for photographs. At every point where Fatima drew the group close, James and Veronica listened with rapt attention – and Brenda rummaged in her bag for water, a fan, or a wad of tissues. All the while, the heat surged at them not only from above, but from beneath their feet and all around. It rose in waves from the flagstone avenues and blasted off the columns and walls. Brenda was slow-roasting in the Ephesus noonday oven.

But when they reached the imposing remains of the Celsius Library, even Brenda couldn't help but be awestruck. Fatima told them about an underground tunnel which was said to have linked the library with the nearby brothel, so the city's menfolk could claim to be stimulating their intellects when in fact they were engaged in stimulation of an entirely different kind. The tunnel, Fatima noted, had never been found, leaving much to rumour and supposition.

The group moved onward and upward, admiring streets, temples, gates, baths, sites of civic significance and stray cats, and immersing themselves in the long-distant past; a past where the once majestic city, the second largest in the Roman Empire, was a vibrant and prosperous metropolis. Fatima strode them up steep inclines and steeper steps as Brenda's knees buckled and her cheeks burned. She felt the sting of sweat trickling into her eyes as she struggled to stay with the group. They passed the new Terraced Houses ('you pay extra to go there later, if you want' said Fatima); they stopped to admire fountains and mosaics, sculptures and carvings, and they listened to grand tales of gods and history told in stone.

At last they reached the site's high point and the other entrance to the city. Travellers arriving at the ancient gate were encouraged to use the public baths to wash away the dirt and grime of their journey. Brenda felt grimy enough for a dip in the baths herself, but all the ruin offered was dry scrub and gravel. James and Veronica might delight in this journey through the age of Rome, but Brenda had seen enough.

It wasn't the same... without Jack.

'Now I leave you,' said Fatima, betraying not a hair out of place or a bead of perspiration. 'You can go where you like, only in permitted areas of course. Look again at magnificent places and work your way back to the main entrance, where Hakima will meet you at half past one o'clock.

Brenda groaned inwardly at the thought of another... what was it... almost 45 minutes before they set off for lunch. She sipped tepid water and bent to shake stones from her sandal.

As she stood, James sidled up.

'I might be wrong,' he said, his voice low, 'but I do believe he's just taken a close-up of your... *puppies.*' He struggled to suppress a grin.

'Who?' said Brenda, looking about.

'The old scroat,' he said.

Henry had been wandering close to, but not within the main group all morning, brandishing a sophisticated camera at everything from people to monuments, from stray cats to wild flowers. Once or twice he'd obliged others by photographing them against the backdrop of a grand gate. As Brenda glanced over he looked away, apparently preoccupied with the gadgets dangling from his camera.

The group traipsed the ruins in twos and threes with varying degrees of enthusiasm. The sun baked the earth, blistering every inch of exposed flesh; flies and other nippy insects grew hungry for blood. Brenda's stomach screamed for food whilst James continued to hop around photographing piles of rocks and colonnades. Slowly, too slowly, they made their way back towards the avenue of trees and liberation.

As they approached the exit, Brenda spotted Henry, perched alone on a rock, mopping his forehead with a stained handkerchief. Though her stomach grumbled in protest, it was an opportunity.

'You go on,' she said to James. 'I need to have a quiet word with our resident paparazzo.'

3

HENRY SAW HER coming up the avenue towards him, but in his fantasy moment he saw not a walk but a dance; a swirling, exotic riot of diaphanous silk fluttering, folds of flesh undulating, skin glistening with sweet perspiration as she floated closer, coming to him.

When Brenda sat by him he imagined he could feel the warmth of her thigh. The sultry musk and jasmine of her perfume mingled with citrus from the moist tissue with which she caressed her neckline. Lust bubbled up like lava inside him. He almost choked on the flood of spittle gurgling into his mouth. He gripped his guidebook like a life-raft, pressing it down on to the uncontrollable bulge in his lap.

'You've quite a passion for photography, haven't you?' Brenda said. It was extraordinary that she was speaking to him. 'I don't know much about it, but that looks like an expensive camera.' She nodded towards his precious apparatus, bristling with buttons and gauges, as it dangled on its strap from his reddened neck. Her manner was warm, friendly; hope strobed in his heart like a hundred flashbulbs popping and popping and popping again.

'It is,' he said and he sat straighter and grew taller with the flood of pride and pleasure. 'Nearly a grand, all told.'

'Is it your job – photography?' she asked.

'Not really, not these days,' Henry replied. 'I work for a regional newspaper. Mostly I do admin, a bit of reporting.' He looked to her for approval, the go-ahead to talk some more. She smiled. 'I used to be the senior hack and do most of the photography too. But—'

'But what?' she asked, open, interested. Overwhelming.

'They hired some spotty kid straight from college. Paid him shit – sorry – so what I do, it's a hobby now.' He breathed through a constricted throat, tight with passion, and terror. This was more words in one go than Henry had uttered since he'd arrived in Turkey.

'I imagine you must be quite good at it.'

'I was. I am. May I show you?' His eyes pleaded with her to say yes.

'I'd like that,' said Brenda.

She wanted to know about his photography. The one thing he loved to do above everything and she, the woman – literally – of his dreams, wanted to talk with him about it. Keeping the guidebook pressed against his trousers, he opened the file on the camera and set up the viewing window. He found the last picture, a pair of Japanese backpackers against the Great Theatre's sweeping curve. He held the apparatus up to his goddess like a sacrifice, making sure she could see clearly, unimpeded by the sun's glare.

He clicked back through one shot after another, all taken as they explored the ruins. She studied each picture, asking intelligent questions about lighting, perspective and framing and dispensing flattering observations about his eye, the balance and depth in the pictures, his use of shadow. He made sure to skim over the occasional shots he'd taken of pretty girls relaxing in the sunshine, dismissing them in a micro-second as 'that one's no good', or 'the settings were wrong'.

'May I hold it?' she asked. 'I think I know which button to press.' And as it felt so good to be with her, to feel the warmth of her praise and appreciation, he let her take hold of his most prized possession.

It was too late. The more she showered him with compliments, the higher he soared, higher than a kite, or an eagle in the sky. Like Icarus, he flew higher and higher. And he quite forgot how near he was to the sun.

When Brenda arrived at the close-up picture of her bent over, shaking grit from her shoe, she stopped. You couldn't see that she was bent over. You couldn't see that she was shaking grit from her shoe. All you could see were a pair of the roundest, plumpest breasts, cleavage glistening with a blend of perspiration and golden-flecked bronzing powder, the dark cavern beneath and the merest glimpse of the lace frame of her brassiere. And as high as he had flown, Henry was suddenly crashing to earth, spiralling, spinning down, round and round like a sycamore seed ripped from the tree.

As Brenda's lips tightened, acid from his stomach washed into Henry's throat.

'Ah,' he moaned, as if struck by an invisible hand. He tried to snatch the camera back but she held it tight. She continued flicking back, more swiftly now, through his pictures from the day. 'Please—' he moaned. He knew what was coming. 'Brenda... stop, please,' he groaned, but she continued scanning, faster now, gripping the camera so tightly he would risk damaging it if he were to wrench it from her hands. *Shit. Shit. Shit.*

Henry felt the blood draining from his forehead. In the flaming midday heat, a chill rattled his spine. He wanted to die. Right here, right now.

But of course, it got worse.

One last picture – of a roadside stall, taken from the back of the coach – and she arrived at the impromptu photo-session from the day before; Brenda and her skinny friend having lunch. She stopped.

'Oh, Henry, no,' she said. He properly, seriously wanted to die.

Shot after shot, one intimate – too intimate – close-up followed another. There were more than two dozen and she stared blankly at each one. Brenda, head to one side, smiling and laughing; Brenda mopping her décolletage; Brenda, eyes closed, appreciating her pudding; Brenda licking her lips; Brenda sipping a drink; Brenda eating bread and hummus; and so, so many close-ups of that lovely, secret plunging valley.

To him, they were beautiful. But as he saw them through her ever more shocked eyes, he couldn't deny the end-of-the-pier peepshow tawdriness of his intentions. No longer intimate, subtle studies showcasing her beauty; in a lurching heartbeat they'd mutated into the squalid snapshots of a Peeping Tom. The blaze of humiliation flared around his neck. He chewed at his lip and felt the iron tang of blood along his gums.

'See... look—' stuttered Henry, 'I'm—' Great blotches of red swelled across his cheeks. His guidebook fell to the ground and he rubbed his hands down the front of his trousers, depositing a clammy stain.

'Henry,' she said, forcing him to make eye contact. 'Your photographs – of Ephesus – they're good. But—'

'It's just that—' blurted Henry. But his tongue had become glued to the roof of his mouth. As he found he couldn't continue, she laid into him, like his mother used to do.

'You can't do this, Henry,' she said. 'You can't take pictures of people – women – like this. I don't like it at all. It makes me feel very uncomfortable. And that's the least of it.'

'What do you mean?' he asked.

'I should say something to the tour operator. Because what you're doing is wrong – it's disturbing – and it makes me wonder what kind of a person you are. It makes me uncomfortable to be around you. Do you understand?'

'Yes?' said Henry, though he didn't.

'I imagine you don't want any trouble.'

'No, no, of course not,' Henry pleaded. A trickle of sweat channelled its way from his forehead into the corner of his eye, making it sting. His fists were so tightly clenched that his knuckles grew white.

'Then you need to do two things.'

'What,' he asked, though it wasn't a stretch to guess.

'Firstly, you have to promise me – faithfully and honourably – you won't take any more pictures of me on this holiday. Not a single one.'

'Okay,' Henry squeaked. He couldn't think of another thing to say.

'Or any of the other ladies, unless you're certain they're okay about it – they've given you their permission. Right?'

'Right.'

'Secondly, you must delete these... offensive pictures of me.'

'All of them?'

'Yes, Henry, all of them.'

'Now?'

'Of course now! I'm serious, Henry, this isn't a joke.'

'I'm sorry. Honestly. It's just—'

'It's nothing. There's no excuse for this. It's deviant and it has to end – now.' Then her voice softened. 'Look,' she sighed, 'there's no need for us to fall out. Delete the pictures and as far as I'm concerned, this is finished. We don't need to mention it again and I won't say anything to the rep. But you must promise to never do this again.' Otherwise I guarantee I'll make a big thing of it. I'm serious.'

'I know, I know,' moaned Henry. 'Really, I'm so sorry I've upset you. I just—'

'I don't want to hear it. I can't think of any justification. Now, are you going to delete the pictures?'

Crushed, Henry had no choice but to comply. He deleted 54 frames in all – Brenda counted each one out loud. He hadn't even backed them up; they were gone for good. Only then did she look up. She didn't look at him, but through him, as if he didn't exist.

'Now, let's get back to the coach before it leaves without us,' she said.

In step but worlds apart, they trod the last hundred yards back to the exit.

Henry boarded the coach and took a seat towards the rear. He knew he'd be left alone to drown beneath a tide of self-pity; nobody ever sat with him. It was all her fault, teasing and tantalising him from the moment he first saw her; giving him hope. Women like her knew how to work their assets and she worked hers so hard she'd worked him up into a frenzy – a frenzy of misplaced lust and desire. Then she'd exposed his private fantasies and belittled them, taking his sweet, solitary pleasures and twisting them until they looked grubby and sinful.

He shrivelled inside. He would not, he could not, let a woman get to him like that, ever again.

4

THE COACH SNAKED into the hills a few miles from Ephesus, the slopes that framed the road abundant with vines, olives and figs. They halted in a gravelled parking area.

'In front of us is the pretty village of Sirince,' Hakima announced. 'Here we stop for one and half hours so you can have lunch and maybe do shopping of nice handmade souvenirs. You see houses ahead and little shops and stalls, lovely winding roads up into the village. Go and explore. Is a lovely place where everyone is friendly and you will find much to interest you and nice photography places too. There are big and little restaurants and you can find what you like to eat. You go now and you come back here at four o'clock exactly please.'

Everyone clambered off the coach. Ahead lay the village, a cluster of pretty white dwellings layering the hillside. Breaking into twos and threes, they moved up the street towards the houses and shops, where stalls overflowed into the streets and awnings offered shelter from the sun.

Veronica announced she wasn't hungry and wanted to spend the time wandering in the market and finding one or two of those *nice photography places*. She looked around nervously, her eyes searching for someone willing to join her. Brenda could think of nothing but food. Henry stepped forward, his shoulders hunched, eyes on the ground. With more obsequiousness than was appropriate, he mumbled he might like to take some photographs in the market too and if it was alright, he'd like to join her. Veronica said that would be nice and James declared his amusement at the 'very funny look' Brenda directed at Henry as the pair wandered off together.

Brenda was a woman on a mission – a mission to eat. Lilly begged to tag along then dragged James and Matt into the crew.

Invigorated by the prospect of food, Brenda strode forth through the crowds of tourists, bypassing every stall inviting them to taste fruit wines, olive oils and nuts, smell handmade soaps and admire hand-crafted accessories. James, Matt and Lilly simply followed in her wake. They passed a couple of prominent restaurants, ignoring the proprietors' pleas to enter. At a shop selling cheese, Brenda stopped to enquire where they might locate a restaurant willing to serve them 'authentic Turkish, not tourist food'. The owner directed them up a narrow alley and the group located a portico festooned with clusters of climbing roses. Their scent mingled with a wave of tantalising odours drifting out into the alley – steamy garlic, coriander and onion, cinnamon, citrus and baked breads.

Beyond the portico they could see three tables set crookedly in grass under the shade of a cat's cradle of vines and ivy. Only one table remained unoccupied. Beckoning them through the portico whilst simultaneously entirely blocking their path was a man as broad as he was tall, wearing three-day stubble and an apron stained with the residue of a dozen lunchtimes. He stood aside to let them squeeze through, beaming a warm welcome.

They stepped into a cluttered courtyard garden, its walls so thick with climbing roses and bougainvillaea that their crumbling plasterwork was barely visible. Under the canopy of vine leaves the air, still and heavy, held in its cloak the aromas of feast and flora. In one corner a sprinkler hissed a fine spray in a back-and-forth motion, creating a glistening semicircle in the grass and drawing a rainbow in the air. A honey-coloured spaniel lay panting against the cool wall of the house.

'This is, like, a private house, isn't it?' said James. 'I mean, it's not a proper restaurant.'

'That's what the cheese man said,' said Brenda. 'He insisted, if we wanted 'authentic' this was the place. Said the man's his uncle and his wife is the best cook in town.'

'Well he would say that, wouldn't he,' huffed James.

'But it's an experience,' said Matt, glancing at Lilly. 'Come on, let's eat.'

They eased carefully on to chairs around the rickety table. Through a narrow doorway, pots of aromatic meat blipped away on a stove. The portly proprietor brought a mound of pides to the table, warm from the oven and dotted with black onion seeds.

'We have good food today,' the proprietor announced. 'I bring?'

'Isn't there a menu?' said Lilly.

'It isn't a menu sort of a restaurant,' smiled Matt. 'Trust me, these places are great – you'll love it.'

They ordered large Efes and James suggested they might enjoy a round of raki, since they were being so 'authentic'.

'What's raki?' asked Lilly as Brenda signalled their request.

'It's like aniseed balls,' said James with a grin.

'Trust me,' Matt said again. 'It's an acquired taste, but it's worth acquiring.'

The proprietor returned with a bottle of raki. He poured a measure into each of four glasses. Matt added water to one of the glasses and the liquid went cloudy. He pushed it towards Lilly.

'Taste it,' he said, a smile crinkling his features.

Lilly sipped tentatively.

'Eeew!' she exclaimed.

'Keep going,' said Matt. 'Now swallow it. There you go. A couple more slugs and there'll be no stopping you.' Matt added water to the other three glasses and everyone toasted a good holiday and a fine meal to come.

The proprietor emerged from the kitchen bearing a platter of vine leaves wrapped around seasoned rice, a mixed bean salad, a bowl of spinach and yoghurt and a dish of creamy white cubes, which he proclaimed to be 'puree of broad bean – very good'. It was all delicious and Brenda and the party feasted. As one dish emptied, another appeared; baked green peppers filled with rice and mince, earthy chicken livers, sautéed and resting on a bed of onions. Through the darkened door, the proprietor's wife – the best cook in town – beamed at them from the steaming kitchen, delighted to see her food so enthusiastically devoured.

'So what's it like,' Lilly asked James, 'working in big business?'

'It's okay,' James declared. 'My Pa holds the reins and that can be a pain. But he's moving me around, for experience and all. I know I should be grateful—'

'But?' interrupted Lilly.

'But, I'm not,' said James.

'Why not?' exclaimed Lilly. 'Sounds like he's giving you a leg-up.'

'He is,' said James. 'Only—'

'It's a far cry from architecture and archaeology,' interrupted Brenda through a mouthful.

'Precisely,' said James, heaving a sigh.

'And what about you, Brenda?' said Lilly. 'What do you do?'

Brenda took a breath. To tell, or not to tell?

'I have a flower shop,' she lied. 'I make bouquets for weddings, wreaths for funerals, displays for hotel receptions. And I help husbands stay on the right side of their wives and girlfriends.'

'Is it doing well?' Matt asked.

'I get by,' Brenda smiled. 'Men always need to apologise for something.'

The next course arrived – slow-roasted spiced lamb, unctuous and tender, with steaming rice and a salad. Brenda savoured one aromatic mouthful after another mopping up piquant meat juices with more bread. Telling fibs about what she did for a living no longer gave her heartburn. The flower shop story was convincing.

'Enough of *What's My Line*,' James mumbled between mouthfuls. 'You and Henry, back at the coach. If looks could kill, Bren.'

'You weren't supposed to see that,' said Brenda. 'That man has been playing fast and loose with his photography, taking pictures he shouldn't. He had quite a few surprises on his camera.'

'You had a word with him?' asked Matt.

'A friendly chat,' said Brenda. 'That's all I'll say. But I didn't want him forgetting our conversation when he went off with Veronica.'

'Anything you need help with?' said Matt.

'I don't think so,' said Brenda. 'Thanks for the offer, but I think it's sorted.'

'I think you handled it, Bren,' James chipped in. 'Poor bloke looked like he'd been tarred and feathered when you two came back to the coach. Made me pray I never find myself on the wrong side of you.'

5

HE STANDS UNDER the shower, his skin prickling under the steaming jets. He washes methodically, soaping and rinsing every undulation and furrow of his flesh, rinsing away daylong sweat. He strokes first shampoo then conditioner through his hair then massages it away under a stream of cool water. He turns the tap off and reaches for his towel; he dries himself inch by careful inch, from ears to armpits, belly to buttocks, the backs of his knees to the creases between his toes. Afterwards, he massages cocoa butter into every pore.

Where his morning ablution is functional, his end of day cleansing ritual is a labour of self-love. It makes him feel like a lion, proud and untamed. He armour-plates his self-confidence with a couple of lines and pulls a fresh shirt from the wardrobe. A sultry evening lies ahead and he will enjoy fortifying his position over dinner. He'll be captivating and charming as always. He'll make the women laugh and make the men jealous. It intrigues him to play them this way, keep them off guard. One or two of the women have been coming on to him. Their looks of lustful desperation nauseate him, yet their overt displays are like trophies, badges to brandish before the others – the amateurs in the game of attraction and sex. He won't need to deal with another one like last night.

It's never been the ones who flirt with him who interest him; it's the ones who don't. They're in awe of him; they understand their lack of status. Whatever, the result is captivating – a reticent glance here, a half-smile there, a quiet sublimation into the background. He lusts after their shy restraint, almost without control.

Normally it's easy to bypass the desperate ones. Plenty of internet dates had been sent home with a disinterested *thanks, but no thanks*. But it had been necessary to deal with the slapper, because of the way she'd behaved towards him.

She wouldn't know for certain what had happened, but she'd know something had gone down – a drunken fuck she couldn't remember perhaps; with him or someone else, it hardly mattered. It'd make her sufficiently uneasy or embarrassed and it would subdue her. She'd get out of his face; that's how it worked.

He stands tall and breathes deeply, welcoming the rush of self-satisfaction into his bones.

Tonight is different. Tonight after yesterday's false start, the games begin for real. He intends to pick up where he was so annoyingly sidetracked. Lilly is the prize; unpretentious and demure. His energies had been redirected last night; later he'll make good, the deferment a minor blip. What was it she'd said the other night? An 'old fashioned' girl? If she meant what he thought she did, it could be a spectacular score; triple-A bonus ball jackpot bonanza time.

If she carries on clinging to Brenda, it could get tricky. But he isn't discouraged by the possibility of a challenge – quite the opposite. He's a lion pursuing a gazelle; all he needs is to separate her from the herd. He'll do it so expertly, they won't even notice.

Dinner is a robust mousaka with rice and salad, but he isn't hungry. He plays his part, massaging hearts and minds over glasses of the engine oil that passes for wine. Whoever he talks to ends up with their eyes on him and their mouth cut into an inane smile; the women all get that pathetic, *please notice me* look. They don't realise how pitiful they are. It's all base behaviour and he's seen it before; a tribe acknowledging a leader, respecting his strength. Wanting his seed.

Whilst it's a diversion, he has the evening's private entertainment in his sights.

When the trip returned, Lilly had let him press a drink on her at the bar. She was a bit tipsy by then; nothing too off-putting, but she'd definitely loosened up and he can make use of that sort of thing.

After the coffees, he orders a round of cocktails for the table. He makes sure hers has a sweet base, sickly the way girls like their drinks. But with the extra shots it packs a punch – she'll never notice beneath all that cream and coconut. It'll dent her *little-miss-perfect* veneer without her realising, but not too much. It'll make her want to say yes when he calls for her to come with them to the big town. And it means he'll be able to get another one into her later, the one that counts.

'Anyone up for taking a ride into Marmaris with me?' he says to the group. 'I fancy slumming it, for a laugh. I want to check out the action, bars and clubs. What do you think?'

A couple of people, but not the girl, accept straight away. It isn't enough – he needs at least five or six so she'll feel safe. He understands the art of persuasion. He begins rounding them up, carefully, so they think they made the decision themselves. Brenda won't be budged, but that might be just as well. He lets it go. The girl gets on board anyway, once there are a few takers. He gets to eight; it's a good number and not too hard to shake off later.

The Turk calls them a couple of taxis and it's in the bag.

6

BRENDA SAT WITH the after dinner stragglers contemplating options. She could return to her room, pick up a book and read on her balcony. The easy option; but it wasn't what this holiday was supposed to be about. She could join the quiet ones at the bar. Mehmet was doing his best to raise the energy level with a collection of middle-of-the-road CDs. An evening of restrained conversation, listening to The Eagles and Elton John? No thanks.

Along the table Adele sat motionless, eyes glazed. She'd made a heavy night of it the evening before but she should have been over it by now, especially having spent the day sleeping it off. She hadn't wanted their usual preprandial and she'd hardly touched her dinner. Now Veronica, hands wrapped around an empty coffee cup, was keeping her company, though there was no obvious conversation. Brenda swept a shimmering emerald pashmina from her chair, grabbed her glass and joined them.

'Right,' she said, 'who's for a few shots down on the front?'

'I... I don't know,' said Veronica, momentarily loosening her grip on the cup, making tremble in its saucer. Tension ebbed and flowed in Veronica like waves on the shoreline. For hours she'd forget whatever made her so nervy, becoming a perfectly pleasant companion, if a little colourless. Then it would surge upon her again and she would twitch and tremble as if she had no right to exist.

'Adele?' said Brenda. 'Don't let the side down.'

Brenda wasn't accustomed to pleading for companionship and she didn't like it. Fortunately, Adele capitulated with little resistance.

'Alright,' she said. 'I could do with a stroll. I'll come, but only for one.' She turned to Veronica. 'Come on, you too, one won't hurt.'

Perhaps because the prospect of being abandoned was more petrifying, Veronica was persuaded. Adele grabbed a clutch bag and Veronica stuffed her purse into a pocket in her shapeless skirt. Brenda shouldered her bulging hobo.

'Now that's a bag,' said Adele, brightening up. 'Staying out tonight?' It was a joke, but Brenda's cheeks coloured.

'Don't be ridiculous,' she retorted, too smartly. 'I never travel light, I can't and that's that.' As a statement it was true, but Brenda hadn't succeeded in eliminating the defensiveness from her tone.

'Prickly,' said Adele, before her eyes widened. 'Oh my god, you're going for the guy in the bar, aren't you? What's his name? You bad girl!'

'Leave it,' muttered Brenda. She wouldn't tolerate her need for Emilio becoming a focus for ridicule.

Waved off by Mehmet, the women waltzed arm in arm along the path, sharing a torch to light the way. Ahead, clouds of insects swarmed in and out of the wandering beam of light. Across the scrubland where the sea met the beach, trails of white surf scudded along the shoreline, beyond which spread an inky blackness broken only by the flicker of a cruise ship on an invisible horizon. Ahead, disco lights pulsed from a few of the bars. In between, restaurants and more refined venues nested, dressed in chains of lights and dots of candle flame. The crisp evening air caressed Brenda's skin, a sublime contrast to the claggy daytime stickiness. Up on the boardwalk the women stopped at the yellow awning. Emilio greeted them warmly.

'Just three of us tonight,' said Brenda.

'Is true, but my eyes see only you,' whispered Emilio, close to her ear.

'Can you squeeze us in?'

'I squeeze you,' said Emilio. Steady now, she thought.

As the trio settled at a table, Emilio contrived to brush his hand across Brenda's shoulders; it stalled on her neck. The simple gesture and her response spoke volumes. Unnoticed by anyone else, Emilio's hand could have been shaken off without embarrassment. But she accepted it, appreciating the pressure and warmth as it rested covertly for a few significant moments.

'Now,' he said to the table, his thumb caressing the nape of her neck, 'how can I serve my beautiful ladies?'

'Cocktails, I think,' said Brenda. 'What would you recommend?'

'You like I choose for each?' Emilio beamed. 'I look in your eyes and I tell you my suggestive.'

'It's suggestion,' said Brenda, 'but it sounds like fun.' Playfulness, just what she needed.

'What you like?' said Emilio, addressing Veronica. 'I think maybe you enjoy sweet tasting long drink, I make with coconut and pineapple, very nice, not so strong, yes?'

'Sounds lovely,' said Veronica who was never going to argue, whatever Emilio suggested.

'And for you,' Emilio said, turning to Adele. 'I think you like more stronger, maybe sharp, with lime and vodka or tequila – I think tequila. I make you special margarita, yes?'

'He's good,' said Adele. 'Yes please, but make sure you—'

'Yes, yes I do salt on glass too, I know how to make it proper, you trust me.'

'I don't imagine any woman should trust you,' murmured Adele, with a half-smile for Brenda's benefit.

'Now, what to do for my special lady?' Emilio turned to Brenda. 'Look at me please,' he said, tilting his head to one side. His dark eyes crinkled as they gazed into hers, as if he were trying to read her mind.

'I make for you with brandy, the colour of your eyes, and cream, because you are soft and sensual. I dress with chocolate, little shaves, for a taste of sweet.' He lowered his deep voice almost to a whisper and he smiled at Brenda, still holding her gaze. 'I make strong and smooth and good taste,' he added.

'Sold,' said Brenda, her cheeks flushed.

'We missed you today,' said Veronica to Adele.

'Yeah. I... I didn't feel well,' said Adele. 'I... it... I don't know.'

'Dodgy tummy?' said Veronica.

'Hangover?' said Brenda. She had little sympathy having pushed through her own stupor to present herself on cue for the early departure.

'Whatever it was, I slept it off. I didn't mean to miss the trip, but I don't think I'd have enjoyed it. I felt crap all day.'

'We had fun,' said Veronica.

'It was a long journey in a bumpy coach and high noon in the ruined city was like being turned on a spit and basted with your own perspiration,' said Brenda.

'Don't be like that,' said Veronica. 'It was interesting, very educational.'

'Right up my street,' said Adele, deadpan.

'We learned all about the history. We got some great photographs too, James and I, and Henry in particular – he's got quite a talent. We went to this delightful village in the hills afterwards. Henry and I took photographs of the shops and stalls, all the cottages. Henry's got an eye for a photograph. He can turn a regular snapshot into something special. Get him to show you.' Brenda couldn't help the snort that escaped her nose.

Adele and Veronica were as good as their word. After a single round, both indicated their readiness to return to the hotel. Brenda would not be pressured into joining them. Emboldened by a potent cocktail of lust and alcohol, she prepared to embrace whatever comfort the next few hours might offer.

It was time to move on.

'I'm staying for another,' she said. 'There are plenty of people here to chat to.' There was no plea or invitation to the women to remain with her.

'We'll be off then,' said Adele. She couldn't resist a knowing smirk. Then she and Veronica left, ambling along the boardwalk and into the darkness, the occasional flash of a torch beam signalling their progress.

Emilio observed their final exchange from the bar and once the women departed he mixed two more cocktails, stirring swirls of cream into generous measures of alcohol and dressing the glasses with shavings of chocolate and cinnamon sticks. He eased through the crowd to where Brenda now sat alone.

'I sit with you,' he said. It wasn't a request.

'Yes,' she replied, as if it was, tilting her head to one side and causing a waterfall of curls to cascade around her shoulders. Emilio set the glasses down and took the seat opposite Brenda.

'You on holiday on your alone? No husband?' Emilio asked.

'Yes,' she said.

'No boyfriend?'

'No boyfriend.'

'You like our Heartbreak Hotel?' he asked. Someone had reported this was the name the locals gave to Hotel Erdem which had been booked for the season by Solasoni Singles.

'Very funny,' she said. 'But it's not bad.'

'Any nice men you play with?'

'Plenty, yes,' she lied, her face dead-pan.

For a moment, he seemed not to know what to make of this remark, which pleased Brenda. It never hurt when a man was uncertain where he stood, even one who was on to a sure thing.

'I want to play,' he said, 'with you,' he added superfluously. His hand extended across the table until it reached the tips of her fingers. When she didn't pull away Emilio pressed forward, inch by inch, parting her fingers with his own, letting his touch connect them, until her whole hand became submerged beneath his, absorbed into his assured grasp. She felt the rhythm of his pulse against her flesh, steady and slow.

'What makes you think I want to play with you?' said Brenda. She wanted; uncomplicated fun in the sun and no predictable lies about commitment and love to deal with. Emilio might have an unfortunate fondness for a cheesy chat-up, but his solid physique, laughing eyes and smoky voice swung the balance in his favour. And his confidence was exhilarating. It might be wrong to want this man, but tonight, she wanted.

'I know,' said Emilio. 'You want, I give you. You will enjoy. I make it good for you.'

7

IT WAS AFTER 1am. Having spent the last few hours loitering on the fringes of the group at the hotel bar, Henry had given up trying to be one of the crowd. He slouched alone at a table across the courtyard in semi-darkness. In a dish, a sputtering tealight neared the end of its life. Around him bedroom lights flickered on and off behind thin curtains. The outline of a woman undressing in one of the downstairs rooms engaged him for a few moments until her blurry silhouette and his imagination were stolen by darkness.

A breeze rustled the climbers which layered the hotel walls. Where stems loaded with bougainvillea dangled, their scent clung to the night air. Sadie would have appreciated that. Every now and again the trill of polite laughter tripped across the courtyard. Girls laughing at men's jokes, keen to please with their smiles and their appreciation; like canaries in a birdcage, pretty and well-behaved.

Henry watched Mehmet serve drinks until all the other guests had drifted off to bed. He washed up, wiped all the tables except the one occupied by Henry, brought down the shutters on the bar and extinguished the courtyard lights, plunging Henry into darkness but for the dying candle. Nursing a half bottle of Efes grown lukewarm in the temperate air, Henry chose not to take the hint; he was in no hurry to vacate. Alone in the courtyard, alone in his bedroom; it made little difference.

The skid of tyres on gravel caught his attention as a taxi drew up by the courtyard gates. Two people alighted. Blinded by the headlights he could make out only that it was a man and a woman. The man seemed to be holding the woman up. She stumbled on the wonky flagstones, probably drunk. As the man approached the concrete steps to the upper bedrooms, he swept the woman into his arms. He carried her up the stairs and moments later a light went on in one of the rooms. Henry didn't know who it belonged to. The curtains were drawn.

He pulled a mini-tripod from his breast-pocket and screwed it to his portable camera. He placed it on the table in front of him, made a couple of adjustments then crouched behind it to position the shot. He pointed it directly at the window where he could identify the outline of the man kneeling on the bed, bent low over the other figure, through the drawn curtains. At least someone's getting some, he thought. Henry pressed the shutter for a slow exposure, capturing a subtle image – a moment of seduction to toy with in his imagination, for when he got home. What Brenda didn't know about wouldn't hurt her. What he did for his own private amusement was none of her business.

He pocketed the camera, downed a last tepid gulp of beer and surrendered his table.

8

SHE'S A DEAD weight by the time he gets her to his room. He flops her down on the bed. She utters a low moan, her eyes roll. He peels off his shirt and kneels astride her on the bed, unbuttoning her blouse, pulling at it to expose her milk-white shoulders. All the time she moans and her head lolls, left and right. He yanks at her bra, tugging at her small breasts until he prizes them out of their cups and the nipples stand high.

He climbs off, rolling her on to her side. He finds a zip at the back of her skirt. One deft move and the skirt hits the floor. He runs his fingers around the top of her panties and smells their fresh cotton scent before grasping at both sides and tugging them down past her knees, over her ankles and feet, dropping them to the floor with the discarded skirt. He pulls her knees up and pushes them wide apart to get his first proper look.

She was so easy, so foolish and trusting; a sweet girl in a big, bad world. He's doing it because he can; because he has the power and no one can stop him. He's on automatic pilot. But then he sees it – it's different from all the others before – and he knows for sure she wasn't joking when she said she was an *old fashioned girl*.

He hesitates for a minute – this is uncharted territory in every sense of the word.

He chucks the unopened condom on the bedside table. He clambers off the bed and slips into the bathroom, returning with a towel. He pushes it under her buttocks. He isn't sure what happens the first time, but if it makes a mess he can always ditch the towel.

One more thing, an exquisite addition to his personal portfolio – a *before* shot. He pulls his camera from the bedside drawer. He points it between her parted thighs and takes three shots, each one closer than the last, all of them engaging the harsh blink of the flash to illuminate her pure, undefended pussy.

Now he can't stop. He won't spoil the prize with his fingers; his cock must be the thing that invades this child-woman, flesh on flesh. He spits to moisten it. Forcing it upward he jabs and stabs until it pushes past the feeble barrier. As he breaks through she lets out a whimper and he presses his hand down on her mouth. He shunts into her again and again until he can't hold back. A deep gurgle surges in his throat as he ejaculates.

He lies across her for a moment before pulling out. A trickle of blood clings to his cock and a couple of spots stain the towel. He clicks off his *after* shot to finish the job, then fetches toilet tissue from the bathroom and dabs at her delicate flesh until the redness subsides.

In the bathroom he washes himself and rinses the towel – that takes care of the blood. Then he dresses the girl and silently returns her to her own room. More than any of the others before, he's confident she'll never realise what happened.

TUESDAY

1

THOSE BASTARD CHAIRS scraping against the flagstones. It's the lemmings waking him up again. One after another he listens to them traipsing down to breakfast, not one of them wanting to miss out on anything, even a slice of cheese and a tomato. Shrieks of laughter, clashing plates, yowling music, the clank and hiss of water heaters all drilling their way into his skull. Louder and louder the racket gets in his head. Rage swells in his throat until he wants to crush something – someone, anyone.

Over years, he's learned to recognise when his behaviour is likely to seem disproportionate to others. He knows when he responds to certain impulses, he will shock and even scare those around him. That's something he can use but for the most part, he has to moderate his behaviour to evade censure. Unrestrained, his anger would detonate. Like the pressure wave from an atomic bomb it would flatten everything and everyone. That's not a desirable outcome in general, so he's learned to control himself. It isn't easy but he's developed strategies which relieve the pressure in his head. Nowadays, no one knows unless he chooses to show them, how primeval his anger can be.

He reaches for his camera; the pictures settle him. They remind him he has all the power he needs; that he can control, take what he wants, when he wants it; that he can compete, challenge himself, and win – every time. He lies back holding the camera up and begins scanning through the images. There are more than 30 photographs, taken one or two at a time each time he'd done it with the drugs. He locates the pictures he took the previous night. He's never had one like that before. The camera caught the bloom of her virgin flesh perfectly.

He masturbates with one hand, scrolling back and forth through the pictures on the camera with the other. Wiping the meagre drizzle of his output on the sheet, he rolls off the bed and into the bathroom.

He showers then fashions a joint. Pushing open the sliding balcony door, he drags a chair to the far corner, out of sight of the courtyard. He flicks the flint on his Zippo and draws deeply on the joint as the tip flares into life. He holds his breath as the drug permeates his lungs then his bloodstream, flooding his body like a long, slow wave rolling on to the shoreline.

2

A FUSION OF laughter and conversation drifted up from the courtyard. It danced with birdsong and the clatter of breakfast dishes. After two hours' sleep, this insistent soundtrack could have been cause for consternation. But Brenda's thoughts weren't yet on the day.

She lay, afraid to stir and shatter the memory of the previous night. She wasn't ready to let it go. Repeatedly she pressed *replay* on her private, mind's-eye home movie, touching, smelling and tasting each moment again and again. She recalled how she and Emilio had talked for over an hour at the table, his broken English forming no barrier to the bond of understanding and mutual desire that tightened between them. He'd hardly unlocked his eyes from her as he directed his waiters to clear up around them, dim the lights and as customers moved on, close up the bar. She'd been as indifferent to their sideways glances, winks and backchat as he and eventually he'd chased them from the premises. She'd watched him gather a mysterious assortment of delicacies from the kitchen, leaving her to wait in the glow of a single candle while he took them upstairs to his flat, before returning to grasp her hand and escort her with a whispered, 'you come with me now'.

She felt again the touch of his hands as they drew her face close to his own and the first, electric touch of his lips on hers, suffused with the earthy scent of his body and the tang of brandy and crème de cacao in his mouth.

Emilio's fingers were warm on her skin as he peeled away her clothes, stroking and kissing as he stripped away her defences. They'd lain on his narrow bed, flesh connecting at a hundred points from their toes to their lips, sipping a honeyed Armagnac from a single tumbler. As they drank, they kissed and touched and laughed. They shared black olives and walnuts, cubes of herbed feta in garlic infused olive oil. He slipped slivers of peach and strawberry between her barely parted lips, letting her taste sweet juices before her tongue engaged with the coarseness of his fingers. Then, his breath heavy with the aromas of their banquet, he whispered in her ear, 'I will sex your body now.'

And he had done it, at first tenderly then urgently and with intensity in his eyes, taking charge, commanding long neglected responses from deep inside her and making her cry out in bittersweet agony.

Brenda stared at the ceiling as she'd stared up at his a few hours earlier while he slept beside her, his arm owning her. As dawn broke, it bathed the room in waves of amber and he'd woken and brought her silently home.

A breeze fluttered the thin curtain and a shaft of sunlight flickered across the wall, a sudden tug away from that room and into this. An unmistakable sickly-sweet odour invaded her consciousness. Someone – she knew who it would be – was smoking a joint.

She reached into her bag and drew out the letter. The envelope was worn, the contents familiar. She knew what would follow but the pull it exerted was too strong. She read from beginning to end; her punishment, an act of contrition, the price for stealing a night of freedom.

'You ruined it all. You forced me into hell – because you and your moral high-ground couldn't let it go. I'll never forgive you for what you did. We won't come back from this.'

There was never any consolation in the letter's incoherent ramblings; no understanding, no forgiveness, only accusation layered on blame. The pages of jumbled vitriol delivered their payload of pain as effectively on the five hundredth reading as they had on the first; and as they had on that first reading, they forced Brenda to question her values and doubt herself and the decisions she'd taken without proper reflection. But still they offered no answers and brought no peace.

Singled Out

She replaced the letter in its envelope. Having suffocated the last vestiges of pleasure from the previous night she arose, clunked the sliding door shut and set about the day.

3

HENRY HAD TO admit, Veronica had come to his rescue the day before in Sirince, being not only willing but happy that he accompany her to photograph the village – even though she knew about his cheeky shots from the day before. Where he might have expected distain, her kindness had poured oil on the waves of humiliation. It had enabled him to stay away from the others without feeling so alone.

They'd had such a good time he suggested they might go out again the next day to take photographs around the town. That he even made the suggestion surprised him. If he'd dwelled on it even for a moment, what little courage he possessed would have deserted him. That she again seemed happy to accompany him – that surprised him still more.

They met up after breakfast. They ambled in awkward silence along the path towards the beachfront bars, the crunch-crunch of their steps synchronising and separating. The air, not yet transitioned from bearable to scorching, was stirred by the whisper of a breeze and birdsong still trumped the daytime cacophony of pounding music and muezzins.

Weighed down with his best SLR, a telescopic tripod and a brace of lenses in another bag, Henry clattered and rattled as he walked. Veronica carried a bag made of quilted floral fabric which looked like it was meant for knitting or embroidery. He'd seen bags like hers amongst Sadie's chapel ladies at home. Veronica wore sensible sandals like Sadie used to, although Sadie would never have gone out without her nylons, even on holiday. Veronica's skirt, ice-cream stripes falling well below her knees, looked home-made, but not in a bad way. Women who knew how to handle a sewing machine took care of the pennies and he'd always had a grudging admiration for Sadie and her ability to knock up a frock for a special occasion or knit him a comfy zip-up.

Most of the bars on the boardwalk were still closed, their awnings furled, verandas shuttered. Of those that were open, garish A-boards boasted combinations of bacon, eggs, sausage and tomatoes and what one curiously described as *Fool English Breaky*. The aroma of fry-up hung in the air – not quite the grease-encrusted odour of rusk and pork rind that Henry was lately used to from the cafe by the station at home, but not far off; certainly close enough to tempt him.

'What a dreadful stink,' said Veronica. It was the first time she'd spoken since they'd left the hotel.

'I was wondering if I had time to grab a bacon butty,' said Henry. He heard a whine in his voice and realised he must sound like a child with his nose against the window of a sweet-shop.

'Really?' exclaimed Veronica. 'But you've had breakfast. Why don't we carry on with what we came down here for then have a nice cup of tea later.'

It felt alright to be organised by Veronica; her mumsy tone was comforting. So he turned his back on a second breakfast he didn't need and the wafts of sizzling bacon which taunted his nostrils. Together they slipped down an alleyway between the bars to the main street. They meandered until they reached a statue of a man in military uniform astride a horse. A plaque proclaimed the man to be Mustafa Kemal Atatürk, whom Veronica announced to be the founder of modern Turkey. An area of cobblestones surrounded the statue. Framing its outer rim was a semi-circle of stone benches.

One bench was already occupied by an elderly woman dressed in black. Her skin was leathery and creviced. Her bulbous nose was pitted and on her cheek a mole bristled with spiky hairs. She breathed heavily, each exhalation extended by an airy wheeze. Her mouth open, it was clear the old crone had lost more teeth than she had remaining.

'Here might be a good place,' said Henry. 'We can set up in the shade and take some shots of the statue and the street and whoever comes along. What do you think?'

'You're the expert,' responded Veronica. 'I'm in your hands.' A wan smile invaded Henry's features. It was in danger of becoming a leer but he reined it in. He didn't know what to say next, so he set down his equipment and fiddled with the clasp on his camera bag. It wouldn't yield.

'Here, let me,' said Veronica and with a click and a twist of her practical fingers, it fell open.

Henry busied himself unpacking and setting up his paraphernalia, examining his camera, cleaning his lenses, checking the light and adjusting dials and gauges. Veronica pulled her pocket camera from its case and sat quietly beside him until he could no longer find a knob he hadn't twiddled or a dial he hadn't adjusted.

'It's impressive, your equipment,' said Veronica, staring at the construction of tripod, camera and lens which now stood between Henry's parted legs. He couldn't resist a private smile but Veronica would likely not appreciate his sense of humour.

'I like what you can do with this kind of kit,' said Henry, moving himself on. 'But as a beginner you can still get some respectable pictures with a half-decent camera like yours. Can I show you?'

Henry extended his hand towards Veronica's camera and she offered it up to him like a sacrifice. He fiddled for a few moments then pointed it at the old woman on the bench. He pressed the red button and released the synthetic *click-click-whirr* of the shutter. He pressed again; *click-click-whirr*. Her attention caught, the old woman focused her milky-grey eyes, full of life and death and age and toil, on him. He took a third snap – *click-click-whirr* – and her time-scarred visage filled the frame. He couldn't tell if the old woman was obliging him or if his attentions had irritated her, but Veronica seemed to realise. She pressed her hand down on his arm, forcing him to lower the camera.

'Enough, I think,' she whispered. The old woman turned away.

Henry scanned the photos. Veronica's camera was basic but it had captured the character of the old woman. He presented the pictures to Veronica, explaining his choice of settings and pausing on each so she could make her appreciative noises.

Veronica was a novice at photography but insisted she was keen to learn how to take better pictures. Using his own shots as examples he delighted in the next hour, showing her how to compose a picture, demonstrating what to include and what to avoid. The town square came to life. Shops, kiosks and bars opened for business, tourists trailed through with garish beachbags, locals crossed their path laden with shopping in flimsy blue carriers or woven baskets. Veronica and Henry snapped away, at ease with one another, companionable; a word of encouragement here, a cautious hint there.

As the sun elevated, the opaque morning light sharpened and heat surged from the cobbles. Veronica suggested they retreat to a bar for a cup of tea and Henry, realising thirst had turned his mouth into a sticky cavern, willingly agreed.

They chose a bar by the statue and settled outside under a parasol. Although Henry would have preferred a beer, he let Veronica order a pot of English tea and a serving of borek for them to share. Though he was still dreaming of a bacon butty, he liked the little cheese and spinach pastries and he was relieved she hadn't chosen those sickly honey and nut concoctions that everyone except him seemed to love.

A waiter brought their order.

'Shall I be mother?' Veronica said and Henry laughed. 'What's so funny?' she asked.

'That's what... oh, never mind,' he replied. It didn't seem right to talk about Sadie. But there was one thing that had been on Henry's mind all morning; a question guaranteed to alter the mood. He needed to pose it even though he wasn't sure he wanted to hear the answer.

'Veronica, do you mind if I ask you a personal question?' Even as he said it, he half wished she would shut him down.

'Go on,' she said. 'But you'll have to excuse me if I decide not to answer once I've heard it.' She stirred the tea; round and round with the spoon, tinkling it against the inside of the china pot.

'It's only... well... you know the other day, I took a couple of snapshots... of you... don't you?'

'Yes.' She hesitated, her smile fading. She pulled the spoon from the pot and set it on the table where a dribble of tea pooled beneath it, then dropped the lid back on the pot with a clink. Henry felt an uncomfortable heat radiate across his chest.

'You'd have been perfectly within your rights to be upset with me.'

'I know,' she said. 'Henry, where's this going?'

'It's... uh... I was wondering, why... after all that... you were so nice to me yesterday up at that village with the shops and stalls. And then today, Veronica, it's been lovely.'

'It has been nice, yes,' she said. 'Look, everyone makes mistakes. Those photographs were wrong. But one mistake doesn't make you a bad person. You seem a bit out on a limb here and I thought you could use a friend. I thought you were maybe better than that unfortunate moment. Does that make sense?'

'I suppose so,' said Henry, although it didn't.

'I was terribly nervous about coming on this holiday. I've never been on holiday by myself before and I didn't know what it would be like. Now I'm here and it isn't easy. Some people are friendly but I'm afraid I don't fit in terribly well. Everyone is so outgoing and loud. They drink so much and love those noisy disco bars where you can't hear yourself think. They're all so much younger too, younger than you and I.'

'I've been thinking the exact same thing,' sighed Henry. 'I'm too old for this.'

'That's why it's nice we're getting along, isn't it?'

'Yes, it is.'

'That's two answers for you. Will that do?'

'It's perfect,' said Henry.

'Now we know each other a little, I hope you won't take any more of those sorts of pictures – of me – will you?'

'No, no, no,' stuttered Henry, 'definitely not. I'm really sorry, Veronica. I wasn't thinking.'

'I can see you've thought about it now. Anyway, no harm done. We can move on, say nothing more about it.'

'Yes, please. I'm sorry I mentioned it.'

'Let's leave it there then. Except—'

'Except what?'

'Except, you could delete the photographs.'

'What, now?'

'It would be the thing to do.'

After yesterday with Brenda he couldn't argue. So Henry pulled out his compact camera. He found the offending pictures and consigned them to the ether, showing Veronica as each one disappeared. He wouldn't enjoy looking at them now anyway – it would feel wrong now he'd made friends with Veronica. It wouldn't stop him harvesting a few more from the holiday – there were girls on the beach every day – but not Veronica.

After their refreshments Henry and Veronica walked some way up the road out of town towards the pine forests. But the trees were home to armies of insects keen to make a meal of tourist flesh. Veronica produced anti-mosquito wipes for them both. He'd have stopped at his arms and legs, but Veronica made him tend to his neck and even his ears, which he wouldn't have thought of by himself.

They pressed on and found a vantage point, a small lay-by with a viewing area bordered by railings, overlooking the beach, the sweep of the bay and the harbour. It gave Henry the chance to show Veronica what he knew about landscapes. They took shots of the wooden boats in the bay, loaded with tourists. He even managed to persuade Veronica to lean against the railings and pose for a couple of proper photos with the sea and the rocks behind her.

Veronica tucked her skirt tightly between her knees but Henry didn't say anything. Her modesty reminded him of Sadie.

4

THE NIGHT WITH Emilio had subdued Brenda's demons, but only temporarily. With the arrival of daylight and her morning ritual with the letter, Brenda's mood crashed. On the patio, her poolside accessories neatly arranged, she'd retreated behind that universally understood holiday blockade of oversize sunglasses, sunhat, iPod, earphones and a 500-page bonk-buster held aloft. She was if not content, at least calm in her private space; until Lilly appeared.

'Mind if I join you?' she asked Brenda's book. Nothing.

'Hello, anyone in there?' Lilly pressed a finger down on the top of the book, forcing Brenda to lower it. Brenda pulled a headphone from one ear, drew her sunglasses down to the tip of her nose and peered over the rim. Lilly's face was flushed. A dewy sheen, beads of perspiration, spread across her cheekbones and the bridge of her nose. Her lips were pallid, her eyes an irregular lattice of swollen blood vessels. She was swaying as if trying to hold her balance on a life-raft.

'God, you look awful!' Brenda said.

'Hangover,' responded Lilly with a wan smile. 'I'm not well.'

'Come, sit down,' said Brenda, motioning to the neighbouring lounger. She proffered a bottle of water. 'Drink,' she commanded.

The girl sat as instructed and sipped the water.

'I didn't think a couple of glasses of raki would do this to me,' she said.

'A couple of glasses of raki wouldn't do this to you,' said Brenda. 'You had more than a couple,' she chuckled, 'and what about later, when you went to town with the others? What else did you drink?'

'I'm not sure,' replied Lilly, 'I had a few more. Matt bought me a cocktail, I remember that. I think James did too. Then they all made me try a fierce thing with coffee beans in it – they set fire to it and you're supposed to drink it straight down. James had one too and everyone was shouting 'drink, drink, drink...' and I didn't want to let the side down. I wasn't going to have any more, but Turner got me another – I don't know what – but it was sweet and creamy like a dessert, not boozy. So I think I let... someone... get me another one.'

'You think? Someone?'

'Matt, maybe. I'm not sure. Heavens, this is so embarrassing.'

'What about the others?' asked Brenda.

'I don't know,' said Lilly. 'One minute we were all together, then... not. I think. I can't remember. All I know is I woke up in my room. Someone must have helped me home but I've no idea who. Brenda, I'm never, ever doing that again!'

'That's what we all say,' said Brenda. 'But everyone goes over-the-top on holiday.' She looked across the pool to where Turner basked, hands behind his head, on a lounger. Beneath his shades it was impossible to see if he was watching them. Yet he must have been as he raised his head, a casual nod in response to her stare. Perhaps he would fill in the holes in Lilly's recollection.'

'I don't usually drink. I've never had a hangover before. I never realised I'd feel so ill.' She clutched at her stomach with both hands. 'I think I'm going to be sick. All this, and the other, too.'

'The other what?'

'Aunt Flo has come calling – two weeks early too.' The girl sniffed.

'Aunt Flo?'

'When I woke up this morning, I was on top of the bed, still in my clothes. But my *you-know-what* had come in the night – sort of. I was crampy and there was blood, right through to the bed in a couple of spots. I had to rinse out the sheet; I couldn't let Defne find blood.'

'I expect she'd have understood,' said Brenda. Defne would have seen a lot worse than the odd spot of blood on holiday bedsheets.

'It's the wrong time though. I'm not due and I haven't got anything with me. Would alcohol bring it on? I shouldn't have drunk like I did. You should have stopped me!'

On a holiday, as anywhere else, people had to take responsibility for themselves. Yet as Brenda recalled the raki they'd pressed on Lilly at lunch – the girl too polite to refuse – she felt a tug of remorse. They'd goaded her for their own amusement and they'd kept up the pace when the party returned to the hotel.

'I need sani-towels, Brenda. Do you have any you could spare?'

'I'm afraid not.'

'Oh,' the girl moaned again. 'I'll have to get something from town. Would you come with me? I'm not sure what to buy here. You'd know, wouldn't you?'

'Yes, honey, I'd know,' Brenda sighed, her weary tone belying the discomfort she was beginning to feel in her own belly.

'We can't go too fast,' said Lilly. 'I won't cope.' Brenda had no intention of taking things at speed. For her any walk, particularly in the high sun, was to be sauntered at the most leisurely pace imaginable. She gathered her belongings. Wrapping her sarong around her bust she tied an efficient knot and pressed it into her cleavage. She would have preferred to change into something more suitable but Lilly's anguish overrode her needs and they set out without further procrastination.

But this wasn't to be the companionable stroll she'd enjoyed the other day with Adele. The women stumbled more than they walked, in near silence. The sun lasered down on them from a sky unblemished by a puff of cloud, searing their flesh like steak on a griddle. The air smothered them and heat rose from the clay beneath their feet and clutched at their throats. It was like trying to breathe through cotton wool. Swarms of biting flies and mosquitoes soared from the scrub, frenzied by the lure of fresh blood. They buzzed and screamed around Brenda's ears and she flapped at them as they attacked in waves. Against her better judgement Brenda tried to quicken the pace, but Lilly seemed not so much unwilling as unable to oblige. She drifted from side to side on the uneven gravel, apologising again and again, offering the humidity and a relentless abdominal cramping as justification for her sluggishness.

As Lilly's evident distress mounted Brenda grew more unsettled. She should have left the girl behind and fetched what she needed from the pharmacy. But they were half way between the hotel and the town and it was too late to turn back. Lilly's top lip was beaded with sweat; her eyes fluttered and rolled. Brenda put an arm around her and Lilly yielded until Brenda felt as if she were supporting the girl's entire weight. They'd been over-ambitious in attempting even this modest walk in 40-degree heat yet Brenda pulled Lilly onwards, anxious to reach a place where the girl – and she – could rest.

'I'm so sorry, Brenda,' Lilly muttered, over and over. 'How could a few drops of alcohol make me feel so ill?'

'Don't you worry,' said Brenda, her voice wavering. 'We're nearly there. We'll take a rest at Emilio's bar.

By the time they arrived at Emilio's, Brenda had as good as carried Lilly for the last hundred yards. Both were exhausted. Perspiration flooded Brenda's forehead and trickled, stinging, into her eyes. Under her sarong, sweat had glued her thighs together as she walked. Now she felt the prickly raw burn of a heat rash spreading between her legs. Emilio, clearing tables for lunchtime customers, spotted Brenda as she reached the boardwalk. He emerged, beaming, from the bar but his smile faded as the women neared. He drew them to a table in the shade and poured water for them.

'My special girl no well?' he enquired, tenderly lifting Brenda's face to meet his own.

'Not me,' she replied stiffly, mopping her brow with a napkin. The last thing she needed was for Emilio to see her in such a sorry state. 'It's Lilly. She's feeling unwell – she nearly fainted. I don't suppose you've got anything to help?'

'I get baklava. Sugar will feel her better.' His concern for the girl was reassuring, giving Brenda hope he'd overlook her own dripping disarray.

Emilio returned with a dish bearing three of the syrupy sweets, which he placed before Lilly. 'You eat, you feel better,' he said. Lilly pushed the plate away.

'Come on,' said Brenda, 'it'll help.'

'I'm so sorry. I'm so sorry,' Lilly repeated.

'It's alright, it's not your fault,' said Brenda; enough with the endless apologising. But something wasn't right. This was more than period pains, more than a hangover. Her instincts were infallible – a curse as much as a blessing. 'In fact—' Brenda said, then hesitated.

'In fact what?' said Lilly, taking her first bite of baklava. Brenda had opened her mouth before fully committing to what would come out. Would she never learn?

'I was wondering if... someone... might have spiked your drink last night.' She couldn't resist poking a stick in the hornets' nest. Why was it always this way?

'Spiked? What, like poisoned me?' squealed Lilly.

'Sort of,' said Brenda. 'In a crowd it could have happened without you knowing. But probably not,' she added, a feeble attempt to deaden the impact of her thought-bomb, too late.

'That's a dreadful thought!'

'You're right,' said Brenda. 'I'm sorry, I shouldn't have said anything.'

On the beach, children screamed; a motor scooter rattled past on the boardwalk, spewing fumes; a waiter emerged from the kitchen holding a sizzling platter aloft. Somewhere in the distance a dog barked.

'It was crowded,' Lilly's voice wavered. 'I suppose—'

'But you were with everyone, weren't you? James and the others,' Brenda interrupted. The hornets were stirring.

'For a while,' whispered Lilly.

'But you said someone looked after you.'

'Someone must have, but I couldn't tell you who. I just hope I didn't make an idiot of myself,'

Brenda was in uncomfortable territory. She'd got herself into it, now she had to get out. The girl was fine. A bottle of water and an Aspirin and she'd be back to normal. Let it go.

'I'm sure you didn't. Anyway, we've all done it. Don't dwell on it; nobody will hold it against you.' Let this be over, please.

'I had some proper bad dreams last night too. Weird ones.'

'How weird?'

'It was like I woke up but I couldn't move. And I saw... I don't know exactly. It made no sense.'

'Put it out of your mind,' said Brenda, willing herself to the same position. 'It's very hot here, your hormones are misbehaving and you had too much to drink. Apart from feeling the worse for wear, you're safe and sound, aren't you? That's what matters. You're not alone, honey. We all get a hangover once in a while, nightmares too. I'd chalk it up to experience, don't let it spoil your holiday.'

'Drinking, Brenda – it's a curse. I'm never doing that again,' sighed Lilly.

A gush of acid washed into Brenda's throat. She swallowed, forcing down instinct and experience. This didn't feel right. Before, she would have pursued, hunted down the truth; ferreted away until she'd uncovered proof and forced whatever it was into the open. But why? To help? For the sake of the truth? To be a rock in troubled times? That's what she told herself, before. Or was it to prove herself right, to have her suspicions vindicated? To show everyone how smart and intuitive and rigorous she was?

After Jack, she no longer knew... anything.

'I'm feeling better now,' said Lilly, returning to the plate to polish off the second baklava. 'You've both been so kind, I don't want to impose any more. Brenda, we should go.'

'Nonsense,' said Brenda. Lilly didn't look any better, just less likely to keel over. She would smother her unease but there was no harm in helping the girl with practicalities. 'Emilio can look after you for a few minutes. I'll go the pharmacy.'

'You come back to me?' Emilio asked. Two questions in one, she imagined.

'I will,' said Brenda.

5

'HOW'S THE KID?'

'Excuse me?' said Brenda. Behind her shades she prized open her eyes. She'd managed a whole half-hour on a sun lounger by the pool without being bothered by anything other than her own unsettled gut.

'The kid. Lilly, right? She didn't look well earlier,' Turner responded. 'I was just wondering, how is she?' He towered over Brenda's lounger, blocking the sunlight and creating optimum conditions for the display of his flawlessly sculpted silhouette.

'Women's trouble, mainly,' Brenda said, making every effort to concentrate, 'and overindulgence. She's up in her room, sleeping it off.'

'Yeah, she was putting it away last night. But that's the young for you, I guess. They don't know when to stop. Get carried away with the atmosphere.' Brenda found herself bristling at the inference that *the young* was a community that no longer included her.

'She can't remember much. She's a bit afraid she made a fool of herself.'

'Nah.' Turner shook his head. 'No more or less than the rest of us. We had fun, that's all.'

'Do you know who brought her home?'

'Sorry, no,' said Turner. 'We started off as a group but the place was heaving. It wasn't deliberate, but we didn't all stick together. You asked any of the others?'

'Not yet, no,' Brenda replied. 'I will though. It might help her fill in the blank spots.'

'That might not be a great idea,' laughed Turner. 'Last I remember seeing her, she was locked in some kind of a tussle with the preppy.' He nodded across to where James and Barry once again sat hunched on opposing sides of their backgammon board.

'You left her with James?'

'Hey now,' Turner said. 'I didn't leave her with anyone. She did what she did. I'm not her big brother. What she gets up to is her business.'

'By the sounds of it, no one was looking out for her,' said Brenda. Turner shrugged his massive shoulders.

'That's what you get on a singles holiday.'

Brenda couldn't deny he was right. That, she was already concluding, was both the bonus and the peril of a singles holiday.

6

LATER THAT EVENING on the balcony, Brenda and Adele chatted whilst Brenda risked fatal damage to her manicure by levering away at the shells on a handful of pistachios. Her second neat spirit of the evening diffused her unease about Lilly whilst shoring up her decision, reached after the conversation with Turner, to stay out of the girl's business. But everything changed when she caught sight of James at the bar.

James was gathering guests around him, much as Turner and Matt had done on the first night. Animated to the point of exhibitionism, his arms circling like the blades on a helicopter, James's voice rose above the others and laughter cascaded round the stone walls. Was he making a contest of it? Turner stood to one side staring at James, his jaw locked.

Brenda sipped her drink and picked away at her pistachios, letting a succession of Adele's pitiless observations on her fellow guests evaporate in the still air. They seemed to fuse with the grinding of the air conditioning extractor until she could no longer distinguish one from the other. As she talked, Adele siphoned alcohol from her glass, suckling it like a baby on the breast. When sharing her caustic opinions on the other holidaymakers, Adele needed little more than a murmured *yes*, *oh*, or *really* from Brenda, effectively liberating her from the need to concentrate on conversation.

Brenda couldn't help it. She had to know what had happened to Lilly the previous evening; even though she was afraid to know, because once she knew, it meant she might have to act. She pressed Adele to drain her glass and all but dragged her from the room to the gathering below. Together they joined James and his cohorts, pretty Chloe, always laughing, Matt and Backgammon Barry.

'Where did you party-animals get to last night?' she queried airily, but with purpose.

'We went to Marmaris, trawled a few bars,' said James. 'Not my kind of place, to be frank, but we had a laugh. Why didn't you come?'

'I wasn't in the mood,' said Brenda.

'Adele?' said James. 'You're a party girl. Where were you?'

'I wasn't well – I felt crap all day,' said Adele, omitting the barbed retort which generally followed an attempt by James to pierce her hostile carapace. 'Something I ate,' she added. James snorted, earning himself a warning glare from Brenda. It had no effect; James was in a puckish mood.

'Nothing to do with the industrial quantity of booze you've been putting away,' he said.

'Piss off, prick,' barked Adele.

'Lilly was with you, wasn't she?' continued Brenda, pressing onward with another question to which she already knew the answer.

'I believe she was,' said James.

'Do you know what happened to her?'

'What do you mean?'

'I mean, do you know what happened to her?'

'We lost the run of her – I think,' said James. 'Why? She's alright, isn't she?'

'More or less,' said Brenda. 'She had too much to drink.'

'We did look for her, didn't we, guys?'

Everyone agreed they'd searched for Lilly but assumed she'd taken a taxi back to the hotel.

'She's here though, safe and sound, isn't she?' said Matt.

'Yes, she's here. But she hasn't been well.'

'That's what you get for a night on the sauce,' Matt smirked. 'Anyway, that's hardly our fault.'

'That may be true,' said Brenda. 'But she's young and she only went to town because you all were going. If you ask me, it was a bit much for her.'

'That's not down to us, Bren,' said James, earning murmurs and nods from the others.

'I know,' sighed Brenda. 'But you haven't seen her. She's been very poorly today, and that's the least of it.' With her serious face on, the mood darkened. She looked askance at James's companions.

'I'll catch up with you later,' said James, as Brenda grasped him by the elbow and steered him away. She guided him to a pair of stools at the end of the bar, positioning herself to discourage anyone else from joining them.

'What else then?' said James.

'I think... someone might have spiked her drink last night. She knows you poured flaming sambuca down her throat but she can't remember much after that.'

'Hold on!' hissed James. 'What the heck are you saying? I didn't spike her drink. Bloody hell, Bren!'

'No, no, I'm... not saying that,' said Brenda. 'But it's a crazy, crowded place and someone did – possibly.'

'What's so bad these days about spiking a drink anyway?' James fired back. 'I've had some top nights on super-charged refreshments. Don't tell me you haven't yourself – when you were... you know, younger. I know she's a bit naive, but if she had a good time, what's the harm?'

Brenda kicked herself. Why did she pick away at things like this? Even knowing where it could lead.

'It's probably nothing,' she said, 'and I know it's not my problem. But I see the nasty side of life so often – in my work. I see stuff other people never encounter. It makes me suspicious.' As soon as she said the words, she realised her error.

'A florist sees the nasty side of life?' James's voice shot up an octave. 'So what, there's a sleazy underbelly to the business of floral art, a nefarious horticultural underworld, a kind of *daffodil mafia*? What's that, a *cosy nostra*? Oh, this is good. Pull the other one, Bren!'

'I'm not a florist,' Brenda hissed.

'What?'

'I'm not a florist,' she repeated, her voice a low whisper. 'I don't sell flowers. At the restaurant yesterday, I lied.'

'Why?'

'Because when they look at me, people expect that to be the sort of job I do; because it's easier than explaining what I actually do.'

'Which is what? If you're not in the business of bountiful bouquets, what do you do?'

'I'm a criminal psychologist,' said Brenda, 'I work with disordered personalities and I teach specialist interview techniques – to the police.' Her words hung in the air.

'Fuck me, Bren. You don't give much away, do you?'

'No, but keep it to yourself. You see what I mean, about not being what people expect?'

'Hell, yes,' James sighed. 'You must have to be mega-qualified – smart as hell – to get into that game.

'I've got a doctorate in criminal psychology and a diploma in cognitive-behavioural hypnotherapy.' The words tripped angrily off her tongue.

'Beats a City & Guilds in flower arranging,' James laughed.

'Quite,' said Brenda.

'So you're *Doctor* Brenda?' he added, his eyebrows heading for the sky.

'I am,' said Brenda, 'for all the good it does me.'

'And hypnotherapy too,' said James. She could see him knitting the facts together in his head. 'You hypnotise people?'

'Sometimes. I don't use it much.'

'But you could?'

'I could.'

'Cool,' James grinned. 'You won't make me bark like a dog or be your slave or anything, will you?'

'No, honey,' sighed Brenda, 'I'm not tempted.'

'Pity, it might have been... entertaining,' said James. 'So what does a criminal psychologist do when she's not playing about on holiday?'

Brenda quietly explained about the work she did with serious offenders – the disturbed and violent, sociopaths, paranoid schizophrenics – in the system, in prisons and secure hospitals. She explained how she used her skills to reveal instinctive responses and get to hidden truths. She professed a fascination in the psychology of the sociopath; she told how she used physicality and linguistic techniques to build rapport and how even the shrewdest and most astute could, with the right approach, be persuaded to betray themselves.

As Brenda talked, a passion she barely remembered challenged the misery and self-doubt of recent months. Beyond the odd flippant aside, James posed questions which evidenced curiosity and intellect. He said he could see she enjoyed her work by the way she talked and he was right. In all its intense, insane diversity, she'd loved her place in the world – before everything changed.

'What on earth made you go into this field,' asked James.

'Believe it or not,' said Brenda, 'deviant personalities intrigue me.'

'You being such a *rules* girl yourself, I suppose; so straight-laced and all,' laughed James.

'If only you knew,' sighed Brenda.

'So,' James said, 'you see bad stuff everywhere, because of what you do. I understand that. But really, here, on holiday? A girl gets off her face and someone slips her a mickey. It's hardly crime of the century, is it?'

'It depends on how you look at it,' said Brenda, stunned that James thought so little of what she regarded as a contemptible act. 'But ask yourself, why does someone spike a drink?'

'For a laugh?'

'A bloody stupid laugh if you ask me.'

'Quite, yes,' said James, colour flushing his cheeks.

'Why else?'

'To have their wicked way?'

'That's a little trite, don't you think?'

'What would you call it, Bren?'

'I'd call it rape. That's the word I'd use.'

'If you want my opinion, I think you're overreacting. You're reading too much into it. She got a bit drunk, that's all. She's alright, isn't she? So come on, put it out of your mind. We're all on holiday, let's get on and enjoy ourselves.'

This appeared to be the last James wanted to hear on the matter and he was itching to rejoin his friends. Brenda's glass was empty and there was time for one more before dinner. Getting involved did more harm than good. None of this was her problem, so why was she picking away at it? She turned to order a cocktail and for the first time noticed Adele, perched on a stool directly behind her, alone.

'One for you?' she asked.

'No thanks,' said Adele, though the glass she clasped in both hands was empty.

'You alright?' asked Brenda.

'Not really, no,' replied Adele, her words rasping.

7

HENRY SAT ALONE sipping on a bottle of Efes. With years as a reporter behind him, he was accustomed to listening in to other people's conversations, even – or perhaps particularly – those executed in barely audible whispers.

Could it have been Lilly he'd seen the previous evening in the shadow of the staircase, drunk or dazed, with a man strong enough to lift her as if she were a ragdoll? It seemed plausible. But Brenda was jumping to conclusions. He'd been the one to see the girl hauled upstairs to a bedroom, not her. Give her credit though, she was sharp. She might be on the right lines. The action in the bedroom's dimmed light, silhouetted against the curtain; it was obviously sex, in one way or another.

But why was it such a big deal?

There was plenty of sex going on at the hotel – or so he assumed. They were all at it with whoever they could persuade to lie still for long enough, weren't they? He would be, if he could. So why would it be a problem if Lilly got a seeing-to? She'd have enjoyed it, wouldn't she? Even though she might not want to admit it in the morning.

But then there was the night before, at the bar. He looked over at Adele, slumped against the counter gulping short breaths, her glass so tightly gripped between her interlocked fingers that her knuckles were white. He'd said nothing about who and what he'd seen and now it seemed something else had happened. But this time it wasn't a mouthy trollop, asking for it from any passing bloke, but sweet young Lilly. They hadn't become friends or anything, but she was a nice lass. He liked her – liked her well enough not to want to see her come to harm at any rate.

Veronica appeared on cue to distract him, camera in hand. Dull, beige and ordinary, she already felt so familiar to him, like a favourite pair of slippers. He beckoned her over. Then he found himself signalling to Mehmet, asking Veronica what she wanted and ordering for her on his tab. Luckily it was only a Coke. Together they scanned through her photographs from the morning. Henry made positive noises whenever he spotted a particularly good shot and pointed out when things hadn't worked, and why. It gave him the opportunity to talk about framing, perspective and the rule of thirds and Veronica lapped it all up – she seemed genuinely interested.

Things were going so well. But then he accidentally called her Sadie.

'Who's Sadie?' Veronica asked.

'Shit, I'm sorry, I didn't mean to—' said Henry.

'It's alright,' said Veronica. 'But who is Sadie?'

'That's my wife's name. Sorry, sorry. It slipped out.'

'I didn't know you were married,' said Veronica, a flutter of disapproval in her tone, and the same look he'd seen that morning when he'd reminded her about the photographs he'd taken of her.

'I'm not. I was, I mean. Just... not anymore. She had cancer. She died.'

'That's very sad,' whispered Veronica. She placed her hand on his arm for a moment. 'Was it recently?'

'Three months ago,' said Henry. Veronica's tenderness was unsettling. 'I thought it would be ok to go on holiday, but apart from you being so kind, it's not quite what I'd hoped and—'

'You're missing her?' interrupted Veronica.

'I... I don't know.'

Until that moment he hadn't considered he might be missing his Sadie. How could he possibly miss her? She'd been such a quiet, frigid woman, with no hobbies outside her chapel circle and no interest in him – physically or otherwise. What was there to miss?

Yet there she was, in pinpoint sharp focus in his mind – her colourless face, tired eyes and thin, almost translucent lips. His wife of over a quarter of a century, pallid and motionless; but he couldn't tell if the vision in his head was Sadie alive, or dead.

It wasn't that they argued. He had to admit, they didn't. For the last decade, they'd hardly talked at all. But divorce wasn't an option thanks to her chapel background. So monotonous years had melded one into another and eventually, despite his blood pressure and niggling angina, it was she who was the first to go, freeing him from their marriage for the price of a funeral.

He recalled the curious rush of exhilaration he experienced when their GP broke the news. She mentioned she was going to the surgery that day for the results of some tests. He didn't ask what tests and she didn't volunteer the information. But then she asked him to sit in on the appointment, which was a bit much. But he did it to keep the peace.

When the GP said the 'C' word, she cried and he patted her hand as it seemed the thing to do. He asked a few questions. Were they planning to do anything, an operation perhaps? How was it likely to go for her? How long would she...? He composed himself carefully to look concerned (like he used to do as a reporter when he went to interview people who'd been burgled or mugged). But it was his own outcome, not hers, that was uppermost in his mind as it meant he could start to plan a future for himself. Six months, the GP eventually said quietly, although he had to work him over a little to extract that vital snippet. And six months it was, almost to the day.

The funeral was held in the chapel and he was surprised how packed it was. Several people, mostly women, came back to the house afterwards. Each one buttonholed him for a few minutes whilst the tea and cakes were being served, to tell him how much they had valued his wife's friendship, loyalty, participation on this or that committee, jam-making or flower-arranging skills, whatever. It amazed him how they all held her in such high regard. He was polite and courteous and eventually they went home and left him in peace. Later he found they'd left him food parcels in the fridge, accompanied by instructions on reheating times and temperatures. He enjoyed a couple of weeks of exceptionally tasty suppers – mostly lasagnes and pies – before they ran out and he had to find his way around the supermarket for the first time. That was the point at which he first dared acknowledge that what he was experiencing might not necessarily be for the better.

Despite the mutterings of the chapel ladies about it being *too soon*, he'd taken himself off on holiday to cheer himself up.

'Sounds to me, it's exactly what you're feeling, Henry.' Veronica placed her hand on his arm again. Her delicate touch arrested his remembrance, pulling him back to this strange foreign place, so far away from home and all its familiarities. A simple gesture, her touch brought the sting of tears to Henry's eyes; tears he didn't want; tears he certainly didn't want anyone to see. He pulled a crumpled handkerchief from his pocket and brought it to his face.

'Oh goodness,' cried Veronica. 'No! Don't touch your eyes with that, please! It's... it's rather grubby, don't you think?'

Henry pulled at the crushed grey-brown square. It was starched with grime, stuck to itself in a dozen places, scarred with unidentifiable stains and pock-marked with a residue of dried nasal pickings. Sadie used to give him a freshly pressed handkerchief every day. This one could easily have been in his pocket for three months.

'It's the only one I've got,' said Henry.

'Right, well you can have my tissues.' And with that, Veronica exchanged a packet of folded white tissues for the fetid square, which she folded and slipped into the side-pocket of her handbag. 'I'll wash it for you and get Defne to give it a press. You can have it back tomorrow.'

It felt good to be looked after.

'Your wife, Sadie, she used to take care of you, I imagine,' said Veronica.

'I suppose so,' said Henry. He rarely acknowledged the lifetime of cleaning, washing, shopping, tidying and cooking his wife had provided, let alone her quiet companionship in the evenings; her simple presence in the room, keeping him from loneliness, the loneliness in which he now floundered.

'I expect she took care of all sorts of things you have to do for yourself these days.'

'Yes?' said Henry, guessing this was the correct response.

'Only... when we don't have someone around to keep us... neat and... clean, it's easy to get a bit lax, wouldn't you say?'

'I suppose so,' responded Henry again. What was she getting at?

'It sounds to me like you're missing a woman's touch in your life' said Veronica.

'Oh, that? No, Veronica, I'm not short of a woman's touch,' blurted Henry defensively. 'There's somewhere I go whenever I need to, you know, do what comes naturally for a man. It's not expensive and the girls are quite clean. I don't go short.'

'I... what? Excuse me?' responded Veronica. She lifted her hand from Henry's and pushed back her chair. The conversations around them all seemed to have ended. Everything was quiet. Even the cicadas' relentless rasping seemed to have stalled in the still air.

'I probably shouldn't talk about it,' said Henry. 'But I know I'm not the only one who pays for it. Everyone pays for it in one way or another.' His voice rose, as if he were challenging the other guests to contradict him. Henry looked around; several guests averted their eyes. A couple of suppressed sniggers were all he got in return. He was right then.

'Henry,' said Veronica. 'What you do for... you know—'

'Sex?' said Henry.

'Yes,' said Veronica. 'It's not something people talk about quite so... openly.'

'Maybe they should,' said Henry. 'Then at least we'd all know where we stood.'

'Henry, it's not nice. Talking about it, I mean. It's especially not nice to talk about going to... *prostitutes*.' Her last word was uttered in a horrified whisper and it dawned on Henry that yet another woman disapproved of him. It seemed when it came to women, he couldn't put a foot right.

'Look, I'm sorry,' he said. 'I didn't mean to upset you. It's this place, it's not turning out like—'

'Henry, I honestly don't want to know,' said Veronica. 'I think we should end this conversation. You're in danger of offending me.'

Every woman eventually ended up sounding like his mother, belittling and patronising him when he said or did something wrong. Veronica's disapproval was obvious but her tone was kinder than he was used to. Veronica was so much more like his wife. Her down-to-earth goodness was transparent. Her workaday plainness was reassuring. Like Sadie.

'Sorry, sorry, I'm sorry,' he said again and again.

WEDNESDAY

1

THE SUN SPANGLED through a thousand peepholes in the canopy of vines, dancing across crumbs and sticky residue, as Brenda sat nursing her third breakfast coffee. It was market day; a promising distraction.

'Beach or pool?' Adele quizzed.

'I might give the beach a go later,' said Brenda. Should she settle somewhere by Emilio's bar for a few hours or would that be too obvious? 'I was thinking of going to the market this morning.' Her own indecisiveness was unsettling.

'Fancy some company?'

'Sure,' said Brenda. One decision made for her, one more to go.

The market took place on a scar of gravel behind the shopping street, away from the beach. One day a week, farmers came from the villages and hamlets in the hills, their pick-ups laden with fresh produce of all shapes and mis-shapes, a riot of colour and a testament to enterprise out of sight of the tourist coastline. Traders moved from town to town, market day to market day, bringing truckloads of goods; t-shirts and trousers, bags and belts, pashminas and pendants, sandals and sunhats all manufactured in anonymous factories far away from the coast or most likely in China. Packets of candy, nuts and spices sat alongside jars of local honey and blocks of cheese; everything was available to buy from trestle tables and rails, all under cover of flapping white awnings – giving the impression the whole market was a trading ship about to set sail.

The two women meandered the length and breadth of the market. They flirted with moustachioed farmers behind piles of wooden boxes laden with runner beans, aubergines, red and white onions, citrus fruits and watermelons; they breathed in the aromas of citronella and cinnamon, fruit teas and fresh herbs, beaten leather, workaday sweat and cigarettes; they bartered with stall-holders over beaded necklaces and gaudily embellished flip-flops; they cooed over a pile of crates crammed with baby chicks, their fluffy down every shade from creamy gold-top to dark chocolate. Brenda stocked up on sugared almonds and Adele found a fake henna kit she couldn't live without. Then, bags brimming, they made for the beachfront and the yellow awning for lunch.

Emilio brought ice-cold Efes and the women quenched their thirst. Mouth wide, Adele gulped at the beer until her glass was dry then summoned another. Head throbbing from the heat and a trickle of perspiration running from her temple, Brenda sipped through parted lips. She pressed the glass, still half full and moist with condensation, against her neck. Her rapid pulse rose up to meet it and she noticed Emilio watching her in the reflection from the mirror behind the bar. She responded; a smile of acknowledgement, a tilt of her head as she drank, leaving moisture glistening where she held the glass to her neck. She saw him smile.

The waves of overheat ebbed in response to the ice-chill against her throat. Exotic music and the spit and sizzle of the griddle teased her ears and the aromas of kofte, seared cod and fresh baked bread taunted her taste-buds. She smiled at Emilio's reflection and he winked in return. With him she had delighted in exhuming the hedonist within her, dead and buried since... since Jack.

'I bet he's hoping for another bite of the, uh... cherry,' said Adele.

'What do you mean?' said Brenda. Had it been that obvious?

'You two did *do it* the other night, didn't you?' Adele lowered her voice to a whisper. 'You wouldn't have gone to all that effort and not got yourself a shag.'

All what effort? Adele's blunt-instrument interrogation shouldn't have shocked Brenda, but it did. Happy to hear gossip about others, her personal life was held private. She felt colour swamp her cheeks and Adele grinned in triumph.

'Was he any good?' queried Adele, without waiting for further confirmation or denial.

'Yes,' said Brenda. 'Yes, he was. Good for me at any rate.'

'I knew it!' Adele blurted, but Brenda put a hand on her arm.

'Don't ruin it for me,' she whispered. 'I need this.'

'What?' Adele lowered her voice. 'You're seeing him again?'

'Maybe.'

'Good for you,' said Adele before the smile melted from her face. 'At least you wanted it, enjoyed it. At least you can remember.'

'What do you mean?' Where had that come from? Far away and quietly, a disturbance began in Brenda's gut; an old air-raid siren, a warning drone cranking upwards.

'I don't know,' said Adele. 'Well, I do. I think I do. I might.'

'I don't understand,' said Brenda. She wasn't sure she wanted to hear it, whatever it was.

'You know you were talking with James last night – about Lilly.'

'Yes.'

'You said you thought her drink was spiked.'

'I overreacted,' said Brenda, attempting to quell the unrest that threatened the day's pleasures. 'She had a headache, that's all. She's not used to drinking like that.'

'I think you hit the mark,' said Adele. 'And with the other thing you said – nearly said – too.'

'What other thing?'

Tray held aloft, Emilio crossed the restaurant and drew close to Brenda as if he could sense her disquiet. He set Adele's second beer and a basket of bread on the table.

'You ladies ok?' Softly, he addressed himself to Brenda and she felt his hand gently squeeze her shoulder.

'We're fine, thanks,' Brenda lied.

Emilio handed them his menus.

'I eat you nice today,' he said. 'Many fish from my cousin's boat this morning and fresh vegetables from farmers. Good tastings. Is food to make happy people.'

'Sounds lovely,' said Brenda.

She opened her menu, creating a temporary barrier between herself and Adele. She scanned the list of gastronomic temptations, anticipating the usual wave of hunger-driven desire to wash over her, but it did not come. Should she have stuffed vine leaves, or borek, or creamy dips to start? Would it be a mixed grill, aubergine piled with spicy ground beef and served with yoghurt, meat pastries curled like Cumberland sausages, or thyme-infused baked fish to follow? Chips or salad? Or both? Or rice? Her eyes found one dish after another, but her senses failed to respond. No rumble of desire in her stomach, no wash of saliva to her mouth.

Adele ordered a tomato and cucumber salad and Brenda chose the aubergine, no starter. She always felt bad things in her gut first and today was no exception. All desire for food deserted her as an invisible girdle of needles tightened around her midriff. She waited for the inevitable. Eventually Adele continued.

'You said Lilly's drink might have been spiked. You asked James why someone would spike a drink, though it's damn obvious.'

'I added two and two and made five,' said Brenda. 'I was wrong.' Why had she gone on about this? Would she never learn?

'I don't think you were.'

'You didn't see her, did you? You didn't talk to her?'

'I didn't need to. What you said made sense. You see, I think it happened to me too, the night before.'

'Really?' said Brenda. 'Are you sure?'

'That's the point,' said Adele. 'I'm not sure, I'm nowhere near sure. But it's possible, definitely possible.'

'What do you think happened?' said Brenda. Wanting to know, not wanting to know. It almost felt like the same thing.

'You'd probably say I drank too much, but I think my drink was spiked. Brenda, I know what drunk feels like and this was different. And—'

'And what?'

'I think I might have had sex. I can't remember it. But you know these things, don't you?'

'I don't know,' said Brenda. 'Who do you think you had sex with?' The words she knew she should use weren't yet ready to come out.

'I can't be certain,' said Adele. 'I was drinking here at the bar and the last thing I remember is one of the guys had his arm around my shoulder. And then—' the unsaid words fizzed in the air, like a faulty electrical connection, perilous to the touch. 'I've got grazes on my knees too. I've no idea where they came from.'

'You could have fallen over,' said Brenda, unconvincing, unconvinced. 'What do you remember that makes you think you had sex?'

'That's just it,' said Adele. 'I don't remember having sex. I *think* I did. But if I did, it could have been... anyone. Matt, maybe? It might have been James. He's a callous shit but I don't think that's his style. Turner? God help me, even one of the others. Or a stranger. I'm not sure and I can't prove anything and I can't exactly ask around, can I? That's too humiliating. But what you said about Lilly made me think and now I can't get it out of my head.' She took a slug of beer and continued, 'I know I had a lot to drink but I've done that a thousand times before. This was different. But there's no proof anything happened to me, or to her for that matter. And if it did what are the odds any bloke would own up to shagging a woman who's so pissed she can't even remember it.' Adele's face tightened. 'It happens on holiday all the time.' To the 18-30s, Brenda thought, not the grown-ups.

'But if you were drugged,' said Brenda, 'and someone had sex with you, that's an assault. No consent, no question of it.'

It's rape, she wanted to cry – *rape* is the word we use for this kind of thing.

'To be honest,' said Adele, picking away at a crusted stain on the tablecloth, 'it's as likely I went along with it; I can't remember. I should probably leave it.'

'Even if you were only drunk, that's still not consent. It still shouldn't have happened,' said Brenda. Stop it, leave it now. Let her believe what she wants to believe.

'Whatever, freaking out about it won't get me anywhere,' said Adele. 'So what about Lilly?'

'If anything happened to her, she doesn't realise,' said Brenda.

'She's better off that way,' said Adele.

'You think ignorance is bliss?' said Brenda. She's telling you what she wants. Pay attention. Listen. For once, listen.

Like you should have listened to Jack.

'Maybe,' sighed Adele. 'Sometimes.'

Brenda wanted to let it go – it wasn't her problem. Having brought the subject up, Adele seemed ready to gloss over what might have happened. And Lilly... What would the knowledge – no, not knowledge, suspicion – what would the mere suspicion that she had been drugged and... What would that do to her?

It should all end here.

Except that Brenda had seen something on arrivals day, as she'd picked her way between the lines of buses at the airport; something she hadn't shared with anyone. It looked innocent enough at first sight, a guest tipping the porter for handling his case perhaps. However it wasn't a coin or two, but a wad of notes passing between the two men, then a package, secreted in a flight-bag. The men shook hands and the porter slipped away. The buyer had seen Brenda, but seemed unfazed. He'd winked, smiled, his eyes full of mischief, and pressed a finger to his lips – and she'd reasoned whatever he needed to help him enjoy his holiday, it was none of her business. But this... this forced her to reconsider.

That same guest had been with the group at the bar on the night Adele couldn't remember, and he'd been with Lilly last night.

What would a devil's advocate say? A lonely, sexually available woman with a drink problem thought she might have had sex with someone, but couldn't remember. Regrettable, certainly, but this was hardly evidence of a crime. And a young woman had gone on a bender, had too much to drink and woken up feeling unwell. What was remarkable about that?

Brenda interrogated herself. What did she know? What *facts* did she have, to back up the slivers of circumstantial evidence and the prickling ache in her gut?

The answer: none at all.

2

ADELE WANTED TO shop before returning to the hotel. As she departed Brenda requested an apple tea. Emilio brought two to the table and slid into the seat opposite her. He took her hand in his and began stroking his thumb back and forth across her skin.

'You no smiling happy today,' he said.

'I'm fine,' she replied. Her sigh said otherwise.

'I make you happy, yes?' he said, head to one side. His knowing gaze drew her in.

'You did – you do – yes,' she replied.

'I sex your body again? You like? Tonight?' He squeezed her hand tightly, preventing her from pulling away though she had no intention. What she wanted to pull away from was the conversation with Adele. What she needed was precisely what Emilio offered.

'I like,' she said, managing a weak smile.

Her body wanted to weep; a release of tears to flood the sinkhole carved by emotional exhaustion; to soothe the ache that flared when she admitted to herself that she craved the fleeting pleasure of a night with a near stranger to escape.

In the cloakroom, Brenda slipped into a swimsuit and tied a sarong sparkling with sequins and silver thread about her midriff. Emilio arranged a lounger under a yellow parasol on the beach in front of his restaurant and brought out a beer for her.

'I come see my lady later,' he said. Guilty pleasure he might be, but she looked forward to the hours with Emilio in his tiny apartment over the restaurant; the bedroom with the shutters that let in shafts of moonlight; the bed that he made with freshly laundered sheets and the vase he filled with bunches of herbs from the restaurant and which cloaked the airless room in aromas of coriander, thyme and sage.

She lay steeped in solitude, basted in Hawaiian Tropic, embraced by the scorch of the afternoon shivering off the hot sand. The love-song of the beach drifted through her semi-conscious state; the laughter of children, the urgent commands of their parents, the wash-wash of waves meeting the sand, the clamour of clashing rhythms from the line of bars and restaurants, the murmur of a hundred conversations and the clink and clatter of plates and glasses.

'Adele thought I'd probably find you here,' said a voice beside her. Brenda prized open one eye to see a grinning James staring down. With his tousled blonde hair and day-old stubble, he looked like a castaway. 'I hope you don't mind some company.'

He looked about for an empty lounger. Without waiting for a response, he dragged it through the sand and positioned it beside her. He waved into the bar behind him. Emilio was already on the sand, notepad in hand. His face wore a fixed professional smile.

'Large beer please and another for my lovely friend here,' said James. Emilio was dismissed to fulfil the order. 'Our man's looking gruff today, what's up with him?' said James.

'I shouldn't worry,' said Brenda. Emilio would bear the intrusion as long as James kept spending. Whether she would, was another matter.

Sat astride the lounger, his toes digging trenches in the sand, James was a barely contained mess of fidgets, ticks, twitches, huffs and puffs. His whole body campaigned for him to be heard, practically begging Brenda for an invitation to speak; an invitation which did not materialise. Eventually his body surrendered and James fished a Kindle from his bag. He turned the cover back on itself and snapped the elastic binding. He read for little more than five minutes; then he went for a swim – several hundred yards across the bay and back; then he lay for a pitiably brief interlude with his headphones on. Finally he sat on the edge of his lounger and played a last, desperate 'please ask me what's wrong' card, exhaling a deep sigh – the sort of sigh to which none but the hardest heart could refuse a response.

'What's up honey?' obliged Brenda at last, holding back the sigh that her own lungs longed to liberate. She heaved herself on to one side and removed her sunglasses.

'Have you ever misread someone – I mean, misjudged someone – or something – so badly, that—' His voice trailed off. 'No, I don't expect you have, have you?'

'You're joking. When it comes to misreading – people, situations, pretty much anything in my personal life – I'm an expert. Take me away from work and it all goes to pot.'

'Really?' said James, brightening. 'You seem much too smart to get caught out misreading people.'

'Don't you believe it,' she said. 'Come on, tell me what happened. Then I bet I can raise you a bigger, more unholy shambles of a misjudgement.'

'It's Adele,' he said. 'I think I must've offended her. She's been down on me since the first night, but I've no idea why. She won't speak to me. I keep trying to talk to her – find out what I'm supposed to have done so I can apologise. But she ignores me or, worse, I get a sarky put-down in front of the others. It was a job to get her to tell me where you were this afternoon. Silly thing is she's the sort I usually get on with.'

'You really don't know what you've done?' said Brenda.

'I don't,' sighed James. 'Do you?'

'I sort of do, yes. But it's not for me to say – it's between you and her.'

'Crap. So there is something. I knew it. Was it on that first night? Or is it something else?'

'James, honey, if you haven't realised, I can't help you,' Brenda sighed. 'You need to find a moment with Adele and sort it out between you. Or you could always just stay out of her way.'

'I know I can be a bit thoughtless, engaging mouth before brain and all that,' said James, 'but if I've upset her I'd rather sort it out – clear the air.'

'It's worth another try then. Have a word with her. But take it gently.'

'I'm not a total emotional cripple,' smiled James. He prodded at his chest with his index finger. 'Somewhere in here lurks a soft-centre. If you think it's worth another try, I'll do it. But only because you say so.'

'It's always worth another try,' said Brenda. 'If you've got the opportunity, take it.'

This appeared to be enough hand-wringing for James for one afternoon. He flashed Brenda a winning smile, all whitened teeth and twinkling eyes, and turned the tables.

'So what unholy shambles of a misjudgement are you guilty of then?'

Had the lunchtime conversation not put her in such a dark mood, Brenda might have made light of his question and found something innocuous to say. As it was, and perhaps because she was ready to burst with the pain of it all – and James was a stranger, someone she would never see again after this week – she took a gulp of beer and a deep breath. In the distance a moped zizzed away, children chattered.

'I was a twin – one of a pair, a matching pair.'

'Christ, Bren. There are two of you?'

'Were. Me and my sister, Jacqueline.'

'What do you mean, *were*?'

'She's... gone' said Brenda.

'Were you close?'

'I thought so, once. Then she married a big shot; went to live in the Cotswolds, all the trimmings.'

'And you?'

'I married my job.'

'Ah, the dark stuff. So, what happened?'

'Jack and I had some... difficulty.'

'What kind of difficulty?'

Brenda gazed over the heads of a hundred sunbathers, far out to sea. On the curve of the horizon a tanker moved slowly, almost imperceptibly, from left to right. It was the sort of vessel that took a three mile circuit to turn around. It couldn't change course in a hurry even if it wanted to.

'Jack's husband was – is – a corporate lawyer. He's away a lot and when he's home, he's not actually *at home*. He has what you might politely call a *pied-a-terre*, a mews house in Pimlico. Somewhere to stay – or play – when he's working late at the office.'

'Oh Bren,' said James, 'is this going where I think it's going? You haven't been getting jiggy with your sister's husband, have you?'

'I know you don't know me,' said Brenda, her voice subdued. 'But no. I haven't, I didn't and I wouldn't have. Ever.'

'Sorry,' mumbled a chastened James.

'Graham is a sleaze, a liar and a cheat. He thrives on success and status, never mind the cost to others. There's nothing he wouldn't do, no one he wouldn't throw under the bus to get the deal. He's a bastard.'

'You don't like him then?'

Brenda's hand drifted to her bag, to the pocket which held the letter. All around them, children played in the sand.

'I was lunching with a couple of colleagues. We were in a decent restaurant for a change, at a swanky hotel in St James's. And Graham was there, having lunch with a woman.'

'That's not so unusual,' said James. 'Colleagues, clients and all.'

'When two people eat together, you can tell if they're workmates or if there's something... more... going on. Even you would notice. I knew as soon as I saw it, long before I watched them share a dessert – one plate, two spoons, feeding each other like infants; and before they left, arms snaking around each other's backs.'

'He didn't see you?'

'He didn't see me.'

'So he was having an affair. By the sound of it, that shouldn't have surprised you, since he's such a prick.'

'That's the trouble. It did. I'd always thought his sleazy side was all about work –rising up the greasy pole. I assumed he and Jack were solid, like she always said they were. I felt so stupid, angry too. Seeing them made me so mad.'

'What did you do?'

'I followed them.'

'Really? You stalked them?'

'What else could I do, James? I had to be sure, for Jack's sake.'

'I guess so,' murmured James, 'though it's not quite—'

'I followed them to Graham's little love-nest. Graham went in through his front door and she went in... next door. She lived next door to him. Five minutes later as I was debating what to do, she came out holding a baby – *a baby!* She waved the babysitter off then let herself into Graham's – she had a key. A key, James, and a baby!' Brenda realised that anger and indignation had elevated her voice to the point where several people around her had paused their own conversations to listen.

'His baby?'

'Yes, his baby,' she whispered. 'I don't think he'd have stood in the window kissing the top of its head otherwise, do you? He admitted it too.'

'Shit, Brenda. What did you do?'

'I took a train down to Jack's and I waited on her doorstep until she got back from her tennis lesson or her horse riding or whatever she was doing that afternoon. Then I sat her down and told her everything.'

'Just like that?'

'She had a right to know.'

'But—'

'I know. *I know.* I've asked myself a thousand times why I did it that way. I was on auto-pilot. All my... my... empathy, my caution, went out of the window. I was so obsessed with seeing Graham get his comeuppance, I didn't reason what the news might do to her. I just needed her to hear the truth about him.'

'What did that do for her?'

'It destroyed her. *I* destroyed her – that's what she said. Me, not him. She said I didn't think about her, *on my pedestal, up there on the moral high-ground* – those were her exact words. I reasoned if it were me, I'd want to know. If I'd stopped for a minute, brought a scrap of my professional sense to the table, I wouldn't have... I—'

Brenda's lips tightened as she fought back waves of sorrow. James put a hand out, but she waved it away.

'People need the truth, don't they? So they can face things, eyes open, everything on the table. What's the point of running away from reality?'

'People run away from reality all the time, Bren. People live their whole lives not facing up to truths they can't cope with.'

'Not me. But I didn't think. Jack's not like me – we're twins, but when it comes to certain things, we are – were – like the flipsides of a coin. I'm black, she's white; I'm steel, she's cotton wool... So then it was all raised voices, tears, flailing and hitting, a dinner service on the floor in pieces.'

'What you told her – it must have been quite a shock.'

'The irony is it wasn't. Between waves of hysteria she told me she knew he had affairs – guessed as much and then spotted clues time and again. But she'd chosen to look away and *not* to see it. She'd decided long ago to live with whatever he got up to, so long as he came home once in a while, paid the bills, maintained their *Horse and Hounds* lifestyle. I'd forced it into the open – and humiliated her, so she said.'

'What about the baby?'

'The baby took it into a whole new league. I didn't consider how much she'd always wanted a baby – everything she'd gone through to get pregnant and not managed it. She told me once how chasing her ovulation cycle had wrung every ounce of spontaneity out of their lovemaking; how he'd tired of the effort a year before – probably around the time his other baby arrived – and retreated to the spare room until she'd promised to stop pressuring him. If I'd only stopped to think, I'd have remembered all the conversations we had over the years when she'd told me she didn't feel either of us were *real women* whilst we remained childless. I never felt it like she did, but I should have realised what the baby would do to her. *I should have realised.*'

'So you told her and now she hates you?'

'Histrionics were the start. She accused me of trying to destroy her marriage so she'd end up sad and alone like me. She said if I thought I was an expert in human psychology, I should think again after what I'd done to her. And she told me whatever kind of expert I pretended to be, a career was a pitiful substitute for a baby and a real life and if I didn't realise that, I wasn't any kind of a woman. Then she said as far as she was concerned, she no longer had a sister. And she shoved me out of the front door and... and that was the last time I saw her.'

'Can't you make it up?'

'It's too late for that. A week later she committed suicide.'

'What?'

'She killed herself. She drank a bottle of single malt and downed enough pills to fell an elephant. Then she arranged herself on her bed, went to sleep and didn't wake up. It was two days before Graham came home and found her.'

'Christ,' said James.

'She did one more thing,' sighed Brenda. 'She called it a parting gift.'

Brenda dipped into her bag and pulled out the curly-edged envelope. She extracted the letter and handed it to James.

'It's her suicide note,' she said. 'Everything she said to me the day we argued, and more, lots more.'

James unfolded and read the letter, one hand clasped over his mouth.

'It isn't your fault,' he said at last. 'She chose to kill herself. She didn't have to go that far.'

'She says I drove her to it, made her feel barren and useless and humiliated. I left her no other option, apparently.'

'She's wrong, Bren. Everyone has options.'

'I hurt her so badly. It was all about me – how I would react, what I would want to know – not her. I didn't consider her feelings for a moment. I could have ignored what I saw. I could have challenged him, not her – forced him to, oh, I don't know what. I just know what I did was wrong – for Jack. And there's no excuse. I relive it every day – I can't help it. And I question my motives too – was Jack right about me being jealous of her?

Did I subconsciously want to destroy her? Every day, James, I bite down on these questions and I don't have any answers.'

'You torture yourself with this every day? For how long?'

'She died two years ago next month.'

'Brenda, you seriously need to get your head sorted.'

'You think?' Brenda moaned.

'You weren't jealous of her, were you?'

'I don't think so. I don't know any more.'

'But you still blame yourself for her suicide?'

'Yes.'

'But you didn't kill her, Bren. She did that by herself. She did it because she couldn't face things.'

'Yes, because I forced her to face them. What gave me the right? I ask myself all the time, why did I get involved? What business was it of mine? And what use am I to anyone when I get things so wrong?'

'You're punishing yourself.'

'Of course. But knowing it and being able to shift myself out of it are very different things.' Brenda gazed out across the sea. The tanker had moved what seemed like a few inches along the horizon. 'I came on holiday wanting to forget,' she continued, 'ready to put it all behind me and move forward – it's time, I know it is. But now I'm here, it's pressing in on me from all sides. We used to holiday together all the time, Jack and I. Graham always said he was too busy so Jack and I came away together two or three times a year. We went all over the place over the years, came here to Turkey a few times. There are memories every day, everywhere. Sights, smells, sounds… they're like stray bullets I can't dodge. They make me miss her so much and wish she was here again and things were back the way they used to be.'

'Sweetheart, you poor soul,' said James.

The pair sat in silence for several minutes, Brenda wiping occasionally at the corners of her eyes.

'So now you know,' Brenda said at last. 'I'm sorry – I didn't mean to heap it all on you.'

'Not a problem. I'm only sorry I don't have anything to offer you.'

'But you did. You listened. It's the first time I've told anyone.'

'A bit cathartic?'

'Maybe. Yes. So... thanks.'

'C'est rien,' murmured James. 'But I'm afraid I need a... nature calls. I have to get back to the ranch. Walk with me?'

'I'll stay a while.'

'You be okay?'

'I'll be fine. You go do what you have to do.'

3

IT'S TOO QUIET. The few guests around the pool are either reading or sleeping – there's no action. The only sound seeps in from the beachfront bars – remote, barely discernible. The air is like wadding soaked in sun oil and a waft of sweaty armpit hits him from somewhere. The sun touches the hills behind the hotel. Soon the mosque will crank up, loudspeaker spitting and crackling and that weird wailing prayer. Like Pavlov's dogs, the chanting makes him thirst for a cocktail.

Then the evening will come and the game will continue. He'd set himself a target for the week – three scalps, he thought would make a good challenge. At this point he isn't sure whether he'll count the tart towards his score. It depends on how the rest of the week goes.

He holds his Kindle high, fending off the sun. They think he's reading but he's not. Eyes hidden behind shades, he's scrutinising the poolside, a one-man undercover surveillance team. He takes in every motion, evaluating its significance in regard to himself, before committing it to memory or discarding it.

The Turk sweeps a long brush across the surface of the pool, mopping up stray leaves and bugs. Insignificant. Two guys slumped over a card game, supping beers and gabbling like simpletons. Insignificant and faintly repugnant. Two women – he hasn't bothered to learn their names – splayed out, glistening with lotion. Both display patches of raw blistering on their backs. Having branded themselves as *cougars* on the first night then gone after some luckless young waiters on the second, he's long since written these two off. Insignificant.

He notices mousy Veronica tip-toeing down the steps from the upstairs bedrooms. So self-contained, she moves discretely across the courtyard wearing her usual curious ensemble; a plain swimming costume with conical cups and some kind of housecoat. The cord is pulled tight around her midriff but the flimsy fabric billows as she walks, affording him glimpses of her egg-white thighs. Every day her routine is the same; she goes into the shade around midday and orders a tuna salad from the kitchen; she consumes the meagre plate then disappears to her room for a couple of hours. Like a grizzly bear on heat, he's alert anticipating her return and she's right on schedule.

She selects an empty lounger and arranges her book, sunglasses and lotion on the flagstones under its shade. The way she twists and pulls at the knotted cord on her robe fascinates him. So many of the women perform some kind of a strip-tease by the pool, unwrapping their gaudy sarongs and sweeping them slowly away from their bodies. This one always looks so shy. She has the demeanour of a woman who undresses in the dark. Her husband probably never saw her naked.

He watches as the robe slips from her shoulders; not scorched red or spray-tan orange like the other women, but pale, translucent like a marble statue. There's no posing, no arranging of arms and legs for optimum advantage. She sits, swings her legs on to her towel and lays back, arms rigid by her side.

She's older than the other women on the holiday, but so modest and restrained. Her lack of worldliness makes her the perfect choice. The thought flickers like a candle flame and his slumbering cock twitches in response.

4

HENRY SAT ALONE at the tables under the pergola, watching out for Veronica. Same time as always; she was a creature of habit. In so many ways she reminded him of his wife; mousy, predictable, meek. He recalled the weird elation he'd felt when he learned from the doctor that Sadie was dying. But Veronica was right; now she'd been gone a few months, he'd begun to appreciate and even miss their dull togetherness. Once the chapel ladies' lunches had all gone he'd been forced to admit he missed Sadie's cooking. They'd never talked much in the evening but they watched telly together, year in, year out, trays on laps. It was companionable in a way he hadn't realised until he sat alone in his armchair, staring at the sunken impression her diminutive behind had left in the other chair.

This holiday was supposed to be fun, but instead he'd been marginalised, ignored by most and beset by unwelcome memories of his wife. Worse still, he'd been humiliated by Brenda's response to his... studies... of her. She'd laid waste to his fantasies, extinguished his pleasure. It was almost impossible now to visualise himself pressed against her breasts when his ears jangled with her put-downs. He recalled with misery the day many decades ago, when his biology teacher had caught him fiddling with himself in the girls' cloakroom at break-time. She made him copy out the chapter in his biology text book that covered ovum and sperm and embryos. By the time he finished with all those flaccid educational words and traced the sterile diagrams, it all but robbed him of the illicit pleasure of his daily ritual. This time as he relived the humiliation though, it wasn't his teacher's face he saw but Brenda's, taut and angry, and her voice, drenched with disgust.

No, the only person showing him the slightest kindness was Veronica and even she'd had a go, furtively slipping a deodorant stick of all things into his camera bag when he wasn't looking. Henry flapped the neck of his t-shirt and sniffed his underarm. Perhaps she had a point. And like Sadie used to, at least she made him feel as if someone cared about him.

He nodded in Veronica's direction and she smiled back; the ingenuous, ordinary smile of a kind and understanding woman.

He gathered his belongings from the table and stood, before noticing the other man, armed with two glasses of orange juice, crossing the scorched flagstones to where Veronica now reclined. His face metamorphosed into a ferocious glare in Henry's direction – one it was impossible to misinterpret.

Henry sat back down.

5

RELIEVED TO BE alone again, Brenda dissolved into the anonymity of the crowded beach. Behind sunglasses she alternately read, dozed and scanned the hazy melange of languor and liveliness that surrounded her. A quartet of perfect beach bodies engaged in an informal game of volleyball; two buff Italian men competing to impress a pair of pin-thin blondes. A trio of children without a common language between them constructed a sandcastle then engaged in a futile attempt to fill its moat by running back and forth to the water's edge, giggling and laughing, toy buckets slopping away their meagre contents. Her senses flooded with the cocktail of aromas – the sea air's crusty saltiness, the bio-metallic bite rising from a tide-line of seaweed and the smoky trails of Gauloises and Havanas drifting the beach. All around, bodies were entwined in one another, kissing responsive lips and caressing warm skin. The flesh of all the world was on parade – old men, their bulbous bellies shiny with sun oil; middle-aged women, cellulite puckering their thighs and stretch marks shining spidery white against tanned skin; young bodies, every movement calculated to show off taut physiques; and the children, children everywhere she looked, sand-blasted and sticky with the residue of a day's play and runaway ice cream.

As the sun lowered, family groups became the first to pack up and exit the sand, infants screeching for tea-time. It grazed the trees around 5pm, a circle of amber casting a lengthening shadow across the bay. All around, the muezzins fired up for the call to prayer, each one picking up the note a fraction behind the last, like a chain of beacons lighting a coastal celebration. The sound rebounded off the buildings and hills and clashed with the battalion of disco rhythms pouring out along the boardwalk.

Now finally she beckoned Emilio to bring refreshment. He perched on the end of her lounger as she drank, stroking the tops of her feet. Having cemented their arrangement for the evening, Brenda crammed her morning's purchases and beach clutter into her bag and made her way back to the hotel.

Later, showered, made-up and glowing in aquamarine and pink, a restored Brenda was ready for her evening. It began with Adele and a fresh bottle of Southern Comfort. Then came dinner and the consolation of food. It was barbecue night; Brenda loaded her plate with chicken thighs and lamb cutlets, bulgur wheat salad and layers of cucumber and tomato. Dessert was three scrumptious slices of halva – chocolate, pistachio and vanilla. And there was wine, plenty of wine.

After dinner Brenda tempted a dozen guests to Emilio's. The bar was a swarm of bodies but Emilio seated them at a reserved table. They each pitched a few notes for a kitty into a glass and ordered cocktails. Adele threw her head back and demolished her first in three gulps.

'Steady on, girl,' said James. 'We don't want to have to carry you home.'

'Fuck off, James,' said Adele. He winced.

'I didn't mean anything by it,' he muttered.

'What I drink is down to me,' said Adele. 'You'd be drinking too if—'

'If what?'

'Nothing,' said Adele.

Adele had started early, kept up the pace through dinner and seemed in no mood to decelerate. We're all grown-ups, Brenda reminded herself. Leave her alone.

Adele hauled herself to her feet and waved for another drink.

'Anyone want to dance?' she said, hips gyrating inside her spray-on micro-skirt. One brave soul stood to take up the challenge. Adele paid him scant attention, favouring instead a dark-haired, youthful local. The young man quickly embraced the mood of Adele's moment, clutching her waist and grinding against her. Trance-like, Adele swivelled and swayed and the Turk matched her rhythm. His tongue found her neck and her earlobes, then he began flicking it rapidly against her mouth, all the while soliciting earthy encouragement from his leering companions. It was only when he began grabbing at her breasts that Adele recoiled. She blew him a kiss, retreated to the table and slumped into her chair.

'Letch,' she spat. She grasped her empty glass and waved it at the bar. 'They're all the same.'

'Who are?' asked James. Always asking for trouble.

'Men,' said Adele, staring directly at him. 'Fucking men.' The venom in her response seemed to shove James back in his seat.

'We're not all bad,' he said. 'Come on, doll, loosen up. We're trying to have a nice night out here.'

'Show me one decent man in the whole world,' Adele slurred. 'Show me one man who's loyal, honest and thoughtful and not just after an anonymous fuck in the dark.'

'I wouldn't say all men were like that,' said Lilly. 'I think you're looking on the bleak side of things. I know a good man, decent.'

'God help you, you poor thing, said Adele. 'You don't know anything and you certainly don't know men. If you only knew—'

Brenda couldn't let it happen, not like this.

'There's a time and a place and this isn't it,' she interrupted. 'Come on, honey, lighten up.'

The music pounded, alternating club classics and contemporary Turkish beats. On the makeshift dance floor bodies sweated, pouted and posed. The young Turk, his attention focused on Adele, approached the table in a grinding parody of a dance move, lust blazing in narrowed eyes. Oozing the reek of daylong sweat, he beckoned to Adele with a crooked finger, then opened his mouth and flicked his tongue rapidly up and down, a lewd and unmistakeable gesture.

'Fuck it,' said Adele. 'If you can't beat them, join them.' With a shrug of her shoulders she levered herself to her feet again. 'Don't wait up,' she entreated, swaying unsteadily. The Turk took her hand and she vanished into the crowd.

'I don't understand Adele,' said Lilly. 'She's got so much going for her, but she always seems so... angry.'

'Sometimes life does that,' said Brenda.

With Adele gone the mood lightened. The party at the table turned into a celebration of holidays past and friends for life made and forgotten. Everyone who'd been on *one of these* singles holidays before had a story to tell, about a love affair that meant everything and then nothing or a bonkers guest whom the tour reps had to manage into submission. Chloe told of a creepy guy on her first holiday who didn't say a word to anyone in the seven days they shared, but materialised like a ghost in all her holiday snapshots. James remembered two women who pretended to be lesbians to scare off some unwanted male attention – not him, he swore it – who ended up more enriched than either expected by the experience. Another woman cringed as she recalled being pursued by a man twenty years her senior. He'd growled like a dog as they had sex and she'd woken up the next morning to find his teeth in a glass by the bed. They all laughed about how you take volumes of pictures of people who become your best buddies for a week, but when you get home you can't remember their names. Lilly's innocent young eyes grew wider with every tale and bonhomie abounded as the drinks flowed. And all the while, Brenda kept her counsel.

A full moon had risen in an arc over the bay throwing an eerie light across the beach, where loungers were stacked in dark towers, parasols furled and bound like sentries guarding the sand. The bars and restaurants emptied, lights were extinguished, music silenced and shutters lowered. Only Emilio's remained open, with a dozen drinkers around a single table, trying to outdo one another with ever taller tales.

Emilio was impatient to close up. He lowered the music, collected empty glasses and stacked chairs, urging the stragglers to depart but without being rude; perfectly judged. He must have done it a thousand times.

'I'll see you tomorrow,' whispered Brenda to James as the group rose to leave.

'You not coming with us then?' he smiled.

'Don't make a thing of it,' Brenda whispered. With a deceptive, 'I'll catch you up,' to the group, she repaired to the cloakroom, where she contrived to remain until the others were absorbed into the darkness of the gravel path.

When she emerged the dirty glasses had vanished, the shutters were down. A single candle flickered on the polished bar, haloing Emilio's expectant face.

6

THERE'S A PREDICTABLE quality to the evening hours. He understands the dynamic and how he needs it to play out. After the food when everyone sits clutching coffee cups and debating what to do with the rest of the evening, one or two people propose going to a bar or grabbing a ride into Marmaris. Lemmings gravitate around leaders. This evening instead of being a leader he hangs back, noticing who joins in and who doesn't before making his decision. Parties disperse leaving a half-dozen stragglers behind; people too introverted – or independent – to join the crowd. Some slope off to bed; others order drinks and sit around.

He bides his time at the tables from which the remains of dinner have been cleared. The lights under the pergola are dimmed and he enjoys being cloaked in shadow. He watches Veronica, alone at a table by the bar reading a book. Her skirt teases her ankles. Around her neck hangs one of those glass *evil eye* beads on a cord, a local trinket. It's supposed to offer some kind of protection against evil, if you believe that sort of thing. It won't do much for her tonight. On the table beside her is an empty coffee cup, no glass. She's not drinking. He'll fix that.

He goes to the bar. The Turk has his back to him, fixing a fresh bottle of vodka into the wall-mounted optics. When he turns there's a moment when unease – or is it fear – shines in the Turk's eyes before his hospitality face switches back on.

'What you have?' he says, voice tight, guarded. It's good to be feared, but sometimes, like now, it's inconvenient.

'A large vodka and tonic and a pina colada please,' he says, placing a smile on his face. The *please* is a nice touch but it won't be enough. The Turk busies himself mixing the drinks. It gives him time to check his wallet. He draws out a wrap of paper along with four 50TL notes. The Turk places the two drinks on the bar; one crisp and clear – the business end of alcohol – three cubes of ice and a slice of lime; the other a creamy yellow concoction adorned with pineapple and a cherry on a stick. A pink straw penetrates the gelatinous mixture. It's an absurd drink.

'I think I should have sorted out my tab before now, got up-to-date with you,' he says, deliberately softening his usual tone. 'I'm sorry about the other day. I didn't have any cash on me and I was embarrassed. We shouldn't have spoken to you as we did. I apologise.' He hands the 200TL to the Turk, whose face melts in gratitude.

'Is ok, is ok, thank you,' blabbers the Turk, pathetic with relief. All they care about is money and he thought he wasn't going to collect.

The Turk turns to the till, giving him the moment he needs to drop the contents of the wrap into the pina colada. It's a practiced move, nobody ever spots it.

The Turk returns with 30TL and change and holds it out.

'You keep it,' he says. That should keep him happy; stop him making a nuisance of himself later on.

He makes his way to the table where Veronica sits absorbed in her paperback.

'I hope you don't mind,' he says, 'but no woman should sit alone on a night like this.' She looks up and he holds out the drink. 'It's a pina colada. I wasn't sure what you liked.' He's seen her ordering this ridiculous cocktail more than once.

The woman smiles cautiously. At first it seems she doesn't appreciate the interruption, but the drink means she can't refuse. It would be rude and she's too well-mannered.

'That's kind of you,' she says, setting aside her book.

She doesn't invite him but he pulls up a chair. He picks up her book – it's not one he recognises. On the front is a picture of a man and woman in period costume, clutching at one another.

'Is this any good?' he asks.

'Yes,' she says. 'But only if you like love stories. It's beautifully written – so tender and expressive.'

'Not quite my thing,' he says, smiling.

7

HENRY HAD NO desire to spend more money drinking alone by the pool. The wave of bitterness that washed over him in that tranquil surrounding late in the evening was too painful; like being marooned on a paradise island with no hope of rescue. As the more gregarious guests moved on he slipped away to his room. Now he sat with the light off on his balcony overlooking the courtyard, thinking of the windswept coastal paths of north Norfolk where he walked in near silence with Sadie, year in, year out, until she went.

He noticed Veronica by the bar, reading a book. Shit. He hadn't realised she'd stayed behind. He thought she'd gone to the bar with Brenda. If he'd realised, he'd have sat with her — kept her company for an hour for the price of a Coke. Now he couldn't. If he went back down he'd look stupid, or desperate.

Two other guests sat together by the pool, the spotty backgammon player and the woman who never stopped knitting. Another man emerged from the darkened dining area and wandered over to the bar. He watched Mehmet place two drinks in front of him. Why two drinks?

Then he spotted that move again — the same one he'd noticed at the yellow bar the other night, when he was sure he'd seen the tart being dragged off by... the same man. He'd never seen a drink being spiked before this week, but he was pretty sure that's what it would look like. Whatever it was, it went into one of the drinks but not the other, just like the other night.

When he saw the man approaching Veronica, it was as if an army of scorpions had skittered up Henry's spine. He sat rooted to his seat as the man pressed the tall glass — the spiked one — on Veronica, then sat at her table. His skin prickled, a cloud of white spots invaded his eyes. Why her? Why?

Veronica took a first sip of the spiked drink and Henry saw her nervy anxiety melt into a modest smile. She nodded then laughed. The man put his hand on hers and she didn't pull away.

He was reeling her in, sip by poisonous sip.

Henry felt as if he'd been drugged himself; he was paralysed from the feet upwards. He could watch – he couldn't turn away – but he couldn't move to help, couldn't cry out; he couldn't alert his kind, sweet friend to the danger she was in. What devil had anointed him with such a yellow underbelly? From the start he'd understood this man's superior status and nothing he'd seen since had betrayed any weakness. Henry saw no hesitancy in his actions only assured confidence, total control.

Henry's foot twitched; an involuntary spasm. His foot, of all things, wanted to leap to her defence where his head and heart were failing him.

She took a second sip.

He's softening her up, watching her drink, waiting for the moment when she starts to fade. Then what? Poor woman can't even say the word *sex* without being embarrassed. What could he want with her? Would he... take her to his room and... fuck her?

She lifted the glass to her lips for a third time.

This is crazy, Henry thought as he pulled the door of his room shut and hurried along the landing to the steps. He descended the darkened staircase gripping the handrail, sliding his palm down the coarse wood. It lodged a splinter deep into his flesh and he hardly felt it.

What was he thinking? He didn't even know what he would do – what he could do – when he got downstairs. He knew he had to do something; he had to intervene. He couldn't let poor Veronica's honour remain undefended. But the thought of standing up to this monster made acid erupt from his stomach. It grazed his throat.

As he approached the table Veronica looked up and smiled. Plain and genuine – she was actually pleased to see him. The man looked up too but there was no sign of a smile on his frozen visage. His eyes narrowed and the furrows around his mouth deepened. Tracklines of anger carved his forehead between the eyes. Bizarrely, Henry found himself picturing Veronica as Little Red Riding Hood, venturing innocently into the cottage where the wolf lay ready to devour her. But it helped, somehow, to see this thing he was doing as not quite real. What didn't help was the sound of his own heartbeat thundering in his ears, and the sense that his voice had utterly deserted him along with all the strength in his legs.

He stumbled as he drew close to the table – it was the only thing he could think of doing. It made him look like an idiot but he didn't care. As he reached out to steady himself he contrived to catch his hand and rock the table so hard that Veronica's tall glass wobbled. It wobbled, but it didn't fall. It took another flustered grab before he could make it tumble. When it did, half the contents ended up on his trousers. Creamy and sticky, like gallons of cum, it dribbled down his thigh, soaking through the flimsy cloth. The rest cascaded to the flagstones and splattered, showering shards of broken glass in a wide circle.

Everyone looked up. The monster leapt to his feet, his features contorted, snarling like a tethered bull mastiff. His fists were clenched, knuckles taut and white and for a moment Henry thought he'd get his face smashed in. But then it was Veronica who came to his rescue. Male fury, like a raging storm at sea, lost all its power when it came up against her soft voice and gentle manner. Lovely Veronica; all she wanted to do was help, and there was nothing anyone could have done to distract her. She found a cloth, moistened it in the swimming pool, then helped Henry wipe down his trousers – he'd have enjoyed it a lot more if he hadn't been so terrified. Mehmet mopped up the mess on the flagstones, scouring a wide circle for splinters of glass. Muttering all the while, he seemed oblivious to Henry's insistent apologies. That was uncomfortable but it couldn't be helped.

Veronica insisted Henry change his trousers and give her the soiled pair to wash, there and then. She wouldn't take no for an answer. She had travel wash – of course she did – and she said it wouldn't wait until the morning as the stain would be dried-in by then.

He hadn't thought this whole rescue thing through, but it couldn't have worked out better.

Henry wanted to cast one of those 'I know what you were up to, you evil bastard' looks as he retreated to the safety of the bedroom block with Veronica, but he'd used up his sliver of courage by then. So he averted his eyes, kept them lowered like he was the weaker, more submissive creature. But inside he felt like a Titan.

He stood in the middle of Veronica's bedroom, his bare legs poking out like matchsticks from his faded y-fronts. As she rinsed his trousers in the basin he saw pity in her eyes, but it didn't matter. He might have looked like Norman Wisdom but he felt like Superman. He'd flown to the aid of someone he cared about, and he'd saved them.

He was King of the World.

THURSDAY

1

THE GULET ON which Brenda and eleven other guests were to spend the last two days of their holiday occupied a berth at the far end of the harbour, beyond the boardwalk. A majestic twin-masted schooner, varnished to a glossy sheen, its hull flittered as the sun's rays rebounded off the lapping water. Tethered to cleats embedded in the walkway, a narrow gangway rattled and bobbed precariously above the concrete. It rose at a steep angle into the rear of the vessel. Beneath it, etched in black and gold script across the polished framework, was the name *Annelise II*.

A man appeared at the top of the gangway. He was perhaps mid-forties but looked older in a sun-bleached, weather-beaten way. A mop of curly salt-and-pepper hair was jammed under a jaunty captain's cap. He wore a navy and white striped polo shirt and his once-white shorts revealed sinewy calves. Shoeless, he bounded down to the gangway's end, sure-footed as a mountain goat.

'Welcome, welcome,' he boomed. 'I am Kaptan Barbar. Is meaning *barbarian* in English. So, I am barbarian sea captain and you are my happy holiday singles. You got your sea-legs ready?'

'We are, and we have,' said James, beaming.

'I thought Barbar was an elephant,' muttered Turner.

'I had a Barbar the Elephant colouring book when I was a girl,' Lilly announced.

'You climb aboard,' Kaptan Barbar said to the group. He turned to Brenda. A bag three times the size of everyone else's carved a channel deep into one shoulder. He held out his hand to her. 'I help.'

Brenda heaved the super-sized bag off her shoulder and held it out for Kaptan Barbar, who took the strain with a theatrical gesture which involved pretending almost to drop the load into the water below. He grasped Brenda's hand and once she had levered one foot up on to the gangway, he pulled her forward, gently and graciously, offering just enough assistance so she could lift her second foot on to the wobbling structure without embarrassment. With one hand in his and the other on the rope which took the place of a handrail but offered unreliable support, Brenda wobbled the five steps it took to arrive inside the boat. She thudded on to the aft deck and swept a hand across her forehead, collecting the beads of perspiration which sprang from her pores.

'That was... fun,' she said to Kaptan Barbar. 'Thank you.'

At the foot of the gangway, Veronica's legs quivered as she grabbed for the rope. Matt offered her his hand but Kaptan Barbar leapt to her aid, guiding her up the gangway. All six men in the party and the other eight women managed the precarious access on to the aft deck unaided. They stood in front of a large wicker basket which contained two pairs of deck shoes and a pair of flip-flops.

To Brenda's relief the aft deck was shaded by an electric blue canvas awning. To either side of where the gangway entered the gulet, a platform area laid with mattresses upholstered in the same canvas formed a comfortable looking area which wrapped around the vessel's rear end. Completing the symphony in blue, matching bolsters were roped along the railings. Dominating the aft deck was an enormous varnished wooden table positioned across the width of the boat. The lip around its rim would ensure the safety of glasses and plates if the weather turned rough. Stacks of plastic chairs were roped to the railings alongside the table. In the centre of the deck a mast rose like a tree-trunk through the overhead canvas and up into the sunlight.

Kaptan Barbar cleared his throat.

'I welcome you to my magnificent gulet for two days – I give you a special time on your mini-cruise. I promise lots of laughter, plenty to drink and good food. We go to quiet bays where the day-boats don't go and you can swim off the side. On-board is plenty of snorkel equipment, a canoe to play with and a deck for sunbathing. But there is one rule, no shoes on-board. So you take off your shoes and put them in the basket. When you go tomorrow back to your hotel, I give you shoes – maybe your own, maybe someone else's. Ha!' He laughed heartily at the joke he probably delivered two or three times a week. Brenda and the others removed their footwear. Brenda waited until all the other pairs were in the basket before placing her jewel-embellished sandals on top of the pile and Kaptan Barbar stowed the basket underneath the rear platform. Brenda felt the sensual caress of warm smooth-sanded wood against the soles of her feet.

'Now I show you around. You come with me.'

The party followed Kaptan Barbar down the steps into the body of the boat. To the left was the steering wheel and control console, where a radio crackled. Kaptan Barbar grabbed the mouthpiece and rattled off a response then shouted something unintelligible at one of the crew on the foredeck, whose legs alone were visible through the forward-facing windows. The legs leapt from the foredeck and there followed a clattering on the rear gangway.

'Always there is something they forget,' said Kaptan Barbar. 'Now, here is our salon.'

The salon of *Annelise II* was the full width of the boat and almost square. The area was panelled in honey-golden teak, its nutty aroma seeping through the tang of fresh varnish. Underfoot a multi-coloured carpet in traditional Eastern style covered the floor. Narrow windows at eye level along either side were framed by velvet drapes tied back with gold cord. Below the windows were banquettes upholstered in shades of blood-red, amber and navy, home to a chaos of cushions in a carnival of colours. Their exotic excess lent the salon the aura of a Bedouin prince's tent.

A pungent aroma seeped across the salon and Brenda glanced around. A couple of steps down behind her a man occupied the tiniest of galleys – more cupboard than kitchen. Wrapped in a grimy apron, he was massaging a spicy marinade into a tray of chicken, squidging and squishing the raw fillets between his chubby fingers. To Brenda the sights, sounds and odours of the kitchen were all to be appreciated equally. But Turner held a lion-paw hand to his mouth and nose.

'I can't cope with this,' he mumbled.

'My gulet only just come back from expensive refit,' continued Kaptan Barbar, oblivious. 'It took a long time and so I miss the chance to do the big cruises with the travel companies this season. Normally my gulet won't be hired for one or two days, but for one or two weeks, and expensive. So you are lucky! But please, I beg you, be kind to my gulet. Treat like you would your own home with greatest respect and I will be happy man.'

Kaptan Barbar led the guests down more steps into the bowels of the gulet and a wood-panelled corridor lit by pulsating night-lights. Doors to the left and right gave access to a dozen cabins, some singles, most designed to accommodate two people. Each guest was urged to throw their bags through the door of one of these cabins. Brenda claimed a cabin to herself as Kaptan Barbar explained how the toilets worked and when they were free to use the showers. He said that despite the good quality of his cabins, guests often preferred to sleep in the open. The crew, he said, would erect a cover above the foredeck, making it comfortable for sleeping out. Not for me, thank you, thought Brenda.

Kaptan Barbar led them back outside and along a side aisle to the foredeck, where he urged them to clamber on to an area directly in front of the windows into the salon. Blue canvas mattresses were arranged in lines across the deck, tied down at the top and bottom with ropes secured to grab-rails at each side. Above them, a second mast soared into the sky. Rigging clanked rhythmically against the wood, as if protesting the absence of a sail. In front of the ranks of mattresses ropes lay coiled, everything arranged, strapped, tied and in good order. With everyone's attention recaptured, Kaptan Barbar made another plea for good care of his gulet, pointing out the new canvas mattresses for special attention and commanding all guests to cover them with beach towels to avoid staining from sun oil.

The gulet did indeed look like new. Wooden surfaces gleamed, polished metal bounced the sunlight around; the ubiquitous electric blue canvas bore not a single stain or spillage; no accidental nicks and cuts scarred the pristine fabric. It was a good deal more habitable than some she had seen before, albeit not spacious below deck. But for two days and one night it was an idyllic base from which to revel in the simple pleasures of the sea and the raw beauty of the crumpled Aegean coastline.

Released from Kaptan Barbar's tour, Brenda went to her cabin to organise her toiletries and change into a swimsuit. A lurch and a rumble signalled the cranking up of the gulet's engine and the odour of diesel flooded the tiny cabin. Brenda heard the steady clank-clank of the anchor being hoisted.

There was a frantic knock at the door. Before she could respond, it opened. Adele levered herself into the cabin, her face contorted into a scowl. She pushed the door shut behind her, squeezed past Brenda and flopped on to her berth, landing on her half-empty bag. Adele's head slumped forward and she clasped her hands to her cheeks as if to stop it from falling off altogether.

'Shit, shit shit,' was all she could manage.

'What's up?' said Brenda. They'd only been on the gulet for ten minutes. What could possibly have happened? Had James put his foot in it again?

'This is going to be a bit bloody awkward.'

'What is?' Come on, honey, out with it.'

'You know last night?'

'Yes. What about last night?'

'That guy. The one I went off with.'

'From the bar?'

'There was only one. Yes, the one from the bar.'

'And?'

'He's here, on the boat!'

'Oh. What do you mean, *here on the boat?*' asked Brenda.

'He's crew. He's the bloody crew,' said Adele, although it came out more like a wail. 'He was the one who jumped off earlier to fetch whatever they'd forgotten, so I didn't realise until now. We're stuck with him – *I'm* stuck with him – for the next two days.'

'And that's a problem because?'

'It's a problem because we messed around a bit last night and it wasn't up to much and... and... I was a bit the worse for wear, okay, I admit it. And I'd rather not see him again, that's why. It's a problem because I don't need to be imprisoned on a boat with him for two days. He isn't even a grown-up; he's a boy, a bum-fluffed deck-hand. It's going to be too embarrassing when the others realise *that's* what I went off with.'

'Honey,' said Brenda. 'I hate to break it to you but they know already. Most of them were at the bar last night.'

Adele moaned and covered her face with her hands again.

'Why do I do it, why?'

'It'll be fine,' Brenda said, her voice softening. 'Kaptan Barbar is his boss, isn't he? He's working, he'll have to behave. What's the worst that can happen? If he makes a nuisance of himself, we can fight him off between us. Cheer up, don't let it spoil the trip.'

Adele sat up and stared into her lap. 'But—' she started.

'No buts,' said Brenda. 'It's not the end of the world. You can handle it.' And I've had about enough self-pity for one holiday, she thought.

'I'm an idiot,' sighed Adele, pulling at one side of her thumbnail with her teeth. Brenda couldn't but agree, so she said nothing. Instead she continued moving what toiletries she could reach between the micro-bathroom and the even more minuscule cupboard.

'What should I do, Brenda?'

'Nothing, honey.' This was becoming tiresome. 'Ignore him and he won't bother you. He won't want trouble. Now, I need to get changed. Do me favour and save me a mattress. I'll be up in a mo.' Adele stared blankly. 'Okay?' Brenda added, impatient for Adele to move. She tugged at the bag trapped under Adele's thigh and it did the trick; Adele stood at last. A hand firmly against Adele's back, Brenda ushered, or perhaps pushed her out of her cabin and returned to the job of readying herself for a day on deck.

2

THE GRINDING CLANK-CLANK-CLANK stopped and Henry heard the engine throttle up. The gulet pulled away from the harbour. On the foredeck he knelt on a mattress, staring out to sea. He hadn't expected to be spending two days on the water but as his lungs filled with the sea air's warm saltiness his heart shuddered with the thrill of it. As the breeze teased shreds of hair away from his scalp he pulled his grubby sunhat hard down to anchor what little remained.

It was an expensive trip and he hadn't budgeted for it. But Veronica had announced she was going as she washed his trousers the night before, suggesting he might enjoy it. Maybe the evening's events had boosted his sense of protectiveness over Veronica; maybe he wanted to spend time with her rather than alone. But he'd gone down to breakfast before everyone else that morning and persuaded Mehmet to call Hakima and book him on the trip. When he realised who was also on the boat, he wasn't sure whether to be relieved he'd be there to protect Veronica, or petrified. Whatever else, he'd keep his eyes open.

'Don't forget what the captain said,' whispered a voice beside him. Veronica held out his towel. Hers was already arranged across her mattress, tucked neatly beneath the ropes at each end. Henry pushed his towel under the ropes. It wasn't large enough to stretch from end-to-end but he did his best with it, smoothing it down like Veronica's. The other mattresses filled up and the deck became a carpet of beach towels with guests fussing around, oiling each other's backs and arranging iPods and books. As the gulet left the harbour the sun climbed higher in a cloudless sky.

Brenda wore a black swimsuit – it squeezed her breasts deliciously. She obviously hated Henry and he hated how she'd belittled him, forcing him to delete his photographs of her; but he was hypnotised by her smothering womanliness. He wanted – no, needed – more pictures of Brenda, to take home; a real woman's pictures to flesh out his fantasies – better any day than the surgically-enhanced ones in his magazines.

He fished out his compact camera. He'd had to leave his proper one behind at the hotel, locked in the room safe. You weren't supposed to bring anything bulky or valuable on the boat. He fiddled with the settings then clicked off a few shots – close-ups mainly; the mast and the rigging, ropes and fittings around the bow, clever angles capturing reflections and shafts of sunlight. He liked how they turned out, enjoyed recalling everything he once learned about light and shadow, focal points and framing on a basic camera. Every now and again he managed a shot in Brenda's direction – a sneak-peak of cleavage, the curl of her golden-brown hair against her skin, beads of sweat glistening on her bosom. But he was super-cautious, fearful of incurring her disapproval again. A second time and she'd show him up in front of everyone, for sure. He couldn't take his time over these ones. But they felt illicit, naughty, and that thought rewarded him with the shudder of a thrill, each one he got away with.

He continued filling his camera with all things maritime – coiled ropes, varnished railings, reflections in the windows, shafts of sunlight bouncing off polished brass. He knelt right at the front of the boat and hung over the edge to capture the bow cutting through the waves, spraying curtains of fine droplets to each side and giving life to a million miniature rainbows.

'Would you take a shot or two of me?' said a woman's voice behind him. He turned to find the slender near-naked body of Adele in his view-finder, so close he could see the downy hairs beneath her tummy button. Unnerved by her proximity, he let go of the camera. Fortunately he'd tethered it to his wrist with a strap.

'What? Uh—' uttered Henry, his cheeks burning. Idiot. Fool, pull yourself together, man.

'Veronica tells me you're good at this photography business,' she continued.

'I... uh... I guess so,' babbled Henry, furious with himself.

'Only, when you come on a holiday alone, you don't get any photographs of yourself – and it would be nice to have one or two,' said Adele. Softly-spoken, this wasn't the potty-mouthed trollop he'd got used to over the last few days. 'If I gave you my email address, you could send them to me?' It was a question not an instruction and he found himself thinking he could probably do that. What's more, he might do the same for some of the other ladies too and that could be gratifying. He wasn't naive enough to think Brenda would go for it, but all the ladies were nice enough in one way or another and he'd enjoy having their pictures to look at afterwards.

'What, now?' he said.

'If that's ok,' said Adele. 'The boat's a great backdrop.'

'Yes it is,' said Henry, hardly able to believe this turn of fortune. The corners of his mouth twitched and he felt them edging towards a leer. He tightened his lips and swallowed down the ejaculation of spittle that flooded his gums.

'Why don't you... sit... here, on the edge?' Henry pointed to a corner of the raised deck. Up by the windows, it rose three feet above the side aisles, necessitating that people haul themselves up on to their mattress in an ungainly manner. Near the bow it tapered to a few inches, comfortable to step on and off and an ideal spot for a lady to pose. It was painted a reflective high white. From this position he could get a backdrop of the boat and the slopes of pine and olive trees to the port side. His hands shook and he inhaled deep breaths in an attempt to settle the fluttering in his gut. From the corner of his eye, he could see Brenda, missing nothing as usual.

Adele sat where he instructed. He began by showing her how to pose to get the best light on her face. He was careful to use only words and gestures, no accidental touching. This was too good an opportunity to risk upsetting anyone. He repositioned her arms and turned her head this way and that, each time clicking two or three shots. Insanely grateful for the advent of digital photography, he knew he could afford to take many more shots than he ever could with film. Relaxed and uninhibited, Adele tossed her hair, smiled coquettishly and then more teasingly, turned one way and another and arched her back at his instruction. He even managed to get her to part her legs a little. But he was careful, so careful, not to draw the disapproval of the ever-watchful Brenda.

Adele proved to be the perfect model. Henry took perhaps forty shots and reckoned to have twenty good ones – for him and for her. He invited her to scan through them and she was so delighted with the results he nearly cried. It filled him with an absurd euphoria, that he could please a woman with something that gave him so much pleasure in return. He explained that when he got home he'd play with the photos a little – that was a moment where he had to take firm control of his facial features – and he promised that if she were pleased with them now, she'd be even more thrilled with the end results.

Adele's little photo-shoot did, as Henry hoped, attract the attentions of the other ladies. Catherine, always so poised and elegant, emerged from behind her sunglasses to see what was causing such a stir. Chloe changed into her favourite bikini and practically begged him to let her model for him. As a result, he spent the rest of the morning in near ecstasy, reeling off shot after shot of lovely ladies in bikinis, swimsuits and sarongs, eyes twinkling, posing for him and generally doing as he bid them; leaning this way and that, opening their mouths, parting their thighs (but only a little), sweeping fragile hands through hair whipped up by the sea breeze and all the while, smiling – smiling at him. He even persuaded Veronica to loosen up a bit and play to the camera. But Brenda kept guard the whole time, casting enough gritty stares his way to persuade him of the wisdom of maintaining his best behaviour. Mostly.

Elated by the whole experience, Henry could have sworn as the morning wore on that her brittle reproach weakened and her features softened. He even allowed himself to wonder if she wasn't a little tempted to ask for a photo-shoot of her own. But she never did.

3

HE LIES ON his front, his aching belly flattened against a towel and the rigid mattress beneath. His heart races, stabbing at his ribcage. Erratic beats pound the wall of his chest right up into his throat. He hasn't moved in two hours, except to demolish three vodka cocktails. They aren't working. Nor are the two lines he'd snorted after breakfast. Behind his eyeballs his head throbs; his gut churns against the boat's motion. He wants to grip the mattress and hang on for dear life, but he knows it wouldn't look right – it isn't the image he desires to project.

So many people put their names down for the cruise that he had to follow suit – no choice – to save being left behind with the dull ones. Hakima made him think the boat trip would be one long party, which would have taken his mind off the relentless pitch and plunge of the waves. But people are just lying around, basted and half asleep. He needs distraction to take his mind off the motion, the sight of land so far out of reach, the horizon's incessant rise and fall, the pulsating engines; the stomach-churning fusion of sun-oil, diesel and garlic.

Then there's that infuriating, scrawny little man; all around him, *click-click*, *click-click*, chasing fawning women with his camera, clambering all over the deck. What's he doing on the trip anyway? His name wasn't on the list last night. He'd double-checked after the creep had screwed with him, throwing booze all over his Chinos, wrecking his endgame, squandering a roofie.

One thing he never tolerates is interference. There would be payback.

Like that day at the coffee bar by the office, when the barista drowned him in cappuccino; an accident, apparently. He knew he'd been set up, the 'accident' organised, probably his team, because he was so far ahead of them, or just some cock-eyed practical joke. But it had screwed catastrophically with his day. So he'd worked out his move and dealt the payback, cold and hard.

He wants to look at the photo but he can't afford to attract attention. So he relives the scene in his mind, again and again, every vengeful thrust he'd delivered in that festering passage, awash with detritus, to a soundtrack of hip-hop and distant laughter. And as his cock engorges beneath him, he inhabits the confusion of anger and arousal.

So deeply engaged is he in his internal snuff-movie, he doesn't immediately realise the boat has slowed. The engine is silent and the anchor is being fed out, rattling into the water. He raises his baseball cap enough to see a cliff face, rocks and a few yards of shingle fringed with stones and seaweed. The boat stops 20 yards from the rocks and a deck-hand plunges into the water with one end of a rope hooked over his shoulder. He swims across then clambers on to one of the rocks and wraps the rope two or three times around, pulling it tight.

Shit. They're not even pulling hard up to this wretched strip of shingle. This means he can't get off the boat. He can't have the one thing his aching, twitching body craves: *terra firma* beneath his feet.

Kaptan Bellyache is lecturing them again. Some crap about stopping here for an hour, so they can jump off the sides and play with snorkels and swim. No shit. In the water? Not a chance. The other deck-hand hooks a stepladder over the side and several people queue up to climb down into the sea. A couple of mattresses along, the posh-boy strips off his t-shirt and stands up. The empty-headed hooray is fit and toned and he attracts attention as he steps to the edge of the raised deck. He lifts his arms above his head and dives out with hardly a splash into the water, which is a good 15 feet down. Then he's off across the bay, so far and so fast that in minutes, he's a speck. There's no arguing with it, when it comes to the water, the prick knows what he's doing.

He endures another swell of nausea as it rolls across his gut for the hundredth time that morning.

4

HENRY COULDN'T BELIEVE how well his day was going. The thrill of being at sea, the fun of having something different to photograph, the unexpected, breathtaking delight of having proper permission to photograph his female companions in their bathing suits; it was all beyond his imaginings. Now the ladies were his friends and he'd been welcomed into the bigger group. This was what the holiday was supposed to be about and at last, it was happening.

'You don't need to keep thanking me,' sighed Veronica after he'd expressed his unfettered gratitude to her for persuading him to come on the trip for the fifth time, or was it the sixth? 'I'm glad you're enjoying yourself.'

He hardly noticed his nemesis who had lain on his mattress, barely moving the whole morning. He hadn't got up to swim like most of the others when they'd anchored in the bay. He'd summoned drink after drink from the crew, with a flick of a finger and barely a glance from beneath his cap. Henry wondered if he might be seasick. That, he mused, would be the icing on the cake of a wonderful, perfect day.

The crew took up the anchor after an hour, once everyone had finished swimming. Now they were heading for a *lokanta* in another bay for lunch. Henry lay, propped up on his elbows, camera in hand, scrolling through the photographs he'd harvested from his new lady-friends. He had several pretty ones which he knew the ladies would love, but he'd also snatched a few cheekier ones for himself – even Brenda hadn't noticed.

The engine slowed again. The boat approached a wooden jetty which ran out 50 yards from land and a narrow beach. At the far end of the jetty stood a white, flat-roofed building flying the red and white insignia of Turkey. A veranda ran along its frontage, decorated at either end with tubs overflowing with pink and yellow flowers. The veranda was set with a table and a hotch-potch of chairs. Overhead a canopy flapped in the breeze, offering intermittent shade. It all delivered a crudely rustic but at the same time, charming impression.

Kaptan Barbar emerged to address the party.

'We are at the restaurant of my brother Hasan and his wife Sophia. Here we stop for a feast especially prepared for you, of all the delicacies of our wonderful country. We stay here for two hours so there is plenty time for food and drink and for exploring the beach or swimming some more. When you hear the bell it is time to return to the gulet.' With that, Kaptan Barbar bounded to the aft deck and rang the dinner bell, clattering the rope attached to the clapper several times. 'There!' he said, returning to the sun deck. 'Now everybody know the sound.'

The party gathered together what belongings they required over lunch and queued to disembark via the wobbly gangway. One by one they made the perilous descent to the jetty, with Kaptan Barbar rendering assistance where needed. By the time they were all on land, the lively rhythms of holiday Turkey could be heard crackling from speakers which dangled from the branches of nearby olive trees.

Henry tucked himself in beside Veronica as the party made its way to the table. As they settled, a plump woman appeared with a tray of dishes. In temperatures which soared towards 90 degrees she wore stockings, an ample skirt layered with an apron, a high-necked blouse beneath a cardigan, and a headscarf. As Henry speculated to himself how uncomfortable she must be under all those layers, she reached over him to deposit some dishes, granting him an unrestricted waft of her all-too-natural underarm odours. Henry coughed so hard he nearly choked.

'Oh, my word,' he said to Veronica and the world-at-large. He clutched at his throat.

'Takes one to know one,' said a voice from down the table. Henry couldn't see who it was.

'Pay no attention,' said Veronica. 'You're doing fine today.'

Henry experienced one of those moments when he felt he should know what was going on, but somehow the conversation had left him behind. The best approach when that happened was to shrug it off. In any case he was having too much fun to let anything spoil the day.

Lunch was a feast which tickled every one of Henry's newly awakened senses. Creamy dips, fresh baked bread, salad leaves and sticky sauces; the sizzle of griddled meats layered with herbs and spices; drizzles of garlic butter and lemon juice; creamy yoghurt, fruits and pungent cheeses. For an hour or more, every space on the table was crammed with a plate or a bowl filled with food. Every time one emptied another replaced it. Henry tried everything, even the things he didn't recognise. Every mouthful challenged his conservative tastes and still he came out smiling. It was hard to believe this rustic dwelling had the capability to deliver such a banquet.

Despite Veronica's plea for restraint, he slurped his way through three Efes and as the beer lubricated his self-confidence it loosened his tongue. He told Adele he thought she would do better for herself with men if she exercised a little old-fashioned restraint. With only the slightest hint of a slur, he told Veronica she was the kindest, sweetest soul he'd ever met – with the possible exception of his dear departed Sadie. He even announced to Brenda that no matter what she said to him or thought of him, he would forever worship her wonderful womanly curves in the privacy of his imagination. Unexpectedly it earned him a guarded upward turn of her plumptious lips – not quite a smile but close – instead of the crushing retort he'd anticipated.

This day, this one day, Henry was having the holiday he'd craved. If it got no better than this, this day alone would be enough.

There was one person his unrestrained tongue hadn't sought out for special mention. Sloshed or not, there were places you didn't go. There was plenty he could say, but, like a smaller, weaker animal facing-off a larger, stronger one, Henry knew his place was to lower his eyes and stay out of the line of fire. A confrontation would only end in trouble.

Yet throughout the meal, the object of Henry's dread seemed only to pick at the mountains of food placed before him. The ebullient persona that everyone seemed to love was but a feeble shadow of its usual self. Bloodshot eyes lowered; the hiss of laboured breathing through a dry mouth. The realisation that the bastard was in some kind of internal hell gave Henry goose-bumps.

As trays of melon, peaches and figs soaked in honey were served, the big man left the table without a word. Henry watched him stumble away from the restaurant and along the beach. The line he walked veered first towards the breaking waves, then across to the trees which edged the beach. At one point he tripped and nearly fell. No wonder, since as he walked, he held his beach bag in one hand and probed urgently within it with the other. He was a good hundred yards along the beach before he seemed to have located what he wanted. He sat under a tree fiddling with whatever he'd found. In due course a trail of smoke billowed around him and he leaned back against the tree. Old stick-in-the-mud he might be but even Henry knew what that kind of smoking was all about.

'Is this yours?' said a female voice close to his ear. At first he didn't hear. 'Henry, your camera. You don't want to lose it, do you?' It was Veronica. He turned to see her holding out a camera towards him. It looked like his – exactly like his in fact. But he drew a surreptitious hand across his trouser pocket and realised his was still exactly where he'd stowed it. But there was another camera like his on the holiday. He'd noticed it one day.

'Oh, yes, it is,' he said and Veronica beamed as she handed him the camera. 'No, I wouldn't want to lose it. Thanks, Veronica, you're a dear. Where would I be without you?'

5

LICKING HER FINGERS after one final honey-drenched fig, Brenda levered her chair back from the table. Hasan brought a tray of apple tea in glasses resting on tin saucers. He set one down for each guest, placing bowls of sugar cubes along the table. Brenda dropped one into her tea, stirring until it dissolved, enjoying the tinkle of spoon against glass. She sipped, inhaling the citrusy aroma. This was genuine apple tea, not the synthetic crystalline *just-add-water* mixative, mass-produced in some factory for the tourist trade. She closed her eyes.

'Come on, Adele, loosen up, sweetie. I'm only trying to be friendly.' Charming though he could be, tact and subtlety were strangers to James. Sensitive enough to acknowledge a problem, well-meaning enough to want to fix it, James had not the faintest notion how to go about the task.

'I'm not your sweetheart' blasted Adele across the table. 'Dickhead.'

'Look, I'm sorry,' said James. 'Honestly, I am. Please Adele, tell me what I did. Or if you won't tell me, can't we put it behind us. You're a babe and you're a laugh and I hate that we're not getting on.'

Adele's features softened to a hesitant smile.

'There! I knew I'd wear you down eventually. Whatever it was, it can't have been that bad. Come on, doll, let it go.' And as smartly as it had materialised, Adele's smile evaporated.

'Just leave me alone,' she pouted. 'You're such an arse.'

Adele grabbed her bag and dispensed a parting scowl before flouncing up the jetty towards the gulet. James flopped back in his chair.

'I give up,' he sighed.

In the distance along the beach, Brenda noticed the silhouette of a man reclining under the shade of a clump of olive trees.

First there'd been Lilly's distress, then Adele's uncertain admission. And there was the trade she'd witnessed at the airport coach park. Brenda didn't believe in coincidences and one person connected these events. Like so many of his type, he was a consummate performer. His giveaways were modest – a vocal inflexion, a flicker of authentic emotion, the hint of an explosive temper – yet she was certain his fabricated charm concealed a contamination.

Until Jack, instinct had always driven her to scratch the itch of suspicions. She'd weigh in without a second thought, hunting down proof, confronting ugly truths. People had to know so they could face things and deal with them. That's what made you strong, dealing with your stuff, not hiding from unpalatable realities.

But that was before... Before Jack, Brenda's world had been black and white, no room for grey. She still didn't fully comprehend what had happened, nor why Jack had reacted as she did. The betrayal had been Graham's after all, hadn't it?

Brenda sat for several minutes watching the lone figure, weighing the options. How would she feel if she turned her back, ordered another apple tea, settled on the beach with her book and an ambient playlist and tomorrow or the next day, realised he'd snared another victim? Experience told her that somewhere, sometime, there'd be others.

Brenda's heart raced as, bare-footed and ankle deep in the sand, she sauntered up the beach trying to look as if she were going nowhere in particular.

'Mind if I join you?' she said as she drew close. Turner pulled himself upright too quickly and, head swaying, tossed something behind him into the sand. Raising his sunglasses, his scowl softened to a studied smile.

'Be my guest,' he said, failing to hide the surprise in his voice. He waved his hand to the expanse of sand and rock.

Singled Out

Achieving a decorous seated position on uneven ground wasn't easy for Brenda. She lowered herself slowly. One after the other, her knees cracked in protest. The weight on those aching joints was nothing compared to the heaviness that bore down on her chest. She arranged herself, straightening rumpled clothes and burying her fuchsia toenails in the sand – the frivolity of those flashes of pink was at odds with the moment. She swept a hand across her perspiring forehead.

'Retrieve your spliff,' she said at last.

'Nah. Plenty more where that came from. Join me?'

This was genial Turner going to work – or trying to. Brenda wanted to accept, gain from the complicity, but cannabis had always given her alarming palpitations whilst delivering little of the pleasure that others seemed to find.

'No thanks,' she said.

'Suit yourself,' said Turner. He pulled a polythene zip-lock from his satchel and slid it open. It contained a fistful of the dried leaf and a packet of Rizlas. An elaborate ritual ensued. Turner deployed the flattened back of his satchel as a workbench and manufactured a mighty Olympic torch of a spliff. He gave the wide end a twist then flicked his Zippo open and fired the flint. The paper flared before settling to a glow. He drew deeply, holding his breath for several seconds before polluting the sea-air with a cloud, at once both acrid and sickly-sweet. Brenda tightened her nostrils and held her breath until the worst of it had dissipated.

'You've not looked well this morning,' she said.

'I didn't think anyone noticed,' he replied, blowing a sigh out along with another payload of smoke.

'I don't miss much.'

'Is that so,' he said, more a statement than a question. Turner lifted his shades again and met Brenda's gaze. For the first time, she scanned his features for giveaways, then let herself be the first one to blink and lowered her eyes.

'What was it, a touch of nautical nausea? An unhappy companion to your coach-sickness?' she said.

The shades dropped again.

'The sea isn't one of my favourite places.'

'You're kidding,' said Brenda, unable to hide her surprise.

'Straight up,' Turner sighed. 'It's not just the waves; it's the salt, the smell, all that shit drifting about, seaweed and slime. And the diesel, that's the killer – I thought this was supposed to be a sail boat.'

'It'll sail – they usually do – but only for an hour or so. That won't be much help.'

'No kidding,' he rasped through a constricted throat. They sat in silence for a few minutes as Turner pulled on his joint, blowing smoke rings.

'Have you tried swimming?' said Brenda. She was certain she hadn't seen Turner swim. The question would nudge at his insecurities. 'It's warm, clean too – mostly.'

'Not my thing. I hate water of any kind – lakes, rivers, pools – it's all the same.'

'You don't swim?' Brenda knew before he answered.

'Like I said, it's not my thing.' Turner exhaled and another bloom of smoke stung Brenda's eyes.

'Oh,' she said. This bulldozer of a man was afraid of water and cowed by motion sickness. That could have been funny – in another time. Even so, she had to rein in the urge to laugh. With anyone else, she'd get away with it, but not him and not now.

'I don't mean to be rude,' she said at last, 'but what are you doing coming on a... boat trip?'

'I've been pondering that precise question myself.'

'And?'

'Why do we do anything in this world?'

'For a laugh? The pursuit of pleasure? To be sociable? Because it's a challenge? For the thrill? To avoid being left behind?' It was a scattergun approach, but it did the job.

'Yep, some of those,' Turner replied. 'Though in retrospect, it was a poor decision whichever way you cut it.' A self-mocking snort escaped his nose. 'It's no fun puking your guts up in a bathroom the size of a matchbox.'

'I guess not.'

Turner's joint expired as it met his fingertips. He ground the remnant between his finger and thumb then pressed it into the sand beside him.

'What about the rest of the holiday?' said Brenda. 'Is it what you expected?'

'Pretty much.'

'You're quite the party animal, aren't you?' Brenda shifted position to more easily focus on his face.

'I like a club night, if that's what you mean.'

'More than that,' she said. 'You're good at getting a crowd going.'

'Place like this, it's not hard.'

'Meaning?'

'It's like kids playing *follow-the-leader*. If you lead, the lemmings – and this holiday is swimming with them – will follow. No need to tell you though, you do it too.'

'I confess,' said Brenda, surprised he'd noticed.

'Maybe we're not so different.'

We are, thought Brenda. We're different.

'What? We're leaders, not followers?' she said. 'We go after what we want?'

'That's right.'

'Are you getting what you want?' Brenda let her voice drop to a whisper. Quiet now. Hold back; give him time to process.

'Are you?' he said.

'Here and there,' said Brenda. 'Could be better.'

'How so?'

'Do you ever feel you've been sidelined? Ever have that feeling that something... interesting is going on and you're missing out? That you're somehow... excluded... from the main event?' He'd have to bite soon.

'You, missing out? I don't get you.'

'Yes, you do.'

Brenda watched gulls circling overhead as Turner massaged the fine sand, letting it trickle through his fingers again and again.

'You're talking riddles,' he said eventually, brushing stray grains from his shorts.

'We should get better acquainted, then you'd understand.' Brenda kept her tone melodic and playful.

'Are you propositioning me?'

'Not exactly. Besides, I don't think I'm your type.'

'You figure? What is my type?' He lifted his shades until they clung to his skull.

'I think—' Brenda hesitated. Was he ready?

'You think what?'

'I think you like your women a little more... passive... than me.'

Her words hung in the air, held aloft by the sudden screech of a seabird. Laughter drifted from the far end of the cove.

His breathing grew shallow. She held her nerve under the weight of the silence, watching an almost imperceptible tick invade the corner of his eye. His jaw clenched and he bit his lip so hard that a bubble of blood blew up against the whitened enamel of his front teeth. He scraped it away with his thumb.

'I don't know what you're getting at,' he said. His hand came to rest on his thigh, his thumb pulsing back and forth as if he were strumming an invisible guitar.

'Yes, you do,' she repeated, and she laughed, confident, challenging him; playful, but with an edge calculated to unsettle. He stared back. A muscle in his upper lip fibrillated. They stared each other down and it seemed as if time held its breath; this time she would not look away.

'You reckon you've got something on me?' he said at last, an acid garnish layering his tone.

'I do. That's why you interest me. What you do – the thing I know you do – intrigues me. More than that, it's... stimulating.' She modulated her voice with skill, maintaining a lilting, honeyed tone, affectingly natural.

'You got nothing. You don't know me.'

Brenda forced confidence into her smile and boldness into her voice.

'So why don't we get better acquainted? How about a little background, a nice, easy *show-and-tell*? You can handle that, can't you?'

He leaned back against the tree again and Brenda watched his face. An involuntary flicker of response invaded his features; a casting about of the eyes, a barely perceptible twitch infiltrating the crease of his mouth. All this told her what she needed to know.

'You asked for it,' he said at last. 'You can have the shitty story of my childhood. Once upon a time... Oh, but my mother wasn't your regular maternal type, not much given to bedtime stories. She was an addict, you see, in and out of prison. So I went in and out of care.' He droned a weary monotone, as if he'd told the tale a hundred times before. 'I had twelve foster homes in as many years. She'd get clean in jail then use again when she got out. She shoplifted and prostituted her wasted body to fund her habit. She was one crazy bitch. She met with a fatal 'accident' on one of her vacations at Her Majesty's pleasure – something to do with a chip fryer. I was thirteen; they didn't tell me for six months.' He shrugged his shoulders and smiled.

It was as if he were reading the account of a deprived childhood from a Social Services file. It was a well rehearsed monologue; the words flowed without hesitation or repetition.

'It's a gritty story,' Brenda said. 'But that's all it is, isn't it? A story.'

'What do you mean?'

'It's a fabrication; a product of your imagination, dangerously overloaded with pathos, if you ask me. I suppose it might be someone's story, but it's not yours.'

'You think?'

'I'm serious,' she continued, her voice soft and uncritical. 'I *get* you. I don't need the pumped-up narrative you use to bait the gullible. I'm not them.' Her heart hammered her ribcage. 'What's so bad about the truth, Turner? Is it too messed-up? Or... oh yes, I bet this is it. Is it too... ordinary?'

'Fuck you,' he said at last, an uncertain half-smile fluttering the corner of his mouth. 'You're a mad bitch. I don't know where you think you're going with all this.'

'Yes, you do,' she said again, almost inaudibly; this time a conspiratorial whisper. 'And do you want to know what else?'

'What?'

'Your thing – the thing I know you do – it... excites me.'

Turner stared unflinching at Brenda, perspiration glistening on his forehead.

'I want in,' she added, 'or I'll *out* you and your dirty little secret.' She looked him square in the eyes and smiled. 'So what's it to be?'

'I don't... You don't... Oh, fuck, get a grip.' Brenda wasn't sure whether he was talking to her or to himself. He dragged himself to his feet, jerked his satchel out of the sand and stumbled off towards the gulet.

So that was it, her opening gambit. He'd been blindsided; he might be intrigued, he'd definitely be unsettled. He'd be forced to properly assess the risk – or the opportunity. Self-preservation and ego would drive him to dig deeper.

She just had to be ready.

6

BRENDA, HE THINKS. Not so fluffy after all. All that pink silk and glitter, hides a sharp-eye, puts you off the scent. That's one smart-ass bitch. But what does she know? Has he been careless? Has she seen something? Is she testing him or bluffing? Can she back it up?

Maybe she's coming on to him. If she is, it's intriguing, not like the other women with their blatant come-ons. But is she flirting, or taunting? Is she playing him, or getting playful?

His brain, fogged by nausea, alcohol and a potent intake of weed, isn't processing.

He realises he hasn't the faintest clue who she is. He'd seen a bold, big-breasted bitch and hadn't troubled to look any deeper. Except to consider whether she was worth a roofie or not – answer, no. She was way too self-assured. Besides, she'd likely need two and then he'd have trouble moving her around; so she'd been de-listed early on and that was that. Now here she is suggesting she's up on what he's been doing. That's a whole different bowl of soup.

It's a dilemma, unexpected, unwanted; it's making his head hurt. But at the same time, it feels like she's challenging him – and one thing he can't resist is a challenge.

As he approaches the boat his stomach curdles. It looks like no one has gone back on board yet, so why is he out there on a metaphorical and literal limb, pacing down the jetty, skull pounding? He intended to be the last one back on board, not the first. Bitch must have properly got to him. He can't believe he owned up to being seasick, told her he didn't *do* swimming. You never – *never* – let people see your weaknesses.

He doesn't want to retrace his steps back up the jetty. That would make him look stupid, like he doesn't know where he's going, can't make a decision. He can maybe take a few photos of the boat, make it look like he meant to walk that way then return to the table and grab another vodka to settle himself. He lifts the flap on his bag and fishes around for his camera. His fingers find the bag of weed, suntan oil, iPhone, book, wallet. They dip in and out of the inside pockets – all empty. His heart rate ratchets up as he digs around to the left and right, searching all the pockets over and over and finding nothing. He pats himself down. Nothing. The camera is nowhere. He knows he had it; he took a couple of shots of all the food.

Shit. It must still be on the table.

He strides along the jetty resisting the urge to break into a run. Laughter echoes around the beach, bouncing off the hills that swell behind the restaurant. The table has thinned out – there are people playing on the beach, a couple more on stools by the bar. Nobody looks over at him – thank god. If they found the camera, at least they haven't got to the pictures.

He approaches the table. The dirty plates have been cleared, leaving only half-empty glasses on the cloth. It's immediately obvious his camera isn't there. The vein in his temple flares. The kitchen – maybe someone handed it in. He swipes the plastic strip curtain aside and enters the darkened interior. As he does, he sets his voice to cheery and nonchalant.

'Hello there,' he says to the owners – he can't remember their names. 'Did either of you pick up a camera off the table?'

They stand, staring at him like village idiots. 'Camera,' he shouts. Nothing. He makes a mime of holding a camera to his face and pretending to take a photo. The couple grin inanely and shake their heads. Nothing. Fuck.

He steps outside again and the sun pierces his shades, scraping at the back of his eyeballs. Almost everyone has moved off – gone exploring or paddling in rock pools like infants. One person remains at the table. It's the posh-boy flopped across the cloth, head in his hands.

'You haven't seen a camera around here by any chance?' he asks, keeping it polite, low-key, even though he can feel acid washing at the back of his throat.

'Sorry, no,' says posh-boy, head still on the table. 'Have you lost one?'

'Yeah,' he says. Dumb question. 'You sure you haven't got it?'

'Positive. Now would you mind going away and leaving me in peace.'

There's a small rucksack close to posh-boy's feet.

'This yours?' he demands, picking up the bag. He rifles through it. Posh-boy lifts his head at last.

'No it isn't. I don't know whose bag it is, but it's not mine. Look, I swam from the boat – I don't have anything. See?' Posh boy pulls out the insides of the pockets in his shorts then waves his hands in the air. 'Now toddle off and leave me alone.'

'My camera,' he almost moans as he turns the rucksack inside out, scattering its contents across the table; lotion, a book, a wallet, a sunglasses case, a couple of postcards; no camera. He flings the bag aside.

'I told you. I haven't got your camera and that isn't my bag. What's got into you?'

'I want... my... camera... back,' he hisses, his face so close to posh-boy's he's practically spitting in his eyes.

'Jesus, calm down, man. It'll show up,' posh-boy wails.

He knows this isn't a productive approach; it's time he got serious. But the weed has an iron grip on his faculties. It can't be helped. He pulls a chair close to the posh-boy and plants himself firmly in front of him. The boy sits up – he's got his attention now. Let's call it payback time. He puts a firm hand round the back of the boy's neck and pulls his face close.

'Here's the thing,' he says. 'I don't give a shit who's taken it, or why. I just want it back, do you understand?'

'Yes?' says posh-boy, trying to shake his head free. 'But what's that got to do with me?'

'Remember that first evening, when you threw wine all over my dinner? You were a prick, but I didn't say a word. Well, this is your chance to make it up to me for being a prick that night.'

'So I spilled a bit of wine,' the boy shrugs. 'Get over yourself.'

'Let me put it this way.' Quiet voice again, staying calm; hand still gripping the boy's neck. 'We're all creatures in the jungle and our job is to survive. Some do it better – we could say, more aggressively, perhaps more ruthlessly – than others. Are you with me?'

Posh-boy's face registers a look he can't read. It's a reaction, so he presses on.

'I'm one of those creatures. I do whatever I need to do. When my shit gets disrupted I react, right? I don't let stuff go by – nobody puts one over on me. Nobody. Ever. I don't lose stuff because I'm careful, so when I lose stuff – you know what I mean – I know it's not down to me, but someone else has screwed with me. When something important to me goes missing, someone has to pay, right? You getting me? Are you keeping up?'

'Uh—' is all posh-boy can manage.

'Think of me like a... Bengal tiger. I'm the kind of character you don't want to be on the wrong side of, see?'

The boy pulls a face and nods, saying nothing. He's learning, that's good.

'My camera is important to me,' he continues, 'and I want you to locate and return it to me – call it the price for your clumsy ass performance the other night. I'd say you're getting off lightly, but if you fail in this, the Bengal tiger will come after you. *Do you get me?*'

'Look, I don't know what you're on about but you don't need to threaten me. I'll ask around, see if I can't track it down. But that's it, ok? Now let go of me! Man, you're seriously fucked up!'

It's an unacceptable show of disrespect and it earns the posh-boy a parting gift – a clenched fist in his gut. Posh-boy grasps at his stomach and utters some kind of a groan. Bit of an over-reaction; he's hardly touching him.

'What is your problem, man?' Posh boy squeals like a stuck pig.

He smiles, withdraws his fist from posh-boy's solar plexus and releases his neck.

'I just don't like you,' he says.

7

KAPTAN BARBAR CLATTERED the dinner bell. Its vintage fire engine *clang-clang clang-clang* rebounded across the bay. Henry and Veronica responded immediately but it took 20 minutes to round everyone else up. At last they were on their way again, engines cranked up, bow churning in the waves. Kaptan Barbar bounced on to the sun-deck, beaming.

'We have wind!' he exclaimed. Everyone looked puzzled. 'We have wind, so we can put the sails up this afternoon,' he said. 'Is fun, yes?' Henry's heart leapt in response to the news. Could this day get any better? 'My lazy deck-hands don't like, as it make them work harder, but we like, yes?' Enthusiastic nods all round. 'Good good! So I shut the engine then you see what my lovely *Annelise II* can do.'

Kaptan Barbar shouted at his deck-hands then returned to the salon and cut the engine, as they leapt into action with as much commitment as Henry had seen from them all day. They unwound the ties around the mainsail and began cranking it up the mast. As it headed skyward, the wind found it and breathed life into the unfurling fabric until it billowed, casting dancing shadows across the sundeck. All around, cleats and tackle clanked and rattled in a kind of anti-rhythm – a timpani of the waves.

The deck-hands unrolled the jib over the bow and the sail on the second mast and high above them squally gusts took hold. The trio of sails ballooned with the strengthening wind of open water; they fought and whipped about, tugging at their fastenings, lifting and plunging the boat forward, cutting into the water and venting salty spray into the air and across the deck. The restaurant on the beach became a speck against a panorama of grey-green scrub and the bay zoomed into the distance. The diesel engine's industrial grinding was replaced by a sublime organic symphony; a blustery flapping of sails, the swish-swash of waves, the metallic pounding of the rigging and the cawing of a seabird. Breathless and eyes wide, Henry lay on his back staring up towards the tip of the mast and beyond into a pristine sky.

Surely this is what life should be about.

All around him lay the near-naked bodies of his new holiday friends, some reading, most dozing in the sun or taking advantage of the shade afforded by the sails. Catherine reclined by the bow, posed and precise, Chloe slept and – this made him chuckle – snored a little; Margaret the knitting queen sat bolt upright against the salon windows, her needles click-clacking away. Brenda lay on her back. Her face was hidden beneath her sunhat so he treated himself to an unrestrained appraisal of her breasts, captive within the confines of her favourite scaffolded black swimsuit – that garment was a piece of engineering genius. Her flesh had darkened in the last few days from the city-dweller's pinkish pallor to an alluring nutmeg.

Although slathered in Factor 30 his own ashen skin was not built to endure this intensity of sun and he could feel the prickle of heat rash invade first his ankles and calves, then his bony forearms. Too many years spent confined in polyester work shirts and woollen trousers. Veronica had gone down to her cabin for a nap. What would she have said? 'Come on now, Henry, get yourself into the shade for a while and give your pasty British flesh a chance to recover.' It seemed the sensible thing.

He gathered his belongings, hopped down on to the aisle and made his way to the upholstered platform at the rear. The canopy offered solid shade. He scrambled up on to the mattresses and arranged himself against the bolsters.

He didn't have an iPod. He was bored with his book which hadn't turned out to be the *roller-coaster adventure ride* it claimed to be on its back cover. He rummaged in his bag and came up with a camera.

For security in case he mislaid it, Henry had scratched his postcode into the metal casing down the side of his camera. He turned this one over and over in his hand, inadvertently rubbing his thumb up and down where the postcode would have been.

No postcode.

This one was identical to Henry's compact camera, yet it felt different. He couldn't explain it but even without the postcode, he'd have known this wasn't his camera. But he knew exactly who this carelessly mislaid device belonged to. He fired it up and held it to his face. Then he summoned up the menu and selected *review*. Up sprang a photo of today's lunch table, laden with platters of fish and meat and surrounded by beaming holidaymakers. He clicked and found another almost identical shot.

He clicked again.

At first he couldn't make out what he was looking at. It wasn't a great photo, technically speaking. A glow in one corner had confused the automatic lighting setting, so the picture was fuzzy. He rotated it a quarter-turn. Immediately the image was obvious.

Henry let go of the camera as if it were a red-hot poker. It fell into his lap. Heat surged to his cheeks. High in his ribcage his heart juddered. Slowly he picked the camera up again, this time looking around to make sure no one was watching.

It was a woman. To be more accurate, it was a woman with her legs wide open and her private parts on view. In fact, the whole picture was a fanny, framed with girlish pubes.

He clicked to the next shot. It was the same fanny but panned out a little. You could see a bit of thigh each side and the hint of a pair of titties at the top of the picture. Henry noticed he wasn't experiencing the usual urgent response in his pants when he looked at these pictures. Something didn't feel right.

He clicked again. Another shot of the same privates but panned out even more. And then he knew; the wide-open legs, the girlish titties; and a face at last, recognisably a face – the face of a young woman. But it wasn't a sexy face, all tongue out and come-and-fuck-me eyes like the photos on those naughty websites he bookmarked. This face was passive in a near-dead kind of a way – expressionless. The eyes were open but the look was vacant, empty – no one home. This was all wrong, so wrong.

He knew this woman. This... girl.

It was Lilly. Heaven help her, it was Lilly.

He recalled the scene he'd witnessed from his vantage point in the courtyard the other night; a man carrying a drunken-looking woman up the stairs in the near darkness; a sexual act of some kind behind the curtains in an upstairs bedroom. There weren't more than one or two men on the holiday who could have carried the dead-weight of a woman's body up those concrete steps without so much as a stumble. Simple and sweet, Lilly would never have let herself get into such a state that she couldn't walk unaided. There was only one plausible explanation; Brenda had hit upon it the other night before James shut her down.

Now he knew for sure he'd been right to intervene the last evening, when Turner had directed his attentions towards Veronica.

His mouth dry, he clicked again.

The next shot was a different woman; a flash-lit photo taken from behind, on grass perhaps. Her smooth bum-cheeks practically filled the picture, and you could see a stringy bit of thong had been dragged to one side, leaving her whole lady-parts, front to back, wide-open and glistening. There were no pubes; this one, whoever she was, was smooth like a baby. He couldn't see a face but the hair was long, trailing into the grass. The one arm in shot seemed to be bent and flopped out to one side, palm upwards – not the way you'd hold yourself if you were... conscious. Then he recognised a familiar flowery mini-skirt, pushed high above the woman's waist and he realised who he was looking at.

Was this photo taken the night they were all at the yellow bar, when Turner had dragged a cataleptic Adele away and no one else seemed even to notice?

Numb with shock, Henry scrolled on. He scanned two dozen more pictures of women in degrees of nakedness, some posed with their legs parted or crudely arched, elevated on cushions, or from behind; others with things sticking into them – a candle here, a dildo there. In one, the tip of an engorged penis, veins flared, oozed over a dead-eyed – there was no other word for it – *victim*.

Enough.

Nausea surged from Henry's stomach. His hands shook. He wanted to weep. The act of having looked at these photographs had burned them into his eyeballs – the strangers and worse still, the ones he knew, Adele and poor Lilly.

The pictures were not unlike the ones he hunted for on the internet – the ones he wanked over on a quiet Saturday evening at home when there was nothing on the telly. Except you knew the girls on the web enjoyed it, didn't they? You could see it in their faces. But these pictures displayed only vacant, dead eyes. One poor woman even had a towel over her face, as if she wasn't a person at all, just an object.

What should he do? Was there a right thing to do? Could he ignore it? Chuck the camera overboard and forget all about it? No one would know if he did, would they?

As Henry's conscience debated with itself, James wandered up from the sun-deck.

'Is that your camera?' he asked.

'Course it is,' said Henry, blood flaring to his neck. What business was it of his?

'Only, Turner misplaced his camera this morning. I thought you might have found it.'

'Nope, sorry,' said Henry, stuffing it into his bag.

'Sure?' asked James. Poncy twerp didn't believe him.

'See for yourself,' said Henry. It was a clever move. He pulled the other camera – his one – from his bag and scrolled through the last dozen or so shots of the ladies, which he'd taken that morning, all open and above-board, mostly.

'Sorry,' said James, who seemed a deal more interested in Turner's lost camera than a fellow holiday-maker had a right to be.

'No worries,' said Henry, pushing his camera back into his bag. He pulled his belongings together and ambled, legs trembling, as nonchalantly as he could manage, down to his cabin.

He slammed the door and slid the bolt. He dropped on to the bed, his head in his hands. He couldn't escape it; Turner's pictures were just like the ones he slavered over on the internet. All the poses were there; it was the expressions – or lack of expressions – which made them different. But why would this make him feel so... soiled?

He pulled out his own camera and scanned the pictures from that morning; there were a few he hadn't planned to show the ladies. But they were just a bit of fun. A pube tweaking out here or there; legs a fraction too wide apart; the red-brown blush of an areola *peek-a-booing* out of a bikini; the barest hint of a nipple. Where was the harm?

But he couldn't avoid the gritty question of those girls round the back of the train station at home. Their eyes weren't so lively and lustful either. Suddenly he wasn't so certain they enjoyed it as much as they claimed they did, as they went down on him in the back seat of his Astra in return for a twenty quid note.

He pulled Turner's camera out of his bag and set it on the bed. For a few minutes he eyed it, motionless, as if it were a wildcat poised to attack him. He picked it up again and located the pictures. He needed to be certain of what he'd seen – convinced he'd not been imagining.

They weren't subtle studies. A second time, picture after picture revealed itself in precisely the same way to him. Still, his normal physical response to photos like these continued to desert him. He stopped at one – a figure kneeling on the ground, on concrete, surrounded by bins and boxes, short hair, head in a puddle. He noticed the shoes first – flat, tan brogues. Then he saw brown ankle-length socks protruding from them. Then he saw hair on the legs and realised. This one was a man – a young man.

His stomach heaved. He swallowed his acid puke back down, but it came at him again. It was almost too fast, but he made it to the toilet. Over the next five minutes down on his knees, he expelled Hasan and Sophia's feast in waves down the bowl until his guts could surrender no more. He swept a hand across his chin to clear trailing dribbles of bile and hauled himself to his feet. The basin could barely accommodate both hands but he crammed them under the tap and splashed and splashed at his face, as if he could wash away the stain of his runaway thoughts. He raised his head and focused on the face staring back at him from the shaving mirror – it wore the eyes of a stranger and they bored into him, condemning his seedy existence.

His little diversions were harmless, weren't they? An innocuous private pleasure, nothing more. You could buy magazines in sweet-shops for goodness sake, so how could there be anything bad about them? These days he got better ones at a private shop in town, but the principle was the same. Then there was the internet and he had to admit, there was some pretty wild stuff on there if you knew where to look. But nobody did anything they didn't want to. Everyone was in it for the fun or the money. They weren't under any pressure, were they? What would be the pleasure in that?

Even round the back of the station, he wasn't drugging the girls; he wasn't forcing anyone. They were just lasses earning a living, supply and demand and all that. He wasn't raping them; he was... helping them out.

So he knew he wasn't a monster, inhuman, like Turner. But why did he feel so sickened? Why was it not good enough that he wasn't Turner?

It was because of another question, one his own conscience was forcing him to face: Was he, with his apparently harmless peccadilloes, on a path that would lead to... *this?*

Was he on some degenerate journey which began with titillation of the sort any sex-starved, red-blooded man might indulge in, but which would one day wind up with him holding a camera up to the private parts of a comatose girl for kicks? A girl he'd forced himself upon whilst she was powerless to fight him off? If he carried on with his little moments of mischief, would he one day end up needing more to excite him? And if he did, is this where it would lead?

He thought of Sadie. What would she think if she'd known what he'd been up to all the time he was married to her? Then there was Brenda. Her censure had angered him, but now he began to comprehend her disgust and understand her mistrust. There was Veronica too. She was kind and decent and he knew she'd feel the same loathing. The prospect of incurring Veronica's condemnation brought a crushing weight to his ribcage.

Shame was not an emotion with which Henry had previously been acquainted; but that day it introduced itself, sending prickling waves of pins and needles across his hands and feet and flooding his forehead with sweat.

He grabbed his camera and scanned the contents. It was easy enough to single out the pictures he shouldn't have taken; they were the ones which he knew would disturb Brenda, or Sadie, or Veronica. He pressed again and again. Delete... delete... delete... and the worst of them were gone. He passed back and forth through the images from the last few days – from the beach, by the pool and on the boat – letting go, one by one, pounding his old-man's libido into submission.

Only when he felt he could, with a clear conscience, put what remained on his camera in the hands of Brenda or Veronica did he consider it was time to stop.

8

ON THE SUN-DECK, propped up on her elbows with her belly pressed into the mattress, Brenda's holiday reading had drawn her into the steamy reaches of the Louisiana bayous and a world of forbidden lust, fractured families and corporate betrayal. Beside her, cross-legged on his mattress, a single white earphone in one ear, James flicked up and down through the contents of his iPod. Every so often he stopped, listened for a moment then continued on, flicking and picking a few seconds here and there. This process was accompanied by the now familiar chorus of huffing, puffing and tutting which told Brenda that James had something he wanted to offload. But this time she was resolved not to bite, not to let her temper be disrupted by another episode of anguished chest-beating from James, especially as it would inevitably involve Adele.

'James, you poor soul, what's up with you?' Staring out to the horizon, her legs curled up under a cotton skirt, sunhat flapping in the wind, Lilly weighed in. Brenda fidgeted her glasses to the tip of her nose. Was there to be no peace?

'I've been weirded-out. Totally. Whichever way I try and rationalise it, it doesn't make sense. I don't know what to think.'

'What are you talking about? What's happened?' Not for the first time, Brenda found herself wishing Lilly would zip-up her good-natured little mouth and leave well alone.

'I honestly wonder if I wasn't dreaming,' James said.

'About what? Come on now, spill the beans.' James had won Lilly's full attention, but it wasn't enough.

'It was so off-the-wall I wonder if he isn't a little... unhinged.'

'Who? Who?' said Lilly, her voice in crescendo as she reached out and tugged the single earphone from his ear. 'In heaven's name, who and what are you going on about?'

Resistance was futile. Brenda set down the paperback and yielded to James.

'What's up honey? Who've you been aggravating now?'

'Oh ha ha, Brenda darling, for once, it's not me,' said James. 'It's him. If anything, he's been aggravating *me*!'

'For goodness' sake,' said Lilly. 'For the last time, James, who?'

'Turner.'

Although Turner was nowhere to be seen, James's voice dropped to a whisper. 'He caught up with me at the restaurant when there was nobody else around. I'd say he crept up on me – I didn't hear him. First he accused me of stealing from him then he picked up someone's bag and started throwing all their stuff around.'

'What a thing to do!' said Lilly.

'Go on,' said Brenda, engaged despite herself. 'What was he after?'

'He was looking for his camera. He accused me of stealing it.'

'Did you steal his camera?' Lilly's tone wasn't calculated to offend, but offend it did.

'Of course not! I didn't know who had it and I told him so. But it didn't make any difference. He snarled at me for a couple of minutes then he told me it was my job to find his bloody camera. Then he landed me a fist in my gut – right out of the blue. I wouldn't say it was a proper punch, but it was well on the way. Then he threatened me! Like I said, unhinged.'

'He hit you?' blurted Brenda.

'Yes, kind of. Bloody hurt too, I wasn't prepared for it. If it wasn't so ridiculous, I'd say he was trying to frighten me.'

'Why?' said Lilly.

'Into finding his camera for him.'

'Did he succeed?'

'Yes. No. No, of course not. But he was so off-the-scale, I couldn't take it seriously. It made no sense – except it was obvious he was mad as hell he'd lost his camera.'

'Has anyone found it?' asked Lilly. 'If he's so upset about it, maybe we should look for it.'

'According to Turner, if I don't find it, he's going to do something bad to me. How messed-up is that? He rambled on about Bengal tigers too. Bonkers. I think he's deranged – manic or something.'

'Should we do something?' said Lilly.

'Like what?'

'Like report him to the police?'

'Don't be soft,' said James. 'To be frank, I think he had some kind of a tantrum. Weird, I know, but what's he going to do? It's a camera for goodness' sake.'

'I don't know,' said Brenda. 'There have been other things too. Remember?'

'Yes, so you said,' responded James, glancing askance at Lilly. 'But what if he's unwell, depressed or something? It wouldn't be right to cause him any trouble. It wasn't that much of a punch. It was so bizarre, it might even have been a joke that misfired – I wouldn't want to pillory him for misjudging a moment.'

'I'm not so sure. It may be more complicated than that,' murmured Brenda.

'In what way?' Lilly, latching on like a kitten tugging at a ball of string.

'Probably nothing,' said Brenda. Second thoughts, keep it to yourself. 'Me and my over-active imagination. Pay no attention.'

'Well, I think he's alright,' said Lilly. 'He probably has some treasured photos and he's upset he's lost it. But it can't have gone far on a boat now, can it? It'll turn up.'

'Unless he dropped in on the beach,' said James.

'Or someone did actually lift it,' added Brenda.

Adele appeared, for once a merciful relief. She clambered on to the mattresses and slid in beside James. Lilly immediately surrendered the few inches of extra space she demanded.

'Don't say anything, lie down,' hissed Adele to James.

'Blimey,' said James, terror and delight jostling for position in his facial features.

'Shut up, just lie down. Put your arm round me or something. Quick.'

Adele didn't need to ask twice. James obliged, sliding one arm under her neck and wrapping the other around her waist. It brought them face-to-face, inches apart.

'Am I allowed to snog you?' said James.

'Shut up,' hissed Adele.

'Can't blame a guy for asking.' James seemed to be warming to the erratic profile of the encounter.

'Go on then. Do it,' said Adele. Not a request. An order.

James made an elaborate show of puckering-up, licking his lips lasciviously before falling upon the bikini-clad Adele with unrestrained if comical relish.

'Do it properly,' said Adele. 'Like you mean it. Make it convincing.'

'Convincing?' queried James, the corners of his mouth twitching with apprehension.

'Just do it. Like you're in love with me or something. Quick, he's coming!'

James pulled Adele's face close and as their lips met the deckhand – Adele's dodgy *quickie* of the previous evening – lolloped towards the gulet's bow like an excitable puppy. As he focused on Adele and James locked in their apparently cosy coupling the fire in his eyes sputtered and died. He turned about and began fiddling with a skein of rope, his cocky smile withered.

James didn't surface for several minutes. His free hand caressed Adele's spine and shoulders and stroked her hair, before gently teasing at the straps on her bikini top and then settling tenderly against the side of her breast. As he worked his magic, the tension visibly drained from Adele's frame and as she responded to James's touch her body seemed to sink into the mattress. At last James pulled back, his eyes remaining steadfastly locked on hers.

Adele's eyebrows elevated, she exhaled slowly and whispered in James's ear.

'Hadn't we better get a room for that?' said James, his default impish grin restored.

The deck-hand stopped fumbling with the ropes and turned, giving James and Adele a last, rueful glance before padding back up the aisle and down into the salon.

Adele sat up and adjusted her bikini as James continued to gaze into her eyes, his face radiant, glistening with a smear of her fuchsia lip gloss.

'Here,' said Adele, handing him a tissue. 'You'll be wanting to wipe that off.'

'I'll be wanting to collect some more,' said James, his ingenuous charm generating a wan smile from Adele.

'James,' she said, her voice unexpectedly soft, 'if only you'd said that to me on the first night.'

'What do you mean?'

'That you wanted more. More of what we had before.'

'Before?' queried James. 'I don't understand.'

'That's my point,' said Adele.

'Please babe,' said James, his eyes pleading with her. 'Tell me. I know I've done something to upset you and I honestly don't know what. I want to make amends. God's honest, I do.'

'You really don't know, do you?'

'I really don't.'

'We've met before.'

'We have?'

'On a holiday, like this, two years ago. In Crete.'

'Christ. Did we? I don't remember.'

'Yeah, I get that.' Adele's tone rippled with sadness.

'Did we—'

'Uh huh.'

'How could I not remember?'

'Beats me.'

'No, I mean it. How could I not remember... you?'

'James, I don't think I can answer that for you.'

'Jesus. I'm so sorry, Adele. I don't know how I could have forgotten you. You're such a... such an amazing girl, so full of life and all.'

James sounded as if he meant it. Brenda could see, even if he didn't entirely believe his own words, his effort to earn forgiveness was genuine. Maybe Adele would cut him the slack he craved.

He brought his face close to Adele's. His hand behind the nape of her neck, he drew her in, his lips brushing hers in a penitent kiss. A solitary tear leaked from one eye and ran down her cheek. He kissed it away.

'I get it, why you were so angry with me. I'm angry with me too. I'm so sorry, babe,' he whispered. 'Will you forgive me?'

'I don't know, James,' said Adele.

'Come on,' said James. 'Let me find you a drink and we can go and talk it over in private.'

Adele let herself be taken by the hand. James led her to the gulet's shaded stern and it wasn't long before Brenda noticed they'd disappeared.

Only the cabins offered true privacy on a boat like this.

9

IT'S TORTURE, THE freaking boat, no other word for it.

It's an unending heaving and tossing, up and down, up and down; now the sails are up, there's a gut-churning rolling, side to side, up and down, lurching one way and another and no remission, no chance of escape. What was he thinking of? He should never have come.

And he should never have put food in his face at lunch. He ate because his empty gut screamed to be filled and because he didn't want to be excluded. Now layers of oily silt curdle in his retching stomach, compounding his problems.

All he wants to do is hurl and shit. He's already expelled half his lunch and he can't even face a vodka. So now he's sober. Sober and sick. Sober and sick and confined to this coffin of a cabin for the last two hours because he can't detach from the toilet. And even that's no picnic – all lurching and grabbing and trying not to puke on your pants.

He yearns for the evening, to be back on solid, unmoving soil again. He needs to know how long it will be before they dock somewhere; before there is earth under his feet. He stumbles out of his cabin towards the salon where Captain Bellyache perches at the wheel.

'Excuse me,' he says, forcing a smile. 'Can you tell me when will we dock for the night?'

'Dock?' repeats the scrawny sea-dog. 'Dock? Ha ha ha!' It isn't a laugh, more a cackle.

'I'm sorry?' Stay calm. Don't upset anyone.

'We no dock. We anchor in a bay for the night. Maybe one hour until then.'

Did he hear right. Christ.

'No dock?' he repeats. A sharp pain courses across his forehead, like he's being pierced by a shard of glass.

'No dock. I show you the wide open waters around my beautiful country. We anchor in a special bay tonight, middle of the water, very quiet, no people. Don't worry, is calm! My cook is busy.' Here the old man points towards the galley where another greasy Turk dices some meat – sickly pink and slimy, chicken or rabbit. The sight of it causes his stomach to heave again. 'My cook make a feast for supper on deck. Then we play music and maybe even I sing!' Captain Bellyache says this like it's something to look forward to. Then more quietly, 'You sick, yes?'

'No,' he says, then, 'Yes, a little.'

'I have good pills. I give you.'

Anything, he thinks. Anything to fight this churning, cramping nausea. He's had headaches before. He's acquainted with the discomfort of travel sickness. He's had a bad rush from overdoing the self-medication. Once he was rendered comatose from a dodgy batch of coke. But this is worse, much worse; because he can't manage his environment; because he's not in control.

The old man jumps down from his position at the wheel and tosses a pile of cushions off one of the banquettes. Lifting the seat he emerges with a dented biscuit tin covered in pictures of London landmarks. He pulls out a box of pills and pops four from their blister pack. He holds them out.

'You take two now and you take two later, maybe two hours time. Then you be fine, much better.'

'Thank you.'

He returns to his cabin and swallows all four pills with the dregs of his last vodka. He braces himself against the bathroom wall, cups his hands under the tap and swallows a couple of mouthfuls of water. They say you shouldn't drink water except from bottles, but he's swallowed worse than that in his life.

From the next-door cabin he can hear a rhythmic *thud-thud-thud* against the wall, the unmistakeable pulse of sex. With all the other banging and clanking going on around the boat, the fuckers probably figure nobody can hear them, which might be true were it not for the volley of sighs and grunts marking time with the muffled pounding. The rhythm quickens and instructions begin, a woman's high-pitched semi-whisper penetrating the paper-thin walls; 'harder... more... yes, right there... oh, oh, yes, do it, do it!' He doesn't know who it is and he doesn't care. He isn't even in the mood to jerk off to it.

He lies down again and closes his eyes. Another hour before the boat stops. Then he'll need to muster all his resources to regain the lost ground.

He wakes with a jolt – how long has he been asleep? There's activity above his head; the thunder of bare feet back and forth and shouting, then a ratchety winding which seems mercifully to signal the sails are being let down. Relief surges through his twitching body. At last he can sit upright and open his eyes without wanting to puke. Maybe the pills are working.

The motor stirs into life and he emits an involuntary groan. Will this never end? But the boat seems to be chugging along with only minimal motion. He tweaks at the curtain across the window and is surprised to see land up-close, a steep rise of craggy rocks and boulders and a scattering of olive trees within a hundred yards. It's evening already; a blood-orange sun half concealed; pinpricks of light flickering on a distant slope. From what he can see the water outside seems calm. He lowers his legs to the floor, hauls himself upright and makes for the bathroom.

He can reach everything in the bathroom without moving. He pisses a brownish-yellow jet into the toilet then points the shower spray into the basin, bends and drenches his head under it. When he looks up the visage that greets him in the shaving mirror is sallow like a death mask, eyes rheumy, lips the colour of raw chipolatas. He smacks his own face a couple of times to get the blood flowing.

He hears the anchor mechanism turning and the chain running out at speed. The engine slows and finally sputters to silence. He can't stay in here forever. It's time to re-engage; or try to.

He emerges into the salon and Captain Bellyache greets him like a long-lost prodigal son.

'Ah, you better?' the man asks.

'A little, thank you,' he returns. 'But I'm still a bit unsteady. Any chance I could have a couple more of your pills to keep me going?' He asks nicely, as if he could survive without them.

'Sure, ok,' says Captain Bellyache. He retrieves the battered biscuit tin from the banquette and locates the pills. There are four left in the pack.

'I could use all four,' he says, shaping his mouth into a polite smile, 'to settle me, later on.'

'These are very strong pills,' says the captain as if he's addressing a child. 'Very important you have no alcohol when you take these. You understand? Is bad for you if you take pills and drink.' He hasn't let go of the pack yet and a mini tug-of-war ensues.

'Yes, I understand.' As he says it, he yanks firmly on the pack of pills. Captain Bellyache relinquishes his grip and it is his. Patronising fuck.

As he exits the salon, up into the fresh air he catches a throatfull of sizzling onions and garlic from the galley. He gags against the fatty odour. There's little enough in his stomach but still it rebels against this invasion, sending another tide of nausea through his body. He sees someone's half-empty water bottle on the table, so he pops the remaining pills and necks it.

10

'WE STOP NOW,' said Kaptan Babar, bouncing up on to the sun-deck. 'The sun is nearly finish for the day and we reach my favourite place on all the Aegean coast of Turkey. So quiet and beautiful – you will love, I know it! Now my cook, he prepare a delicious meal for evening, with salad and some chicken kebabs and fish we catch ourselves – very tasty, not heavy, good food. You will like! I will ring bell to eat soon. But now is time for cocktails, so I take your order.'

He pulled out his battered notepad and began to work his way around the deck, leaving no one out. It wasn't a question of whether one wanted a drink, but only which drink. Brenda preferred a wash and brush-up to a cocktail, so whilst Kaptan Barbar's back was turned she slipped away. On the aft deck she passed Turner slumped across the table, his fists curled around his head.

'You alright?' she asked.

'Fine,' he mumbled without looking up.

Even Brenda could see there was little point in attempting her usual ablution and make-up routine, although she'd brought with her every bottle, jar, palette and brush she typically deployed. There was neither the room to execute this marathon exercise in even modest comfort, nor any point in so doing, only to end up sticking out amongst the sand-blasted hair and the shabby shorts and t-shirts, like Cinderella at a barn dance.

So after an uncomfortable shower, she restricted herself to her favourite age-defying moisturiser, illuminating foundation, concealer, blusher and lipstick – two shades but without a lip-liner – to achieve the most un-made-up of her make-up routines.

She glossed her hair with a finishing spray and her lightest floral perfume then worked it into a silver scrunchie high on her head, creating a healthy looking ponytail. She draped a single accessory around her neck, a multi-faceted crystal pendant shaped like a teardrop on a long silk cord. Without her usual shimmer of sequins, seed-pearls or diamantes she felt barely dressed, but she was appropriate – and that was what mattered.

She emerged on to the aft deck, where Kaptan Barbar stood poised with the dinner bell. The table was laid for twelve. Along the centre were baskets of bread, dishes of garlic butter, bowls of yoghurt and two wooden tubs exploding with coarsely-chopped salad. Two mats lay empty and as Kaptan Barbar pounded the bell into submission, the cook appeared with platters piled high and steaming. The first contained skewers crammed with char-grilled meat and vegetables, glistening in the blue-grey evening light. In the other lay at least a dozen whole fish, striped with grill-scars and scattered with knobs of butter and parsley. Simple fare it might be but this was a mouth-watering table.

'Mmmm,' said Brenda to no one in particular. 'Smells lovely.'

Kaptan Barbar smiled and pulled out a chair for her in the centre of the table.

'You smelling lovely too,' he murmured, as the guests gathered around the table.

'You casting your spell on another local?' said James as he flopped into the chair next to Brenda. 'What will Emilio say?'

'Don't be daft,' said Brenda, feeling blood swell her cheeks. 'I'm not... it's not like that.'

'Whatever it is, don't let it get in my way. Pass the bread, I'm ravenous!'

'At least you've done something to work up an appetite,' she said.

'A bit of healthy one-on-one? Nothing wrong with that,' James retorted.

'Except we all rather shared in your... exertions.'

Adele slithered into the seat beside James and pushed her hand down between his thighs.

'What have we here lover-man?' she said.

'My little fellow, pleased as punch to see you again,' said James.

'I meant, what's for dinner?' said Adele. 'I'm ravenous.'

'That's how James is feeling,' remarked Brenda.

'We've been—'

'We all have a pretty good idea what you've been up to,' said Brenda. A triumphant grin broke across Adele's face.

One by one the guests settled at the table and despite having done nothing since their lunchtime banquet, they managed to pass the next hour filling their stomachs and emptying every platter, bowl and dish. No longer sidelined by the gathering as a grimy letch, Henry, extracted from his once odious shell, proved to be an engaging dinner companion. He recounted tales from his career as a regional newspaper journalist, about holding councils and politicians to account, rooting out fraud and dodgy dealing and exposing the transgressions of local dignitaries and minor celebrities. Catherine and Chloe, both beneficiaries of his photographic skills that morning, hung off his every word. Lilly and Margaret the knitting queen, held a spirited debate on the money-saving benefits of making your own clothes. All the while James and Adele endeavoured to feed one another their entire dinner, oblivious to every censorious grimace.

Coffee served, the ubiquitous Turkish Delight consumed, it was time for the main event.

'You want I sing for you?'

Kaptan Barbar stood by the raised gangway, legs apart, hands on his hips, head high. It was a look that suggested he was unaccustomed to this invitation being declined.

Cue an obliging volley of whoops, whistles and vigorous table-banging.

'We go up front,' he bellowed. 'I have guitar. We have jolly singalong!'

The diners, one or two rubbing over-stuffed stomachs, headed for the foredeck. James and Adele held hands, unwilling or unable to let go of one another.

'Aren't you coming?' trilled Lilly.

Apart from Brenda, only one other person remained at the table – Turner; or perhaps not quite Turner, more his sickly, subdued alter-ego.

Turner had barely touched his dinner. For upwards of an hour, he'd pushed a couple of lettuce leaves and a teaspoon of yoghurt around a plate. He succeeded in disposing of three vodkas, but these had made little impact on his general demeanour. The gregarious party animal was a shrivelled husk, eyes bloodshot, hands twitching.

'No, you're alright,' replied Brenda. 'I'm going to stay back here for a while.'

Turner looked up, his lips tightening.

'You look like you need some help – pharmaceutically speaking,' said Brenda, deploying her most empathetic tone. The promise of chemical assistance should get him onside.

'You've got something? Brenda, babe, whatever you got, I need it.' The follow-through smile was less charmer, more starving street-urchin.

'Stay here,' said Brenda. She took the few steps to her cabin, returning with a bottle of cloudy, milk-like liquid and a packet of capsules.

'Here,' she said, passing the bottle across to Turner. 'This'll turn you around. You're not supposed to drink with it though.' She watched as Turned necked the whole bottle, swilling back the remnants of his cocktail glass to wash it down. 'Still, you're a big boy, I'm sure you know what you're doing.'

'It's disgusting,' rasped Turner, dragging the back of his hand across his mouth. 'It's gotta do some good. What is it?'

'K&M. Kaolin and morphine,' said Brenda.

'Morphine?' queried Turner.

'Don't get too excited. It's an over-the-counter treatment,' said Brenda. 'But you should probably stop drinking. The two don't mix well.'

'What else you got?' he asked, pointing to the pack of capsules.

'These? They'll help too, but you shouldn't take them all at the same time and not with booze either.'

'Give me a couple,' said Turner. 'For later.'

Brenda dropped two capsules into his outstretched hand and he immediately swallowed them. He waved to the cook who was resting, feet up, in the salon below. 'Get me a large brandy, will you.' He turned to Brenda, 'and for you?'

'I'll have the same.'

'And another for the lady,' he shouted to the cook.

Brenda pretended to inspect her fingernails as she probed her conscience for a flicker of guilt. She'd warned him three times about mixing drink and drugs. It wasn't her responsibility that he chose to ignore her – even though she knew he would. Her conscience was clear. Clear enough.

From the bow came the sound of Kaptan Barbar's guitar being tuned. Then two chords strummed and a coarse vocal took flight across the bay. It was at once resonant and raw, like rusty corrugated iron wrapped in burlap. A wave of whooping and hollering settled and rose again as Kaptan Barbar fired up a rousing sea-shanty to get the party going.

The chef brought two brandy glasses to the table, poured a measure into each and deposited a dish of peanuts. He set a line of tealights in glasses along the centre of the table. This added an unexpected touch of the romantic, one which Brenda could exploit.

'Thank you,' she said.

'Leave it here,' instructed Turner. The cook set the bottle between them.

Turner picked up his glass, threw his head back and downed it in one. He unscrewed the cap on the bottle and poured a refill. Brenda cupped her own in both hands, circling it to swirl the syrupy liquor and allow it to warm.

'I gotta pee,' said Turner. 'Don't go anywhere.' Holding the table, he levered himself to his feet and clomped down the steps towards the cabins. As she waited Brenda swirled and swirled her brandy glass and gazed into the night. Moonlight glanced off the water, casting shivering patterns across the canvas above her head. In the distance she could just make out where the sea met the land. The dark shadow of uneven hills was broken by a speckle of lights from dwellings and the occasional car gliding through the night. Where the outline of the hilltops broke against indigo sky, a festivity of stars spattered the natural canvas. On the foredeck, Kaptan Barbar launched into a soulful melody and as his audience fell to silence, from the nearby shore a million cicadas became his chorus. On another night, it would have been... perfect.

It was five minutes before Turner returned. When he did so, eyes bulging, his breathing was tight and shallow. As he sat he sniffed sharply, wrinkling his nose and blinking. He took a swig from his glass and exhaled a hissing breath through his teeth.

'What you said,' he began. 'What you said, after lunch. What did you mean by it?'

11

THE POWDER SHOOTS upwards like a hundred thousand shotgun pellets, connecting with the fragile blood vessels at the back of his nasal passage, dead centre between his eyes. It uploads into his system and screams through his veins. He wants to get back upstairs and get under Brenda's skin but he can't stand up so easily so he has to sit on the cot until things stabilise. He's used to handling his shit better than this. Must be the ocean's swell, crippling his sense of balance.

His mind is foggy, probably from the pills, but he's still sharp enough to work her; find out what she thinks she knows – if anything. Most likely she's trying to push his buttons with nothing to back it up. He hasn't given anyone a reason to suspect him of anything. He's been a perfect gentleman, the perfect holiday companion. He's had them eating out of his hand.

But there's something about her, he can't put his finger on it. And what with the stuff she came out with, it's been gnawing at him and he can't get past it.

He can move now and he's feeling strong again. He can deal with this like he deals with everything. Holding on to the shelf, he hauls himself to his feet and makes his way out to the deck. Christ, the boat is still rocking. At least the nausea has gone.

She's still at the table and there's a look in her eye; steely, kind of sexy too. But that's ridiculous. She's a heaving lump, must be years older too; how is that ever sexy? But there's that something – that thing you can't put your finger on. He runs his tongue over his bottom lip. Was she coming on to him on the beach? If so he could always play along, figure out what she's after then maybe give her one to shut her up.

He sits back down, because he needs to know where she's coming from and why she baited him. He needs to know if he's put himself at risk; if she's a problem he has to deal with. This is serious, so he goes straight for it.

'What you said, after lunch. What did you mean by it?'

'I'd have thought that was clear.'

'You're going to have to spell it out for me,' he says, still opting for friendly over threatening, but it's a close call. 'Humour me.'

'Ok,' she says and she takes a breath. 'Look around you, all the good people on this holiday. There are one or two exceptions, but most of them hold back. They wait for others to get things going then they go along. They don't want to be thought of as too... anything. They're afraid of earning the disapproval of strangers. Maybe it's shyness, lack of confidence. You might say they're afraid of life.'

What she's saying is true – he knows it. They're the lemmings. Even with that computer salesman bobbing around, he knows he's been the centre of their universe all week and he's hardly broken a sweat. He's had whoever he wanted – men and women – eating out of his hand, like people always do when he turns it on. He can see it from the way they look at him, how they smile, laugh at his jokes, trail along after him to lunch, to the bars and clubs.

'But then there's you,' she continues, 'and me.'

He's perplexed. This anomaly of womanhood – lardy fat and sweating one minute, fabulous and sensual the next, by days bookish and remote, by night a social butterfly – insists on aligning herself with him.

'You and me?' he says, realising too late he sounds like a simpleton.

'Yes,' she continues. 'I saw it in you the first night; actually, before that, at the airport.' Some kind of a non-smiling smile breaks across her face; the look is a cross between Victoria Beckham and the Mona Lisa. Like she's stumbled on a bag stuffed with money but doesn't want anyone else to notice.

'What did you see in me?' he asks. He wants to hear her say it. Her acknowledgement of his potency is tweaking at his cock.

'You go for it – life, what you want – you grab it by the balls. Life is all about the challenge for you. You crave an explosion of experience and you don't care how you get it. You're not a passenger – you don't wait for the bus. You make things happen.'

'I do,' he concurs, gulping from his glass. As her words suffuse his consciousness his ego swells. She seems to get what he's about. Instead of anxiety at the prospect of being seen – of being known – so clearly, the feeling overwhelming him is strange and unwelcome, but he can't escape it. It's *relief*. For once, he's not alone.

'It's not only about being at the centre of things,' she continues, her voice a caress against his shredded senses. 'You don't let anything get in your way.'

'I see what I want and I take it,' he says. 'That's how it works.'

'And screw the consequences?'

'No,' he corrects. 'Manage the consequences.'

'Manage – that's a neat perspective,' she says, smiling right into his eyes, sharp and soft at once. He notices her voice has evolved a hypnotic timbre. 'So maybe when what you want isn't – oh, you know – entirely... kosher. You have to be mindful of not getting – what might we say...?'

'Made?'

'Made,' she echoes. 'That's the perfect word.'

He gulps more brandy and refills his glass. The chaos of pharmaceuticals, alcohol and coke jolts through his body like a chain of electrical surges. His vision drifts, fuzzy one moment, ice-clear the next. For a second, there are two Brendas, then three, then one again.

'You don't get *made*,' he slurs, 'unless you get careless.'

She's playing with her pendant, a faceted, pear shaped crystal, twirling it between her fingers. He's mesmerised by the way it catches the light from the moon and the flickering candle flames and showers it around the boat in a blaze of refracted light. It twirls round and around in her fingers, first one way then the other, slowly at first then faster and faster.

'I can see the real you,' she continues; her voice is mellifluous. 'You have what some people might see as extreme needs; drives and urges you don't ignore. You entertain them, you feed them. It's like a mission for you, to respond to what your body – and your mind – demands. Certain men have to do that – be who they are, meet their own needs, wherever it takes them.'

The way she looks at him – he knows this look. It's the one that says she respects him, even admires him; admires the way he hunts down what he wants and takes it. She's a stranger, yet with every word she validates him.

And she's coming on to him hard, pushing at him. But it's not the desperate flirting of a woman past her prime. In fact it's not flirting at all, more a meeting of minds. And it's putting him in the zone.

He's connecting, and it feels good. As he gazes into the crystal as it flashes and flickers and twirls in front of his eyes he can hardly make out her face any more; just an aura and a voice, soft and low. It draws him closer, like a magnet he can't pull away from – doesn't want to pull away from. His breathing steadies for the first time in hours; the taut cliffs of his shoulders release and in a moment he's hardly aware of, her undulating voice seems no longer to be coming from the other side of the table, but from inside his own head.

It's such a relief, to relax and yield.

12

'YOU'RE SHARP,' BRENDA continued. 'I imagine most people underestimate you. I don't though. I know what I see.'

His eyes homed in on the crystal teardrop as she spun it clockwise then anticlockwise, casting a thousand rainbow shards of light into orbit around her.

'You have pinpoint focus,' she continued. 'You focus on the light, focus on the thing that matters to you.'

Round and around it spun as his eyes locked on to it.

'You focus your mind. The world goes round and around, round and around, but you keep your focus on the light. The colours and the light bring such a sense of peace to you – a sense of release and openness.' She watched his suppressed synapses calibrating her instructions. 'You're so peaceful; you can let every muscle in your body relax.' She pressed on. 'Your arms, your hands, to the tips of your fingers. Your shoulders, your neck—' His head dropped forward then suddenly jerked upwards. His eyes jolted open and he glared at her.

'I don't believe it. You're trying to hypnotise me!'

'Oh, that's funny,' she said, camouflaging her dismay. 'Why would I want to hypnotise you?' Even loaded and disoriented, he'd fought it. It was worth a try, but it would have been almost too easy.

'To get me to talk,' he said.

'What about?'

'Oh—' Turner hesitated, as if confused by his own thoughts. 'I don't know, whatever.'

'No need for hypnosis,' Brenda said, forcing sensuality into her tone. 'You've been longing to talk to me.'

'You think?'

'I know. You're curious; you can't work me out and you don't like it.' She arranged a confident smile across her features.

'What makes you think I give a shit about you?'

'You've been in your cabin all day feeling sick as a dog. Yet here I am and here you are. You've forced down a cocktail of drugs to keep yourself going. That wasn't to join in a singalong.'

Turner's forehead glistened with sweat. He wiped a hand across it and shook his head, as if to restore his senses.

'You think you're one smart bitch, don't you?'

'No,' Brenda said. 'But I don't miss much.'

'So?'

'So, you're maxed out on pharmaceuticals – over-the-counter and whatever else you've taken. Coke?' She didn't wait for a response. Turner sniffed, wiping a thumb across his nose. 'And you've drunk enough booze to sink an armada.'

'Says you.'

'You're obviously used to it,' she responded, 'but everyone has their limits, even you.'

'I'm not even close,' he said, throwing back his head and emptying the glass down his throat in one giant gulp as if to prove a point. A few bubbles of drool appeared at the corner of his mouth.

'Maybe I was trying to save you – from yourself. A non-invasive remedy.'

'What, hypnosis?' he grizzled.

'That word sounds so... *light-entertainment*. I prefer to think of it as relaxation – deep relaxation. It's a great way to get someone to, oh, you know, loosen up, let go a bit.'

'I don't know jack shit about hypnosis,' Turner retorted. Brenda winced at his inadvertent use of her sister's name. Focus, focus, she ordered herself.

'You know about getting people to let go though, don't you?'

He stared at her, unblinking, the forefinger of his right hand picking away at a hangnail, flaring red and peeling from his thumb.

'In many ways,' she continued, 'hypnosis is a bit like, well, drugs – tranquilisers or sedatives. If you use it properly it can help with nerves, stress, anxieties, addictions, that sort of thing.'

'And if you use it improperly?'

'You can have someone docile and biddable in a few seconds. You can make them do anything you want. Then you can see to it they can't remember a thing afterwards. You know what I mean, don't you?'

Their eyes connected across the table. His mouth twitched, tightened, and she was glad there was an expanse of wood separating them.

Laughter ebbed and flowed as Kaptan Barbar hammered out tune after tune on his guitar, accompanying himself in a half singing, half shouting vocal. The guests joined in when they recognised a song and when they didn't they clapped, thumped and stamped to keep the rhythm.

Turner bellowed for the chef to bring more brandy. When he failed to respond, Turner dragged himself out of his chair and stumbled down into the salon. He threw the cushions off the banquette, lifted the seat and burrowed in the clutter of its contents.

It would have been easier had Turner been more receptive to her little play with the crystal. But with a mind like his – especially with a mind like his – there were other strategies. Quietly, Brenda pulled her mobile phone from her pocket, placed it on the table, tapped 'record voice message' then slid it under a stray napkin left over from dinner. Then she threw the contents of her glass overboard. This would take a while and she needed a cool head.

'Bingo,' she heard him say and a moment later he clambered triumphant from the salon, an unopened bottle of spirit held aloft like a trophy. The most reliable way to get any man to keep on drinking was to hint he that should stop.

Turner dropped into his seat, his lungs expelling a heave of alcoholic breath across the table. He cracked the screw-top and held the bottle out. She presented her empty glass. Turner's arm swayed as he poured, leaving a sticky trail across the table. He poured for himself, clashing the bottle against his glass as he did so. He downed the contents in two gulps and poured again.

'Tell me something,' said Brenda. 'If you're so sure I've got nothing, what are you still doing here? Why aren't you in your cabin nursing your nauseated carcass?'

'Maybe... you interest me too.' He said it as if the words surprised him, almost as much as they surprised her.

'You haven't made your mind up about me yet?'

'I haven't,' Turner concurred. He sighed and took another gulp from his glass. 'You didn't buy it then?'

'Buy what?'

'Back on the beach. My tragic upbringing.'

'You over-egged the pudding,' Brenda replied. 'There might be a grain of truth here and there, but you dress it up too far. You can't help yourself. I guess it works though. Makes a certain type of woman want to rescue you?'

'It does,' he said, his eyes narrowing.

'I don't need the bullshit,' continued Brenda, on a roll now. 'Like I said before, I *get* you. I get what you're about. More than that, I'm intrigued by who you are. You're good looking and successful. You're clearly intelligent. But then there's an edge. It's that part of you that's so unexpected, that's what's... interesting... to me.' He stared unblinking into her eyes, his gaze intense and intimidating. Was he ready? 'So how about the truth, Turner – the real truth?' It was the first time she'd said his name all evening. It grazed her vocal chords like acid.

'You're some kind of a bitch,' Turner drawled, with something that was probably meant to be a smile. 'But I appreciate directness and I like a challenge. Shit, but you're growing on me.' His glass drained, he took a swig from the half-empty bottle.

'So?'

'You were right. Mine was an ordinary, pitifully dull childhood; a semi in suburbia, box trees and bay windows; a father who washed his own car and a mother who spent her weekends cooking for the freezer; They didn't do drugs and they didn't do shoplifting.'

'Where did the drugs and the shoplifting fit in?'

'Patience, sweetie, I'll get to that.' Turner's eyes narrowed. 'So I was wretched, bored to death. School was tedium, lessons so dull I was embarrassed for the teachers. Breaking the rules was so easy it wasn't even fun. And at home the happy-clappy parenting made me want to stick someone.' Turner held his fist aloft and made repeated stabbing motions in the air.

'That's an extreme thought for a young boy,' said Brenda.

'Is it?' he replied, as if the idea hadn't crossed his mind before. 'I thought about it a lot. I worked out all the detail until I had it perfect in my mind. I'd imagine my parents in that squeaky bed of theirs. I'd wait until he'd finished his business and she'd stopped making those little, baby *oh, oh, oh's* she dished out when she wanted it all to end. You know how women are.'

'No,' said Brenda.'

'You all fake it. You think men don't know that it's all an act for them. Anyhow, it was my dad she cheated all those years. He was the patsy. That doesn't happen to me.'

'What happens to you?' said Brenda.

'Don't you want to hear what I planned for my folks?'

'Go on,' said Brenda. He was rolling now, desperate to showboat.

'I'd catch them right when they were helpless – him all out of breath and panting, her looking into his eyes like he'd actually done something for her. Then I'd do it, with a blade from the knife block in the kitchen; I'd stick them both, him first, then her.' Teeth gritted, Turner sawed the air with his clenched fist. 'Then I'd stand and watch until they went cold.' He paused.

'There you go,' he said at last, bringing the bottle hard down on the table. 'That's what a cosy middle-class upbringing and a good education does for you. It was all their fault.'

'Is that what you figured? Why?'

'They were in my way. They made everything safe, too comfortable, I hated them for it.'

'Did you kill them?' Brenda asked, struggling to deliver the impression of excited curiosity. She scanned his face for clues, for once uncertain of his response.

'No of course not,' he said, a fine spray of spittle casting across the table. 'That would have been stupid. You see stories in the news all the time about idiot sons who do their parents in. It never turns out right for them.'

'So what did you do?'

'I stayed out of their way. I was still a child after all, technically speaking. Then at around twelve or thirteen, I figured out what my dick was for and that, you know, commanded a significant allocation of my attention. Then I started sampling the shit on offer at the school gates.'

'What? Hot dogs? Ice cream?'

'Brenda made a joke.' Turner smiled, a lopsided half-grimace.

'How did that work out for you?'

'I went a bit crazy for a while. I tried everything and most of it got me high. But you can't maintain a habit on pocket money.'

'Is that where the petty crime came in?'

'Jeez, bitch! You wanted this, but I'm doing it my way. Don't you push me now.' Turner rose to his feet, his chair fell back. He leaned across the table towards her, fist extended. Brenda's body jerked as she fought its instinctive response. Did he see her flinch? Blood throbbed in her ears. She lifted her glass and took a slow sip, buying a few seconds. As she lowered it, her eyes connected with his. Forcing herself to visualise Emilio across the table from her, Brenda managed to get her eyes co-operating with her lips and delivered a smouldering response.

He withdrew, his eyes still locked on hers. He retrieved his chair and flopped into it. Brenda let out what was left of her breath. Keep going, keep going.

'Still, none of this is a revelation. A teenage boy plays with himself and does a bit of dope. So very *so-so*. I want to know what makes Turner tick and you're still playing safe with stories about stuff that never happened. You haven't shown me anything real yet.' She needed more – much more.

'You have everything going for you,' she continued, 'looks, mental strength. I don't know what you do for work, but you carry yourself like a successful man.'

'I am a successful man,' he responded. 'I hustle. I part the rich from their money and I'm good at it.' He leant back in his chair and put his hands behind his head, interlocking his fingers. 'Big ticket investors, the moneyed classes.'

'All very respectable?' Brenda queried.

'Depends what you mean by respectable,' Turner responded with a snort. 'I'm a broker in the City; it's the upper echelons of the hustling game, but it's hustling all the same.' He struggled over the word *echelons*. 'It might not be proper in some people's eyes, but it's legal.'

'How's that working for you?'

'Pretty solid. Promotions, the kind of bonuses that make the news. All the trappings.' He picked up his glass again and waved it from side to side as if to emphasise the scale of his success. A trickle of its contents overflowed along his fingers.

'That's nice. But is it enough for you?'

'What do you mean?'

'Success. Money. Is it enough – for a man like you?'

'What, my Aston, my Shoreditch penthouse? Is it enough?' He paused, looked out across the bay for a moment, smiling. 'Yes and no. It's great, of course. But... sometimes it seems too... easy.'

'And when it's easy, there's no sense of achievement.'

'You're right.' Turner banged his glass on the table so hard that it made Brenda jump. Did he notice? He slopped more spirit into it from the bottle. 'No challenge, that's the problem.'

'How come?'

'It's easy to get what I want. People can't keep up with me. You know, it's not so hard to make money when you know what you're doing.'

'Most people would appreciate a little *easy*.'

'Not me. When there's no challenge, all it is, is an... un... an... un... unremitting daily grind.' With each mouthful of liquor his speech grew more laboured, each word more imprecise. Brenda feared for the recording and prodded at the phone under the napkin, moving it a few inches closer to her target.

'So you need to get your buzz in other ways.'

Turner stared at her; a penetrating gaze, eyes engorged with arrogance; his wariness was submerging under a hunger for recognition. A sheen of sweat coated his cheeks. She stared back, unblinking. He was at a tipping point. If he went for it, she'd get what she needed. But rage crackled beneath his skin.

'You're a piece of work,' he grizzled under his breath as he at last averted his eyes. She waited. Minutes passed before his ego took the helm again.

'So, I challenge myself, okay?' he blurted, the words finally breaking free of his mouth. 'Certain scenarios *excite* me and I pursue them. I do it to feel *connected*. What's the harm in that?'

'What scenarios?' Brenda held her breath.

'You keep saying you know. You tell me.'

She wanted to beat the table with her fists and cry, the scenarios where you dope a defenceless woman in front of everybody, then cart her off somewhere, do god knows what to her and then revel in your violation and her confused ignorance the next day; but whatever got said, he had to say it, for the recording.

Turner's head swayed, his addled brain-cells would be struggling with what to say, what to hold back. Even drunk, it took time to prize open the trapdoor on a mind like his – but time was not on Brenda's side. Soon the party on the foredeck would break up and if she didn't have what she needed by then it would all have been for nothing.

'I thought you were smarter than this, but you still don't get it, do you? I want to see what the little boy who pictured murdering his own mum and dad has become. I'd imagined there might be more to you than childhood fantasies you couldn't even follow through on. I want to assess if the grown man is any kind of a match for me. Never mind what you need, I want to see if you've got what I need, if you've got anything for me. So are you going to tell me something real or shall I take myself to sleep?' She swept her cabin key off the table as if preparing to depart.

He shifted in his seat. Again he seemed to be weighing something up. He took a deep inward breath and the air hissed through his teeth.

'It'll shock you,' he said. 'More than that, if I tell you, there'll be no going back. And you need to know, if you want to play this game – and I'm serious about this – you get into bed with me on this, you don't get out. You understand?'

'Of course I understand you,' whispered Brenda. His ego drove him forward; it trumped the vestige of caution that lay buried under the landfill of drugs and alcohol.

She could smell victory. Her heart pounded against her breastbone – would he notice? Adrenaline surged, delivering a swell of out-of-body giddiness. She knew all about these physiological responses. The racing pulse; the trickle of sweat which glistened in her cleavage; short breaths from a parched throat. She was well aware of that intense place that fear or stress or excitement – which was it this time – took you. It was exactly the way she'd felt...

As the realisation hit Brenda, the breath was all but sucked out of her.

It was exactly the way she'd felt... when she'd gone far beyond where she had a right to be, to excavate the truth about Jack's husband and blurt it out to her sister without regard to the consequences.

She read Jack's letter, so drenched in blame and condemnation, every day. But she hadn't connected with it until that moment. For Brenda, it had been about the thrill – the thrill of the kill. The sudden self-knowledge yanked at her like a choke chain.

13

'THERE!' SHOUTED TURNER, elated. 'I knew you weren't for real! I've spooked you, haven't I? You aren't up for this, and you never were. You're a fucking fraud.'

Brenda glared at Turner, the whole evening, all her efforts hanging over a precipice. She wanted to run and hide from the shame of what had just slammed into her. She needed time to process – to recover. But she was so close, too close to quit. She drew a hand across her cheek, as if to wipe away the streak of tears. There were none, they were all in her mind.

'I need a comfort break, that's all,' she rasped. 'Don't go anywhere.'

She stood. Realising she couldn't recover the phone under the napkin without drawing attention she said a silent prayer that it would still be there when she returned. Down in her cabin, Brenda splashed cold water around her neck. Gradually the blotches across her décolletage subsided. The sting of guilt still prickled.

She dug the letter out of her bag for the second time that day and read it as slowly as she could bear. The waves slapped against the hull; Kaptan Barbar pounded his guitar overhead; feet stamped and hands clapped as Brenda rocked back and forth, clutching the crumpled pages and fighting the urge to scream.

When she could put it off no longer, she re-applied her lipstick and returned to the table.

'Welcome back,' Turner said.

'You'll have to go much further than that to shock me.' Brenda wasn't going to let anyone else down tonight.

'Do you want this then?'

'I do,' Brenda insisted. Get it and get out. He was pushing it to her now, no stopping. She just had to get out of her own way. 'Give it all up,' she commanded.

The noise from the foredeck had stilled to a melancholy chanting. Turner cleared his throat and hawked a gob of spittle over the side of the boat.

'A man like me,' he began at last, 'needs the thrill of constant challenge. I must channel that need, else I'd go crazy. If I didn't, never mind fantasising, I might actually kill someone.'

'So it's a survival strategy?'

'Kind of.'

'What else?'

'A buzz. I have to have it.'

'I knew it. Like an addict?'

'If you like.'

'So what do you do?'

Silence.

'What do you do?' A second time. She willed him to respond. She needed this to be over.

'I *take* women.'

'So?' Brenda held her breath.

'I *take* women,' he repeated, 'without them knowing.' He stared directly into her eyes, challenging Brenda for a reaction. One corner of his mouth lifted and his tongue, shiny with spittle, pushed outward and ran across his lower lip from left to right, leaving it glistening grotesquely in the moonlight. He shifted in his seat, his hand pressing into his groin. The confession stimulated him and he needed to see it had the same effect on her. Only once he did would he give up the detail. He must be made to believe. It might not be the professional approach, but this wasn't a police interview room; there were no rules here.

'I know,' she said slowly, her voice slow and sensual. 'Keep going.' She forced down a swell of disgust, parted her lips and allowed her eyes to meet his. He drew himself upright in his chair, puffed up like a peacock.

'It took me some time to arrive at an... activity that achieved my objective, in sufficient style, whilst allowing me to... you know... mitigate the risk of exposure.'

Activity. Objective. Mitigate. He spoke slowly, annunciating every syllable, his words disconnected and clinical. Knowing what kind of a mind was at work, she should not be surprised.

'What do you mean?'

'I had to explore a few possibilities, weigh up the pros and cons, before I settled on the perfect challenge.'

'It's a challenge? To have sex with women without them knowing?'

'Not the sex,' he said. 'The execution, the process.' He licked his lips again.

'Explain it to me,' said Brenda, manufacturing a look of lust to her eyes, sweeping her hand across her neckline as if to wipe away the glow of sex. 'Every detail, so I can feel what you feel. You understand, don't you, what that'll do for me?'

He looked at her for several seconds, all the while his hand in a steady motion out of sight below the tabletop.

'You know, this isn't about being some kind of a monster,' he said at last. 'It's more... process driven than that. Each time is a project, an exercise that requires... stuff.'

'What stuff, Turner?' she said, her voice solid and assertive.

'Intellectual skill, a knowledge of the environment, tactics. Stuff like that. And the practical application of some *under*-the-counter pharmaceuticals.'

'What's the process? Where's the challenge?'

'The challenge is to get my mark to a state, chemically speaking, and a place, geographically speaking, where I can do the business, have my photo-op and get out, without leaving a trail. It's about the right place, right time; making the right kind of moves, an approach that opens up the opportunity; it's about getting the information I need so I can decide whether to do it at her place or somewhere else; it's about timing and execution and escape. It's *all* about tactics. That's what makes it fun.'

'Fun?'

'Fun, exciting – whatever. Adren... adrenalin rush. The buzz, yeah? Like I'm a tiger hunting prey; stalking, circling, pouncing at the right moment. That's the thrill. Don't you get it? The sex isn't the thing. It's... kind of a bonus.'

Brenda struggled not to choke on the lump which engulfed her throat.

'Tell me about the... projects.'

'What, all of them?' He sniggered. 'That would take us all night and you remember what I said, don't you? We're getting into bed together on this. Now you know what you know, now we're in it together – complicit – we're going to have... so much more fun.' His hand continued its rhythmic rise and fall between his thighs. His glass empty, he reached for Brenda's, gulped down the remainder and pushed it back across the table towards her.

'What's yours is mine, right?' he said.

Before he could let go the glass, Brenda reached out and cupped her hands around his. Her thumb pressed firmly into his, stroking back and forth.

'I told you. I want to feel what you felt – when you did it,' Brenda replied. 'Bare outlines isn't enough, I need detail. You want me? You're going to give me some... stimulus. You will give me what I need – all of it, everything.'

Beyond the conventional perceptions of hypnosis, suggestion came in many forms. Brenda could get results from them all.

'Well damn. You really are getting off on this!' exclaimed Turner. He wet his lips with his tongue again in an exaggerated gesture. So dry was Brenda's own tongue, it seemed glued to the roof of her mouth. She needed water but she couldn't interrupt the lava flow of his ego.

'Tell me what you did to them,' she said, her parched throat forcing an unexpected huskiness into her tone. The scorch of lust fizzled in Turner's eyes.

'The first one was a temp from work,' he began. 'I don't remember much about it. I was more nervous than excited. There's a confession for you. It was one I had to get out of the way – break my *drug-fuck duck*, you might say.' He laughed to himself as he recalled the memory.

'What happened?' said Brenda, for the recording, for the recording.

'I took her home, I got her into the bedroom, I fucked her, I took a picture, I left. She didn't have a clue.' Turner laughed. 'What else is there?'

'You tell me,' said Brenda. 'But that's nowhere near enough. I expected so much more from you. I thought you were the real deal.'

'Okay, okay,' said Turner. 'You want it? Fine. I picked her because I knew she lived alone. It was a Friday, someone's birthday, so everyone went for drinks after work. It's not my usual thing, but—'

'But what?' Brenda said. Keep the momentum, keep it moving.

'I'd... acquired my first stash of roofies that week and I was itching to give them a try.'

'What happened?'

'The bar was crowded and it was tricky getting the stuff in her drink. But I did it and it felt... amazing. From that point, I knew it was going to work. I still get that buzz even now. I found her address and door keys in her handbag. By then she didn't know which way was up and I had to walk her out fast, before she'd need to be carried. We made it on to the street and I shoved her in the back of a minicab. Filthy, it was, stank of sweat and curry.'

'Now you're getting it,' Brenda said. 'I... appreciate the detail. Go on.'

'Detail? How's this for detail?' Cold laughter hissed between Turner's teeth. 'I told the cabbie she was my girlfriend and she'd had one too many. Then what d'you know? We only passed the whole journey sympathising with each other about our girlfriends' shortcomings. Two blokes together, moaning about our bitches!'

'And what about when you got her home?' Brenda whispered, as if the words didn't want to escape her mouth.

'They're not supposed to remember a thing afterwards, that's what I was told. But I wasn't so sure that first time, so I covered her face with her shirt. Then I was just careful. I didn't want to leave any... evidence behind.'

'That was it?'

'Pretty much. She was quiet, just the way I like it. But you know the wildest thing? On the Monday she came looking for me at the office. I saw her come out of the lift and get directed over to my desk. I thought, heck, I'm in trouble now. But she only wanted to pay me back the cab fare! She was embarrassed because she thought she'd got drunk and I'd cared enough to see her home. How about that?'

'So you pulled it off, that first time,' Brenda said, pressing her sadness back down. 'What next?'

Number two was older, a bit too old, to be honest – no offense.'

'None taken.' Brenda was fairly sure there was little or no age gap between them. That she could still be stung by an offhand remark from this man astounded her.

'I met that one on a dating website. I've done five or six off websites.'

'How do you work that?'

'I fake an identity. You can be anyone you want on the internet.'

'And?'

'I put up a profile, nice normal guy, *blah, blah.*'

'Do you post a picture of yourself?'

'You think I'm an idiot? Of course not!'

'So how come they go for you?'

'Oh, this part is good. I had to congratulate myself when I hit on this idea.' Turner leaned back in his chair, poured the dregs from the bottle into his mouth and throated it. He let the chair drop forward and stared into Brenda's cleavage. 'I downloaded this picture of a cat – cute, fluffy, big eyes – and posted that instead. My headline was, *Love me, love my cat.* I'm a cat lover and that makes me irresistible to women!'

'Do you like cats?' Brenda asked.

'No,' said Turner. 'But women love men who love cats. It's a tool in the toolkit. Hell, it doesn't work on everyone but it works often enough. It works on the type I'm looking for.'

'What type?'

'Quiet, shy, not many friends, not so sure of themselves. I don't like the noisy ones or slappers. They have to be a bit demure, private.'

'Why demure and private?'

'I don't want the women who would give it to me anyway. I want the ones who wouldn't.'

His words pierced the still night air like shards of glass all aimed into Brenda's heart and all pricking and stabbing away at once.

'So what happens when you find one? What do you do then?'

'I do the email thing to warm them up. I make sure they know I don't like jeans and I love it when a girl shows off her legs – that guarantees I can get what I want without having to fight my way in. Then I arrange to meet them somewhere where they don't know anyone. They're so nervous and so buzzed to be wanted, they'll let anything happen to them, *ya-da-ya-da*.' Cold eyes challenged her for a response.

'Then what?' she asked. Keep him on the leash, tethered to his egotistical confession.

'I get them home, I give it to them whichever way I want on their own bed, I take the snapshot and I leave. Then I send them a brush-off email and I'm done. It's easy to evaporate from a dating website too; no trace no trail. They don't have a clue what happened so there's no comeback.'

'Are you sure?'

'I'm still here, aren't I? Three years and counting.'

'Three years? And it still challenges you?' asked Brenda.

'At first, yes,' said Turner wistfully. 'Now, not so much.'

'So what now? Have you moved on?' She noticed his hand had sunk back down against his groin. Once again it motioned up and down with a steady rhythm. She sipped at her drink, desperate for the purity of a glass of water but not wanting to interrupt the moment.

'I mix it up a bit. But mostly I've moved on to what you might call face-to-face projects,' he said. 'It's more risky, but the potential for jeopardy makes things more... engaging. Every time, a test of my mettle.' Turner's head drooped again as he battled the onslaught of alcohol.

'What kind of face-to-face projects,' she said, her voice clear and assertive again. She would do it; she would get to what happened to her friends, even if it killed her.

'I trawl the internet. I find places advertising meet-ups for lonely hearts – there are dozens every night. There are so many, I've never been to the same place twice. And I've been at this game a while, so that's a lot of lonely hearts, believe me. You get maybe fifty, a hundred or more in a room at once, all eyeing each other up, looking for love. That's a joke for starters. I go for the ones who are properly on their own. They're easy to spot – they hide in the toilets to get their nerves in check. I pick a spot nearby and eventually they come out. It's like shooting fish in a barrel.' He laughed, cold and disassociated.

'And when you get one?' said Brenda.

'A friendly smile; an easy question – a micron up the scale from *do you come here often*, but not too far because they can't handle it. I have to find out if they live alone too, don't forget.'

'I imagine they're relieved to have someone to talk to.'

'They are. I buy the drinks of course. Talking of which... I need more medication.' He grabbed the table so hard it grazed against the wooden deck and Brenda feared they would attract the attention of the foredeck singalong. So far nobody had interrupted them. How much longer could that last?

Turner heaved himself down the stairs to raid the drinks store again, returning with another bottle. This one she recognised; raki, generally her tipple of choice on sultry Turkish nights. Turner fell into his chair, cracked the seal on the bottle and poured the two glasses. He took a swig from his own then shoved the other one towards her.

'Are you man enough for this?' he said.

'I'll have water with mine,' said Brenda.

'Pussy,' said Turner, a half-smile creeping across his features. Her demand necessitated another laborious climb down the steps into the salon. Moments later he emerged, a bottle of water with the top removed in his hand. He stood behind Brenda, pressing himself into her back and forced the chilled bottle, damp with condensation down the low neckline of her t-shirt and between her breasts. Was it the shock of the ice-cold bottle or the chill she felt at being so close to him that made her shudder? Turner laughed, withdrawing the bottle. He flopped into his chair and slopped the water into Brenda's glass until it all but overflowed. The liquor clouded and she brought it to her lips. She took several gulps. This was tougher and more painful than she'd signed up for.

'Good?' said Turner, a curious smile tugged at his mouth.

'A favourite,' said Brenda, gulping again. She was beyond trying to keep a cool head. She craved the wraparound comfort of inebriation.

'Drink up, sweetie,' whispered Turner.

She gulped again, anxious for relief from the tension. The alcohol swept through Brenda's veins, numbing her pain but diffusing her purpose. It slithered into her brain like a snake through grass. Like a snake... a snake in the grass... forked tongue, fangs loaded with venom... venom, poison... drugs. Was she...? Had he...?

Brenda's pulse fluttered like a trapped moth. She felt oddly spacey, drifting; her eyes seemed to be outside of herself, looking on. All the saliva was siphoned out of her mouth. A weak moan escaped her lips.

'You don't know, do you?' he said slowly, staring. His eyes narrowed to glassy slivers; the inky pinpricks of his irises gleamed in the candlelight.

'What?' she breathed.

'You don't know if I spiked it.' He smiled. 'Are you going under? Do you think?'

'Jesus,' she said. 'You didn't—'

'Might have,' he said. 'You're playing with me. Maybe I thought I'd play with you too. Maybe I'm going to sort you out, whether you want it or not.'

'You wouldn't,' she said, trying to sound assertive, in control. Her tongue seemed to swell in her mouth as the candle flames throbbed in time with the drumming in her chest.

'Wouldn't I?' he laughed.

'No,' she said, her mind overflowing with doubt. 'You wouldn't.'

'Ah...' he sighed. 'You want to know the truth? You're, how shall I put it? You're a big girl and I wasn't sure how it would work on you.'

'So?' Brenda held her breath. She felt as if she were drowning, spinning down into a whirlpool of her own careless fabrication. 'So?' she repeated, more insistently. Desperation laced her voice, she knew it, but she couldn't fight it.

'So you can cool your ass down. I didn't put shit in your drink.'

'Truth?'

'Scout's honour. Fucking relax.'

A panic attack. Her body had rewarded the evening's labours with a panic attack. He could have, but he hadn't. But if he had, she'd have fallen right into it. *Stupid. Stupid. Stupid.*

'I believe you,' she said, the words clinging to her constricted throat. Anxiety wrapped itself around her like a concrete cloak. She was off her guard. It wasn't the right time to be jousting with a mind like his. But this was the time she'd been given. She had to recover her ground, fast.

'Sss... so,' she hesitated. 'You've got the girl. What next?'

'It amazes me even now, how many bitches let a man they don't know buy them a drink in an open glass. It's almost a duty, to show them what a risk they're running. But they get that one the hard way. Like you nearly did,' he laughed.

Turner held his glass out, swirling it around and around, staring into it. Brenda sipped at what was left of hers, gripping it so he couldn't see how her hands trembled. It was the cheapest raki, shaken with fear, and the alcohol stung her gums. He was right. The thrill of the kill had blunted her to the risks. He'd have had her and it would have been entirely her own fault. And she would have deserved it, deserved to pay for her carelessness and over-confidence and all her other crimes. How was that for a day of reckoning?

'Then you take them home?' she continued, weakly.

'Sure, usually in a taxi. It's nice to see where they live, have a bit of a look around.'

'Whilst they're unconscious?'

'You know, they're not unconscious as such,' said Turner, brightly. 'That would be weird. They're kind of there, but not. Eyes open usually, but not seeing anything; and definitely not remembering. But I look after them.'

'What do you mean?'

'When I'm finished. I tidy them up; I wash them, sort out their clothes. Leave them looking respectable. Like they got a bit pissed and fell asleep without getting undressed. I'm not a monster.' It was the second time he'd claimed this.

'You mentioned photos,' said Brenda, forcing herself to return to his throwaway remark. 'You have photos of your... projects?'

'Sure I do,' he said. 'I take a photo, sometimes more than one. I like looking through them.'

'A bit like a trophy cabinet?'

'Exactly like a trophy cabinet.'

'What kind of photos?' she asked, clutching at this glimmer of hope. Unlike a secret recording, which would only go so far, photographs could be used by the police. Turner swigged back a mouthful of liquor from the bottle, licked his lips and grinned, broad and dirty.

'Oh, you know, naked and wide open mostly; the usual. Sometimes I get something else in the shot. Women leave stuff lying around in their bedrooms – vibes, candles. I like a little variety in my portfolio – a different look; a stocking top, a flash of colour, an accessory, you know. It helps me recall the specific occasion when I'm looking at them later.'

'Time to go... you know,' he said through a lopsided grin. As he rose from his chair, his penis full against his trousers, he staggered back into the wooden mast behind him. 'Shit, where did that come from?' he exclaimed as he struggled to regain his balance. 'Don't move an inch, I'll be back. Then it's your turn.'

Brenda sat impassively for minutes whilst Turner relieved himself. She heard him mount the steps from the salon behind her. Suddenly his massive hands were on her shoulders. Once more she had to fight the urge to flinch as he slid them downwards and cupped her breasts. A stale wave of alcohol enveloped her face as he bent close to one ear.

'Speaking of variety,' he whispered, 'I did a bloke once.'

'What?' cried Brenda.

'Gotcha!' said Turner cheerily. 'I knew I could shock you eventually. You want I tell you about it?'

'Of course,' she breathed. She should win an Oscar for her performance. She eased his hands from her breasts. How thrilling it would have been to have them there just a few days ago.

'A certain situation demanded a response. And... it was an... insightful experience too.' He lurched from one word to the next as he eased himself into the chair beside her.

'What do you mean?' She stared straight ahead as he brought his hand down on her thigh and once again drew close to her ear.

'I would say... the night I shoved a man's head face down on the ground and plundered his... passage, was one hell of a learning experience,' he hissed. That was the point I realised it wasn't only the challenge. It wasn't the thrill, and it certainly wasn't the sex. *It was the power.* I didn't even care it wasn't a woman.'

'Why did you—?'

'It was payback,' Turner interrupted. He leant back, hands behind his head.

'For what?'

'The bastard humiliated me, caused me a considerable loss of earnings and damaged my credibility. You don't let that kind of thing go for nothing.'

'What happened?'

'He's a barista at a coffee bar by the office. I was picking up my mid-morning triple and he shoved a tray of cappuccino off the counter and down my suit. I caught the whole load; four *grande* buckets.'

'Sounds like an accident to me.'

'Fucking wasn't an accident. He'd been put up to it. One of the guys at work – maybe all of them – paid him to do it.'

'You think so?'

'I know so. Look, I know how these things work. He apologised, *blah blah*, and stumped-up for my dry-cleaning. But with my suit swamped in cappuccino, I had to go home and change. I missed a meeting, lost two big-ticket investors to a colleague. Whatever he paid, the guy got his money's worth. You know though, I might even have done the same. But the barista – he had to be taught a lesson. So I taught him.'

Some kind of a sound came out of Brenda's mouth, but it wasn't a word.

'How many have there been, in total?' she said.

'Projects or photos? I'm up to number 33, but I took more than one photo sometimes, so it's probably about 20 maybe 25. I can't recall exactly.'

'Up to when?'

'Up to right now, babe,' Turner whispered. 'Up to a couple of days ago.' A note of triumph; a broad grimace of satisfaction and pride, devoid of humanity.

He'd got there at last. Soon, soon it would be over. She cleared her throat.

'Here. I knew it.' She forced her voice to co-operate; her tone once again became complicit, loaded with the pretence of admiration.

'So you were right,' he said, 'what you were poking around for on the beach. Actually it's been interesting.'

'How so?'

'It's like... it's like I scored at both ends of the *drug-fuck continuum*. At one end, I sorted out the biggest slapper on this trip. Not my usual thing, I admit, but she was begging to be dealt a lesson. Not so different from the barista.'

'And at the other end?'

'I scored my first straight-up bona-fide whiter-than-white... virgin.'

Turner's boastful, celebratory tone released a wave of nausea within Brenda. She wanted to scream. She wanted to pound her fists into his over-inflated chest.

'Adele,' she said at last. 'And Lilly.'

'Bingo. Sweetie, you're smarter than you look. How d'you figure it?'

'Educated guess,' she responded. But she'd had enough. There it was. With those words, she had proof.

'They don't know, do they? They don't have a clue, right?'

'Right.'

'See. That's the epitome of success to me. I executed those two projects under everyone's noses. Nobody knew. Careful planning, confident execution wins the day.'

'What about the pictures? Did you get pictures – of them?' Brenda fought her revulsion. She hadn't known about the photographs, but they would be vital.

Turner stared at her, his face rock-set into a scowl.

'Yes, but there's a problem,' he said at last. 'As of this afternoon, I appear to have *mislaid* my camera.'

'You've lost your camera?'

'Yes. I've lost it. Why, did you take it? Is that how come you know so much?' he said abruptly. His eyes bored deep into hers.

'No,' she said. 'I've no idea where it is. It can't have gone far, can it?'

'That's what... someone else said. But I have my suspicions. I'll handle it. I'll deal with it in the morning. You watch me. Someone's gonna pay.'

Brenda was exhausted. Her whole body seemed to be in a spasm, an internal tremor she struggled to control. She could not connect with what Turner might or might not do in the morning, in pursuit of his missing camera. She'd done enough. She'd got what was needed.

Turner sat back and smiled.

'So what do you think now,' he hissed. '*Am I the real deal or what?*'

'You're something else, I'll give you that,' said Brenda.

They sat in silence. A lilting lament, borne on Kaptan Barbar's gravelly voice, seeped into the evening air like mist and drifted across the bay, playing with the cicadas and the slop-slap of water against the hull.

'You know what comes next, don't you?' said Turner. 'Time for me to collect.'

Whatever fight Brenda had left inside her, it wasn't enough for this.

'What, now?'

'Of course now,' he grizzled.

'Are you sure?' she said, thinking as fast as her exhausted faculties would allow. She reached out for his hand again and let her thumb work his pressure point, stroking back and forth. 'I mean, you've been struggling with the motion, the up and down of the waves, that incessant swell, the swaying back and forth, that endless, undulating, rolling around, all day long. And what's it like in your cabin, so stuffy and stifling down on the water line, and it's so cramped and claustrophobic. And, well, it must reek a bit too, what with you being so... poorly today.'

'What are you saying?' He scowled, tight-lipped, on the cusp of anger.

'Wouldn't you rather collect... tomorrow?'

'Tomorrow?' he repeated, as he digested the thought.

'You've earned... what's coming,' she continued, still stroking. 'It's been... enlightening. You're going to get the full payback, I promise. But here?'

'You might have a point,' he finally admitted. 'My cabin isn't exactly wholesome at present.'

Turner's head lolled forward, mimicking the vessel's motion. As she withdrew her hand he heaved and swallowed. Beads of perspiration squeezed out across his temples as the impact of the evening's excesses tightened its grip. He reached for the stray napkin under which lay the mobile phone. Brenda got to it first, sweeping the phone up with it and slipping it unnoticed into her pocket.

'Here, let me,' she said. She poured water on to the napkin, wrung it out and passed it back to Turner. He wiped it across his forehead and heaved another nausea laden sigh. She stood, slowly, backing away the two or three paces to the steps down to the cabins. He must not follow her.

'Tomorrow,' he murmured. 'But don't sleep too easy. Happen I'll come for you anyway.' Brenda descended the stairs on tiptoes, hardly daring to breathe.

14

BORED WITH THE singalong and exhausted by both the day's activities and his disturbed thoughts, Henry excused himself from the crowd on the foredeck. His bare feet made no sound as he padded up the side aisle towards the aft deck and the steps down to the cabins. He was so quiet the two people talking at the big table did not hear him. Henry drew closer, hidden in the shadows.

He loved to listen to Brenda, providing she wasn't telling him off. Her voice made him think of warm bath towels, bowls of steaming soup, marshmallows and soft toffee bonbons. He didn't intend to pay any attention to the conversation, just immerse himself in Brenda's voice. But what he heard brought a rush of blood to his head.

Henry listened for minute after minute, mouth agape and hardly able to breathe for fear of his presence being exposed. His ears reddened and sweat oozed into his palms as Turner poured out his vile accounts to Brenda. Not only did Brenda listen; she seemed to be captivated, enthralled by the confessions. Like a nightclub hostess on a mission to fleece the gullible, she worked every seductive ploy to extract the details.

It may have fooled Turner but to Henry it was obviously an act. He knew for certain once he saw the look of disgust on Brenda's face as Turner staggered off to fetch more drink. The interplay between them wasn't so much a conversation, more an exotic dance. He knew why Turner responded, because she'd played a game like that with him only days before. This time he couldn't help but admire the way she moved in on Turner, laser-focused, acting the part as if her life depended on it. But why? What was this about? The snooping reporter inside him pleaded to be let out – there were so many questions and no answers. And he had to stay hidden.

Turner had a job holding himself together. Slopping his drinks, his head drooping one minute, arms flailing the next; his words became so slurred it was hard to make them out. But like an armour-plated tank with the enemy in its sights, Brenda rumbled on.

The music on the foredeck stopped and Kaptan Barbar encouraged an extended round of applause, cheering and whooping. An encore was cried for, but the impromptu concert would soon wind up. There was a crumpled napkin on the table. Henry thought he could see something hidden in its folds but in the near darkness he couldn't make it out. When Brenda retreated to her cabin she pocketed whatever it was.

Henry backed away a few inches to avoid being spotted. He couldn't let either of them realise he'd been listening, let alone how much he'd heard – and what he now understood. A spasm shuddered his chest.

Turner intended to deal with his missing camera problem in the morning. It wouldn't take him long to get around to Henry, maybe even put two-and-two together, especially if Veronica mentioned the camera she'd found on the table at lunch. If Turner came for him, especially after the incident with Veronica and the spilled drink, it would be... His head swarmed with images of grim TV dramas; contorted corpses, blood spatter, ligatures and lacerations... That was ridiculous, wasn't it? Or not? A chill ran through his stomach. It was one thing to play-act a bit of clumsiness but he could hardly defend himself against... Christ, if that bastard did come for him it wouldn't end well.

Turner's head lay like a boulder on the table lolling between his biceps, a grizzle escaping through his lips. Suddenly he hauled himself up, hands splayed, grabbing for the rim of the table. He lurched against the almost imperceptible motion of the lapping waters, like a skiff caught in a liner's wake. As he turned, he reached for the back of his chair but missed and stumbled towards the edge of the boat. A strained gurgle escaped his throat and he heaved a gallon of liquid vomit over the side, then swayed again, grasping for the railing. But it was too late and he was off balance, top-heavy. Turner's flailing skull thudded against the wooden frame above the railing not once, but twice, and he toppled forward, folding over the low barrier. As music once again rang out from the foredeck, Turner uttered no sound as he fell towards the water.

There was no cry for help, only a splash, like that made by a seabird diving down to catch a fish. Henry peered over the edge. Turner had dropped head down into a circle of his own viscous vomit. He lay still in the water, his face submerged, arms floating to his sides.

Henry held his breath as the seconds ticked by and waves of applause and laughter breezed from the foredeck. Turner's body drifted a few feet but appeared to be hugging the side of the boat. Still no cry for help; still no splashing to alert anyone.

He stared at the inert form for another thirty seconds to be sure, before taking the few steps down to his cabin, where he silently turned the key in the door and didn't switch on the light.

15

BRENDA CLOSED THE cabin door behind her and turned the key. She sat on the bed and only then did she let go. Silent tears of rage ran down her cheeks.

She'd kept going, working through layer after layer of depraved confessions, keeping up the pretence that she revelled in the salacious detail. It had worked, perfectly. So why did she feel so devastated? She'd interviewed dozens of people like him before, so why had this one made her feel so... dirty? It was all tangled up with Jack.

A commotion above drew her attention; people shouting, a high-pitched scream, several pairs of feet thundering back and forth; muffled *'oh my god's'* in several different voices; a woman crying.

Brenda dabbed her eyes dry, double-checking in the mirror to erase evidence of tears before stepping out of her cabin. The aft deck was a chaos of people – guests and crew. Some hung over the side of the gulet, others stood around, eyes wide. Kaptan Barbar hollered commands in Turkish and someone threw a lifebelt into the water. Someone else, waving a torch back and forth across the water, shouted 'over here'.

James ripped off his shirt and plunged into the water. Only then did Brenda look over the side. A body floated face down in the shadows close to the hull. James splashed frantically towards where the torch directed him. There were too many people straining to see what was going on, so Brenda stepped back. She looked around in vain for Turner.

The splashing and shouting moved toward the stern where the crew had let down the gangplank. Kaptan Barbar bobbed unsteadily at the foot of the fragile structure. Then, with a strength that belied his sinewy frame, he pulled and heaved at the dead-weight which James pushed upwards towards him from water. Slowly, laboriously he hauled the body clear of the waves and dragged it aboard. Kaptan Barbar rolled the mass on to its back and as she recognised the drowned man, Brenda's throat constricted.

Kaptan Barbar knelt down, linked his fingers then pressed his palms hard into the unmoving mound of Turner's chest; rhythmically he pressed and pressed, then stopped, then pressed and pressed again, all the while his lips moved as if he were muttering some kind of a prayer under his breath. Every few seconds he put his mouth against Turner's and breathed into him.

It must have been only moments but everyone held their breath as Kaptan Barbar worked on Turner. There was a choking and spluttering, a groan, a retching cough; a cry or two and hands gripping Kaptan Barbar's shoulders. Someone shouted for a blanket and as they hauled Turner upright Brenda stepped back into the shadow. More murmuring and Kaptan Barbar and Matt hooked Turner's arms over their shoulders and attempted to stand him up. It wasn't an easy manoeuvre but they dragged the semi-comatose hulk down to his cabin. As the guests followed, Kaptan Barbar shooed them away, *'Show's over, he fine. Go to bed, all go to bed'*. He would remain with his charge, leaving the cabin door ajar.

Unnoticed and unaided, James had clambered out of the water and retrieved his shirt. At the table Brenda found him alone, sipping from a glass of brandy in the chair Turner had occupied for most of the evening. His damp shirt clung to his chest, his forearms were a forest of goose-bumps. Brenda pulled out a chair and he greeted her with an ashen smile. He pushed the glass toward her, but she shook her head.

'If I'd known it was him, I'd have let the bastard drown,' he said.

FRIDAY

1

HIS EYELIDS ARE glued. As consciousness screams into his brain, he can't open them even a crack. He can hear breathing and rustling – there's someone in the room with him. He lies still, pretending to be asleep until he can figure out what to do. From the smell – sweat and saltwater – it's a man.

His clothes are clammy; the mattress is damp. He hears the water slapping against the wall beside him; he must still be on the boat. Has there been an accident? Are they sinking? His heart stutters at the thought. A swell of nausea rises as far as his gullet and an involuntary moan escapes through his nose.

'Ah, you waking up,' says a voice. It's Captain Bellyache. Why is he here? 'How you doing?'

Why the question? How's he supposed to be doing? He can't summon the energy to answer.

He raises a hand to rub the congealment from his eyes; it makes them sting. His knuckles feel like sandpaper against his eyelids. His nose tightens against the odour of seawater – it's coming from his own flesh. He licks a finger and his tongue tastes salt.

His brain is taking longer than usual to calibrate. As he forces his eyes open, he takes a breath to speak. The only noise that comes out of his mouth is a rasp, chased by a stinging cough. His lungs are on fire.

'Hold on, hold on my friend,' says Captain Bellyache. The man's leathery forearm encases his neck and he is heaved upright. Cool and smooth, a glass presses against his lips. He splutters in response to the chilled water but it eases the acid burn in his throat.

His eyeballs are two pebbles rattling inside his skull. He recoils from a shaft of sunlight which pierces the flimsy curtain.

He wants to hurl. Captain Bellyache thrusts a tin bowl under his chin. 'Is ok,' he says, 'You be fine soon.' Another wash of vomit wells up from his gut and this time swills into the bowl. He sweeps a salty wrist across his lips.

'What happened?' he says at last. The words come from his mouth but the voice is a stranger's.

'You fall in the water,' says Captain Bellyache. For once his voice is subdued, serious. 'You nearly drown to death.'

'Drown?' he says. A sharp pain gnaws at the inside of his head. Drowning. His worst – his only – fear. 'I don't remember.'

'Is good,' says Captain Bellyache. 'Better you no remember, better to get over the shock, no?'

'I guess,' he says. 'Did you... someone—'

'You lucky man, says Captain Bellyache. 'Young woman see you in the water and Mister James, is good swimmer, he dive in and rescue you – he your big hero'

'Oh,' is all he can manage. Why did it have to be *him*?

'I sit with you all through the night, make sure you ok,' says Captain Bellyache.

'Thank you,' he says. He is genuinely grateful. 'I'm fine now. I need to sort myself out.'

'You sure?'

'Yes, thank you. You've been kind.' It seems the right thing to say.

'Is ok. So long as you fine, I happy. I no want people coming to bad accident on my gulet – no good for business.' There's an edge to the laugh that follows.

'I promise you, I won't say a word,' he says. He's certain he will never discuss this humiliation.

'Ok, is good. I leave now. We go slowly today, stop for lunch then back to harbour. You be fine.'

'I might stay down here,' he says. 'But I can take care of myself now. Thank you.' Another expression of gratitude. That's enough now, the man needs to fuck off and let him get his head straight.

Captain Bellyache gets up at last and pulls the cabin door shut behind him.

He takes short, tight breaths, his muscles aching for release.

He reaches for his stash; there's enough left for a couple of lines. He stares at it for a moment, then carefully re-folds the paper wrap and presses it down into his bag. Later, perhaps.

He struggles to remember what happened. He was drinking but that's nothing new; he can handle alcohol. He was overwhelmed with seasickness all day. He remembers sitting at the dinner table with the others, trying to pretend he was fine but feeling like shit. He recalls drinking with Brenda, just the two of them. He remembers staring at her tits; he thinks he even made a grab for them at some point. Christ. He remembers her twirling necklace; telling her his growing-up sob-story – he's told that a hundred times; he thinks they talked about work. They flirted. Why did he entertain that? Disgust seeps into his brain. Did they... did they...? If they did, he can't remember. That's definitely for the best. But then what? How come he ended up in the sea? Did someone catch him off-guard, push him over the railing? Who would have done that? Was it her? Again and again he ram-raids his brain for answers but comes up with... nothing. He has a dozen snapshots of the evening in his mind, but his recollection is riddled with gaping holes. Snapshots... photographs? Did they talk about taking photographs?

He slumps back on his cot, resigned to the fog of over-indulgence. But the cabin swirls around his head and forces him upright again. He emits another volley of yellow-green vomit into the bowl before stripping off his crusted clothes and struggling into the bathroom. He folds himself on to the toilet and lets the shower trickle down on him until he can't smell the seawater and the puke any more.

He rubs himself dry then folds the towel into a square and places it over the damp patch on the cot. He pulls on a pair of shorts and sinks on to the towel, his head in his hands. The more he dwells on it, the worse he feels. He knows he should be thankful – at least the posh boy is good for something – but instead a fire smoulders inside him. It's the thought of being pulled out of the sea by that prick. He sees himself, a dead-weight, being hauled into the boat. He imagines posh boy's arms wrapped around his chest and his flesh shivers in response. He can almost feel the bastard's breath against his ears. If he had any more puke left in his gut he'd bring it up, but there's none left to garnish his revulsion.

He knows he's worked himself up into an irrational place; he needs to settle himself. He reaches into his bag for the camera – it's a Pavlovian response. Looking through his photos always works. He lifts the bag on to his lap and stares into the opening; a t-shirt, his shaving kit, wallet, the zip-purse containing his weed. He digs deeper toward the bottom and his fingers bypass sun oil, a book, his Blackberry. Then they connect – the camera case. At last.

He yanks at the strap and the case flies out of the bag. It's light – too light. He snaps open the catch to reveal... nothing. The case is empty.

Where's the fucking camera?

2

BY LATE MORNING the sun dripped from a cloudless sky. The gulet, powered by its engine, cruised a few hundred yards from the coastline. The motor chugged rather more than it rumbled, an easy counterpoint to the swish-swash of the water rippling against the hull.

It wasn't the most picturesque view but Henry, in awe of the whole gulet experience, didn't want to miss an opportunity to capture every panorama, every facet of the trip on his camera. He could make out sheep and goats on the hillside, here and there a clutch of olive trees with their shimmering grey-green foliage and the odd car or truck gliding along an invisible road. Through his zoom lens he homed in on a goat tugging at a branch, the angular outline of a villa embedded in the hills, a solitary couple embracing on a scrap of beach.

Exposed to the day's heat for the last two hours, Henry's neck was scorched earth. A vest covered his back; he'd been thorough with the sun lotion on his arms and legs, but he'd forgotten to do round his neck. Where earlier there'd been a touch too much colour, now it was puckered and raw.

Veronica sat cross-legged on the mattress next to Henry's reading a book. Her skirt covered her legs and a sunhat shielded her face and neck. Given her limited wardrobe she'd come well prepared.

'I'm feeling warm,' he said to her. 'I'm off to find some shade at the back.'

'I'll come with you,' she said with a limpid pool of a smile that sent a more pleasurable glow erupting across his cheeks.

Together they settled on the platform at the aft end, reclining against the canvas bolsters like a sultan and his princess. Kaptan Barbar brought a lemonade for Veronica and a beer for Henry –

it was ice cold against his fingers and when he brought it to his lips it slithered down his throat like honey.

This would all be perfect, were it not for *the camera* – and the fact someone had played the hero last night. Like the kraken, the camera's slumbering owner would wake soon enough. Henry wanted to disown the thing, throw it overboard, but he couldn't do it. What he could do – what he must do – was make it someone else's problem.

'Veronica,' he said, gatecrashing the companionable silence.

'Henry?'

'Something's been bothering me. I'm not sure what to do about it.'

Veronica peered over her sunglasses.

'What have you done now?' she said.

'Nothing... nothing,' he replied. Why did everyone always think he was up to something?

'So what is it?'

'You know yesterday, when you found my camera after lunch?'

'Yes.'

'Well, as it turns out, it wasn't mine. It was someone else's.'

'Did you know that, Henry, when you took it from me?' Veronica's tone brought to mind a barrister in a court of law. This wasn't the timid mouse of the holiday's early days. And this wasn't how the conversation was supposed to go.

'That doesn't matter now,' he responded too hastily. 'Just understand it isn't mine and it's here in my bag.'

'Whose camera is it?'

'That doesn't matter either.'

'Do you know whose camera it is?'

'Yes.'

'Then why don't you return it? Come on Henry, you can't keep hold of things that aren't yours. I don't understand your problem.'

'It's not as simple as that,' said Henry. 'There are pictures on the camera – bad pictures; nasty, awful pictures, Veronica.'

'But they're someone's private pictures!' exclaimed Veronica. 'You have no right to look at them, nor judge them for that matter.'

'Look,' said Henry. 'I can't explain it. You'll have to trust me. I know something about the pictures – and the person who took them – something I wish I didn't know. But now I know it, this thing about them, I can't just give the camera back.'

'Henry, whatever it is, it can't be that bad. Come on. Let me see what you're talking about.' Veronica reached for Henry's bag, but he gripped it so hard his knuckles flared white to the bone.

'Oh my Lord, I can't let you Veronica, I can't,' Henry spluttered. 'You mustn't see things like this. Not you, it wouldn't be right.'

'This has really upset you, hasn't it?' Veronica's tone softened. 'Look, maybe I'm not the best person to ask. Why not try Brenda. She's a worldly-wise sort. Maybe she'll know what to do.'

Stunned by his own stupidity, Henry berated himself. Why hadn't he thought of Brenda? Why hadn't he taken the camera straight to her this morning? He could have dumped it on her and been done with all the worrying. How stupid and reckless of him, to hold on to it all this time. After last night, Brenda would understand. And Veronica was right; she'd know what to do.

What Brenda might not appreciate however, is how he'd taken charge of the camera when he'd known it wasn't his. What if she came over all severe again and made him feel like a naughty schoolboy? Another dose of that medicine would be unbearable.

'I don't know, Veronica. She'll react like you; have a go at me for taking it when I knew it wasn't mine.'

'Honestly, Henry, I don't know why that should worry you. Don't tell her that part. It might not come up and if it does, you can say you assumed it was yours. They're identical, aren't they?'

'More or less,' said Henry. Was sweet Veronica actually suggesting he tell a lie?

'Well then, get yourself down to her cabin and have a word. She's been down there all morning fretting about something or other, I don't know what. You'll make quite a pair today.'

On any other day, such a thought would have given Henry something to play with, but not today. He knew exactly what was exercising Brenda.

'Right,' he said, 'right.'

The first time he knocked, she didn't hear him. It was hardly surprising – his knock was more of a tap, a dusting of fingertip against wood. His second attempt connected more audibly. Brenda pulled open the door.

'Oh,' she said, as she realised who it was. It was a neutral, bland *oh*, devoid of the warmth she showered on everyone else.

'Can... can I come in,' he stuttered. 'There's something I have to talk to you about. It's important.'

She stood aside, which he read as consent. He took control of the lascivious musings threatening his composure and squeezed past her into the cabin. He was immediately caught up in a cloud of her intoxicating scent – the one she'd worn the day he first encountered her. It draped the air like an invisible cloak of delight. Tightly wound as he was, he couldn't permit himself even a moment's pleasure in the experience.

Brenda pointed to the bed, which he took to mean he could sit. He perched on the edge, where the wooden frame bit into his scrawny buttocks. Astonishingly, she sat beside him. As she did so she secreted two items under her pillow – a mobile phone and a notepad. She clutched a biro, which she spun around and around in her hand.

'What is it, Henry?' she asked. Neutral again.

'I don't know where to start.'

'What's it about?' she said, this time softer, more muted.

'Who,' he corrected. 'It's about Turner.' The pen spun faster and faster between her manicured fingers, twisting this way and that. '*I know.*'

'You know what?' Brenda queried, the beginnings of a scowl fluttering across her features.

'Look,' said Henry. 'I don't want you getting all snarky with me again. It wasn't deliberate. I wasn't stalking you or anything. I didn't mean to—'

'Didn't mean to *what*, Henry?' Here was another conversation in danger of going off the rails. Why did this always happen?

'I heard you talking with Turner last night. I honestly didn't mean to, Brenda. But once I'd caught on, what you were doing, I couldn't interrupt.

'What do you mean, what I was doing?'

'What you were saying and everything.'

'Saying? Come on Henry, what do you think you heard?'

'I know exactly what I heard,' Henry's voice wavered.

'Well?' Her jaw locked tight and her mouth twitched. She was angry now, or was she upset? He couldn't tell which.

'You... you were dragging stuff out of him. Making him tell you stuff. Bad stuff.'

'And?' Her eyes bored into his skull with an intensity that was almost terrifying. Keep going, keep going, he told himself.

'I'm not stupid, Brenda. I could see what you were doing. I know it wasn't, you know, for real.'

'What do you mean?'

'What you were saying. You know, pretending to enjoy it. I know you... someone like you... wouldn't, you know, enjoy that sort of thing. But he bought it, didn't he?'

'So it seems,' she said, her voice softening. She looked away. 'And you heard all that?'

'Most of it, I think.'

'You heard Turner telling me about all his—'

'Yes.'

'And about—'

'Yes. Yes. Adele and Lilly. Brenda, I heard everything. I was right behind you down the side of the boat. I was stuck. I couldn't barge in, and I couldn't go back to the others either.'

'Did anyone else?'

'Hear what you were saying? No.'

'Well it makes no difference now,' said Brenda. The sentence came out as a long, sad sigh. 'I tried, but it didn't get me very far.'

'What do you mean?' asked Henry. Brenda pulled the mobile phone from under her pillow. She turned it over and over in her hand. 'Brenda, I know what you think of me, but you can trust me, I promise.' It was a line he'd used as a reporter when people needed a tiny jog along to persuade them to speak. It always amazed him it worked as well as it did. This was the first time he'd meant it.

'I couldn't get it out of my head that he was up to something. So I... I persuaded him to talk about it and I tried to record what he said. But it didn't come out. I think I cut the recording by mistake. All I got was the first few minutes, nothing of any significance. I've been writing down as much as I can remember, though I doubt it'll do any good. You could maybe help with that, if you were listening.'

'I could,' said Henry. 'But I think I've got something better – something that'll help – prove it all.' He pulled out the camera. 'Please don't be angry with me,' he added, and the squeak in his voice reminded him of when he was seven and pleading with his mother not to scold him when he tore his trousers climbing a tree in the park.

'Is that what I think it is?' said Brenda, her eyebrows reaching for the ceiling.

'Yes.'

'Where did you find it?'

'Someone gave it to me yesterday. They thought it was mine.'

'And?'

'Brenda, it's got everything on it. Everything.'

'Even—'

'Adele and Lilly. Yes, I'm afraid so.' Brenda's left hand cupped her mouth as she held her right hand out for the camera. Her breathing slowed as she scanned through the pictures. When she reached the ones of Adele and then Lilly, a tear bloomed in the corner of her eye.

'I'm sorry. You shouldn't have to look at things like that. Only, it will help, won't it? It's evidence, isn't it?'

'I don't know. Things work differently here. But it might.'

'I know this sounds stupid, Brenda, but I'm scared. Of Turner.'

'Why? Does he know you have his camera?'

'I don't think so, but he'll figure it out. And he's already angry with me for something else.' Henry hesitated. 'I probably shouldn't ask this, but would you mind taking care of it? I can't, I can't—'

'Alright. But for god's sake, don't let him know I've got it, will you?'

'No, no, no, I won't. I promise. What will you do?'

'I'm not sure, Henry. It's a nest of snakes whichever way you look at it.'

'What about the police? Shouldn't we... shouldn't you take it all to the police?' He'd done enough; he didn't want to be involved in what came next.

'Probably. I don't know.' Brenda sighed. 'Henry, whatever happens you've done the right thing.'

'I know you don't approve of me, Brenda, but I'm not a total loser.'

'I know you're not.' She looked straight at him when she said this, gifting him a watery half-smile. His heart rattled in his chest.

'And despite what you might think,' he said, 'and any impression I might have given, I do know right from wrong.'

'I believe you, Henry.'

'Come on,' he said, daring to let his hand pat her arm, just twice, no more. 'There's not much you can do until we get back later. How about you come on deck and have a drink with Veronica and me before lunch?'

'Thanks Henry, but I think I'll stay down here for now. I want to write down everything I can remember.'

3

'HERE IS THE final day of your mini-cruise,' Kaptan Barbar bellowed, louder than was necessary. 'Today we enjoy a barbecue on the beach prepared by our own chef from fish we catch this morning while you were all fast asleep! We set up the cooking and in one hour, lunch is ready. Before then you can stay on my lovely *Annelise II* or you can go to shore, as you wish.'

An inviting crescent of white sand curled like a sleeping feline. At its head a cluster of rocks and boulders lay jammed together. A cliff sprayed with scrub, grasses and wildflowers rose behind the beach. Olive trees clung inexplicably to its craggy surface, growing outward before heading up towards the sun. Toward the far end of the beach, a tail of sand twitched away to nothing, where the rock wall plunged downward and blue-green water nibbled at its fringes.

As the anchor chain clattered one of the crew swam the hundred yards to shore and secured a rope around a boulder. An upturned rowing boat lay close by, its bleached hull scarred by stripes of peeling paint. The deck-hand righted it, slotted the oars into place and pushed it into the water before clambering aboard and sculling back to the gulet.

'Do we have to swim?' queried Lilly.

'Ha! No, of course no, you don't have to swim,' chuckled Kaptan Barbar. 'You can swim if you want but if not, our rowboat will take you to shore. My crew, he come back and forth for anyone. If he on beach, you wave and shout and he come for you!'

'You lot can take the boat if you like, but I'm going for a dip,' said James. 'The water looks amazing. Someone take my t-shirt?'

Singled Out

With no intention of swimming anywhere, Brenda took James's t-shirt and crammed it into her bag. James leapt off the railings and began powering towards the beach.

After some debate, Lilly and Adele also elected to swim, leaving Brenda in charge of more clothes and towels. The women proceeded through the water more sedately than James, keeping up a dry-hair doggy-paddle until their feet could touch the bottom, then wading through the shallows. Along with Veronica, Henry and Margaret the knitting queen, Brenda clambered uneasily down the steps into the rowboat.

The water shimmered like molten silver. Sunlight easily penetrated, revealing a landscape of smooth pebbles and rippled sand. Shoals of tiny fish wibbled back and forth.

James reached the beach before the boat. His shorts clinging to his legs he stood, feet buried in the sand, poised to drag the rowboat ashore. Brenda clutched her bag to her chest. It couldn't be allowed to get wet. More importantly it must not leave her sight as it held, wrapped in a plastic bag and then a t-shirt, a camera, a notepad and a mobile phone. As the shifting sand underneath her feet threatened her balance, James proffered his hand.

The boat made a second trip to the gulet and a quick check revealed only Turner remained unaccounted for.

'He sick,' said Kaptan Barbar. 'He fine in his cabin. I lock away the drinks, ha!'

Kaptan Barbar unloaded coolboxes and cooking utensils from the rowboat and Matt made a joke about the assembled party looking like survivors of a shipwreck. Some guests spread towels on the sand while others wandered off to explore.

'One hour you be back,' hollered Kaptan Barbar. His command was acknowledged with a smattering of *yo's*, nods and waves.

James and Adele headed for the far end of the beach. From a distance, shadowy recesses in the rock suggested there were caves.

'Wait up, you two,' said Brenda, struggling to get traction in the hot sand. James turned, pulling the sort of face which would discourage a less assertive individual. Brenda, sweat trickling down her temples, laboured to catch up – this was important.

'Adele, honey,' she said as she drew close. 'I need to have a word – in private if you don't mind.'

'About what?' Adele queried, James's hand still tightly in her grasp.

'It's personal; something we talked about a couple of days ago. It's important.'

'Oh that,' she said. 'James knows about it – I told him.'

'I don't think—'

'It's fine – whatever you want to say, he can hear.'

'If that's what you want,' said Brenda.

'Brenda darling,' said James with a theatrical flourish, 'I am the soul of discretion.'

The trio reached the rocks and James helped both women scramble up to the first of the caves. They had to duck their heads and enter one by one. As the entrance cast its shadow the heat of the beach cut abruptly to a dank stillness. They took a few steps into the cave and as Brenda reached out in the gloom her palm connected with the uneven clamminess of the cave wall. Something ran across her fingertips and she jerked her hand away. Further into the darkness a drip-drip of water feeding a rockpool bounced back and forth around the walls. The cave had the feel of a medieval dungeon and the mustiness of undisturbed air clung to her flesh like a prisoner pleading for release. As her eyes acclimatised and she could make out crevices oozing creeping spindles of vegetation and limestone residue drizzling into stalactites above, it felt no more inviting.

James guided the women to perch on a rock and flopped onto the cave's floor beside Adele, his arm coming to rest protectively across her thigh. Brenda pushed her feet into the sand. This would not be easy.

'Shoot,' said Adele through tight lips.

'You know what you said the other night – about not being sure what you'd done?' said Brenda.

'Uh huh,' said Adele.

'I know what happened.'

'What, were you spying on me?' snapped Adele.

'No, honey. I can't explain, but I got to the truth.'

'And?'

'You weren't dreaming and you weren't drunk. It was Turner. He used a date-rape drug on you.'

'No shit,' said Adele. 'You think I hadn't worked that out?'

'Oh babe,' groaned James, reaching for Adele's hand.

'I thought you should know for certain,' said Brenda.

'You thought... Right, now I know. Thanks. I think I'll get on with enjoying my holiday now, if it's ok with you.'

'What do you mean?' said Brenda. 'We can do something about it.'

'Like what?'

'There's evidence. We can go to the police.'

'We? *We?* Brenda, this didn't happen to you. It's got nothing to do with you.'

'Adele—' pleaded Brenda.

'Stop it,' Adele spat. 'This isn't your problem. Best thing you can do is butt-out and leave me be.'

'But there's... proof,' said Brenda. 'You've got to do it. You have to do something, to stop him doing it again.'

'And exactly what does that do for me?' said Adele. She gripped James's hand so tightly that her fingernails burrowed into his flesh, but he didn't resist.

'I don't understand,' said Brenda. 'You know what he did and we've got proof. We can... you can go to the police!' The word *police* bounced around the cave walls. When it came to a stop there was silence, but for the drip-drip of the water somewhere distant, endlessly filling a rockpool.

'What proof?' Adele said at last.

'Photographs,' said Brenda. 'He took photographs. I've got them.'

'Christ, Brenda,' said Adele. 'You want me to look at photographs of myself being... being—'

'I think you need to leave us alone now,' said James suddenly. 'Brenda, can't you see, Adele wants nothing to do with this.'

'But, I thought you'd—'

'No buts, Brenda,' said James, more firmly than she'd heard him speak before. 'If you want to do Adele a favour, delete the photographs. Get rid of them and forget all about this. She doesn't want this, can't you see?'

'But he has to be stopped!'

'What can I say to make it clearer?' said Adele, her voice monotone. 'I don't want to deal with this. I want it to go away and I don't want to be stuck in a police station on the last day of my holiday when the damage is done already. So leave it.'

'But—' Brenda pleaded.

'I don't like to say this, Bren, but I'm going to,' said James. 'I know you mean well, but it's time you stopped interfering. You need to get a grip on your own problems, leave others to deal with theirs. Now go away, leave us alone.'

A shiver coursed through Brenda's body, an involuntary response to the cold rock – or the chill in the atmosphere.

'Would it make any difference if I said I know for sure it happened to Lilly too?'

'Poor cow,' said Adele. 'But no, it doesn't make any difference.'

'Does she know?' said James.

'No,' said Brenda. 'I haven't spoken to her yet.'

'Yet?' said James. 'You're going to tell her?'

'Yes,' said Brenda. 'She has a right to know.'

'You think she has a right to have her life ruined by... *you?*' said Adele. 'She doesn't realise anything happened, why put her through it? You can see what she's like. What do you think it would do to her? Do you think she could cope with knowing... *that?*'

'I think she'd need help with it,' sighed Brenda.

'You think she'd get that in a tin-pot village in Turkey?' said Adele. 'From a tour rep and a bunch of holidaymakers? Or from those self-important yuppies she works for? Or from *you?* You can't tell her.'

'Adele's right, Bren. She isn't hurt, is she? And she hasn't a clue about it. If you've got any feeling at all, leave her be. Remember Jack.'

'Who's Jack?' said Adele.

'Who hasn't a clue about what?' said a voice behind them.

Brenda turned to see a silhouette in a halo of light in the cave's entrance. Wrapped in a diaphanous sarong, Lilly's slender legs looked almost child-like as shafts of sunlight threw them into relief.

'Who hasn't a clue about *what*?' she repeated.

4

BRENDA WASN'T THE only one with little appetite for the mouth-watering barbecue the chef presented on the beach. Whole fish dressed with herbs and lemon, sprinkled with olive oil then griddled to the precise moment where the skin went crispy yet the flesh remained succulent; bowls of tomato and cucumber, aubergine dip, yoghurt and mint dressings and potato salads were spread around a canvas square laid on the sand like a picnic rug. It was plentiful food and under other circumstances, it would have been tantalising. But the fetid notes of failure and rejection coated Brenda's taste buds, preventing her from drawing any pleasure from the feast.

She'd been shocked that Adele and James had implored her to keep Lilly in the dark. But with Lilly stumbling upon them, she'd had no alternative but to accede, at least temporarily. With James's granite-set *don't you dare* stare boring into her skull, they'd colluded, deflecting Lilly's inquisition.

Throughout the afternoon's drift along the coast Brenda's mind ranged back and forth. Was it right to hide the facts, to protect one girl's sensibilities? Or should she force Lilly to confront the reality because there was a greater need at stake. Turner had to be stopped, but for that to happen Adele or Lilly would have to go to the police and Adele had already emphatically refused. But who had elected her, Brenda, to the role of moral arbiter? What gave her the right to force other people to hear what she wanted them to hear, or do what she wanted them to do, at whatever personal cost? What kind of a person did that make her? *What would Jack have said?*

And yet... and yet...

There was no respite for Brenda even as the harbour and boardwalk grew close and the gulet manoeuvred into its berth.

Singled Out

Kaptan Barbar threw open the basket of shoes then bounded down the gangway to help his guests disembark. He bowed to the men and kissed the hands of the women, urging them all to come and stay on his beloved *Annelise II* again next year.

'I love all my friends from England!' he shouted as he waved them off. Veronica and Henry, deep in conversation, disappeared towards the shops. James and Adele walked in silence, arms linked. The others including a subdued Turner made for the path to the hotel.

Brenda hung back. The muscles in her neck were twisted into a rope of knots drawing her shoulders tight; waves of pain circuited her skull. Ahead, the yellow awning caught her attention; it was the one place where her fractured composure might be soothed.

Emilio stood by the entrance of his restaurant like a sentry. As he spotted Brenda a smile ruptured his leathery features in a burst of crinkles and creases.

'I see the others,' he said. 'I pray you come to me alone.'

He ushered her to a table. As the sun seeped towards the horizon, a game of beach volleyball was getting underway by the water's edge. Sunbathers were packing up and an attendant shuffled around the loungers picking up litter. Emilio brought a tray to the table – a creamy cocktail dusted with cinnamon for Brenda and a chilled beer for himself. She would have preferred his beer but sipped at the velvety concoction without complaint. Shots of brandy and crème de cacao melded with the sweetness of vanilla. Its unctuousness washed over her. It was the sort of drink normally served in a martini glass – two sips and it would be gone. But Emilio had presented a globe the size of a fishbowl with two scoops of ice cream bobbing like golden islands in an opaque sea.

'You look sad,' he said. 'Is because you go home tomorrow?'

'Yes, I'm sad about that,' she replied. It was the right thing to say. 'But—' her voice trailed away. It wasn't fair or right to share what disturbed her.

'Is more, I think,' he whispered. He placed his hand over hers, stroking his fingers back and forth. The tenderness of his gesture made a lump swell in her throat.

'Something happened,' she began. 'Something bad. I tried to help, but I think I made things worse.'

'Something happen to you?' said Emilio.

'No, to someone else. Two people, in fact. Two women.'

'A bad thing?'

'Very bad, Emilio. About the worst thing that can happen to a woman.'

'I think I know what you say,' murmured Emilio, his rough hands now gripping tight on to hers. 'Is done by a man, yes?'

'Yes.'

'You know who does this?'

'Yes.'

'The women must go to police.'

'They won't. One wants to forget the whole thing and the other, she doesn't know what happened to her.'

'How is this possible?'

'It's possible, believe me, Emilio.'

'So you cannot stop this... bastard... from doing what he do again?'

'That's the problem, Emilio. I have some evidence but without the women who were... I don't think anyone will be able to do anything. I can't force them, can I? That makes me as bad as—'

'No,' said Emilio. 'You stop that. You're a good person, you try to help.'

'He's done it before too. In England.'

'How you know this?'

'He told me.'

'How he tell you?'

'He just did, every detail.'

'How you know he was not lying, maybe playing a game on you?'

'I know, Emilio. I know how to do these things. I know he was telling me the truth and there's other proof too, but it's no good. I can't see what I can do without involving the women.'

'My brother can help, maybe,' said Emilio, leaning back in his chair.

'Your brother?' said Brenda.

'He local police captain. Maybe he know what to do, even without your friends. Always he have something, good idea. Not always what the rules say, but he give good sense.'

'Good sense. I need some of that, Emilio. I'm not sure of anything anymore.'

'Come, I think we go see my brother.'

5

FOR THE SIXTH or seventh time he pours the contents of his canvas bag on to the bed. For the sixth or seventh time he turns the bag inside out, pressing his fingers into every pocket and crevice. Each time he searches he wills the outcome to be different. Still nothing. He turns to the miscellany on his bed. Maybe he can't see for looking. He stares at each item in turn, picking it up, as if acknowledging its existence and the fact it is patently not a camera, before returning it to the bag. He searches his wardrobe, in between every folded t-shirt and pair of shorts. He pulls his suitcase from under the bed and unzips it, feeling around the pockets, the lining, the seams, even though he knows it could not possibly be there. He keys the code into the safe and empties it on to the bed; a wad of Sterling, passport, keys and his stash. He knew before looking it wouldn't be in there.

This is fucked up. He's missing the pictures but it's more than that. He has no idea if the camera is buried in the sand somewhere or if one of the lemmings got hold of it. He doesn't know if this will become a problem and the uncertainty is agitating. The familiar throb of his pulse pounds his temples.

He fetches his shaving mirror from the bathroom then sits on the bed and rips into what's left of the packet of white powder in his stash. Scooping it on to the mirror, he fingers it into a rough line then rolls a note and hoovers the powder up his nostrils. As it overruns his veins he salvages an alternate possibility. If anyone found it, what's it to them? They're pictures of women with their legs open; could be pictures of any bloke's girlfriend, playmates of the month, whatever. The picture of the one with the shirt over her head wouldn't help, nor would the one of the boy by the bins. But out of context, it wouldn't make any sense.

But analysis is no help – there are too many unknowns. He doesn't know how it happened but he's left himself exposed; it's anyone's guess how badly.

He surveys the empty package and notes with a passing satisfaction that he judged the quantities perfectly. It's the last night and it's all gone, nothing wasted. He soaks the paper wrapping to a pulp in the basin then flushes it down the toilet – screw the Turk's plea not to put paper down the toilet. He washes the plastic bag with soap then ties it to the towel rail to dry.

Laughter outside signals the other guests are gathering for the last night cocktails and dinner. He wants to crush his worries, forget the last two agonising days and enjoy a few drinks. But before he joins the others he needs another shower to rid himself of the stench of the sea and the grimy wooden boat. As he stands under the jets of steaming water he counts the white ceramic tiles, first one wall, then the other, horizontally, then from top to bottom; a distraction.

Apart from this week's, the pictures are all backed up. He can get another camera.

6

HENRY STOOD AMONGST the pre-dinner drinkers by the bar. That in itself was something. He'd been accepted into this gathering of men and women from all walks of life, their ages spanning four decades. Whilst not quite in the inner circle, he'd been promoted from outcast – the one everyone went to lengths to avoid being stuck with – to the elevated position of group photographer and general photographic adviser. And it was all because of Veronica.

This evening was the last with his new friends. He would be in touch with one or two once he got home, mainly so he could tweak the photographs he'd taken of them, but it could never be the same again. As Henry listened to laughter and music, enjoyed the aromas of griddled chicken, garlic and lemon and contemplated the return to his daily life, he felt his heart lifting and then plunging into a pit inside his chest.

Veronica, always one of the last to come down for dinner, was yet to arrive. James and his backgammon buddy were arguing about who was the better player and making plans to play online once they got home. By his side, so close you couldn't slip a sheet of tissue paper between them, Adele clung to James, her arm hooked like a lobster claw around his elbow. She wore the skirt he recognised from the photograph on Turner's camera. Did she realise? Was it an act of defiance or ignorance? He felt sure if it were him he'd have burned the offending clothes. But then he wasn't a woman and he never understood how their minds worked.

Away from the bar Turner held court around two tables pulled together. The man wore his high-energy social persona like a costume. He spoke fast and too loudly, eyes flashing, hands waving, taking theatrical gulps from his glass every time he stopped for breath. Still his attendants responded to whatever he said with smiles and laughter. He was as Dr Jekyll to Mr Hyde, so cavernous was the distance between gregarious, charming Turner and the grizzled creature Brenda had gone into battle with on the boat.

Mehmet banged a bottle on the bar counter three times. The guests knew the signal by now and moved to the dining tables. Veronica wandered across the patio from the bedrooms, timing it perfectly as usual. Her reluctance to circulate with the pre-dinner crowd had annoyed Henry at first, but now he simply looked forward to her arrival. He greeted her with a smile and a barely perceptible nod of his head. He took a deep breath.

'Veronica,' he said. 'Might I say how lovely you look tonight?' She looked much the same as always but he thought it worth the risk of a put-down since it was the last night.

Veronica looked at him for a second longer than he'd hoped for before smiling and acknowledging his compliment. But it wasn't a put-down, so that was good.

'Where's Brenda?' said Veronica.

'I don't know,' said Henry, 'she's not come down yet.'

'I haven't seen her since we got off the gulet. I thought she went to see her friend at the yellow bar.'

'Ah,' said Henry, stifling a snigger. 'Maybe she decided to stay there for a bit of—'

'If she did, then it's none of our business,' interrupted Veronica.

'No. Of course not.'

As they settled at the dinner tables, a commotion arose. By the gates a police car crunched to a halt, sending a shower of gravel across the flagstones. Two policemen in uniform strode in; behind them a third man in a crumpled suit, an uneven moustache plastered to his upper lip like roadkill. They bypassed a shocked Mehmet and made for the tables.

'Who is Turner?' said the moustache. A low murmur like distant thunder rumbled around the tables. Everyone looked down at their empty place settings. An age passed before Turner stood up.

'I am,' he said, his face set like stone.

'You must come with us,' said the moustache.

'Am I under arrest?'

'You must come with us. Now,' he repeated.

'Why?'

'We want to talk with you. No more argue. You come now.'

'What is it? The weed? All this for a bit of weed?' One of the police moved his hand over his sidearm.

'Okay, okay, I'm coming,' said Turner.

Turner pushed back his chair and turned to the other guests. 'I picked up a bit of herb at the airport, to chill out, you know,' he said. 'I bet it's about that. I'll get it sorted.'

The two uniformed officers positioned themselves either side of Turner and marched him across the patio and through the gate. Beyond sight of the guests at the tables, they handcuffed him before bundling him into the car. Henry watched, mouth agape, heart racing.

'Veronica, I'm sorry,' he said. 'I have to know what's going on. I'll be back later, I promise.'

'Henry?' breathed Veronica.

'I'm sorry, I can't explain, I have to go. Enjoy your meal and I'll see you later.'

Once through the gates Henry picked up speed. He trotted along the darkened path with his eyes fixed on the boardwalk. Once he reached the strip of bars he slipped up an alleyway towards the town square and the police station. Outside the entrance stood the police car, empty. Turner would be inside already; it would have taken the car only a couple of minutes to reach the station.

Henry stood, debating with himself how to find out what was going on without getting involved. He could pretend he'd lost something. That would get him to the counter, then maybe he could ask casually. He considered pretending he was Turner's friend, but that was ridiculous and would only heap suspicion back on him. He wasn't getting very far. But then the police station's doors swung open and he saw Brenda and her friend the bar owner emerge. She shook the hand of a man he couldn't clearly see inside the door, who held on to it for some time. The bar owner grasped Brenda's elbow as they descended the steps. They set off across the square walking side by side, Brenda's whole body rigid, absent of its customary voluptuous fluidity.

Henry stayed several paces behind them as they headed towards the beach. They made their way on to the sand, where he had to move closer to keep them in view as the evening shadow enveloped them. He stood against a wall at the far end of the boardwalk and watched as they found a cluster of rocks. The bar owner swept the rocks with his hand and Brenda sat. He perched alongside and wrapped his arms around her. As she rested her head against his shoulders, her whole body shook. As it convulsed, he gripped her tighter, stroking her hair, cupping her cheek with his hand, caressing her arm. For several minutes he held her shuddering frame until the tremor subsided.

And still he held her, unmoving, protecting, soothing.

7

HE CAN'T FIGURE out who or what has given him away. Maybe someone at the hotel – the scrawny Turk perhaps – took a dislike to him smoking on his balcony. He shouldn't have given him a hard time over the bar tab. Maybe they had eyes on the porter at the airport. But if they had they'd have come for him earlier, when he had a bag full of the stuff and a lot more besides.

It doesn't make sense.

The room they've put him in is sparse and shared with a guard reeking of acidic aftershave; the sour ooze hangs in the air. A strip light dangling on chains from the ceiling flickers – it does little to alleviate the gloom. There's a table, the chair he's using and two more opposite. A slit of a window is covered with a metal grill. It's open but too high to see out of. Outside he can hear two male voices in conversation. He can't understand what they're saying but it's a smoke break; the odour of cheap tobacco seeps through the window. A truck rumbles past coughing diesel fumes; a couple of cars then several mopeds honking their horns, scaring pedestrians. The bars by the beach are in full swing, pounding out a clamour of conflicting rhythms.

The heat is oppressive, like being smothered in a steaming blanket. In a cell nearby a man retches then hammers on his cell door, roaring for attention. Without moving, the guard hollers a response and the man is silenced.

His capacity for coherent thought is in shreds. The coke has evacuated his bloodstream and he's down. He's lost track but it seems like he's been here for hours. He needs to get this over with, find out what it's all about. What's keeping them?

There are voices in the hallway and the metallic shunt of a lock being drawn. The guard stands aside as the door opens. Two men enter, neither in uniform. Are they what passes for detectives in this hole? The older of the two is dressed like a vagrant; his trousers are two sizes too big, held up by a scuffed leather belt; his shirt is missing a button and belly flesh fights for freedom. Patchy black and grey stubble coats his face and he wears a forest of a moustache which plays host to the remnants of his dinner. The other younger man is urbane Euro-chic; he wears a suit the colour of clotted cream like a second skin and a white shirt open at the neck. He carries an envelope containing something bulky. The two men sit. The suit opens the envelope and places the contents on the table.

What the—? It's the camera.

It doesn't make sense. How have the police got his camera? He didn't report it as lost property – he's not a moron. Even if someone else had done it – the dumb posh boy maybe – he wouldn't be in a cell if they were returning it.

He doesn't need to be a genius to realise; this is serious.

'You like my country?' says the one dressed like a vagrant. Crumbs tumble from his moustache. He surveys the table before wiping a sleeve across his face.

'Yes.'

'You enjoy your holiday? Up until now?' The vagrant bares his teeth.

'Yes.' *Where the fuck is this going?*

'You have good time?'

'Yes.' *Say as little as possible*, he orders himself. *Until there's a brief in the room.*

'Do you enjoy taking photographs?' The suit speaks at last. In contrast to the vagrant, his is a clipped English accent. *This one's not a local. What does that mean?* He feels the vein in his temple begin to swell.

The suit picks up the camera. He turns it over in his hands, finds the viewer and after a few attempts, locates the scroll button. A couple of clicks and he'll reach the pictures – the trophy shots. When he does, his eyebrows elevate as if he hasn't seen them before. *Theatricals; do they think he's stupid?* He shows the vagrant then sets the camera, screen up, on the table.

Lilly's pristine pudenda moments before he pierced it, leaving nothing to the imagination.

'Not quite the usual run of holiday snaps,' says the suit. 'What do you say?'

'Those... that?' he says, forcing out a blokeish snigger. 'She's my... uh... girlfriend. On the holiday. Bit of fun, a little holiday romance, you know how it is. Those... that picture. It was a little something to remember her by.'

The vagrant writes something on his notepad and underlines it, twice.

Immediately he realises his mistake, and it's a big one. He's as good as admitted the camera belongs to him. He should have denied all knowledge of it. He's no idea where it's been since he misplaced it. For all he knows it could have been through dozens of hands.

Stress blunts his judgement.

The two men stare him down as the vein in his temple thuds like a bass drum against his skull and a dart of pain shoots across the back of his eyeball. It seems like minutes pass. They don't scare him; he's got rights, even here.

'No,' says the vagrant at last. 'You lie.'

'Don't muck about,' says the suit. 'She's not your girlfriend, anyone can see that. There isn't the faintest whiff of a nice holiday romance about this picture or any of the others.'

'So?'

'I'll tell you who she is. She's your victim.' He pauses. 'One of them anyway; one of several I'd say, judging by this.' He prods the camera as the power-save kicks in and the girl's fanny fades to grey.

'Do I need a lawyer?' Stay in control, keep it polite.

'I don't know, Turner. Do you?'

'This is shit and I'm not saying another word till I get a brief.'

'Well, if you insist. Tomorrow it is then,' says the suit, deadpan. Or was that a flicker of a smile that flashed across his face?

'What the fuck?'

'After hours,' explains the suit. 'Too late to get a legal down here. There won't be anyone here to hold your hand until the morning. Don't piss your pants. We'll find you... somewhere... to while away the hours.' His voice is laced with contempt.

The vein in his forehead pounds its alert. This is all wrong.

'You're kidding me,' he shouts, rising to his feet. Alarm flares, stampeding through his self-control. 'I want a brief. Now, this minute. I'm flying home tomorrow.' The guard reaches for his pistol. Sit down, calm down. Keep your head, he orders himself.

'You're not going anywhere,' the suit says. 'Not until we've had a proper chat about this... material. That's going to need sorting out. Unless there's anything you want to say now, without a lawyer here to hold your hand.'

'Fuck you,' he says. This is all to shit. These donkeys have got him tucked up for now. A brief will have him out in minutes. If he gets here early enough he could still make the flight. All he needs is to get through a night in the cells. How hard can that be?

The vagrant and the suit exchange words in Turkish, low voices, serious faces. The vagrant leaves the room whilst the suit picks up the camera and scans through more shots, his features taut. In due course the vagrant returns.

'Busy here tonight,' he says. 'Few cells, many people. Not like your country, eh?' The vagrant laughs, a dense, wheezy exhalation.

'I wouldn't know,' he murmurs.

The suit slides the camera back into the envelope and leaves the room without another word.

'Come with me,' says the vagrant. He's taken to a cell. The guard unlocks the door and guides him inside. It's larger, windowless; a pile of grimy blankets occupies one corner alongside what looks like a plastic bucket topped by a toilet seat. A clammy stench snatches at the back of his throat; a cocktail of piss, excreta and sweat.

But that's not even half the problem.

Three men stand facing him. They're stupid looking thugs, pock-marked and riddled with scabs and scars. One has a stump instead of an index finger. The vagrant pokes his head round the door, utters a few words and one of the thugs nods in response, then smiles, lips flared like a bull mastiff. The door bangs shut.

The realisation surges up on him, like a wash of puke you can't hold down.

This is a set-up. This is trouble.

SATURDAY

1

THE QUEUES FOR Immigration and Passport Control were more clusters than lines, an unholy scramble to reach the baggage carousels before the suitcases. A few feet ahead of her, Brenda spotted James and Adele, arms linked, like police officers facing off a line of rioters. Neither had spoken to her in the coach, nor as they waited at Dalaman. At the gate, Adele had avoided eye contact.

As if aware of Brenda's gaze, James turned. He delivered one of those tight smiles, eyebrows elevated, that hints at apology before turning to Adele and kissing her cheek. Behind Brenda, Veronica and Henry trundled towards the queue's tail.

'I lost track of you at the airport,' said Veronica. 'I wanted to thank you.'

'For what?' Brenda queried.

'When I came away I was a hopeless bundle of nerves. You were so kind, so friendly that first night. I want you to know it really helped settle me down.'

'It was nothing,' smiled Brenda. 'Now you won't be afraid to come on another one.'

'At least I'll know what to expect,' said Veronica. 'But my next trip is closer to home. Henry and I are going on a photography weekend in the Lake District.'

'You are?' said Brenda, surprise etched too deeply in her tone.

'Separate rooms,' blurted Henry. 'Just friends, no funny business.'

'Henry!' exclaimed Veronica.

'I'm happy for you,' said Brenda and she meant it.

'There's Margaret,' said Veronica. 'I'll pop and say goodbye. Keep my place for me, will you, Henry?'

'Of course,' said Henry and Veronica wandered ahead to where Margaret stood alone.

'Was it you that got Turner locked up?' said Henry once Veronica was out of earshot.

'Yes,' said Brenda, staring into the distance.

'Did you give them the camera?'

'Yes,' she said, 'and the recording and my notes. But nothing much will come of it.'

'Why not?'

'I know how these things work, Henry. Any half-decent lawyer could drive a truck through what I gave them. The recording is almost inaudible and doesn't contain the... most important material. As for the camera, Turner's smart – he isn't recognisably in any of the photographs and there's no proof the camera is his. If he's got any sense he'll deny it. And without a victim, what can they do?'

'Adele and Lilly are victims, aren't they?'

'Adele won't press charges and Lilly... doesn't realise what happened to her.'

'That might be for the best,' said Henry, placing a hand on Brenda's wrist, then just as quickly removing it.

'Do you think so?' asked Brenda, surprised to find herself seeking Henry's opinion. 'Don't you think she deserves to know the truth?'

'What good would it do?' said Henry. She's a young girl with her life ahead of her. From what I've seen, knowledge like that can ruin lives.'

'You think I should keep it from her?'

'You're asking me?' said Henry, his cheeks flushing. 'Yes, I do.'

'That'll mean there's no victim – so, in theory, no crime.'

'So what then? A few hours in custody and he'll be back home, free to do it again?'

'Between you and me,' said Brenda, 'the local police don't take well to outsiders corrupting the good reputation of their town. I got the impression they planned to give him a bit of a turn on the spit, even though it won't get them much. Someone told me they'll give him something to think about, whatever that means. Even so, without a victim's statement he'll likely be home in a couple of days.'

'He's done it before. Aren't you afraid he'll do it again?'

'Of course I am, but what can I do? I'll talk to the police in London of course; tell them what I know, connect them up with Turkey. I've already set the ball rolling. Turner might not have been as careful as he thought. There's a chance – small, but a chance.'

'I think you're very brave,' said Henry, 'doing what you did.'

'Thanks,' Brenda said. 'Others would say I was interfering.'

'I understand why you did it,' said Henry. 'I know I'm not in the same league as you, but some of the stories I used to pursue as a reporter; it wasn't only for the paper. They were things I knew were wrong, that demanded to have a light thrown on them, where I couldn't let go until something was done. I know what that feels like.'

Brenda smiled at Henry, so different from the man she'd assumed him to be a few days ago. They bid their goodbyes with an amiable handshake.

In the baggage hall there were hugs, waves and smiles, promises to keep in touch; a steady exodus. Familiar faces dissolved into strangers as everyday life blistered then burst the holiday bubble.

Brenda emerged into the heaving arrivals hall. Ahead amongst the throng she spotted Lilly, as clearly as if the girl had a spotlight beaming on her. Brenda watched as Lilly chatted on her mobile. Everyone felt it was better that Lilly remain ignorant of what had happened to her. Everyone that is, except Brenda. The previous day when Lilly stumbled across them in the cave, James and Adele had secured Brenda's co-operation only temporarily; it had seemed prudent in the moment. But here was another day and another moment. This could be her last chance.

When the call ended, Lilly slipped her phone into her bag and looked around. Her eyes connected with Brenda's.

'You look lost,' said Brenda, approaching her.

'Not lost,' said Lilly. 'Danny's meeting me, but he's been held up. I've a half-hour to kill before he gets here.'

'I'm in no rush,' said Brenda. 'Fancy a coffee?'

At the coffee bar Brenda purchased a latte for Lilly and for herself a concoction layered with syrup and whipped cream that looked more like a dessert than a beverage. They found an empty table, sticky with the residue of a hundred hastily slurped drinks and pushed aside a jumble of crockery and a half-eaten sandwich nesting in its plastic cocoon. All around them people came and went, jerking suitcases noisily between the tables; children screamed and announcements blared. The atmosphere wasn't conducive; but it was what she had.

'Danny's coming for me, I knew he would. I can't wait to see him!' sighed Lilly, oblivious both to the turmoil around her and the tornado of revelation which would shatter her bliss. 'He said he'd try to make it, but if he couldn't get away I might have to get on the bus. But I knew he wouldn't let me down. Brenda, I can't wait!'

'I remember you saying you were spoken for,' said Brenda. 'Was that Danny you were talking about on the first night?'

'Yes of course,' said Lilly. 'He's the only one for me. He's been so kind and patient, what with me being kept so busy all the time.'

'Are you engaged? Will you be getting married?' asked Brenda.

'I'd like to say yes,' said Lilly. 'But I don't have the ring yet, so it's a way off. Danny knows how important marriage is to me. He knows I won't do... well, you know what, before I'm properly married. But it's a question of money and we don't have enough yet. He says I'm the one for him, but money is so tight he can't afford to get me a ring yet, or even think about a wedding. He keeps saying he wants to marry me though, and why don't we... you know what. But I won't. It's just my thing. I won't let him touch me before we walk down the aisle. I couldn't.'

'Because you're an old fashioned girl?'

'Because it's the most important thing, Brenda. Because saving yourself for one person is the most special you can be. And because once it's gone, you can't ever get it back. You can't give it to your special person if you've already thrown it away, can you?'

'And he's okay with that?'

'He's a man,' laughed Lilly. 'So no, he's not okay with it. But he understands and he knows he has to live with it. And I'll tell you another thing, it's made him think. I know he's looking forward to being with me, you know... in that way, because of how special it is.'

Brenda sipped her sickly drink through a straw. Blobs of sweetened whipped cream washed hot coffee down her throat. It did nothing to diminish her dilemma.

'He's the one for you then?' she asked, though the answer was obvious.

'You know, when you've found your one, don't you?' said Lilly, her face glowing.

'I guess,' said Brenda, but she didn't. She'd never had a 'one'.

'I want it all to be perfect,' said Lilly, 'and there's no reason it shouldn't be, is there?'

'No, honey,' said Brenda, a leaden weight pressing on her chest, 'there's no reason.'

The girl's phone pinged with a text message.

'He's outside!' cried Lilly. 'I have to go. I've had such fun on this holiday and it was lovely meeting you. You take care now!' And with a hug and a wave, Lilly evaporated into the crowd.

Brenda stared into the dregs of her coffee. How could she rob someone of their happiness when doing so delivered no conceivable benefit? How could she wilfully rain down trauma and distress on such a delicate flower as Lilly? Had she learnt nothing?

She pulled Jack's letter from her bag and removed the sheets from the envelope. As baristas clattered and coffee machines clanked and customers squeezed around her, tutting and huffing, she read it one more time from beginning to end. Finally Jack's message was getting through; the distress, the sense of abandonment, the pain of betrayal that ran through every sentence. Finally, Brenda understood the damage she'd done, by putting her own selfish needs and rigid values so far above any concern for her sister's emotional welfare.

Helplessly she clutched the crumpled letter as tears welled in her eyes.

'Jack,' she whispered, 'I'm so sorry.'

'Are you on your way?' said a voice beside her. She looked up to see a man bearing a toddler in a sling, clutching a tray overflowing with drinks and snacks.

'Excuse me?' croaked Brenda. The noose of reality constricted her throat.

'It's busy in here,' said the man. 'You've finished your drink. How about you give up the table?'

'Yes, sorry... sorry,' said Brenda. Still holding the letter in her fist she gathered her belongings and stood. A woman and two more children appeared, overwhelming the table.

Brenda wheeled her case across the arrivals hall looking for a sign for the courtesy buses. Stopping by a news stand she noticed a waste bin. She released her clenched fingers, freeing Jack's letter and smoothed it flat between the palms of her hands. It was time to let go.

Brenda held her breath as she made the first tear, straight across the centre fold of all three pages. She tore again, from top to bottom, and again, and again. When she could tear no more, she held her hand over the bin and let the confetti of tiny squares flutter into the waste beneath.

'Bye, sis,' she said. 'I get it now. I get it.'

Back to reality, Brenda thought. Back to the daily grind; move along, nothing to see here... She dipped into her bag and brought out her mobile phone, still dark after the flight. She pressed the button and it powered up. There'd be work to attend to no doubt; something to engage and distract. It'd be a relief to focus on something to which she wasn't intimately connected.

Singled Out

The phone found a base station and emitted a loud *ding-ding* followed swiftly by another and another; three text messages.

> Hi Brenda welcome back. Big case real piece of work. Need you and your clever talk. Call soon as you land DCI 701 Davis

> Hello my special lady. Your bad man let go of police fly home tomorrow. Will you come soon again? Emilio want sex your body xxxxx

> Hi Brenda don't hang about i said it was urgent i meant it. Might have something on your date-rape guy too. Not sure need more info DCI 701 Davis

Brenda scanned her contacts, located the number she wanted and dialled as she strode towards the exit.

'Hi Kieran... yes, great thanks... no problem... what you got for me...? Sure, I can be there in an hour... Yes, it's fine, I know it's important... What about the other thing...? Really...? There's a photofit...? Can you ping it to me? Alright, yes... Get the coffee on, will you? No... if I'm honest, it hasn't been much of a rest.'

EPILOGUE

MEHMET RINSED A cloth under the tap and rung it out then smeared it across the bar and around the bottles on the wall. He always relished the few hours' peace and quiet he got between one lot of guests departing and the new lot arriving; everyone in transit and he, a solitary man in his kingdom, with only the birds, the cicadas and the odd stray cat for company.

And Defne of course. Always Defne.

He watched as his wife heaved a bundle of sheets and towels over the balcony of one of the upstairs bedrooms. They landed with a thud on the flagstones. Luckily for him, Defne took care of all the rooms. He hated the idea of the clean-up on changeover day. All those soiled sheets – all that making out, pairing-off. It was what they came on holiday for, wasn't it? Sometimes he lay in his bed at night alongside his exhausted wife, thinking of all the sex going on around him. Everywhere, except in his own room.

It had all got a bit strange last night, with the big man being taken off to the police station. What was that all about? Everyone else packed up and left this morning but he hadn't seen the big man again. Then the police came and cleared out his room. They'd asked a few questions but he couldn't say much, except the man had an outstanding tab at the bar. The police wouldn't pay it, would they? That was a lost cause. He wondered if his friend Emilio had a handle on what had gone on. His brother worked at the police station, maybe he would know.

Down in the town, Emilio had been having a bit of fun this week. Lucky bastard. He knew what he was doing, making a play for the fat one. Turned out she was well up for it from what Emilio had reported. After the first night though, he'd gone quiet. That wasn't playing the game. It was Emilio's job to report back, letting Mehmet share the vicarious thrill whenever he managed to get a tourist into his little attic room. He'd made a joke of it and was surprised when all Emilio would say was, 'This one is different, I like her, I like her.' And that had been that, nothing else all week.

He wished his wife was back in Antalya like Emilio's, not forever hovering around him, like a fly you can't swat away. That way he might get laid once in a while himself. If he did, he'd be sure to let his friend know about it, maybe give him an itch he couldn't so easily scratch, make him the jealous one for once.

* * *

A MESSAGE FROM THE AUTHOR

THANK YOU for reading Singled Out – I hope you enjoyed it. If you did, please do consider leaving a review on Amazon.

Word-of-mouth and positive reviews help to generate interest and enable an independent author to gain traction beyond their circle of supportive friends, relations and blog subscribers. The goal is *discoverability* – for a new author to be *found* in the vast on-line global bookshop. Discoverability builds when people who enjoy a novel tell others about it. It's that simple and it happens one reader at a time – which is why *every single reader* is a very important person.

It took me five years to write, edit and refine Singled Out, but I aim to publish my next novel within 12 months. If you'd like to keep in touch with progress, visit my website at **www.julielawford.com**. You can read and subscribe to my blog from there and can also email me and join my mailing list. I love hearing from readers and I respond personally to every email. I'm on Twitter **@julielawford** and I have a Facebook author page too: **JulieLawfordAuthor**.

I'm truly honoured that you have purchased and taken the time to read Singled Out. It's a thrilling thing, to know that a story that came together in my head over the weeks and months, is being enjoyed by readers around the world.

Printed in Great Britain
by Amazon.co.uk, Ltd.,
Marston Gate.